otherworld chills

BY KELLEY ARMSTRONG

Women of the Otherworld
Bitten
Stolen
Dime Store Magic
Industrial Magic
Haunted
Broken
No Humans Involved
Personal Demon
Living with the Dead
Frostbitten
Waking the Witch
Spell Bound
13

Men of the Otherworld
Tales of the Otherworld
Otherworld Nights
Otherworld Secrets
Otherworld Chills

The Darkest Powers trilogy
The Summoning
The Awakening
The Reckoning

The Darkness Rising trilogy
The Gathering
The Calling
The Rising

The Nadia Stafford Adventures
Exit Strategy
Made To Be Broken
Wild Justice

The Cainsville series
Omens
Visions
Deceptions
Betrayals

Shards and Ashes (with Melissa Marr)

Age of Legends trilogy
Sea of Shadows
Empire of Night
Forest of Ruin

The Masked Truth

City of the Lost

otherworld chills

KELLEY ARMSTRONG

www.orbitbooks.net

ORBIT

First published in Great Britain in 2016 by Orbit

1 3 5 7 9 10 8 6 4 2

A CIP catalogue record for this book
is available from the British Library.

ISBN 978-0-356-50068-3

Printed and bound in Great Britain by Clays Ltd, St Ives plc

Papers used by Orbit are from well-managed forests
and other responsible sources.

MIX
Paper from
responsible sources
FSC
www.fsc.org   FSC® C104740

Orbit
An imprint of
Little, Brown Book Group
Carmelite House
50 Victoria Embankment
London EC4Y 0DZ

An Hachette UK Company

www.hachette.co.uk

www.orbitbooks.net

CONTENTS

CONTENTS

BRAZEN

BRAZEN

1. NICK

When Nick Sorrentino's alarm went off at 5 a.m., he bolted upright, certain it was his phone ringing, some emergency unfolding. Five years ago, he would have figured it'd be Elena or Clay with a Pack problem. These days, his first thought was "the boys." Reese or Noah was in trouble and needed his help. Or they'd been out drinking and needed a lift. Even with werewolves, the second was more likely, particularly if the werewolves in question were twenty-two and nineteen.

But it wasn't a phone call—it was the alarm. Why the hell would he set it for 5 a.m.? It must have been one of the boys, playing a sadistic . . .

As he reached to shut the phone off, he realized it wasn't on the nightstand. Well, yes, it was, but there was an obstacle in between him and it. A woman.

She groaned, fumbled for his phone, and handed it to him.

Right. That was why he'd set the alarm. He needed to get home in time to take Noah to school because Noah had been forbidden to use his car, which was, Nick had to admit, turning out to be more of a punishment for *him*.

At least he'd had the presence of mind to set the alarm. That alone was an accomplishment, given that he hadn't decided he *wasn't* heading home until he'd been in the back of a cab, with Jacinda undoing his zipper. Maybe it was a sign that he'd really had one too many women go down on him in the back of a taxi if

3

he could still pause to think, *Huh, I should set my alarm.* That, or he was getting old.

"Are you going to turn that off?" It was a woman's voice . . . but didn't sound like Jacinda. Nick turned his head to see her friend, Heidi, curled up on his other side. Right. Huh. Well, maybe he wasn't that old yet.

He shut off the alarm. Then he checked his e-mail, making sure he didn't have an angry message from Frank Russell. Russell was the client he'd taken out last night on a double date with Jacinda and Heidi. Nick looked from one woman to the other. Not the way a double date was supposed to work.

He did have an e-mail from Russell, but it only thanked him for the evening out and asked for Heidi's phone number. Russell had apparently left with Heidi, but he said that she'd had an emergency and taken off. Which must have been when she'd hopped into the cab with Nick and Jacinda, just before it pulled away from the curb. At least Russell hadn't figured that out.

Nick climbed over Jacinda and started pulling on his trousers. Heidi rolled from bed and stumbled into the bathroom.

"Where are you rushing off to?" Jacinda asked as she watched him dress. "You never start work before nine, which means we have plenty of time for another round. Or two."

She tugged back the covers, showing him what was on offer. It was, he had to admit, a very nice offer. Tempting, though? Well, that was the problem. Ten years ago he would have already been back in that bed. Now, though, he felt only an answering twitch in his groin and a spark of regret.

"I'd love to," he said. "But I need to take Noah to school, and it's an hour drive home."

"The kid has his license, Nick. He even has a car."

"He lost his privileges. He drove after having a beer."

"*A beer? One?*"

Nick pulled on his shirt. "That's the rule."

"Since when do you follow rules?"

Since always, he could say. Maybe not the ones most of society lived by—grow up, get a job, marry, have kids—but he obeyed the laws of his kind, of his Pack. Imposing them on Noah was as important as sticking to them himself, no matter how inconvenient.

"If I set out a punishment, I need to follow through with it."

Jacinda shook her head. "I'm not sure I like this new Nick. The old, irresponsible one was a whole lot more fun."

"Could have sworn you had fun last night. Or maybe that was just Heidi."

She gave him a smile for that. "Okay. But still, taking in those cousins? And going to work every day? That's not the Nick I knew."

"I haven't been that Nick in years, Jace."

"I know, but it's getting worse. How long has it been since you called me? I'm beginning to think I might need to bring a friend more often, just to keep you interested."

He bent to kiss her. "You know better than that. Adding Heidi to the mix was your idea. I'm just flexible and accommodating."

"You are indeed."

She caught his hand and pulled him closer. Her other hand went to his waistband, but he peeled her fingers off.

"Don't tempt me, Jace. I really do need to leave."

He gave her a last quick kiss and started for the door.

"Were you even planning to come back?" she asked.

He glanced over his shoulder at her.

"Last night," she said. "Before I jumped you in the cab, were you even planning to come back to my place?"

"If you wanted me to," he said, which was the truth, even if it didn't quite answer the question. "Get some more sleep. I'll call you."

"Soon?"

He hesitated. He could lie and say yes. Most guys would. But that was never how he'd done things.

"I'll call when I can," he said, and slipped out the door.

*

As Nick drove home, he left a voice mail with his admin assistant to say he might be late. He worked for his father at the family business, which just happened to be a multinational corporation. Nick's corner of it was small, by choice. There was no way in hell he could run a business like that—he had neither the aptitude nor the interest.

Nick's niche was graphic design and client services. He had an eye for what worked and an unerring instinct for knowing what people wanted. It wasn't a cutthroat ability to pander and manipulate, but a genuine desire to please.

When he disconnected, his phone pinged with a text message for an entirely different sort of business. Pack business.

Nine months ago, Elena had become Pack Alpha. At almost the same time, they had discovered that a long-dead member was actually very much alive. Between shifting Pack dynamics, regular Pack business, and raising six-year-old twins, Elena and Clay had little time to search for Malcolm. Nick had offered to do it.

Malcolm Danvers. Estranged father of Jeremy Danvers, the former Alpha. Nick remembered Malcolm well. And not fondly. No one remembered Malcolm fondly. They weren't searching for him to welcome him back. They needed to find and kill him. Preferably before Jeremy found out he hadn't already been dead for twenty years, as they had thought.

Werewolves are, by nature, violent sons of bitches, as Clay would say. Clay had been bitten at the age of five, rescued and brought up by Jeremy. The first time Nick met him, Clay knocked him flying. His way of saying hello . . . and establishing dominance.

Nick didn't have much use for dominance. He was happier obeying orders than giving them. Except now that his best friends led the Pack, he'd realized it was time for him to step up and do more. Hence offering to handle the hunt for Malcolm.

A hunt like this wasn't Nick's area of expertise. While he was a fine fighter, he didn't feel the usual drive to hunt, to protect territory, to fight for his place. Elena teased he satisfied that urge in his romantic pursuits, yet the truth was that he didn't really pursue there, either. Like hunting, he enjoyed it and he'd rarely turn down an opportunity, but it wasn't a driving force in his life.

Malcolm was different. He'd always pursued fights and women with equal vigor. And with the same ferocity. Women were prizes to be conquered and then discarded. Or worse. Nick's grandfather, Dominic, had believed Malcolm killed Jeremy's mother. Not that the old Alpha had turned him out of the Pack for it. Malcolm was too good a fighter to lose over a dead woman. Another Pack, another time.

Now, Malcolm was back and very much alive. And finding him was Nick's job.

2. NICK

Nick left his car in the drive, and stopped on the front porch to text Noah and ask if he was ready. He could just open the front door and holler, but these days, text messaging seemed the way to go, even within the walls of your own home. Given that the walls of that house encompassed ten thousand square feet of living space, Nick had to admit that hollering from the front door wasn't practical, no matter how good a werewolf's hearing.

It was a massive house, on a huge chunk of property, sixty miles north of New York City. And yes, an estate that size within commuting distance *did* bring the occasional enterprising real estate agent to the gate on behalf of some billionaire or other. You had to be a billionaire to afford property like this. Or you had to have family who'd bought it three hundred years ago when they emigrated from Italy. The house had been rebuilt twice in the interim, but it was an ancestral home. A communal home, too. That was how werewolves lived, all generations under one roof. For years it had been just Nick and his father, Antonio. Now there were the boys, Reese and Noah.

Reese and Noah were permanent residents. A third young werewolf—Morgan Walsh—made it his home base. Morgan was older than the other two, and even more skittish about settling in, particularly into someone else's home. Morgan was on one of his walkabouts, this time staying with the Russian Pack for a few months. He'd be back, though, and was already hinting about finding work in New York and "renting" a room at the house. Rent wasn't necessary. If it made him feel less awkward, though, they'd take it. Young werewolves needed a Pack, but they needed a family and a home, too.

When Nick opened the door, Reese greeted him. Coffee in hand, bleary-eyed, Reese looked as if he hadn't gotten a moment's sleep. He hadn't. Reese would have just gotten in after a night shift at one of the family factories. His choice—Antonio would never make his dependents work for a living, as Nick well knew. Reese was studying for his MBA and in the meantime he wanted to learn the business from the ground up. Which included working night shift at a factory. Nick didn't interfere, even if he would like to see the young man be a little less mature and responsible, enjoy his youth.

Nick plucked the coffee from Reese's hand. "Thank you."

"Uh, that was mine."

"I know. But you should be heading to bed, which means you do not need caffeine. I do." Nick leaned into the next room. "Noah!"

"He's coming. Slowly, as usual. He said you stayed in the city. You should have texted me. I'd have given him a lift to school. No need to end your date early."

"I had to come home and change anyway."

Reese lifted one eyebrow. "Um, no. You keep a bag in your car."

"I took it out last time we went to Stonehaven."

"That was a month ago."

Nick shrugged. "I forgot to put it back in."

Reese stared as if Nick had left behind his cell phone for a month. As Nick walked into the kitchen, Noah came around the corner, running his hand through his hair. That, along with brushing his teeth, constituted his idea of proper grooming.

"Are we shaving today?" Nick asked as Noah grabbed an apple.

"You can. I can go another day."

Nick couldn't argue. Noah did only need it a few times a week. He didn't look nineteen. Or eighteen, which was his official age, the Pack having aged his ID down a year when they'd taken him in, to help him catch up, academically and otherwise.

Nick could say Noah just took after his father. Joey Stillwell had grown up with Nick and Clay, and he'd always been small, always looked young, even for a werewolf. With Noah, though, there were other problems. Namely an alcoholic mother who hadn't stopped drinking during her pregnancy. Add in a rough life with a brutal stepdad and Joey almost out of the picture, and you ended up with a whole slew of issues, not just delayed maturity but learning problems and a hair-trigger temper. The last two had much improved since Noah came to live with them, but there was nothing that could be done about the first. At least Noah had finally started his Changes a few months ago, which helped.

"So I guess your date went well," Noah said, brows waggling as he took a bite of his apple.

"Do Nick's dates ever not go well?" Reese said, reaching for a banana. "How about Russell? Did his date go well, too?"

Nick hesitated. He didn't mean to—Reese wasn't fishing—but it took him a second to think up an answer that wasn't an actual lie. That second was all Reese needed.

"Ah," Reese said. "Russell's date went home alone."

Again, Nick wasn't nearly quick enough. Or maybe a flicker of guilt gave him away.

Reese burst out laughing. "Whoa, no, his date did not go home alone. Was it a trade-up? Or did you take double dating to a whole new level?"

"Noah?" Nick said. "Where's your knapsack?"

"What?" Noah looked from Nick to Reese as Reese sputtered with laughter. "What do you mean, take double dating . . .?" His eyes widened. "No . . . You mean . . .?"

"I *mean* get your knapsack," Nick said. "Reese needs his sleep. These night shifts are making him giggly."

"So you . . .? *Both?* How . . .? I mean, how does that come up? You ask if they're game?"

Nick could ignore the question. But that wasn't his policy with the boys. Ask him anything. That was how Antonio raised Nick. It also meant never ignoring the opportunity to pass along a lesson or advice.

"No," Nick said. "It has to be their idea. Otherwise there's going to be hurt feelings afterward."

"Uh-huh," Noah said. "So you wait for women to offer you a threesome? Outside of porn flicks, in what world does that actually happen?"

"In Nick's world," Reese said. "Which can bear a marked resemblance to a porn flick. Kind of a James Bond high-end porn-flick crossover."

"No kidding," Noah muttered. "I bet if his car broke down, he'd knock on the nearest door and find sex-starved college girls having an orgy."

"Of course not," Reese said. "In the Nick version, it's classy grown women holding a Tupperware party, which turns into an orgy after he arrives."

"Okay, ha-ha," Nick said. "Are you going to school today, Noah?"

Noah found his knapsack. Nick had to remind him to actually put his homework in it, but five minutes later they were off and Reese was headed to bed.

As they walked out the door, Noah said, "So, um, not that I'm likely to ever need it, but do you have any advice on threesomes? Like what to do, what not to do, and how not to piss one of the girls off. Are there guidelines?"

"There are."

"And you'll tell me?"

"Yes," Nick said. "When you're twenty-one."

"What? There's an age restriction?"

"Yes. It's twenty-one. Before that, it would just be awkward and messy. Get in the car."

At two that afternoon, Nick was driving across town. Very slowly, as one usually drove across New York on a weekday. Normally he'd have called a driver, but the instructions from Rhys Smith's security team had been clear. Use your own car. Bring no one with you. He hadn't even been given directions until he was on the road.

All very cloak-and-dagger, which would amuse the hell out of Reese after his James Bond joke. The truth was, Nick's life resembled that of the international spy only superficially. Yes, he had no problems with women. Yes, he had money and knew how to dress, what to drive, and so on. He could hold his own in a fight or a car chase. But when it came to true espionage, he left that to the experts. Which is what he'd done with the search for Malcolm.

When Elena and Clay learned Malcolm was alive, they'd known exactly where to find him. In Nast Cabal custody, where he'd apparently been for the last decade, serving a prison term as a thug or an assassin—whatever use they had for a psychotic werewolf. Malcolm was a prize, and they'd kept him under the tightest security. So he should have been there when Elena negotiated for his return. Except he wasn't. Elena and Clay had seen Malcolm while he was being escorted from his cell . . . and while the entire Cabal building was in chaos, after the CEO had been murdered. After they parted, it seemed Malcolm seized an opportunity, murdering his guards to escape.

Finding out Malcolm was alive had been bad enough. Alive, free, and knowing that Clay would come after him? That was a challenge Malcolm wouldn't ignore. He would be biding his time, waiting for the Pack to lower its guard. Then he'd go after someone—Jeremy, Elena, the kids—to preempt Clay's attack.

All this meant they couldn't just keep their ears to the ground and wait for Malcolm to surface. They needed to pull in whatever resources they could. For Nick, that meant hiring Rhys Smith's team of supernatural mercenaries.

Rhys's team had been on the job for two months. A guy named Ness was in charge of Nick's case. Though Nick had met a couple of the agents actually tracking Malcolm, he'd only communicated with Ness by text and e-mail. Now Ness was in New York and had an update for him. He wanted to meet face-to-face to discuss it.

The directions led to a motel. As he pulled in, he had to text again for "final instructions," which turned out to be a room number. He was told to park in front of the room. He did . . . eventually. First, he pulled into the restaurant lot next door and left his car between two rigs, while he slipped out and checked behind the motel room. There was a man there, not visibly armed, though Nick was sure he had a gun tucked under his jacket. Rhys's agents didn't rely on their supernatural powers alone.

Nick got downwind enough to catch the guy's scent. An ID check of sorts. It was no one Nick recognized, so he just filed the information.

Next he checked the front of the motel. A guy sat in a pickup reading a map. He'd been reading it since Nick drove in. Another operative.

Nick returned to his car, parked in front of the proper room, and walked to the door.

3. NICK

When Nick knocked, a man opened the motel room door. Mid-forties. Trim. Well dressed. This, Nick presumed, was Ness. Yet no introduction was offered. The man brought him inside, and Nick noticed a second possibility—a fifty-something guy with a slight paunch.

There was a third person in the room. A woman. All Nick could see of her was her ass. He wasn't complaining, though. It was a very nice ass, a perfectly rounded curve under a pencil skirt as she bent over a table, writing. There were legs, too, even if they weren't the first thing he noticed. Black nylons with seams running down shapely calves. Black heels, high enough to be sexy, but not imprac-tically so. And there was hair, dark, curling waves tumbling almost to the desk as she wrote.

The first man cleared his throat. Nick thought he'd been caught ogling, but the guy only seemed to be getting his colleague's atten-tion. The woman finished what she was doing, straightened, and turned, and the view didn't get any worse. She wasn't young—maybe late thirties. She wasn't classically beautiful, either, but it would have been almost a disappointment if she'd been twenty and gorgeous. This was far more interesting—a striking mature woman with the body of a '40s pinup.

She extended a hand and walked over. "Vanessa."

It took a moment for him to make the connection, and mentally kick himself for his presumption.

"Ness?" he said.

She smiled. "Yes, but in person, it's Vanessa, please."

They shook hands.

"Normally these guys would give you a pat-down, but considering what you are, you don't need a weapon to kill me. So I think we can skip that part."

She dismissed the two men, who left to stand guard outside. Vanessa waved Nick to a table with two chairs. He took one. As he sat, she flipped through a sheaf of pages.

"I'm sorry to call you in on such short notice," she said, "but I was in town on business, and there's been a break in your case. It seemed like a good opportunity for us to meet, rather than send another agent to update you."

"Thank you."

"You have been pleased with the agents I sent to update you, though, haven't you?"

She continued flipping pages, her gaze down, but there was a note in her voice that made Nick tense.

"I know they were pleased with you," she said before he could answer. "*Very* pleased."

Now Nick intentionally didn't reply, waiting and gauging her voice, her posture.

Vanessa lowered herself into the remaining chair. "I'm wondering if there's a specific type you'd like me to send next time, Mr. Sorrentino. Blonde? Redhead? Brunette?"

Shit.

She continued. "I debrief my agents after they meet a client. They don't hold anything back. Whatever happened regarding a mission I hear about it."

Nick straightened. "I don't know what Jayne told you, but I can assure you, I did not take advantage—"

"Oh, I know. It was mutual. There's no question of that. I'm just curious how I could send you two of my best, most *professional* agents, and you manage to have sex with both."

"I didn't have sex with Tina."

"No?"

He tried not to squirm. "Technically, no. There was . . . intimacy. But she offered."

Vanessa stared at him. "During a client information meeting? How does that work? She updates you on the case and then offers you a parting blow job?"

"There were a few steps in between."

"I should hope so."

The words sounded shocked, but her dark eyes glittered with barely contained laughter, leaving Nick feeling like a cheerleader who's been caught screwing half the football team.

Nick cleared his throat. "If there was a complaint—"

"Far from it. Both agents are eager—very eager—to work with you again."

"Then if I've broken some code of client conduct—"

"If you have, it wasn't one you were informed of. There's no issue with your behavior, Mr. Sorrentino."

He met her gaze. "Then why are we having this conversation?"

She blinked. Silence fell, and now she was the one who looked uncomfortable, as if she'd been called out for gossiping about the cheerleader.

Nick continued. "If there is a problem with my behavior, I apologize. Either way, it will not happen again. Can we move on to my case?"

Vanessa updated him on his case. Nick kept the meeting coolly professional, and she followed suit. She told him what they'd been doing, and he asked questions. All business.

"The main reason I called you here is to tell you we're following up on a rumor that Malcolm was spotted in Detroit," Vanessa said. "We heard he'd made contact with a half-demon there, someone he'd worked with at the Nast Cabal."

"And the reliability of this rumor, on a scale of one to ten?"

"Eight."

Until now, Nick had been only half processing. The update had seemed like mere customer service, making sure the client knows you're using his money well.

"Give me the details on this half-demon," Nick said. "Name. Bio. Address. I can be in Detroit tonight."

"There's no need for that. I've sent Tina. Once she has visual confirmation of Malcolm Danvers, she'll report back."

"That's not what we agreed on. I said—"

"Yes, I know what you said, and I was told not to argue the point. I did not, however, agree to it. You hired us to find Malcolm Danvers. Once we have accomplished that, he's all yours. But it's our job to confirm it."

"And as the client, I'm relieving you of that responsibility. I have the right—"

"No, I'm afraid you don't, Mr. Sorrentino. The contract states that we will provide confirmation."

Nick folded his hands on the table. "I am asking you to reconsider. I would insist, but I would prefer to ask. I'm sure Tina's a good agent, but Malcolm is unlike any targets she's had."

"Tina successfully tracked a werewolf on a mission in Germany. That's why she's on this case. She is prepared."

"For a *werewolf*. Not for Malcolm Danvers. He'll be on to her before she gets visual confirmation. He was the best fighter in the North American Pack—"

"*Was*. Past tense. Very past. Malcolm is eighty-five, Mr. Sorrentino. Yes, I know werewolves age slowly, but he's an old man."

"No, he's not. The Nasts were experimenting with cryogenic freezing. Elena says he doesn't look much older than Jeremy. So shave off twenty years for that. Shave another twenty for a werewolf's delayed aging."

She leaned back, and he could tell she was mentally calling bullshit on the cryogenics. Just as Rhys had. The Nasts were denying it, and even among supernaturals, cryogenics was a little too *Star Wars*.

"I said Malcolm was the best fighter in his time," Nick continued. "These days that title goes to Clayton Danvers. Who faced Malcolm nine months ago. Clay would be the first to say it was a real fight. A real *challenge*."

"Clayton had just finished dispatching a dozen Cabal security officers. He wasn't in top condition. The only person Malcolm had fought that day was Elena, who bested him before Clayton arrived." Vanessa picked up her file and pretended to leaf through it. "I'm sure that's the story you provided in our intake session. Elena turned Malcolm over to Clayton. They faced off. Clayton won, but he was interrupted by the arrival of the guards. That's why you hired us. Not because Clayton couldn't kill him, but because he missed his chance."

"That doesn't change the fact that two werewolves fought Malcolm and both agree he's not a doddering old man—"

"We don't expect him to be. But you hired us for a job, Mr. Sorrentino. I'm going to ask you to let us finish it."

"If Tina goes after Malcolm, he will see her coming. If he sees her coming, he will kill her."

"I disagree."

"And you're willing to stake your agent's life on it?"

"She's not going to confront him. We've established a fifty-yard guideline. Once she receives visual confirmation and provides photographic evidence, Malcolm Danvers is yours. Until then, we have a contract to complete."

Nick called Elena on his speakerphone. She was in her own car, on her way to get the twins from school.

"I could go over her head," he said when he finished filling her in. "But I'm not sure Rhys would do anything about it."

"He won't," she said. "If she's blocking you, it's on his orders. Rhys might think he's above stereotyping werewolves as dumb brutes, but he's sure we have a little too much confidence in our ability to kick the ass of any other supernatural. He thinks we're an insular group, distrustful of others, and so we'll want to wrest back control the moment we can." She paused and he heard her turn signal click as she took a corner. "All of which isn't exactly untrue. But in this case, we're not exaggerating the danger. We'll never convince him of that, though."

"So, your advice . . .?"

"If they want to take the risk, we have to trust that they know what they're doing. They could even be right. Malcolm is the Pack's bogeyman. Maybe we've built him up more than he deserves. You warned them. Now we hang tight and pray they don't screw this up and lose him."

An uncomfortable pause as tension zinged along the line, and Nick pictured Elena fighting the impulse to add, "Are you okay with that?" She was Alpha, which meant this wasn't a democracy. Her word was law. Which was fine with Nick. Elena struggled with it.

"Works for me," he said, and she gave a soft sigh of relief.

"So, otherwise, what's up there?" he asked, and they spent the rest of their mutual drives talking.

4. VANESSA

Vanessa Callas had a routine. Once her niece headed to her room to study, Vanessa mixed a gimlet, drew a steaming hot bath, lit a candle, and settled in with a book. Tonight, it was past nine and she was sitting in her hotel room, cell phone by her elbow, trying not to gaze longingly at her novel and the hotel bar menu. The candle she'd brought from home sat on the table. She put her finger to the wick, using her Aduro powers to light it, and then snuffed it out. Lit it. Snuffed it again.

She was waiting for two calls. One anticipated; one dreaded. The anticipated one was from Tina. After Nick Sorrentino left, she'd phoned and told Tina to take the night off. She was sending in Jayne tomorrow, and the two could tag-team confirmation on Malcolm Danvers. Tina hadn't been pleased, but she'd promised to call once she was checked into her hotel. That had been an hour ago.

The dreaded one was from Rhys. She was sure Nick had contacted him the moment he got out the door. Nick would complain, and the boss would be pissed. Not because Rhys wanted her handing the case over to Nick. He was the one who'd forbidden it.

"If it was Elena or Clayton, sure," he'd said. "They're used to handling situations like this. But Nick? He's used to *helping* them handle situations like this. Outside the Pack, Nick is known as Clayton Danvers' friend or Antonio Sorrentino's son. He has no reputation himself. He's an omega wolf."

The man Vanessa had been working with remotely had not seemed like an omega wolf. The man she'd met this afternoon absolutely did not seem like one. He'd taken charge just fine. But taking charge in a meeting and taking charge in the field were two different things.

"Bottom line," Rhys had said, "we take the risks here, no matter how much he argues. He's the Alpha's BFF. If we get him killed, it's a shit storm of trouble for us."

So Rhys wouldn't call to give her crap for refusing Nick's demand. He'd call because Vanessa hadn't kept the client happy. And in this case, she'd had every intention of keeping Nick happy . . . and the memory of that—and the colossal fuckup that ensued—was why she really needed a gimlet. Possibly two.

Vanessa Callas did not take unnecessary risks. Not in her job. Not in her life. She was smart and she was careful, so smart and so careful that when she did decide to take a chance and do something crazy, she had no idea *how*, and usually ended up making a complete fool of herself. Like she'd done today.

Vanessa was in charge of five agents. Four of them were women, not because Rhys hired her to play den mother but because, after a few months on the job, female operatives usually requested her as their handler. She'd found the balance between boss and bossy older sister, and her agents took comfort in that. It was a closely knit team, and overnight meetings often resembled sleepaway camp. Which is where Jayne, after a few glasses of wine, started gushing about Nick Sorrentino. Tina pounced on the next Nick update and got her chance, and then she was the one gushing, though it appeared she hadn't been quite as successful as she'd let on.

Nick Sorrentino. The perfect one-night stand. A werewolf with a model-perfect face and athlete-perfect body. Young enough to have the energy for an all-nighter; old enough to realize his partner should also enjoy that all-nighter. Experienced and attentive. And a nice guy. That was, for her operatives, perhaps the most shocking part of the package.

That's when Vanessa made her decision. She was going to get some of that. God knows, she *needed* some of that.

Vanessa was thirty-eight. She'd come to work for Rhys seven years ago. Before that, she'd been with the FBI, zooming up the ranks with such single-mindedness that after a while she no longer even cared about the end goal, wasn't even sure what her end goal was, only knew that it was higher than wherever she'd been. Then she met Rhys and realized a career could be more interesting and fulfilling, especially for a half-demon.

She worked her ass off, which hadn't left much time for more than passing relationships. That seemed fine, until she hit thirty-four and the doctor said if she was planning to have children, she was reaching the end stretch. At first she'd been furious—who was he to presume she wanted kids? The more she thought about it, though, the more she realized she did want something, not children but the relationship they sprang from. An intimate bond with someone who could be both lover and companion.

As she was realizing that, a friend introduced her to Roger. At twenty-five, she wouldn't have given him a second look. There was a spectrum of elements she'd wanted with any potential mate. Looks, yes. Success, yes. But also intelligence, wit, and personality. Score on three out of five, and it didn't really matter which three, you had a winner. Roger . . . Roger was adequate in all categories, outstanding in none. Vanessa had decided that was good enough. At least it was at thirty-five, when it seemed a woman was still expected to present an appealing package and then be thrilled if it attracted anyone at all.

Roger was all for a long-term relationship, even if he did wish she'd drop a few pounds. She had—which was a struggle, given her figure—and she hadn't even pointed out the fact that his spare tire was rapidly becoming tractor-sized. Though he had two kids from his previous marriage, he wanted more. She wasn't set on them but wasn't set *against* them, either, so she said sure. Then, on the day they'd been supposed to move in together, he announced he'd found someone else. A twenty-five-year-old who was, it seemed, in possession of a more reliable set of ovaries.

That was the end of Roger.

Vanessa hadn't dated since, too angry and disillusioned. The problem was, if you weren't dating, you weren't getting sex. Twice in the last few months, she'd found herself in a hotel bar, seriously considering an invitation from a fellow traveler. Which meant the situation was growing dire—in her line of work, you know better than to ever go back to a stranger's room. What she needed was a hookup that came with a "not a psycho" stamp of approval. What she needed was Nick Sorrentino.

So when Tina got a solid lead on Malcolm Danvers, Vanessa made an overdue business trip to New York and combined it with the chance to deliver this update to Nick herself. She'd bought a new dress—a little vampy but revealing nothing more than curves—and tried not to regret the ten pounds she'd gained back post-Roger. She'd left her hair unpinned. She'd taken extra care with her makeup. Then she'd formulated a plan of seduction. Except, well, her experience with seduction was . . . nonexistent. Still, from what Jayne and Tina suggested, Nick didn't need serious wooing. She would let him know she was game and perfectly fine with the concept of casual sex. It had seemed like the easiest way to convey this message was to bring up Jayne and Tina.

There was a moment, when she first saw Nick, where she doubted the wisdom of her plan. It was not because his bio photos didn't do him justice. In person, Nick Sorrentino looked like he'd just stepped off an ad for Armani or Ferrari. Tall and slender, flawless olive skin, dark wavy hair, deep brown eyes . . . He might be fifty but, being a werewolf, he looked a decade younger. And Vanessa was sure Nick Sorrentino would still turn heads when he *did* look fifty. And sixty. Probably even seventy.

But it wasn't his looks that made her hesitate. It was him—his manner and his bearing and his demeanor, quiet and professional, polite and thoughtful. She hadn't expected a smarmy playboy, but maybe, yes, a hint of that, an air that said he was a player and proud of it. When she didn't detect any such sign, she realized her plan might be . . . unwise. But by then, it was too late. She'd played her hand and insulted him and made a fool of herself.

Now she waited for a call from Rhys, telling her their client was not pleased and he wasn't sure what the hell she'd done but she was off the case.

When the phone rang, she reached over with trepidation. Then she saw the caller ID. Mayfair Flowers. Tina Mayfair's code name.

"I can't imagine Detroit is such a tourist hot spot that it took you ninety minutes to find a hotel room," Vanessa said on answering.

When silence returned, she continued, "Tell me you're at a hotel . . ."

"I made visual confirmation," Tina said. "Just as I was about to leave my post, he came out of his contact's house. It was too dark for a distance photo, so—"

"Did I tell you not to approach?" Vanessa said. "Did I *order* you to stand down?"

"But he was right there, and it was dark enough for me to get closer for a photo."

"So you got it?"

Silence. Then, "It wasn't as easy as it seemed. I've been following him—"

"No!" Vanessa said. "I don't care if he's twenty feet away standing under a streetlight. Back down. *Now.*"

"I would, but . . ."

Vanessa gripped the phone. "But what . . .?"

"Somehow, I lost him. I got myself into this blind alley and I feel like an idiot."

No, you didn't get yourself there. Malcolm Danvers got you there.

"Get out now," Vanessa said. "Whatever it takes. Just—"

A sharp intake of breath. Then a clatter, as if the phone had hit the pavement.

"Mayfair?" Vanessa called. "Mayfair!"

Another clatter. Then a male voice. "Hello?"

"Who is this?"

"Who is *this*? Did you lose your phone?" the man said, his voice soft. "Or did you lose something else? Yes, I believe you did. Such a shame, too. She's not gone, though. Not yet. I could return her. Would you like that?"

Vanessa struggled not to snap a reply. "Yes, I would."

"I thought so."

The line went dead.

Vanessa sat clutching the phone. Two choices. One, cover her ass—and her employer's. Save them the humiliation of admitting they'd underestimated Malcolm Danvers. Request backup, jump on the next plane to Detroit, and pray she could get her agent back.

Option two? Well, option two would result in huge personal and professional embarrassment, and quite likely cost Vanessa a job she loved. It also gave Tina her best chance of survival.

Vanessa picked up the phone and dialed.

5. NICK

It was almost nine-thirty, which in the Sorrentino household meant dinner hour, since it was late enough that everyone was finally home, at least temporarily. No one even considered the possibility of separate dining times. In this house, the evening meal was the one chance for everyone to be together, if only for an hour or two.

Tonight dinner started even later than usual, Nick having picked Antonio up at the airport. He hadn't needed to—Antonio would be the first to say he could grab a cab. But after his father had been away for a week, Nick knew he'd much prefer a lift and an hour spent catching up. So Nick always made sure he was there, waiting.

They were partway through the meal when Nick's cell phone buzzed. He was about to shut it off—work or friends could wait. But then he saw who it was and said, "I need to take this."

Nick took the phone outside, where Antonio wouldn't overhear his conversation. Vanessa told him what happened—that Tina had apparently been trapped and then kidnapped by Malcolm.

"He wants something," she said. "He's holding her hostage until he gets it."

The only thing Malcolm wanted from Tina was amusement. As for trading Tina's life for his freedom, that was ridiculous. Malcolm wouldn't trust any promise to call off the hunt, and he'd never think himself in serious danger anyway. Malcolm intended to kill Tina, but he would keep her alive until she'd served her purpose.

Nick didn't tell Vanessa that. He could hear how upset she was, and he wouldn't take away her hope, no more than he'd say, "*I told you so.*"

"You know him," she said. "You understand how he thinks."

Nick doubted any sane person could understand how Malcolm thought, but the Pack knew better than to underestimate Malcolm, which was where outsiders failed.

Nick checked his watch. "I'm going to see if I can still catch a flight tonight."

"You can. There are seats on the last plane to Detroit, leaving just before midnight. Your ticket will be waiting. I'll meet you at the gate."

"Meet?"

"It's my agent. I'm coming along. I'll see you at the airport."

She hung up. Nick hesitated, then glanced at his watch again. No time to call her back and argue. They'd settle this at the gate.

Antonio had no idea Nick was spearheading the campaign to find Malcolm. If he did . . . well, Nick was a little old for his father to forbid him to do anything, but in this case, Antonio would sure as hell try.

Antonio knew Malcolm was alive. He thought, though, that Elena and Clay were hunting him with Nick just helping out. Antonio would even be fine with Nick liaising with Rhys's team, as long as any involvement stopped short of Nick getting within a hundred miles of Malcolm.

There was a reason Nick lacked a reputation in the werewolf world: because his father had done everything in his power to keep Nick from the fights and challenges that would earn him one. When Nick was young, he'd even been forbidden to travel without other werewolves, for fear some mutt would decide to see what Antonio Sorrentino's son was made of. Nick used to beg Clay to set up challenge fights for him, as he watched Clay climb the ranks himself. A few times Clay did have a challenger to spare, but even then, when Nick won his bout, all he heard about afterward was Clay.

Traditionally, in the werewolf world, if you didn't have a rep, you were invisible. Then Jeremy became Alpha. Jeremy, who'd rarely fought a bout, because Clay would quietly intercept all challengers to protect him. In the past, the Alpha had to be the strongest werewolf in the Pack. But times had changed and Jeremy had other qualities that made him the perfect leader for the twenty-first century. With his ascension, the pressure to gain a reputation eased, and Nick had relaxed. His Pack valued him. Any mutt he encountered discovered he was a perfectly fine fighter. And Antonio could rest easy, knowing his son was safe, which was the main thing.

Nick was going to let his father keep resting easy, for as long as he could. So he made his excuses—Pack business, Elena needed him to check something out—and then grabbed his packed bag and took off.

As Nick drove down the long lane, he spotted a blond figure leaning against the gate, and for a moment he saw Clay, half a lifetime ago, staking out the end of the drive, waiting for him.

"You going somewhere, Nicky? Not after that mutt they spotted in the city, I hope."

But it wasn't Clay. It was Reese.

Nick pulled over and put down the window. Reese leaned in.

"Where is he?" Reese asked.

"Who?"

"Malcolm." Reese raised a hand against his protest. "Yeah, I've figured it out. You need to work on your stealth skills, Nick. You aren't very good at it."

Nor was he any good at denying it, especially given his pact of honesty with the boys.

"He's been spotted in Detroit," Nick admitted. "I hired Rhys to find him, and there's a problem. I'm going to sort it out. Elena knows. Antonio doesn't. Obviously, I'd prefer to keep it that way."

"Sure."

The agreement came quickly. Nick must have looked surprised, because Reese shrugged. "I know how he is. And I know you're not heading off to take on Malcolm yourself."

Nick gave a short laugh. "No. I'm not that stupid. Once I've confirmed the situation, I'll bring Clay in."

"Good."

Reese walked around the car and opened the passenger door. Nick caught and held it.

"I'm coming with you," Reese said. "Yes, it's basic recon work. Yes, you can handle it. But you should have backup."

"I do. One of Rhys's agents."

"Doesn't count," Reese said. "This is werewolf business."

Nick hesitated. He had vowed not to be his father. He would protect the boys, but he wouldn't coddle them. Yet as he paused, his gaze went to Reese's two maimed fingers. Chopped off by a couple of mutts in Anchorage, partly a warning, but partly just because they could. These days, Reese would have been prepared for those mutts. But he sure as hell wasn't prepared for Malcolm.

"Not this time," Nick said. "Not with Malcolm."

"Because he's a badass. And a psychopath. I've heard the stories. Hell, I even heard them in Australia, long after he was supposed to be dead. All the more reason for you to have backup."

"Which I will. Clay will join me as soon as I've confirmed the situation. I can handle this, Reese."

"I never said you couldn't."

As Nick stared him down, Reese dropped his gaze, grumbling slightly, knowing that if he insisted, he *was* saying Nick couldn't handle it.

"I'll call if I need you," Nick said.

"Bullshit."

Nick met his gaze. "If I say I will, I will. You know that."

Again, Reese grumbled and looked away, but he nodded, saying a "Fine" that insisted it wasn't fine at all, then shut the door and let Nick drive away without him.

6. NICK

Nick had less luck persuading Vanessa to stay behind. Admittedly, he didn't try very hard, after telling Reese he'd have an agent backing him up. He'd already strained the truth with Reese by suggesting Elena knew exactly what he was up to. He'd texted her to say that Rhys's handler lost touch with her agent so he was flying out that night. Once he had visual confirmation of Malcolm, he'd call Clay in. All technically true. He'd just left out the part where that MIA agent had almost certainly been kidnapped by Malcolm.

Vanessa had bought them first-class tickets. Probably assumed he wouldn't fly coach. Not necessarily true—he was as flexible in that as in everything else—but yes, given the choice, he'd take the extra leg and elbow room.

Their seats were together, which was less comfortable. He hadn't forgotten that this whole mess could have been avoided if she'd listened to him. Also, while he wasn't one to hold a grudge, her early mockery still stung. If it wouldn't have been rude, he might have switched his seat. As it was, he just worked quietly on his laptop.

Halfway through the short flight, Vanessa cleared her throat and said, "Tell me about Malcolm Danvers."

He glanced over. She had her laptop out. Malcolm's dossier was right there on the screen, and he wanted to tell her to read it instead, but that was being pissy. She followed his gaze, though, and said, "That's his bio from Elena. Heavily redacted."

"I'm sure she didn't remove anything you need to identify him. Or to understand what he's capable of."

"No, but it's like reading the arrest file for someone who was never charged with a crime. Without a trial, there's nothing in-depth. No motivation. No insight."

"I'm not sure I can provide that, either. I knew him for half my life, but we weren't close. Malcolm had his favorites. Thankfully, I wasn't one of them."

"Who was?"

Nick hesitated, but the answer did explain more about Malcolm, which would help her.

"Antonio—my father—and Clay were his favorites," he said, "Jeremy was . . . not the kind of son Malcolm wanted. So he looked for substitutes. Antonio was a fighter, and that always topped Malcolm's list of requirements. But when Clay came along . . .?" Nick shrugged. "My father isn't aggressive. There's no edge. No anger. He fights for pure physical challenge. Clay has edge. He was bitten as a child. He embraces his wolf side more than any of us. Malcolm was fascinated by him. He didn't understand him, though. Whatever Clay's rep, he's no psycho. If you threaten his family, he won't think twice about killing you. But otherwise? He's never laid a finger on anyone for kicks. He wouldn't understand that, any more than a real wolf would. Violence is for problem-solving. Malcolm didn't get that. When Clay wouldn't hunt mutts for sport, Malcolm blamed Jeremy's influence. It didn't matter how much Clay hated Malcolm—and he hated him more than anyone—Malcolm never stopped pursuing him."

"As a substitute son? Or . . . more?"

"Antonio always thought there was more to it when Malcolm chased *him*. There was no shortage of women in Malcolm's life, but he had nothing but contempt for them, and humans in general. So maybe there was some confusion there. Looking to make a con-nection, whatever that connection might be."

"Is Elena in danger, then? If Malcolm wanted a woman of his own kind, there is one now. Only one."

"He won't go after her like that. It'd be easier if he would—lay a trap for him. She might be a werewolf, but to him, she's just a woman. Weak."

"Except she kicked his ass."

Nick smiled at the thought. "True, but that's only going to piss him off. Elena belongs to Clay, so she's relatively safe. Same with me."

"Because you're Antonio's son."

He nodded. "Malcolm never pursued me, but he treated me well for Antonio's sake. I'd say that means he won't come after me, but I'd never make that presumption. It only means I'm unlikely to draw his immediate fire."

"He'll think twice before attacking you."

"No, but he'll think twice before *killing* me."

"According to the GPS from Tina's phone, she was somewhere around here when she called. It was shut off after . . . Nick?"

They'd arrived in Detroit an hour ago, rented a car, and drove to this neighborhood. They'd been walking for about ten minutes as Nick followed the trail. He'd moved away while Vanessa had been talking. Now he lifted a hand, telling her to be quiet as he listened. The night was still and silent. Nick could see signs that it hadn't always been like that. There had been shops, but they were long closed and boarded up. An empty block, inhabited only by homeless people and vermin. Vermin of the animal variety—even gangbangers and dealers didn't see profit in a place without buyers. Contrary to what the news reports might suggest, the whole city of Detroit wasn't like this, but there were pockets of it. A modern-day ghost town.

Tina should have taken one look around and known she was being led into a trap. But she'd been too cocky. He'd gotten that vibe from her when they met, and it was part of what made him decide they wouldn't spend the night together. Here, she would have looked around and thought this was the perfect place to catch her prey, without ever considering Malcolm might be thinking the same thing.

"Stay close," Nick said as he set out.

"We should do this methodically," Vanessa whispered as she jogged to catch up. "Tina said it was a blind alley, so if we cover the area strip by strip—"

"No need," he said. "I have her trail."

"Trail? Oh, right. Scent. Okay. I'll cover you."

Vanessa had a gun. A legal one she'd checked at the airport. While she'd readily admitted that she hadn't been in the field for a few years, she seemed to know what she was doing, so he left her to it and focused on Tina's scent.

Even without the trail, he could have guessed where Tina was heading—he could see two burned-out streetlights ahead and a dark roadway that seemed to lead to a dead end. Only her trail entered the blind alley, though. That gave him pause, but he continued following the trail until—

A scent hit him so hard that he stopped in mid-stride. It was no stronger than Tina's, but it felt like cold fingers reaching deep into his brain to pluck out a memory long buried.

"Malcolm," he murmured.

"Are you sure?"

"Yes," he snapped, with more impatience than he intended.

"Sorry, but it's been twenty years since you've been near him," she said. "And you expected to smell him here, so—"

"Werewolves don't forget Pack scents." Nick walked to the building on the left. "He was on the roof. He jumped her. Then . . ." He followed Tina's scent back to the road.

"He took her that way." Vanessa pointed the direction they'd come.

Nick shook his head. "I only smell Tina."

"She escaped?"

"No, he let her go."

Vanessa walked back to the road and looked down it. "That's not possible. She would have called as soon as she found a pay phone."

"He didn't release her. He let her run so he could chase."

"Why?"

"Because that's his idea of fun."

7. NICK

Malcolm had let Tina run because it amused him, but Nick knew it was more than simple sport. Presumably there was no place nearby he'd deemed suitable to hold her and it had saved Malcolm the hassle of transporting her out of this neighborhood. It might be empty here, but there was life a few blocks over. Also, a quick capture lacked challenge.

As a trained agent, Tina wouldn't flee to the authorities. With her ego, she'd be cursing herself for getting jumped. Also, Malcolm wouldn't simply have released her—he'd have allowed her to "escape," so she'd think she bested him. That would give her confidence. She'd want to repair her failure. To turn the tables and catch him. And all the while, he'd be herding her.

The trails confirmed Nick's guess. They'd converge and separate, and he could see Malcolm driving her along a preordained path, one that funneled Tina where he wanted her to go, giving her few options to divert from the path and driving her back onto it when she did.

Vanessa watched his back in silence as he tracked. He considered Changing to wolf form, but the trail was clear enough.

Too clear? That was the question.

Had Malcolm laid this trail for someone to follow? The only person who *could* follow it was a werewolf, and Malcolm wouldn't suspect that one of the Pack had sent Tina after him. Werewolves didn't hire outsiders to do their dirty work. He'd presume Tina was from the Nasts, so he just hadn't worried about hiding his scent trail. Still, Nick kept an eye—and an ear—on his surroundings.

Eventually the trail led to an empty building, abandoned so long that it was impossible to tell what it had been. Maybe a small factory or even a school—a two-story rectangular box without a window left intact.

Nick glanced around the neighborhood. Not really a neighborhood so much as a piece of land with buildings on it, some homes, some commercial, some occupied, some not. At this hour, it was silent. He took one last listen and then led Vanessa through a doorway.

Inside, the only light came from the moon shining through broken windows.

"Can you see?" Nick whispered to Vanessa.

"Not well."

He gave her credit for admitting it. "Stay close. If you can't see me in front of you, let me know. I'd rather not use flashlights if we can help it."

"If I need to, I have this." She lifted her fingers and they started to glow.

"Then use it," he whispered. "Better than tripping in the dark and making noise."

"I know."

There was no annoyance in her voice, but he murmured an apology nonetheless.

Even inside, Nick couldn't tell what purpose the building had once served. Anything that could leave a hint had been stripped. It was all empty rooms. Well, not really empty—there was plenty of junk, but most of it seemed to have been brought in by squatters over the years.

Now, though, he could hear no signs of life. When he passed one room, he caught the scent of a corpse. A recent one. Human. Male. He smelled blood, too.

As they passed the room, Vanessa lit up her fingers and waved them inside, illuminating a corpse, sitting up, throat ripped out.

"Werewolf?" she whispered.

Nick didn't answer right away. It was a classic werewolf kill, which made him slow to reply. It's not easy to tear out someone's throat when you're in human form, so there was a moment where he wondered if it could be an animal's work. But then he caught the scent, and when he moved closer, he found a few dark hairs caught in the man's ripped flesh. Wolf fur. Malcolm had Changed form and cleared the building, scaring out those who would run and killing those who wouldn't.

When Nick told Vanessa, she gazed down at the body. Not horrified but disgusted. Thoughtful too, before she turned to him and said, "I'm sorry."

"For what?"

She nodded at the body and then waved around the building, and he knew what she meant. Sorry that she'd thought he was exaggerating. Sorry that she'd underestimated Malcolm.

"Let's find Tina," he said.

She nodded and followed him out of the room.

They found a second body. A girl. Maybe seventeen. A street kid. She lay on her back, long sleeves ripped as if she'd tried to protect her throat as the wolf leapt on her. That death hit harder, and it took a moment to move on. When they did, Nick heard the whisper of fabric on concrete, so faint he thought he'd imagined it until he made Vanessa stop moving and he caught the noise again. It sounded like something being dragged across the concrete floor.

He followed the sound. They were on the second floor and the noise seemed to come from the middle. When he approached, his arm shot out to stop Vanessa. He motioned for her to light her fingers. She did and looked around. Ahead, part of the floor was missing, and they could see down to the first level . . . where a body lay in the middle of the room.

"Tina," Vanessa whispered.

Nick caught her before she could move closer to the hole. She leaned and strained to see better.

Tina lay on her stomach. Drag marks led to a blood pool ten feet behind her.

"Is she . . .?" Vanessa asked.

He was about to say he couldn't tell when Tina moved, one arm slowly reaching out as she propelled herself forward. That was the sound he'd heard—Tina dragging herself toward the door.

Vanessa exhaled. She started forward, but this time caught herself.

"It's a trap, isn't it?" Vanessa whispered.

Nick nodded.

"But we can't leave." She straightened. "I have an agent down. That's my priority, above my own safety."

She looked over, as if expecting him to argue. He didn't. If it was a Pack brother, he'd do the same. He waved her back to the hall, where they could come up with a plan.

8. VANESSA

Leaving Tina was one of the hardest things Vanessa had ever done. Even if she knew she wasn't abandoning her, that's what it felt like. Her agent—her friend—was lying in her own blood, badly injured, and Vanessa had walked away.

She'd screwed up here worse than she ever had before. It didn't matter if Rhys had refused to let Nick take over. It didn't matter if Vanessa had warned Tina off and called Jayne in to assist. She did not accept excuses from her team and she would not make excuses for herself. Whatever had happened to Tina—whatever was happening now—it was Vanessa's fault.

Nick stayed upstairs to stand watch over Tina and to avoid spreading his scent through the building. She had to struggle to factor scent into the equation. It required a bigger mental leap than she would have imagined. A werewolf could track his prey, no matter where she ran. A werewolf could smell someone nearby, even if they were silent and hidden. A werewolf could recognize another by scent. Thinking that way was as normal for them as using her built-in flashlight was for her.

Rhys had a werewolf on the team, and Vanessa had prided herself on thinking she knew all about them because she'd once spearheaded a huge operation with him. Now she realized that was as ridiculous as saying you understand another culture because you have one casual friend from it.

As she continued across the first floor, she didn't detect anyone else around. She kept her gun in one hand, the fingers on her free hand lit, not just for light but to jump-start her powers if Malcolm leapt at her from the shadows. That's what he seemed to have done to Tina. Werewolves didn't use guns—even the one on Rhys's team balked at it. According to the Nast file, Malcolm had refused to use anything but fist and fang. They'd send him out with a gun or blade, only to find he'd left it behind, as if even carrying a weapon spoke of weakness.

So Vanessa kept moving, as quickly as she dared, poised for attack. As she turned a corner, she heard a scratching sound. She wheeled, her back to the wall, gun ready.

She continued, inching along the wall now, struggling to check her speed. The sound grew louder. Vanessa moved to the open doorway and stopped.

There was Tina, sprawled on the floor, a few feet farther from that puddle of blood. One arm was outstretched to drag herself along, but only her fingers moved, scratching the concrete floor as if her strength was gone and she was too far into shock to realize the futility of it. Vanessa gripped the wooden doorjamb so hard she smelled smoke. She only gripped harder, struggling not to race into the room.

That's what he wants. You see her there, dying, and run to her.

Now came the time for faith. To trust that a man she barely knew would watch her from above.

She walked forward with her gun out, fingers blazing, knowing that was still not enough to save her from Malcolm. Only Nick could do that. She had to walk into the middle of that floor, an open target.

"Tina?" she whispered.

Tina kept scratching at the floor.

Vanessa moved to her side and lowered herself on one knee. She could hear Tina's breathing, shallow and labored. When she touched the woman's shoulder, Tina didn't tense, didn't react at all, just kept scratching the floor.

She gripped Tina's shoulders with both hands, her fire extinguished, her gun on the floor, intentionally leaving herself vulnerable. Tina still didn't respond. Vanessa carefully turned her over and—

She sucked in a breath. Tina's throat was . . . Vanessa had seen Malcolm's other two victims, their throats savaged, a bloody mess of tissue and gore. He hadn't done that to Tina. He'd slit her throat just enough to let her bleed out. Slowly.

Vanessa's burning fingertips flew to Tina's neck, pulling the flesh together and then cauterizing the wound to stop the bleeding. Field medicine learned from another fire half-demon on Rhys's team.

She closed the wound, but when she looked at Tina, she knew it was too late. The critical blood loss was back there, a dozen feet away. Tina still breathed, heart pumping, but her eyes were empty, her hand flexing as if she was still scratching at that floor, the instinct for survival outlasting all other mental functions.

Vanessa told herself she was wrong. Had to be wrong. Tina was alive. Just in shock. The wound was cauterized and now they just needed to get her to help.

She whipped around, looking for Nick, annoyed that he wasn't already here to help. When she caught a flicker of motion, she remembered *why* he wasn't and grabbed for her gun, but it was only Nick, leaping from the second floor as easily as if it'd been a two-foot hop.

"We need to get her help. There's a clinic—"

"She's gone, Vanessa," he said softly.

"No, she's breathing. She's alive. She can get a transfusion. Help me lift—"

"Vanessa?" He took her shoulder and, before she could throw him off, turned her to look down at Tina, lying unmoving on the floor.

"No," she whispered. She dropped to her knees and looked into Tina's eyes, wide and staring blankly. Then she heard a rattle, deep in the woman's chest.

"She's alive. She . . ."

Tina's lips parted, and she exhaled. Then she went still.

Vanessa's hands slammed down on Tina's chest, pumping, starting CPR. She knew it was useless. She'd known she couldn't save Tina from the moment she saw that hole in her throat and that look in her eyes. Tina had been lost before they even made it to the building.

That didn't stop Vanessa from performing CPR, even as she swore she could feel Tina's body cooling. At last, she felt Nick's hand on her shoulder, fingers resting there, telling her what she already knew—they had to go.

Vanessa pulled back and stared down at Tina. The hole in her throat was almost medically precise in its placement. No knife had made it, though. The edges were jagged, as if Malcolm had . . . She wasn't even sure how you'd do that. Bite? Rip? Whatever he'd done, there was no way Tina sat still and took it. Yet it would be impossible to be that precise with a struggling—

She bent and ran her hands over Tina's head. There it was. A goose egg, also expertly placed. He'd brought her here, questioned her, knocked her out, and then cut her throat. That's why there'd been one blood pool. Tina had been bleeding out and then regained consciousness and crawled away.

Vanessa rose. Nick had moved off now, scouting the area and occasionally dropping into a crouch, presumably sniffing.

"It was definitely Malcolm," he said, though she knew he was checking for her benefit only. He knew who this was. No one else would be this sadistic.

"It wasn't a trap for us, was it?" she said. "He didn't even stick around to watch her die."

"It would seem not," he said slowly, looking around.

"You don't detect any sign of him, do you?"

"No, it's just . . . It seems odd."

"Only if you presume he knew someone would come after Tina tonight, which would have been nearly impossible if we weren't relatively close already." She reached down to touch the pool of blood. It was already tacky. "It's been at least an hour. Maybe two."

"And he tired of waiting, I suppose. I'll hide her body for now. You have someone who can come to retrieve it?"

"First thing in the morning. For now, I need to notify Rhys."

Vanessa retreated to a corner to do that. She kept her back to Tina's body. It was the only way she could focus. Seven years on the job, and she'd never lost an agent. She'd been so proud of her record, and now she realized it'd been dumb luck. No matter how many precautions you took, it was never enough. There was always something to miss, blame to take—

She pushed away the thought and went to notify Rhys.

9. NICK

Nick circled the room as Vanessa texted Rhys. There was no reason for Malcolm to give Tina that slow death if no one would witness it. Had Malcolm known her backup was coming? Having been an operative himself, he'd know that the phone call he'd interrupted would have triggered backup, possibly even from someone already in the city.

So why wasn't Malcolm here? Nick was quite certain he'd left— the trail he found was cold, and when he followed it as far as he dared, it continued on toward the back of the building. There was no trace of Malcolm's scent in the surrounding rooms to suggest he'd lain in wait.

This was, admittedly, the point where he'd normally turn to Elena or Clay and say, "What do you make of this?" That would be the extent of his responsibility.

He circled the room one last time. Then he stopped short.

"We need to go," he said, turning to Vanessa.

She was still on the phone and raised a finger, telling him to hold on.

He strode over. "No, we need to leave. It's a trap. We're in a building with at least three dead bodies and—"

As if on cue, he picked up the distant creak of a floorboard.

"*Now*," he said.

She signed off. "We need to move Tina—"

"Too late. Someone's coming."

"We should wait," she said. "Hide and see what's going on."

"I know. But not here. Come on."

*

Nick and Vanessa watched as three people stood around Tina's body. Three men dressed in dark clothing, two holding guns, the third a knife. Big guns—.45 caliber, he'd guess. The knife wasn't small, either, and judging by the bulge under the guy's jacket, he had a gun there, too.

They weren't werewolves. Nick could tell that from their hiding spot, the men's scent drifting far enough to pick up. They looked like . . . Well, that was the thing. To the untrained eye, they looked like commandos or mercenaries, like guys who'd work for someone like Rhys. Except, having met people who worked for Rhys, Nick knew that real mercenaries dressed and acted like ordinary people. Blending in.

These guys looked like they were in a mercenary role-playing game. They were physically suited to the role, at least the stereotype of it. None over forty years old or under six feet tall. All square-jawed and bristle-haired. It'd be an amusing spectacle, actually, if they weren't standing over the corpse of a woman he'd known.

It'd also be more amusing if those guns weren't so damned big.

One dropped to his knee beside Tina.

"Looks different than the others," one of his companions said.

"Different but the same. Still a werewolf kill."

Nick tensed. They knew they were stalking a werewolf?

The guy continued. "Seems as if he got interrupted here. Started tearing out her throat and something stopped him."

"Think he heard us coming?"

The kneeling guy, who seemed to be the leader, touched the blood trail. "Nah. It's dry."

"She's different, too." That was the third guy, his hair so short he might have been bald. "That's no hobo. Are we sure it's our target's handiwork?"

"No," the leader said. "It's some random dude who just happened to slit her throat in the same building where two people had their throats ripped out by our target. Of course it's him. We have two kinds of victims—those who won't be missed and pretty women." The guy rose. "Okay, let's fan out. See if this bastard left any clues."

This was, one could argue, the point at which Nick should get the hell out of Dodge. He was a werewolf, and these guys were looking for a werewolf. Bounty hunters of some type, he guessed, on Malcolm's trail. *That* was the trap. Let Tina die slowly, knowing these guys were coming. Either they'd find her alive and slow down to help—or, if her handler had dispatched backup, the arrival of three armed bounty hunters would throw a wrench into the works. Either way, it let Malcolm slip off scot-free.

So Nick should go after Malcolm. And he did. He followed the trail out of the building, over two blocks, where it disappeared at the roadside, meaning Malcolm had hopped into a car and escaped. There was no tracking him after that.

"I want to know who those guys are," he said to Vanessa as they walked. "If they've separated, I can grab one. Question him."

"That's what I'd suggest," she said. "Except for the part where *you* question him."

As the leader said, they'd split up. Vanessa left Nick in charge of tracking. He knew which one he wanted. The bald guy. More brawn than brains. He'd fight the hardest, but he'd break first, too. That's what Clay always said, which is why, in a fight, he often left the biggest guy to Nick.

Now Nick was tracking his target, with Vanessa as backup. It didn't take long before he could hear the guy, who made no effort to hide his footfalls. Soon she could hear their target, too, in the parallel hall. They continued on to the next adjoining corridor. Nick veered off to intercept as Vanessa carried on.

Nick came out behind the guy. He moved cautiously, rolling his footfalls, and closed the gap until he was a few feet behind his target. Then he slowed and listened. After a moment, he heard Vanessa's footsteps. A few seconds later, the guy heard them, too.

The guy stopped. Nick halted behind him, barely breathing. The target raised his gun and dropped his free hand to his side, brushing his radio. He must know he should notify his team, but he couldn't bring himself to call in backup. Straightening, he strode forward just as Vanessa turned the corner in front of him. Surprised, the man stopped short.

That's when Nick lunged. His pounce was silent, he was sure of that. But the guy must have sensed something behind him. He spun, gun rising. Nick slammed a fist into the side of his head. The guy flew off his feet and hit the ground.

"Nice," Vanessa murmured as she knelt, confirming the man was out cold.

He let Vanessa bind the man's hands with plastic cuffs, blindfold and gag him, and then Nick loaded the limp body over his shoulder and carried him out of the building.

10. NICK

Nick hauled the bounty hunter into the equally empty building next door. By the time they found a room, the man was kicking and grunting against his gag. Nick dumped him on the filthy floor.

Vanessa warned the man that she was going to remove his gag and there was no sense calling for help—lying that they'd taken him far from his companions. The moment the gag came off, though, he started to yell. Vanessa pistol-whipped him in the exact spot where Nick had punched him and Nick yanked the gag back into place.

Vanessa repeated the warning. This time, the man seemed to decide he ought to listen, maybe because he now realized Vanessa wasn't alone.

"Who's your partner?" he said, whipping his head about as if he could peer through the blindfold.

"An associate."

"I saw him when he clocked me. I've seen him before, too."

Nick tensed.

"And where have you seen him?" she asked.

"I dunno. But I got a look at him right before he decked me."

"Describe him, then."

The guy stammered and blustered, saying Nick had dark hair and he was a "really big guy." Nick had to smile at the second part. Obviously, that line drive to the head had colored the man's recollection.

Nick let her handle the questioning. He had some knowledge of interrogation techniques. Well, the kind Clay used, at least, which usually involved his fists. Clay would prefer something more intellectual—the guy was a PhD, after all—but as he'd said many times, that wasn't the language mutts spoke.

It was different with this guy. Vanessa used the classic good-cop routine, claiming she was only doing her job, regretted it even, and sounded as if she genuinely did.

"Look, I overheard you guys in there," she said. "You're hunting a werewolf. I have no issue with that. Filthy, murdering scum. Did you see what one of those bastards did to my colleague?"

It took a moment for him to realize she meant Tina. "She was with you?"

"Yes. I have a feeling you and I are after the same guy. But you aren't authorized to take him out. I checked with my superiors. There's no record of an alternate license being issued."

"License . . . ?"

"For hunting werewolves."

"Since when do we need a license?"

"Since when *don't* you? The Cabals regulate the hunting of all werewolves and vampires. And if you pretend you don't know what a Cabal is . . ."

"Of course I do. But I don't know nothing about them regulating werewolf hunting."

"Then I'd suggest you look into it, because if you're caught? The penalty is stiff, as you might imagine."

He paled.

Nick mouthed a question to Vanessa, who nodded.

"So that's what you're doing, then," she said. "Hunting vermin? Or is it a bounty?"

"Both."

"Hunting *vermin* for a bounty? Or just this particular werewolf?"

The man shrugged. "Any werewolf would do. The guy just wants them exterminated, and he's willing to pay to see it happen. Win-win."

"Exterminated?" Vanessa said.

"Well, controlled. You can't just wipe them out, right? Not that I'd argue if you could. World would be a better place without those brutes."

Nick tried not to react. This was something he couldn't get used to. When he was growing up, the Pack had kept itself separate from the greater supernatural world, so he'd never had cause to wonder what others thought of them. Then the Pack rejoined the interracial council, and he'd found out exactly what they thought.

"So someone's putting out bounties on werewolves," Vanessa said. "Besides general cleanup, what's his motivation?"

The guy's face screwed up in confusion. "Motivation?"

"Did this guy lose someone to a werewolf?"

"Not that I know of. He just doesn't like them. He considers it his . . . what's it called? Civic duty. As a supernatural."

Nick mouthed another question.

"Let me step back, then," Vanessa said. "Do you know who you're hunting?"

"It's not a who. It's a what. Werewolves aren't human. You can't think of them that way."

Nick rocked on the balls of his feet.

"Let's pretend it's a who," Vanessa said. "For simplicity's sake. Do you know the identity of the one you're hunting now?"

A pause. A long one. Then, "Pete does."

"Pete?"

"The team captain. He gets all that intel. We're not supposed to ask."

"Do you know *anything* about it? How he found out the guy's a werewolf? Who told him where to find him?"

More silence. Then, defensively, "That's not how it works. The team doesn't get details."

Vanessa prodded, but more wasn't forthcoming. The facts seemed clear enough. Someone was putting out bounties on werewolves and had set these guys on Malcolm's tail. Then Malcolm discovered he had two groups to contend with—the bounty hunters and whoever Tina worked for—and used one to distract the other while he fled.

11. VANESSA

Tina was dead. Murdered horribly. Vanessa kept thinking, *What if we'd been a few minutes quicker? What if we hadn't been so careful?* It wouldn't have made a difference. She knew that. Yet logic didn't help, because she'd seen Tina alive, seen her moving, and there was part of her that insisted her operative could have been saved. That she'd failed.

Dwelling on that was self-indulgent, though. There was a job to do—stopping Tina's killer. Grief would come later.

It wasn't just Malcolm they needed to worry about now. Vanessa was with a werewolf . . . and there were three idiots in town on a werewolf hunt.

Vanessa could tell that conversation had upset Nick. No one wants to think another person would hunt them down as "vermin." But she hadn't expected him to seem quite so shocked. Because she wasn't. That's when she realized that no matter how liberal she considered her own views, she still supported the stereotypes by *not* being shocked, not being outraged.

As they walked out of the building, she wanted to tell Nick she'd never heard of such bounties, that these men were clearly thugs of the lowest order. Except she'd be lying. Not about the thugs part. They obviously were. But supernaturals *did* hunt werewolves and vampires. Not often, and they usually weren't successful. Given that there were only a few dozen of each on the continent, more than the very rare death would be noticed, and the werewolves and vampires would retaliate.

They *should* retaliate. Put an end to it. It wasn't as if the hunters would fight back. They were like humans going after big game. They knew, if their prey got within ten feet of them, they'd be dead. So why didn't werewolves and vampires put a scare into the hunters? Because people like the Cabals and Rhys's teams didn't bother to warn them. Didn't want to stir them up, because that would just be inconvenient.

As they neared their rented car, Vanessa said, "It does happen." Nick looked over, his dark brows gathering.

"Hunting werewolves," she said. "And vampires. I've heard of it." She braced for him to ask why they didn't tell the Pack.

"I've heard of it, too," he said. "But not in North America. It's a big problem in areas without a Pack, and there are plenty of those. Supernaturals go there to hunt. Elena even found an encrypted Web site offering tours." His lip curled. "We'd never heard of it here, though. I'll have to let Elena know."

And that was it. No blame. No accusation. He didn't complain because it was exactly what he'd come to expect. This was how werewolves were treated.

"You should have been told," Vanessa said. "Your Pack, that is."

Nick shrugged and opened the rental car door. "We'll handle it." They got into the car.

"It shouldn't happen in the first place," she said. "They're redneck idiots. If they were human, they'd be out hunting illegal immigrants or small-time crooks. They just need an excuse."

"Oh, I know. It's not like werewolves have never done that themselves." He started the car. "Historically, we hunted mutts—outside werewolves. They'd say it was to keep them in line, but really, the Pack wolves were like these guys. They wanted to hunt, so they came up with an excuse."

Nick drove out of the parking spot. "We have a Pack member now whose dad was killed in a mutt hunt when he was fifteen. The hunters knew his father had a kid. Didn't care. They wanted to kill him, too. He's lucky he escaped." He glanced over. "Want to guess who was in charge of that hunt?"

"Malcolm."

"Yep. So that's another Pack wolf we aren't telling about his return. Too many folks lined up to kill the bastard already." He reached the road and turned left. "Speaking of Malcolm, that's my priority here. If Elena wants to come out and handle these losers, fine, but I'm guessing she'll see it as a wild-goose chase. Easier to get to the root of it and work from there."

"Find out who's laying the bounties instead of hunting down three knuckleheads taking them." Vanessa nodded. "She's smart."

"That's why she's Alpha. Our instinct is to hunt them down. But these days? There are other ways. The point, though, is that my goal is Malcolm, and his trail is warm. He came to Detroit to visit a contact, right?"

"Yes, from his days with the Nasts."

"Then I'm going to pay a visit to his contact. You don't need to come along. It's been a long night, and after Tina . . ." He shrugged. "I can drop you at a hotel and check back with an update in the morning."

"I should go along, as backup."

He said nothing.

She continued, "I won't interfere. After what happened to Tina, you're in charge here. You're the one who understands what we're dealing with."

"Then just tell me where we need to go."

12. NICK

Before they reached their destination, Nick pulled over. He had to update Elena, and he wanted to do that in private. Vanessa had her own call to make. She'd texted Rhys, but her boss wanted to speak to her about getting Tina's body back.

Nick had hated leaving Tina behind. At the very least, he'd wanted to hide her body, but the arrival of the hunters quashed that plan.

He left Vanessa in the car so they could make their respective calls.

Elena put him on speakerphone—she and Clay hadn't gone to bed after he told them he was leaving for Detroit. Jeremy had taken the twins to Charleston, where Jaime was doing a show, so they didn't have to worry about him overhearing.

"So it's definitely Malcolm," Clay said after Nick explained about finding Tina. "Good."

Elena sighed. "What he means is, 'Damn, it's a shame Malcolm killed that poor woman.' Did you know her well?"

"I'd met her. We had drinks. It's harder on Vanessa. She's holding up, though—she hasn't had much time to process it."

He told them about the bounty hunters.

"Son of a bitch," Clay said. "Bounties? Here?"

"Vanessa said it happens."

"And no one bothered to tell us?"

"I'll raise a stink," Elena said. "Right now, we need to make sure these guys don't pick up your trail. Did they get a look at you?"

He told them what the bounty hunter had said.

"So he's probably seen your picture somewhere," Elena said.

Clay grunted. "Hopefully on a list of 'werewolves you do not fuck with or you'll bring the whole Pack down on your head.'"

"Hmm," she said. "Did they seem to *know* you're a werewolf?"

"No," Nick said. "I'll keep my eyes open, but they're on Malcolm's trail. Which is still inconvenient. They don't stand a hope in hell of taking him down, but there's always dumb luck."

"You want me to hop in the car?" Clay asked.

Nick was about to answer when he realized it wasn't him that Clay was asking.

"It's up to Nick," Elena said. "If he wants to get rid of Vanessa, you can back him. Rhys will squawk, but he doesn't have much leverage here. He screwed up not letting Nick take over."

"I'll grab my bag," Clay said.

"Hold on," Nick said. "I didn't answer yet."

Clay made a noise, as if to say this was merely a formality. Of course Nick would want him there.

"Let's wait," Nick said. "We've got werewolf hunters in town, and you're the most recognizable werewolf in the country."

"So? They come after me, we end the problem."

"And have three bodies to bury?" Elena said.

"Nah. One, maximum. I'll just scare the shit out of them and make them realize this werewolf-hunting thing isn't as much fun as they thought."

"While Malcolm escapes?"

Silence.

"Fine," Clay grunted. "But my bag is already packed. Find Malcolm. Then give me a call."

"I will."

*

They were in the suburbs, outside a house big enough to hold a family with five children and two dogs. As Nick surveyed the place from the idling car, he said, "So Malcolm's contact doesn't live alone."

"Just him and his wife."

"Kids grown?"

Vanessa shook her head. "No kids. He took advantage of a really bad real estate market." She waved down the road. "Half these places are empty. Foreclosures everywhere."

Which explained why the street was so dark. They'd driven through other neighborhoods that seemed to be thriving, but this— like that downtown street of vacancies—was what people thought of when you said "Detroit" these days. Nick looked at the huge house. It'd be less of a bargain when they were paying to keep it heated during a Michigan winter.

"Any idea which houses are empty?" he asked.

After a minute of flurried typing on her phone, Vanessa said, "I can tell you."

"Direct me to one, and we'll park there."

13. NICK

They found an empty house, and Nick snapped the garage door lock and parked inside. Then they crossed backyards to the contact's house.

The contact was Richard Stokes. A sorcerer, married to a half-demon named Sharon. According to Vanessa's sources, Stokes worked for the Nasts as a hit man, which is how he'd gotten to know Malcolm. They'd done a few jobs together—the Nasts sending them out as tag-team assassins.

From all accounts, Malcolm did not like partners. His first two had suffered unfortunate and fatal accidents during their missions. Malcolm had barely bothered disguising what he'd done, and his excuses had been perfunctory at best. That was Malcolm flexing his muscles and nudging his boundaries, seeing how badly the Cabal wanted him.

With Stokes, the Nasts found a partnership model that worked, mainly because it wasn't a partnership at all. Stokes figured out that Malcolm shouldn't theoretically have a problem working with someone. Wolves were pack hunters. The issue was one of hierarchy. Stokes had let Malcolm take the lead, and it turned into a beautiful friendship. Or at least a functional working relationship.

In the Pack, every wolf who ran with Malcolm was never allowed to forget what a privilege that was. In the last decade, though, Malcolm had lacked his usual posse of sycophants. He'd had only one: Richard Stokes.

When Malcolm escaped, then, it wasn't long before he'd showed up on Stokes's doorstep demanding payment in services, information, and money. That put Stokes in a very ugly position. If the Nasts found out that he'd had contact with their valuable escapee, they'd kill him. If he ratted out his former partner, Malcolm would kill him. So Stokes had played both sides. He did help Malcolm. Meanwhile, he told the Nasts and got the Cabal to agree to let him keep aiding their escapee until Malcolm lowered his guard enough to be safely brought back in. A mole in the Nast Cabal had passed all that along to Rhys.

Now Nick and Vanessa were at the Stokeses' back door, under cover of night, wearing gloves from Vanessa's kit, evaluating the situation.

The dark house meant Stokes and his wife had gone to bed. Which made things easier. It did, however, increase the chance they'd startle the two and get hit with a combined blast of spell and half-demon power.

The first potential obstacle was a security system. Luckily, Vanessa had a device to detect if one had been installed, and the skills to disarm it. When the detection device came back negative, she hesitated.

"That doesn't seem right," she said. "Stokes is a professional killer. He knows the value of security."

Nick shrugged. "Maybe he thinks being a hit man means he doesn't need it."

"Hmm."

She picked the lock. It opened easily. In fact, the entire door opened, the deadbolt having been left unfastened. Nick looked at that and then craned his head through the doorway to see a security alarm, flashing green.

"Bolt not used, alarm turned off. Shit." He stepped into the house and inhaled deeply. "I smell blood."

Vanessa moved past him to survey the dark kitchen. Nick dropped to a crouch and inhaled again.

"Malcolm," he murmured.

"Since we last saw him?"

"I can only judge the relative age of a trail, but it's fresh, meaning it's not from earlier."

"All right, then. Let's go see what he's done."

She lifted her gun and started forward. Then she stopped.

"Yep," Nick said. "The guy with the nose and the night vision should lead the way."

They reached the dining room door. Then Nick smelled something else. Burned meat. He turned back to the kitchen and sniffed, but there was no trace of the scent there.

"What's wrong?" Vanessa mouthed.

He shook his head. If it was what it smelled like, he wasn't telling her until it was absolutely necessary. He crept into the dining room. She covered him with her gun. He paused and inhaled, picking up only the smells of blood and burned flesh. He started forward again. He was approaching the next doorway when a board creaked. He stopped and glanced back at Vanessa. She was poised in the kitchen doorway—standing on ceramic tile.

Just as he lifted his foot, he heard the brush of a stockinged foot. It came from the left. He turned to see another doorway, this one with stairs beyond it. A second swish of fabric on wood. Too far away to be the hall. It must have come from the opposite side of the house.

As the noise came a third time, he remembered a similar sound, heard only a few hours ago. Tina dragging herself along the floor.

He could definitely smell blood. Had Malcolm repeated his trick?

He backed them into the kitchen and looked around. There was a second door, closed. He'd noted it earlier and presumed it led to the basement, but he should have checked. As soon as he looked in that direction, Vanessa cursed under her breath, as if chiding herself for the same thing. She motioned that she'd guard while he checked.

Nick cracked the door open. It led to a home office. Through it he could see a second door, leading to the other side of the house. That was where the noises came from.

Nick inhaled. A man's scent permeated the office. Stokes's scent. Strong. No hint of Malcolm's.

He backed up and told Vanessa his plan.

14. NICK

Nick waited while Vanessa got in position. As he went back through the dining room, Vanessa shuffled loudly, announcing her position in hopes of luring their target in her direction.

Nick moved silently through to the front hall. The stairs were to his right, the entry door to his left. He paused and inhaled. Definitely more of Malcolm's scent here. Two trails. One led back the way he'd come. The other went upstairs.

Nick slipped to the foot of the stairs. The stink of blood was stronger there and seemed to come from upstairs. He retreated. A leaded glass door opened into a formal living room. Malcolm's trail didn't cross its threshold. When Nick listened, though, he caught the brush of fabric on wood again, heading toward Vanessa.

He cracked open the leaded glass and inhaled. No recent scent other than the homeowners'. No blood, either. Yet he did detect the burned flesh smell, which gave him pause. Either Richard or Sharon Stokes *was* here, injured and moving toward Vanessa. That burned smell . . .

Although Sharon Stokes was a half-demon, her power was minor hearing enhancement, not fire. Which meant the smell . . . Nick didn't want to consider what that meant.

He eased through the doorway and crossed the big living room. On the other side, if his calculations were right, lay the home office.

Nick moved on the far side of the half-open office door, where he couldn't be spotted. The room had gone silent. Every few minutes,

Vanessa would make a soft, seemingly accidental sound. But when she did, there was no answering sound from the office, which seemed to confirm his suspicion. Whoever they were dealing with wasn't in any shape to deal with them.

He reached the half-open door and angled for a glance through. No sign of a figure. His gaze dropped. There were a few hard-to-see spots, but he could make out enough to be sure someone wasn't lying on the floor.

He definitely smelled Stokes, though. So where was he?

Nick's gaze surveyed the floor. Then he spotted an area of darkness beside the desk, with a sleeve protruding from it, the rest of the body tucked back in the shadows.

One last glance around, and then he zipped toward the desk, ready to find—

It was a sweater that had fallen off the back of the chair.

A faint click behind him. Nick wheeled as a closet door swung open. He dove, and a bullet hit the wall beside him. The gun fired again while Nick lunged. The bullet sliced through the back of his shirt as he dropped and hit his assailant. Another shot. This one from across the room. His attacker fell over him, his gun sailing off to the side. Vanessa snatched it up as Nick pounced on his fallen foe.

The man had twisted as he fell and now lay on his stomach. Blood seeped from his right sleeve, where Vanessa's bullet had hit his arm.

"It's Stokes," Vanessa said. "Grab his hands so he can't cast."

A sorcerer cast with a combination of words and gestures. If the guy knew any witch magic, though, restraining him wouldn't help. As Nick caught the man's hands, he braced for a spoken spell, but Stokes only grunted in pain when Nick yanked on his injured arm.

Why hadn't Stokes cast earlier? Sure, he had a gun, but a trained killer would use every weapon in his arsenal, and there were sorcerer spells like knockbacks and blurs that would have made Stokes's closet attack much more effective.

Then there was that smell . . . Even stronger now, as Nick pinned Stokes. One split second of *What did Malcolm do?* passed through his mind. Then he knew. And his stomach clenched.

He grabbed Stokes by the shoulder and flipped him over. The man didn't react to the pain now. Nick could see why he'd barely reacted after the shot. His eyes were glazed over. Dulled by painkillers. There was blood on his mouth. And that burned smell blasted out on his breath.

Vanessa walked over, gun still trained. "Were you expecting someone else tonight, Richard? Is that why your alarm was off? You were lying in wait for Malcolm?"

"Malcolm's already been here," Nick said. "And Stokes can't answer. Malcolm cut out his tongue."

Vanessa rocked back before catching herself. She quickly recovered but couldn't mask the horror in her eyes.

"For snitching," she murmured. "He cut it out for snitching."

"With the added bonus that it robs Stokes of his power."

He released Stokes's hands and started to rise. Out of the corner of his eye he saw something flash. A knife. Nick wheeled, but Vanessa was already in motion, grabbing Stokes's wrist, her fingers blazing. Stokes let out a grunt, more surprise than pain, as he dropped the knife. Before Nick could react, Vanessa had Stokes pinned on his stomach again, hands behind his back. She motioned for Nick to hold them while she used plastic cuffs.

"You're fast," he said.

A shaky laugh. "My field skills are coming back. Slowly."

"We aren't here to hurt you, Stokes," Nick said. "Malcolm's gone. We're on his tail."

Hate blazed through the man's drug-bleary eyes. This wasn't an innocent victim, Nick reminded himself. As much as that horrible injury made him want to feel pity, Stokes almost certainly deserved it. From what Vanessa had said, he'd made a very good partner for Malcolm. Equally vicious and ruthless.

"I'm—" Nick began to introduce himself, but Stokes cut him short with a guttural growl.

Stokes jabbed his chin at the desk and, with his hands bound, managed to mimic writing. Nick got a paper and pen.

"You're right-handed, I take it?" Vanessa said.

He nodded. She undid the cuff and tied his left hand to the desk leg. He didn't like that—clearly he expected to sit up and write his message—but after some glowers failed to move Vanessa he snatched the page and started to scribble a message. He wrote it in a combination of text and haphazard shorthand that Nick deciphered as: *Want my help? Find my wife. He hurts her? I'll hunt you down and do worse than cut out your goddamned tongues.*

"Charming," Vanessa said. "Your bravado is admirable, Stokes, but you're an idiot if you think you should threaten someone with a gun at your head."

He scrawled, *Find my wife or no Malcolm. I'll hunt him down, and you'll never find him.*

"All right," Vanessa said. "So Malcolm took your wife—"

He cut her short with a wave and wrote, *He said someone would come for him, and if I didn't kill whoever came . . .*

He stopped there. Nick didn't care to imagine what Malcolm said he'd do to Sharon Stokes. The look in Stokes's eyes was enough. As soon as he read the words, though, Nick stopped and looked up, toward the second floor, and that sick feeling in his gut returned.

Shit. Oh, shit. He wouldn't . . .

Hell, yes. He absolutely would.

"Did you see Malcolm leave with your wife?" Nick asked.

The haunted pain in Stokes's eyes vanished in a snap, his lip curling as if to say, "What a fucking pointless question."

Nick repeated it and waved at the pad. Stokes wrote, pen strokes hard now, anger and frustration mounting.

If you're asking if I stood at the fucking window and saw which way they went—

"No, I'm . . ." Nick struggled for a way to word the question that wouldn't reveal his suspicion. "Malcolm did that to you. And then what? Was your wife with him? Was she conscious? Did he drag her out? I'm a werewolf, and I need some idea of what kind of trail I'm looking for. Walk me through it—quickly—so I can go after them."

Stokes still simmered, and it was obvious he considered Nick a flaming idiot, but that idiot was the guy he was counting on to bring his wife back alive. He wrote quickly, the words nearly illegible in his haste.

Broke in. Knocked her out. Knew I'd been talking to the Nasts. Said I set him up. Told me what he'd do if I didn't kill whoever came here after him. Then he cut out my tongue and cauterized it. I passed out. When I woke, they were gone.

Taking Stokes's wife was too much trouble. That was the problem. One Nick wasn't about to explain to this mutilated killer, seething with rage, frantic for his wife's safety.

"I need to go upstairs," Nick said to Vanessa.

Now Stokes didn't bother with the paper. He didn't need to. Nick could decipher his garbled words just fine.

"What the fuck? No. *Fucking no*," Stokes said as he jabbed his free hand at the door, telling them to go, get on his wife's trail, bring her back.

"I really need to go upstairs," Nick said. "To check her scent."

Fresh dismay in Vanessa's eyes told him she knew what he was really checking.

As Nick headed up the stairs, the smell of blood grew stronger. He could tell himself it was from cutting off Stokes's tongue. It wasn't. The smell was much too strong for that.

The stairs led to a wide hall with four doors plus a double set that presumably led to a linen closet. Nick went through the open door first. The master bedroom, stinking of fear and sweat and blood and burned flesh. This was where Malcolm had done it, surprising the couple as they slept.

The sheets were soaked in blood. On the floor lay the remains of Stokes's tongue, tossed aside. Nick walked to the bed. While it was a lot of blood, it wasn't enough for what he'd smelled.

Nick backed out and checked the double doors. As he expected, it was a linen closet—a walk-in one, but still small enough to search with a visual sweep. The next door led to a spare bedroom that smelled as if it'd never been used. A bathroom was next. Also empty. Then the third bedroom, which seemed to be a second office, smelling of Sharon Stokes. No blood, though.

Nick returned to the hall and looked around. He could mentally map out the upper level and tell that all space was accounted for. The blood, however, was not.

He walked to the middle of the hall, trying to pinpoint the location of the scent, but it seemed to come from all directions. He crouched again, to follow Malcolm's trail. As soon as he bent, the smell grew fainter. He rose. Stronger.

Nick looked up. There, in the ceiling, was an attic door. Nick went to the linen closet and found a hook hanging on the wall. He used it to snag the strap on the attic door. It opened, steps sliding down.

15. NICK

As Nick climbed those steps, there was no doubt the blood scent came from up there. The attic was nearly pitch-dark, though, and he had to pause for his eyes to adjust to the light coming from the hall below.

The attic was empty. Completely empty. Nick didn't have to move from the top of the steps to scan the entirety of the massive open space. And to assure himself there was nothing up here except the smell of blood.

As soon as he walked into the attic, he spotted the blood pool, glistening on the dust-covered floor. When his footsteps subsided, he picked up a sound. A very soft *plink*. Then silence.

He circled the blood pool. It was perfectly formed, with no sign that whoever bled here had crawled or been taken away. Yet there was clearly not a body.

Plink.

This time he saw the drop hit the pool. He looked up and saw only the black roofline above. When he blinked, his night vision adjusted and—

Sharon Stokes. Spread-eagled on the ceiling, her throat and wrists bloodied.

Nick took out his phone and shone the light up at Sharon's body. Only then could he see how she'd been fastened there, and when he did, his stomach lurched. He lowered the light and noticed the tools hidden in the shadow by the wall. A nail gun and a ladder.

Malcolm nailed her to the ceiling, cut her throat, and let her bleed out, hanging there.

Had she regained consciousness? God, Nick hoped not.

He stared up at that body, and there was part of him that couldn't quite believe it. Yes, the Malcolm he'd known was a sadistic son of a bitch, but this? And cutting out Stokes's tongue? What had the Nasts done to him? Nick wasn't sure he wanted to know.

Nick found Vanessa and Stokes where he'd left them. Stokes lay on his back, both hands fastened again. Vanessa stood over him with her gun.

"Your wife's gone," Nick said.

Stokes screwed up his face, and Nick knew what he'd say if he could. *Of course she's gone, you fucking moron. That's what I told you.*

"I mean she's dead. Malcolm killed her before he left."

Stokes went still. Then his face hardened as he bucked up, managing to get to his knees.

As soon as Stokes pushed to his feet, he lunged at Nick. Vanessa grabbed his bound hands and yanked him back. He shook her off and settled for glaring at Nick with all the hate he could muster as he mouthed, "Liar."

"I wish I was," Nick said. "But think about it. Is Malcolm really going to bother taking a hostage? All that mattered was convincing you to kill us for him."

He could see in Stokes's hesitation that he knew Nick was right. He just didn't want to believe it.

"Where is she?" Stokes mouthed.

When Nick didn't answer fast enough, Stokes figured it out and turned toward the living room. Nick moved to swing into Stokes's path, but Vanessa stopped him.

"Let him go," she murmured. "He's not giving us what we need until he sees for himself."

"I know." Nick lowered his voice. "But he shouldn't see her like that."

Nick broke into a jog to catch up with Stokes, already cresting the top of the stairs.

"Let me bring her to you," Nick called as he loped up behind him.

Stokes was on the extended attic steps. When Nick grabbed for his pant leg, Stokes wheeled and kicked. Nick caught his leg. Stokes yanked, managing to keep his balance with his bound hands again but ready to topple.

"Let him go," Vanessa said again.

Nick wanted to haul Stokes's ass down those stairs, pin him on the damned floor, and tell him he wasn't seeing his wife that way. That no matter what a vicious asshole Stokes was, he obviously loved his wife, and that shouldn't be his final memory of her.

But Elena would agree with Vanessa. Their goal was Malcolm, and his trail was cooling fast.

Nick released Stokes. The man stumbled up the stairs. He flipped a switch with his teeth, and a row of lights flickered on as Nick climbed the steps. Stokes saw the blood immediately. He walked to it, gaze tripping across the floor, looking for Sharon. When he reached the edge of that perfect puddle, he turned and glared at Nick as if to say, "Where the hell is she?"

Nick crossed his arms and glared back. Beside him, Vanessa inhaled sharply. Stokes heard. He looked at Vanessa and followed her gaze.

Silence. Ten long seconds of silence. Then Stokes screamed, a horrible, wordless scream of rage. He wheeled on Nick and stood there, bristling like an enraged boar.

"Get her down," he mouthed as he gestured.

"Fuck you," Nick said.

Stokes charged. Nick slammed him in the gut and sent him flying, coughing and choking. He hit the floor. Nick advanced on him as he rose.

"I told you she was dead. I offered to get her down before you saw her. I'm not doing it now. If you want revenge, tell us whatever you can about Malcolm. Then we'll cut you loose, and *you* can get her down."

Stokes snarled and raged, but Nick didn't budge. Despite being bound at gunpoint, Stokes clearly considered himself the Alpha here. Nick was an idiot. Vanessa was a woman. They'd damn well better jump when he said jump. And if they did, he'd see no reason to give them what they wanted.

So Nick watched Stokes rage and waited, until his anger and grief began to sputter.

"Let me repeat myself," Nick said. "You tell us what we want. We let you go. Otherwise, we walk out of here, and I pick up Malcolm's trail on my own, and you can figure out how the hell you're going to call for help without the use of your hands or tongue."

Stokes struggled in his cuffs, but Vanessa had bound him well.

Nick turned for the hatch. Stokes lunged at him. Nick spun, caught him in the gut with another right, and left him on the floor, heaving for breath.

They made it halfway down the main stairs before Stokes came after them.

16. NICK

They let Stokes sit at the desk and type the full story on his laptop. As they knew, Malcolm had come by earlier that day. He wanted Stokes's help, though he'd insisted he was offering Stokes an opportunity. Stokes played along.

Malcolm needed money. He'd mooched some from Stokes already, but he was smart enough to see that income stream wouldn't last forever. So he'd found a job on his own. Malcolm had called it assassin work; Stokes called it thug work.

The job was lucrative, though. Stokes had asked for details and said he'd consider it. They made plans to meet the next day. Then Malcolm left the house, with Tina on his tail, and that's when it all went wrong.

While Stokes didn't know where Malcolm was staying, he listed a few hotels of the sort Malcolm favored these days, upper end but not luxurious, balancing his budget with his ego. He provided the make of the car Malcolm was driving, but he was certain Malcolm would have ditched it by now. Stokes had taught him a few things about being a hired killer.

They asked for details about the job then, as another route to Malcolm.

West-coast client, Stokes typed. *No name. Sorcerer. Suspect he runs a cut-rate Cabal-wannabe operation.*

Nick looked at Vanessa.

"There are a few dozen of them," she said. "Anything from million-dollar operations to borderline street gangs."

73

Expect this one to be in the middle, Stokes wrote. *Up-and-comers. Malcolm said—*

Stokes stopped. Nick looked toward the window, where he could pick up the distant wail of a siren. He'd been too preoccupied to notice the faint sound sooner.

Vanessa motioned subtly for Nick to check it out. "Keep going," she said to Stokes. "What did Malcolm say?"

Nick walked through to the next room. He could pick up the sirens better.

"Ambulance," he called back softly. "Maybe a midnight heart attack. I'll take a look."

It was impossible to get any kind of wide view from the front windows. Nick walked to the front door. The outside lights had been on when they arrived. He flicked them off and eased open the door. He could hear the siren, coming steadily closer. And more now, the growl of engines and the rumble of tires. More than one vehicle. There was a second siren too.

Was that a fire engine?

Uh, yeah. What was the chance of a fire in the neighborhood right now?

Pretty good . . . if Malcolm set it to draw attention to Stokes's house. To frame his former partner for murder.

But that was a roundabout way of doing things. Malcolm was never roundabout. If that's what he wanted to do, he'd just call and report someone was seriously injured—

"Shit!"

Nick raced back into the house. As he did, he heard Vanessa tell Stokes to "Sit your ass down in that chair." He hurried through the living room. Vanessa was arguing with Stokes, her back to Nick, gun pointed at Stokes, who was standing.

"We need to—" Nick began.

She glanced over her shoulder. Stokes tensed. Before Nick could say a word, Vanessa had twisted back to her target, but Stokes was already in flight. Stokes grabbed her in a choke hold and went for the gun.

She flipped the chamber open, emptying the gun so deftly that Nick heard the cartridges hit the ground at the same time he saw her toss the gun aside. Then she clamped down on Stokes's arm with ten blazing fingers. He snarled, but either the painkillers hadn't worn off or he just didn't give a shit.

Stokes backed up, his arm tightening around Vanessa's neck, her eyes bulging. Nick could smell her fingers burning into his arm, but he didn't relax his hold until Nick had him in a choke hold of his own.

"What the hell do you think you're doing?" Nick said. "The cops are on their way. Malcolm called them in. We're trying to save your ass."

Vanessa wrenched free, gasping as she spoke. "He doesn't want to be saved. He wants us to decide he's too much trouble and put him down."

She struggled to catch her breath. "His wife is dead upstairs. He knows Malcolm will have framed him as his final revenge—hopefully exacted *after* Stokes has helpfully killed us. But his timing was a little off."

Nick gave Stokes a shove. "You need to run."

Vanessa grabbed her gun and slapped it back together as she asked, "How far off are they?"

"Maybe a couple of blocks. We'll need to—"

Stokes snatched the knife from earlier. Nick wheeled, ready to block his attack. Only he didn't attack. He drew the knife back and plunged it into his heart.

When Nick lunged for him, Vanessa grabbed the back of his shirt.

"He was going to do it," she said. "It was just a question of whether he took us along."

"But the cops wouldn't have thought he cut out his own tongue."

"Doesn't matter. Malcolm wasn't letting him walk out of this. Let's just hope *we* can."

*

The ambulance had indeed stopped at the Stokes house. So had two police cruisers. The cops had gone in first and called to the paramedics, presumably when they found Stokes dying on the study floor.

"Wait," Vanessa said. "Wait . . ."

Nick could point out that he hadn't given any indication that he planned to do anything *except* wait. They were in the yard behind the Stokes house, waiting for a chance to run through the rear yards to the car. The trick here was to time their departure just right.

One pair of officers had already circled the property. A perfunctory search. Stokes had obviously stabbed himself. It wouldn't even be clear that there'd been an intruder until they realized their victim was missing his tongue.

The officers had gone, but Vanessa still held off, making sure they didn't pop back out to check something.

"Still clear?" she whispered.

"Yep."

"All right, then. Let's go."

Nick steered them through this yard and the next. There were fences to scale and it was obvious Vanessa was out of practice, but she didn't pretend otherwise, letting Nick help her as they went.

At the halfway point, Nick stayed on the fence after he'd helped Vanessa down. He rose, balancing, to get a look back at the Stokes house. It wasn't a clear angle, but he could see enough of the road to be sure no new emergency vehicles had joined the others. As he readied himself to jump down, though, he saw two police cars pass.

Nick crouched on the fence until the cars pulled in with the others. Two detectives went inside. Two uniforms stayed on the front lawn.

He jumped down and told Vanessa.

"They're guarding against curious neighbors," she said. "They may have shut off the lights and siren, but people will have heard the vehicles. Any minute now, every occupied home here will have someone peering out, trying to see what's going on. Which means we need to move. Fast. Nosy neighbors are worse than cops."

They jogged across the back of the yards, and got through two before it seemed as if half the neighborhood lit up. When a door opened, they dove behind a shed.

"Go on," a voice muttered, thick with sleep. "Be quick about it, Mitzie."

Nick swore.

Vanessa whispered, "We're fine. City pets are used to people nearby, and any pooch named Mitzie isn't going to be a world-class guard dog."

"Which doesn't matter when one of us is a werewolf," Nick whispered back.

He'd barely finished before the dog started wailing louder than a police siren. Vanessa was right about one thing—Mitzie was no guard dog. She'd caught one whiff of Nick and started throwing herself against the door to be let back in before the monster devoured her.

"Take the lead," he whispered to Vanessa.

She scaled the rear fence, which left them blocked by the shed. A door opened, Mitzie's owner muttering, "What the hell?" as the dog barreled inside. The door shut, but as soon as Nick topped the fence, a deck light turned on in the yard he was climbing *into*.

"Go!" he called down to Vanessa.

Nick jumped. A muffled shout from inside the house told him he'd been spotted. He made a run for it—in the opposite direction. Back over the back fence. Then through the yard where Mitzie's owner had, thankfully, retreated indoors to tend to his distraught pet. Hop the next fence. And then circle around into the yard of the empty house where they'd parked.

Vanessa had the car running and the garage door up. He raced to the passenger side and jumped in.

"Go!" he said.

"That neighbor saw you run into this yard," she said. "If we back out now—"

"I went the other way around." He rolled down the window. "The witness will tell the cops I ran *toward* the Stokes house. Now go."

17. NICK

With the headlights off, the car rolled down the driveway. Once they were sure no cruisers were ripping after them, Nick pulled his knee up, rubbing his calf and wincing.

"I think I pulled something back there," he said. "Five fences in five minutes. I'm too old for that shit."

Vanessa gave a shaky laugh. "Five fences in *twenty* minutes was too much for me. I've been too old for this shit for a while. Out of practice, too. I need to get out in the field more. I can't believe Stokes got the jump on me back there."

"You handled it," Nick said. "And he *is* a professional killer."

She screwed up her nose as if to say that wasn't an excuse. Nick watched her as she drove, her gaze fixed ahead. She was a beautiful woman . . . which was almost certainly not what should be going through his mind at this moment.

Vanessa cast an anxious glance in the rearview mirror.

"I'll hear anyone coming after us," Nick said. "My window's cracked open."

"I know."

"We're fine." He paused. "Relatively speaking."

She gave a tight laugh and loosened her death grip on the wheel, flexing her hands, only to squeeze it again with both hands, her gaze staring into the night.

"You know what we need?" he said. "A drink."

"Oh, yeah."

"Think we can find one at"—he checked his watch—"three-thirty in the morning?"

She glanced over. "You're serious?"

"I am. We've made our getaway. We aren't going to track down Malcolm tonight. We need to rest and convey our updates to our respective bosses. And then we need a drink. Or three."

Her laugh loosened then, as did her grip on the wheel. "If you really are serious, I won't argue. I'm sure we could find a corner store and grab—"

A phone buzzed.

"Speaking of bosses," Nick said. "That must be yours."

"Um, no. When I'm in the field, I don't even put it on vibrate."

"Well, mine *is* on vibrate and . . ."

He trailed off as they looked at each other. Nick whipped around, clicking his seat belt off as he looked in the backseat. The phone kept ringing. He pinpointed the sound, coming from under his seat. He reached down, feeling around until his fingers touched plastic.

He pulled the phone out. A blocked number showed on the screen. He was about to answer when Vanessa grabbed the phone from him and yanked the wheel, braking hard, but not before the car lurched up over the curb.

"Out!" she said. "Now!"

She scrambled out. He followed. The phone kept ringing. Then, as the car doors slammed shut behind him, the ringing grew muffled, and he realized she'd left the phone in the car. She prodded him until they were fifty feet away.

"Cell phones are used to set off bombs," she said before he could ask.

They stood on the curb and watched the car, still running. They were on the edges of the suburb now. A lone truck slowed as it approached. Vanessa waved her own cell phone, telling him it was fine, they'd called a tow truck.

The other phone kept ringing.

"We're assuming Malcolm put it in there, right?" Nick said. "That he was watching Stokes's house and planted the phone, and I was in too big a hurry jumping into the car to notice his scent in the garage. Is there any other explanation?"

"No. It's Malcolm."

"Okay, then I'm ninety-nine percent sure it's not a bomb. He'd never use one."

Vanessa shook her head, gaze still trained on the car. "Anyone can adapt—"

"Not Malcolm. He really is an old dog. Using a bomb is a trick he couldn't learn even if he wanted to, and believe me, he wouldn't want to."

The phone stopped ringing. A few seconds of silence passed. Another car slowed. Vanessa waved it on. The phone started again.

"He's trying to make contact," Nick said. "That's his style. Engage the enemy." He looked around. "And the alternative is that we leave the car running, with our stuff in it, and walk away." He looked at her. "You stay here while I check the phone—"

"No. I might be able to tell if it's been tampered with."

Nick followed her back to the car. She flung open the passenger side then backpedaled, as if ready to dive aside. When no explosion came, she retrieved the phone and ran from the car. When they got fifty feet away again, Vanessa held the phone out gingerly, turning it over in her hands as it continued to ring.

"Stand back," she said. "Please."

Nick did, only because he knew she wouldn't answer otherwise. Once he was about ten feet away, she hit the talk button.

"Hello."

Nick could hear the voice on the other end, and it was as chilling as picking up Malcolm's scent, like being sucked into a time warp back to a place you'd rather never visit again.

"Please put Nicholas on the phone," Malcolm said.

"I don't know who you—"

"I was in your car. I smelled him. I'm sure he's right there. Just look around. Handsome fellow. Terribly charming. *Not* terribly bright."

Nick resisted the urge to scowl at that. If—like Stokes—Malcolm considered Nick an idiot, it would only make him easier to catch.

Vanessa looked at Nick. He held out his hand.

"Hello, Malcolm," he said into the phone.

"Nicky. How are you, boy?"

Not exactly a boy anymore, but Nick knew that wasn't what Malcolm meant. Like the diminutive, it was meant to put Nick in his place.

"So where is he?" Malcolm asked.

"Where's who?"

Malcolm laughed. "Are you that dense, boy? Your partner-in-crime. The brains *and* the brawn."

"If you mean Clay, he's at home. Probably sleeping."

Another laugh, infused with impatience now. "There's no way he'd send his pup out alone. I remember when you were boys, how you followed him around, just like a puppy. And as helpless as one. Clayton's not only your friend—he's your protector. If you're there, he's nearby. Guaranteed."

"Would you like to wager on it?" Nick paused. "I've got a new car back home. A Jag. I remember you liked Jags. Mine's top-of-the-line. If Clay's here, you can have it. I bet you'd like that. Not a lot of fancy cars in your life these days."

Silence.

"Yes," Nick said. "Clay looked after me when I was young, because he was a full werewolf long before I was. And, yes, that's not the only reason. I'm not my father. I'm not a warrior. But I'm not a boy anymore, either, and neither is Clay. His mate is the Alpha. He has children. Do you really think he's going to come running after you? Do you really think you're worth it?"

More silence. Then a laugh. "Yes, I do, because I saw his face at Nast headquarters. He's not going to let me live out my retirement in peace."

"No, he's going to kill you. But first you need to be found, and that's really more trouble than he's willing to expend on you."

More silence as Malcolm seethed. Vanessa motioned he might not want to antagonize Malcolm, but Nick knew what he was doing. No way in hell would Malcolm leave town if Clay wasn't here. Running from Nick Sorrentino would just be humiliating.

"Clay may have given you his grunt work," Malcolm said after a minute. "But he'll show up. You're in over your head."

"Slaughtering humans is par for the course with you, Malcolm. Unless you've got a posse at your command, you like easy prey."

"Oh, it isn't me you need to worry about, Nicky. It's the guys on the other end of the GPS in that phone you're holding."

Nick went quiet.

Malcolm chuckled. "That shut you up. Let me help, or you'll be there all night figuring it out. Those three werewolf hunters you saw earlier are just one team on the prowl. There are two others, and they're all in Detroit. And someone has helpfully provided them with the GPS in that phone. So you have two choices. Either you run back home to Daddy or you call Clayton and his bitch to come rescue you. Because otherwise—"

Tires squealed a couple of blocks over.

"In the car!" Nick said as he smacked the phone off. He drew his arm back to pitch the cell, but Vanessa grabbed his elbow. "They're tracking the GPS," he said. "He gave it to the werewolf hunters. Three teams of them."

She took the phone from him. "Then we'll have better luck throwing them off track *with* this. Get in and drive."

18. NICK

Nick peeled off the curb and hit the gas, but it wasn't exactly the sort of car he was used to, and when he looked into his rearview mirror, he could see a pickup bearing down on them.

"I've got their license number," Vanessa said. "That'll help later for ID, but right now, we need to lose them. Stay on the straight-away."

"But they're gaining—"

"This is no deserted back road. They'll follow until they can find a place to push us off the street. Just give me two minutes to scramble this."

"Scramble?"

"The signal. That won't help with these guys, but it'll keep the other teams from catching up."

The truck got about three car lengths behind them and stayed there. While the road wasn't busy, the occasional other vehicle meant their pursuers weren't taking a chance. They were waiting for Nick to make his getaway by veering down a quiet side road.

"And . . . got it," Vanessa said. "They'll still see a GPS signal, but it'll send them on a wild-goose chase. Can you lose these guys?"

"In this car?"

She chuckled. "It's not a Jag, but there's a distinct advantage to having an ordinary car—it'll be much easier to lose them. Do you want to switch spots?"

He glanced over.

"We can do it," she said. "I have before. Mid-car-chase driver switch." A flashed grin. "It's fun."

"I'm fine with driving. You navig—"

The truck shot forward, narrowing the gap between them.

"Damn it," Vanessa said, twisting to watch the truck. "The idiots are getting restless. Can you go any faster?"

"I can. But *that's* the problem." He waved at the red light ahead—with cars going through.

"Make a hard right at the light. Join the traffic flow. Try not to hit anyone."

The last part was the toughest. The road ahead wasn't jam-packed, but it wasn't empty either.

"Nick! Brace—!"

The pickup bumped them. Nick smacked against the seat belt. He hit the accelerator. The light ahead was still red, with no sign it'd turn green anytime soon. Nick played with the acceleration, easing back and jolting forward, judging the traffic flow ahead, trying to gauge . . .

He hit the gas. There was a split second where the engine hesitated, as if to say, "You want me to do *what*?" Then it revved, and while they didn't exactly fly back in their seats, the car did accelerate, engine whining.

Nick glanced over his shoulder. He could see the driver's face, screwed up in confusion, the passenger's eyes wide, mouth open as he said something, likely some variation of "Slow the fuck down!" as they barreled toward the intersection.

"You need to slow—" Vanessa began.

"Got it."

"You can't take the turn—"

"Hold on."

He gauged the traffic flow, slowing just a little. Behind him, he could hear the pickup's passengers shouting, "He's going through! Goddamn it, Ted, don't you dare follow—!"

Nick braked hard, sending the car into a skid and then steering out and around the corner, wide enough to make a car in the opposite lane veer. He heard the other driver yell an obscenity. Completely unwarranted, considering that Nick probably saved the guy's life, because as the driver veered, he also slowed, and the guy in the pickup—still thinking Nick was going straight through—kept going, narrowly avoiding a T-bone.

There was still plenty of honking, and a squeal of tires. Nick accelerated again, zooming up on a transport. He weaved to see past it. Then he swerved into the opposite lane—and into the headlights of an oncoming car.

"You don't have time—!" Vanessa began.

Nick hit the gas. She was right—he didn't have time. But presuming the person at the wheel wasn't asleep, the oncoming car would brake. Which it did, tires protesting as Nick's car veered in front of the transport. Both the oncoming car and the truck laid on their horns.

Nick put the pedal down again, passing the next car and then making a sharp right at the light and another at the next, taking them back the way they'd come. He crossed the first road they'd originally been on and continued into the night, the pickup long gone.

"You *can* drive." Vanessa grinned over at him, eyes sparkling, and for a second he knew she'd forgotten the horror of the night.

"So, do I get that drink now?" she asked.

"Several. I think we've earned them."

They continued in silence for a few minutes. Then she said, "I need to call Rhys."

"And I need to call Elena. Just let me get where we're going."

"Which is . . .?"

"Someplace we can get a drink."

She smiled and relaxed in her seat. They reached the highway, and she watched out the window, saying nothing for about five minutes, and then, "We need a plan."

"I know. Just . . . let's rest a bit."

Nick left the highway two exits before their turnoff, intentionally. He glanced over, waiting for her to ask where they were headed, but she had her eyes closed. When she opened them ten minutes later, she shot forward in her seat.

"Why are we at the airport?" she said.

"Getting a drink. If anything's open. Then getting you on the first plane home."

She twisted to face him. "Hell, no. You're not—"

"Yep, I am."

"If this is because Stokes got the jump—"

"It's not." Nick pulled into the parking garage. "We're chasing a psychopath who'll grab you the first chance he gets. Then he'll kill you—horribly—to teach me a lesson."

Her face hardened. "I'm not some date you brought along—"

"I know that." He pulled into a spot. "You're accustomed to bad guys who will kill you if you get in their way. But that's not Malcolm. He knows I'm with a woman, and he's going to target you because, if you die, I'll blame myself. That's how he operates. He kills those who don't matter. And he hurts those who do. He *will* come after you."

"Then we'll know how to catch him."

"No."

Vanessa sat there, poised, as if waiting for him to elaborate.

He looked her in the eye. "No."

"Then I guess we'll have to split up and do this on our own. You call Elena and have her send Clay. I'll get Jayne and a few others, and we'll go after Malcolm separately. Then we'll pray it doesn't turn into a huge cluster-fuck, attacking each other and those damned werewolf hunters, while Malcolm circles until he can take out Clayton."

"After that fight at Nast headquarters, Malcolm knows Clay will—and can—take him down. The minute Clay's here, he'll bolt. Elena knows that. She won't send him."

"So she'll come out herself? Even better. Malcolm would love that. You said he likes to hurt his enemies."

Nick shook his head. "You're not drawing me into this argument, Vanessa. Stay or go. Your choice, but only because I can't force you onto a plane."

He left her the keys and got his bag from the trunk. Vanessa caught up with him halfway to the parking garage exit.

"I'm not trying to be a pain in the ass, Nick," she said. "But this guy killed my agent, and that gives me a reason to go after him. I can do that with my own people, but I'd really rather do it with you. You know Malcolm. Bring in whoever you want, and I'll work with them, too. But I have experience and tools that your people don't. Like checking for a security system or scrambling that phone signal."

"I don't want to take responsibility—"

"You're not *bringing* me. You're teaming up with me."

When he didn't respond, she said, "How about I call Rhys? Get his word on this. If he wants to recall me, he can."

He stopped walking. "Fine. You'll make that call here, where I can hear both sides. But before that, I'll phone Elena. If she insists we split up, I have to do that."

"Understood."

19. VANESSA

Vanessa went into the terminal and used the restroom while Nick phoned Elena. She could have also placed an advance call to Rhys to tell him what was up, maybe even massage the facts to be sure he'd let her stay. Nick hadn't foreseen that because he wasn't underhanded by nature. She'd given her word. He expected her to stick to it. So she'd honor that trust.

When she got back, Nick was done his call. Elena had agreed to let Vanessa help him, if that's what Rhys wanted. In the meantime, Elena was driving to Detroit with Clay, ready to jump in the moment Nick needed them.

Elena's decision didn't surprise Vanessa. If Malcolm did go after Vanessa? Well, let's be perfectly objective here. That was better than risking Nick or any of her Pack. And in coming after Vanessa, he'd get close enough for Nick to act. A cold hard assessment. And the same one Vanessa would make if an outsider volunteered to assist a member of her team.

Vanessa called Rhys next. She admitted Stokes got the jump on her, since she'd have to put that in her report. He said the same thing that Nick had—Stokes was a trained killer, and she'd handled it fine. If she was comfortable staying, then she could stay. Like Elena, though, he wasn't sitting back to wait for an update call. Jayne and Rhys were both coming out. Like Elena and Clayton, they'd hang back and wait for a distress call.

When Rhys said he'd wait for a distress call, he meant it—part of her kit was a short-range SOS alert with a GPS. Now that someone would be in range soon, she was expected to wear it.

It was not easy to find alcohol at five in the morning. Apparently, state liquor laws meant that even the corner stores stopped selling it at 2 a.m. Or they did for most people. Nick sussed out a store with a thirty-something woman behind the counter, asked Vanessa to stay in the car, went in, and came out with alcohol.

It wouldn't have been a hard sell. Even after a night of narrow escapes and filthy buildings, all it had taken was five minutes in a restroom for Nick to look like he'd stepped off a magazine cover. Vanessa was sure with only a modicum of charm—and perhaps a generous bribe—he'd been able to convince the clerk to break the rules for him.

Before he'd gone into the store, Nick had asked what she drank and she'd joked about missing her nightly gimlet. In all seriousness, she said a fifth of gin and a bottle of 7UP would be fine. At the hotel, she discovered he'd grabbed good gin and a packet of Rose's lime mix. Vanessa suspected he'd looked up the recipe on his cell phone. A guy considerate enough to do that for someone he didn't particularly seem to care for? Well, they didn't make many men like that in Vanessa's world, which only made the "didn't particularly seem to care for her" part all that much harsher.

When they'd gotten on that plane together, she'd known he'd rather be with just about anyone else. His opinion seemed to have improved since then, but she suspected she'd have had to work very hard for it to get worse. Since Nick had a reputation for being nice to just about everyone . . . well, that didn't exactly mean he'd want her number when all this was over, not even as a professional contact. Meanwhile, the more time she spent with Nick, the more time she *wanted* to spend with him, and it had nothing to do with the fact that he was very nice to look at. Put him in a dark room and she'd still be happy. Of course, if she was in a dark room with Nick, she'd probably be *very* happy . . .

Oh, hell.

She knocked back the rest of her gimlet and let Nick mix her a second. It didn't help that there was a king-size bed beside their table. The hotel had apparently been out of double beds. When she said "apparently," she wasn't implying that Nick had lied. As nice as that might have been for her ego, Nick would never pull that. She'd been the one asking when the desk clerk had said there were only king rooms left, all the while giving Vanessa a look that said, "This better be your brother, sugar, or you're out of your mind for *wanting* two beds." The room had a pullout sofa, though, and Nick had gallantly offered to take it, though she planned to flip him for it when the time came.

At least they weren't drinking in awkward silence. Nick was being his charming self, making conversation. He seemed in no rush to get to sleep, and she needed the drink as much as she'd joked she did. She'd started a very rare third as he asked about her move from fieldwork to team leader.

"I'm a half-assed field agent," she said. When he started to make the obligatory protest, she raised her hand against it. "That's not humility. I'm better suited to supervising. As you may have been able to tell, I'm not a twenty-five-year-old kick-ass martial-arts fighter. Never was, even *at* twenty-five. Getting through basic training was a bitch. Marksmanship? No problem. Academic? Technical? Easy-peasy. Running, jumping, climbing? Hell, no. I just don't have the body for it."

His gaze dropped, and she'd like to think he was checking out aforementioned body, just as she'd really like to think that the spark in his eyes was an appreciative assessment. When he said, "Nothing wrong with that," there was a flicker of hope that he was complimenting her, but he followed the comment with, "Not everyone's cut out for everything," and she took another gulp of her drink.

Stop acting like a schoolgirl with a crush.

Oh, but Nick Sorrentino was so crush-able. In every way.

Another long drink, this one draining her glass. He went to take it then stopped, looking her in the eyes, head tilted, as if assessing her sobriety.

"I'm fine," she said. "I have a high tolerance."

His lips quirked in a smile. "And you're a lousy liar. I'm good at reading the signs, and it's time to cut you off."

"Spent some time tending bar, have you?" Even as she said it, she wanted to slap herself. Nick Sorrentino had most certainly never been a bartender, not unless he'd played one on a friend's yacht.

Before she could retract the comment, he laughed and shook his head. "No, nothing like that. I'm just . . ." He shrugged. "Careful. If a woman's had too much . . ." Another shrug. "I'm careful."

In other words, he'd learned to read the signs so he wouldn't take advantage of a woman who'd overindulged.

Damn, she thought, looking at him. *Why hasn't someone snatched you up by now?*

Again, it was a stupid question. If a man like this was snatch-able, some woman would have done it twenty years ago. He wasn't interested in that. Why would he be? For a guy like Nick Sorrentino, there was no upside to a committed relationship. It wasn't like he'd get more sex if he had a steady girlfriend.

And maybe, for five minutes, you could stop thinking about Nick and sex?

"I'm not going to stop you," he said. "But if you really aren't accustomed to that much, you'll pay for it tomorrow."

He held out a bottle of water. She took it and put her empty glass aside. He deserved backup that wasn't hungover tomorrow.

"We should be getting to bed." Her cheeks heated. "I mean, getting to sleep."

"I know what you meant." He cleared his throat, the easy humor falling from his eyes. "I also know you might not be comfortable sharing a room, given what you think of me."

"What?" She looked up, startled. "No, I—I have absolutely no qualms about sleeping with you." *Oh God, did she just say that?* "I mean, sleeping in the same room as you."

His head tilted again, another searching look, cooling fast now. When he spoke, his tone was clipped, uncharacteristically formal. "If I make you nervous, I can assure you I did not suggest a single room because I plan to seduce you."

"I know that. And you didn't suggest it—we agreed on it. For safety." She forced a laugh. "It's not like you need to trick a woman into a hotel room to get laid." *Stop talking. Stop talking now.* "That didn't come out right. I just mean—"

"You made it clear this afternoon what you meant, Vanessa, and if we can avoid resuming that conversation, I'd appreciate it."

"I was flirting."

The words slipped out before she could stop them. No, not slipped. Blurted. She'd seen that she was losing any ground she'd gained and the only solution—after three gimlets—seemed to be this. Honesty.

She expected him to blink in surprise. Laugh maybe. Relax certainly. Instead, he pulled back, his gaze shuttering. He thought she was mocking him.

"I was flirting," she said. "I . . . Jayne and Tina . . . well, they talked, and I . . . You sounded like a nice guy."

"Nice?"

Her cheeks heated. "Among other things. I know how terrible this sounds, but I didn't know you, and it's been a while . . ."

"Been a while?" he repeated.

Now her cheeks seared. *Shut up. Just shut up.* But she couldn't. Not while he was giving her that chilly look. She had to get traction. Somehow.

"Sex," she blurted. "It's been a while. I've never had a one-night stand, and you seemed . . . I wanted . . ."

"Some of what I appeared to be freely offering?"

"Oh God, even plastered, I know how bad this sounds. I'm sorry. I'm really sorry."

Was she imagining things or did he seem to be relaxing? A hint of a smile in his eyes? Nope, she was imagining it. She had to be.

She plowed forward. "I didn't know you. Yes, that's a lousy excuse. If you were a woman and I was a guy thinking that, it'd be wrong and insulting, so it still is, and I apologize. I'm just trying to explain why . . . I didn't mean to offend you this afternoon."

"You were flirting." Definitely a hint of a smile in his eyes now.

"I . . . I thought if I talked about you and them, you'd know I was okay with it, that I wasn't a prude or anything. I was trying to open the door."

"I see." He watched her for at least ten seconds, then burst out laughing. When he recovered, he said, "Not a lot of experience with flirting, I take it?"

"None."

"You may want to work on your technique."

She sputtered a laugh. "You think?" They both laughed.

Then Vanessa sobered. "I *am* sorry. I think you're a great guy, and that was a lousy thing to do. I was wrong to presume . . . well, to presume anything. The point is that I'm not the least bit concerned that you brought me here to seduce me. You wouldn't do that, and not just because you don't need to. You'll be a gentleman because that's what you are."

He shrugged, pulling back as if uncomfortable with the compliment. "It's basic respect."

"I know. I'm just saying that I appreciate it." She forced a smile. "And that I know I have nothing to worry about, even without that 'basic respect.'"

A smile played on his lips. "Oh, I wouldn't say that. Since we're being honest, I'll admit that I possibly was playing to type this afternoon, checking you out when we met. Which doesn't mean we'd have ended up in bed. I'd like to think there's a little more to my decision-making than, 'Damn, she's hot,' but there *was* that, and I'll admit it, even if it makes me seem like exactly what you expected."

"You aren't what I expected." She met his gaze. "At all."

He pulled back again, as if not displeased with the implied flattery but not comfortable with it, either. Then he smiled and shook his head. "I think three gimlets is past your limit."

"It is." She paused. "Wait, did you say I was hot?"

He laughed. "*Definitely* past your limit. Let's get you to bed. Alone."

"Damn."

He leaned forward and she thought he was going to say something. But he kissed her. The shock of that almost made her pull back. Luckily, she recovered fast enough to return it. When she tried to put her hands around his neck, though, he caught and held them, and kept kissing her, a gentle kiss that promised more but did not deliver on that promise. Sweet and careful, like a first kiss after a high school date, a kiss that said simply, *I like you.* It also said, quite clearly, *This is all you're getting*, but added a subtle . . . *for now.*

"Time for bed," he said when he pulled back. "For sleep."

"I know. You take it. I've got the sofa."

He shook his head. "Absolutely not. I'm taking—"

She cut him off with a wave, walked over, and pulled out the sofa bed. He hurried to help.

"This is mine," he said.

"Mine." She flounced down onto it and lay back. "And I'm not moving. So unless you want to share . . ."

His gaze traveled over her, and she swore that gaze was like gas-
oline, her demon fire igniting and searing a path down her body.
She reached up and undid the first button on her shirt. Then the
second. He watched, his breath coming faster. When she undid her
front bra clasp, he yanked his gaze up to her eyes.

"You're drunk," he said.

"Doesn't matter."

A wistful smile shattered the lust in his dark eyes. "Yes, it does."
He walked over to the sofa, leaned down, and kissed her again,
that sweet promise of a kiss. "I appreciate the offer," he said when
he pulled back. "I would *love* to accept, but . . ."

She lifted up and kissed him, that same kiss, in it nothing except
promise.

"Thank you," she said, then fastened her shirt and watched him
retreat to his side of the room.

20. NICK

When Nick woke to sunlight streaming into the room, he bolted up, certain he'd forgotten to set his alarm for driving Noah to school. Then he saw the half-closed curtains . . . which were not his curtains. The night rushed back and he sat there, propped up, taking a moment to process it. Then his gaze swung to the sofa bed where Vanessa was . . .

The sofa bed was empty.

Now he did jump up, his legs swinging out, feet hitting the floor. Had she left? Woken sober, remembered the gimlets and the conversation and the kisses, and slipped out in embarrassment? He paused. No, Vanessa wasn't stupid. She wouldn't run off when Malcolm was on the prowl.

A noise sounded across the room. He noticed light under the bathroom door, exhaled, and lay back down.

He shouldn't have kissed her. She'd been drunk and from the way she'd been blushing furiously when she admitted she'd hoped to seduce him, he had a feeling she was regretting that kiss.

But he couldn't help himself. She'd been so flustered, so anxious to apologize, even if it meant embarrassing herself with her confession.

Last night, he'd seen many sides of Vanessa. The cool leader and the tough agent, certainly, but also the pain and grief and blame over Tina, and the blame and self-recrimination over Stokes. In spite of that, she'd been determined to see this through.

He hadn't fought very hard when Elena and Rhys decided she could stay. He still wished she'd gotten on that plane—for her own safety—but he wasn't exactly gritting his teeth and counting down the hours until they could go their separate ways.

Yet they would go their separate ways. Eventually. And there'd been a moment, lying in bed last night after kissing her, when he'd tried to figure out how to see her again. He supposed the answer was easy—just *say*, "Hey, I'd like to see you again." But he had no idea where she lived, and if she wasn't a short drive from New York, then "getting together" involved serious effort, which would imply that, well, he was serious. That wasn't a message he'd ever send. Not on so short an acquaintance.

The bathroom door opened. Vanessa walked out, dressed in her button-down shirt and, from what he could tell, nothing else. If he'd pictured how she might look the morning after sex—and yes, let's be honest, he had—this was it, her long hair mussed, falling over the half-buttoned shirt, her full breasts pushing against the fabric as she walked, her long legs bare, shirt riding up enough to give him teasing glimpses of full hips and . . .

And he was staring. Also . . . He tugged at the sheet to hide his rising interest.

"Sorry," he said, pulling his gaze away.

She smiled. "If I objected to being watched, I'd have put my pants back on."

So he watched, since that implied permission and perhaps even invitation. She walked to the side of his bed and stood there, smiling as his gaze traveled down her.

"I'm sober," she said.

"So I see."

She put one knee on the bed, her shirt riding up enough to show her panties, very simple white cotton trimmed with lace, but small enough that he couldn't help thinking how they must look from the rear, if she bent over, that lush ass—

The sheet didn't really help now. He could shift, try to hide it better, but Vanessa had her hands on the bed now, moving slowly onto it, watching him for any sign that she should retreat, and he decided hiding his interest really wasn't in his best, well, interests.

"Is this okay?" she asked, one foot still on the floor.

He glanced down, directing her gaze. When she saw the obvious tent in the sheets, she grinned, her eyes sparkling with delight and, yes, surprise, as if she somehow figured she could walk over half naked and he'd be yawning, really wishing she'd just let him sleep. If that's what she expected, she'd clearly been hanging out with men in rather desperate need of a little blue pill.

He moved over, letting her onto the bed. While she was still climbing in, he undid the remaining buttons on her blouse. It fell open. He reached in and cupped her breasts. She let out a soft hiss as his thumbs rubbed across her already-erect nipples. She shrugged off the shirt and damn, she was gorgeous, hair tumbling down over breasts he could barely get his hands around, full and soft.

If it was possible to get any harder, he did, his cock pushing urgently against his briefs now, as he gripped her breasts and pulled her down into a kiss. She kissed him back—hell, how she kissed him back, nothing like last night, hard and rough and hungry, leaving no doubt where this was leading, but . . . As much as he hated to ask the question, he knew he had to.

"I know you're sober," he said. "But are you sure? If you've never had a one-night—"

"I shouldn't start now," she said. "I know. You're right."

Shit. He shouldn't have asked if she was sure.

But he had to, didn't he? He exhaled and started easing back. So did she. Instead of crawling off him, though, she only lifted up on all fours, then leaned down to kiss him again, her hard nipples brushing his chest.

"I can't have sex with you and walk away," she said as she tugged the sheet down. "Maybe I could have, before we met, but then I got to know you and . . . one night—or morning—wouldn't be enough."

"I—"

"And I know you don't do more than that," she said, lowering her mouth to his chest, tongue flicking his nipples, teeth nibbling them before she raised her head. "Or a sequence of nights, equally casual."

"I—"

"I'm not asking you to say this is different. It'd be a lie, and you don't play that game." She hooked the sides of his briefs, pulling them over his hips, his cock jumping free. "You're a decent guy. Your terms are clear. Casual sex or no sex. Which means, as much as I'm going to regret it, no sex."

"I—"

"That's not an ultimatum," she said, looking up at him. "I wouldn't crawl naked into your bed and tease you into agreeing to something you don't want. I'm crawling naked into your bed to say *thanks but no thanks*, in the most appreciative way I can think of."

She shifted down, curls and breasts tickling his chest, then his thighs as she moved down over his cock, her lips parting as she lowered them to it.

"You don't have to—"

She grinned, cutting him short. "Oh, believe me. I want to," she said, and went down on him.

21. NICK

Vanessa might not have had any experience with one-night stands, but that certainly didn't mean she was inexperienced. If anything, he mused later, the fact that she was accustomed to long-term relationships seemed to actually have its benefits. You could get away with lazy or inattentive sex on a one-nighter. With a long-term partner, more skill was required . . . and the time to develop that skill was provided. In short, it was the best blow job he'd had in years, and when she finished, he showed his appreciation by reciprocating, which she certainly seemed to appreciate in return.

Now they were in bed, finishing a room-service breakfast and struggling to keep their attention on planning their next move with Malcolm. Or Nick was struggling. The food had helped as a temporary distraction. He'd been starving, and since Vanessa knew what he was, he didn't have to hold back. He'd gotten two breakfasts, eaten them both, and she'd only teased about a werewolf's legendary appetite.

The meal over, they'd started planning, and that's when the food settled and he noticed Vanessa was wearing the panties and shirt again, the blouse left unbuttoned, modestly hanging almost closed but with enough of a gap to tease whenever she moved. She looked even sexier now, sated and smoky-eyed, lounging in the bed, completely at ease.

"The problem in finding Malcolm"—she said—"is that we *can't* in a city this size. We know he's around, and you suspect he'll make a move for me—"

"He will."

"Which leads to problem number two. With that phone scrambled, he's not going to find *us*, either."

She shifted, blouse falling open, revealing a generous curve of breast and—

He pulled his gaze away. *Focus*. What had she been saying? Right, the phone.

"Should we unscramble it?" he said. Before she could answer, he shook his head. "No, obviously not, or it'll bring those werewolf hunters running."

"Also, Malcolm would smell a trap."

"True."

She reached for her own phone, blouse stretching open now, one breast showing, nipple erect and—

"We kept the phone so he could call," Nick said quickly. "Can we call him? I know the number was blocked, but . . ."

"That's just what I was checking," she said, tapping her phone. "I set someone on it last night, reverse-tracing the number. Still nothing, but that's still our best bet. The trick, again, is how to work it so he doesn't smell a trap."

Nick shook his head. "No, the trick is to let him smell a trap, but one as clumsy as he expects from me. One he figures he can easily thwart."

"Okay, let me grab my notebook. I brainstorm better on paper."

She climbed from bed and crossed to her bag. When she bent over it, her blouse fell open and rode up to her waist, her ass on full display, those tiny white panties covering just enough to—

Nick took a deep breath and tried to steer his thoughts elsewhere. It didn't work, probably because he was still looking. She rummaged through the bag, full breasts hanging free, ass moving as she shifted, inviting him to rip off those panties and—

She straightened and turned. "Okay, I—"

Her gaze dropped to his crotch, cock straining against his boxers. A slow grin. "Should I bend over again for you?"

He let out a low growl.

Her grin grew. "That legendary werewolf appetite isn't just for food, is it?"

He said nothing as she walked back to the bed, an extra swing in her hips, blouse left half open, eyes glittering with the confidence of a woman who knows a man's watching her and that he's enjoying the view immensely.

She stopped at the side of the bed. "We do need to get to work, however inconvenient the timing. That leaves two options. Either I get dressed, or I . . ." Her gaze dropped to his crotch. ". . . take care of the problem I caused."

"I'd hate to ask you to get dressed."

She laughed, eased onto the bed, and tugged down his boxers with one hand. The other hand reached in, her warm fingers wrapping around—

The phone rang. *His* phone.

"It's mine," he said as she paused. "Just ignore . . ." He struggled to finish the sentence. *Ignore it. Keep going.* But it could be Malcolm. Or Elena. And he shouldn't be . . .

Ah, shit.

"Answer," she said, pulling up his boxers. "I'll give you a rain check. Redeemable at any time, anyplace."

She grinned wickedly, and the thought of all the places he *could* redeem that rain check gave him pause. It also made him think whoever was calling could wait a few minutes. But Vanessa was already handing him his phone from the nightstand. When he saw the number, he swore. Reese. It *could* have waited.

No, he realized with an inward sigh, it couldn't have. Even if he'd known that it was almost certainly nothing more urgent than, *Hey, where'd you put the TV remote?* it didn't matter, because it *could* be more urgent, and there was no way he was focusing on sex while worrying about that.

He answered.

"Okay," Reese said. "I give up. I need an address."

Nick flipped to his messages, seeing if he'd missed a text. He hadn't.

"What?" he said.

"I'm breaking down and admitting that I'm a lousy detective. I can't find you. I need an address."

Nick went still. Before he could ask what the hell Reese meant— *and please don't let it be what it seems to be*—Reese continued, "I've been here for two hours. I've called every bloody five-star hotel and even a few of the fours. I've used your name and both your aliases. My master plan to show up on your doorstep has failed."

"You're in Detroit . . . ?"

"Um, yeah. Kinda the gist of what I was saying."

"What the hell are you—?"

Nick clipped his question short. As he paused, Reese continued, talking fast, rambling, as if he could distract Nick from the why with details of the how, explaining that he'd told Antonio that Nick called to say Reese could join him on his mission. Then he packed a bag, drove to Detroit overnight, and spent the last few hours trying to figure out where Nick was staying.

"You told Elena, right?" Nick said. He knew the answer, but he asked anyway.

A long pause.

"Let me rephrase that," Nick said. "You *asked* Elena. That's a statement not a question, because she's the Alpha, and you would never do something like this without checking with her, and if you have, then Clay is going to kick your ass all the way back home for being so damned disrespectful that you didn't even think to ask."

Silence, then a quiet, "Shit." A pause. "Should I . . . ? I'll call her now."

"Where are you?"

"Some diner—"

"Where *exactly* are you? Name and location."

The pause seemed to get even longer this time, though the question was a simple one. "What happened?" Reese said finally.

"Give me the damned address."

Reese did.

"Now stay there. Understand? Do not leave that table, not even to take a piss. I'll be there in half an hour, and I'd damned well better find you still in that seat."

"Um, what's up?"

"Did you hear me?"

"Sure. I just . . ."

Reese trailed off, and Nick could hear the concern and uncertainty in his voice, as he had when Nick first demanded the address. Yes, at home, Nick set the schedules and the boundaries, and he doled out the punishments, but he never snapped orders or raised his voice.

"Just stay there," Nick said, taking it down a notch. "Whatever happens, remain in that seat."

"I will."

22. NICK

Nick drove as Vanessa gave directions from her phone. He could feel her casting worried glances his way as she'd been doing since he'd hung up and started getting dressed. She'd figured out what happened from his side of the conversation. She'd said little since. Worried he'd bite her head off, too? Thinking now that maybe he wasn't such a nice guy after all?

"I know you're worried," she said finally. "I'm trying to figure out how to say this without pissing you off even more . . ."

"Left or right?" he said, waving at the road, which ended ahead. She checked. "Left."

Silence until he made his turn.

"It's a city of a million people, Nick. I know you realize the chances of Malcolm finding him . . ."

She went quiet. Nick kept his gaze straight ahead, but his gut churned. If Malcolm found Reese . . . He clenched the steering wheel. Going after Vanessa would be a dagger to Nick's back. But Reese? That would be standing right in front of him and driving the blade through his heart. Given the choice, there was no question who Malcolm would pick.

"He won't find Reese," Vanessa said, her voice low. "Not this quickly. He'd need to know he was here, and start looking, and even then, Reese would have to do something stupid, like check into a hotel under his own name. He just got here. He drove around in his car and then he went for breakfast. Malcolm cannot find him."

Silence.

"Nick . . ."

He eased his foot a fraction off the pedal.

"He's Australian, right?" Vanessa said.

Nick glanced over sharply.

"I'm trying to distract you," she said. "If you want me to shut up, tell me to shut up. But this will go better if your blood pressure is lower by the time you get there. So, if you can, tell me about Reese."

He did, awkwardly at first, spitting out a few facts, then relaxing and talking—maybe even bragging. He didn't reveal anything too personal, but he did talk.

"And there are two more, right?" she said. "Morgan and Noah?"

"You did your homework."

A wry smile. "I was hoping to seduce you, remember? In retrospect, I think I'd have gotten further talking about your kids, not your conquests."

"They aren't—"

"I know. They're not *your* kids. They aren't even kids, technically. But they're your family of choice."

He managed a faint smile. "I wouldn't exactly call it a choice. They landed in my lap and were stuck with me."

"But you chose to take them in. To give them a home. Three total strangers."

Nick shifted. "Noah wasn't—"

"I know. He's the son of an old friend. But you know what I mean. You just don't like taking credit."

"Because I didn't do anything to deserve it. We have money. We have a big house. I have time for them. I wanted to do this. It was my choice, and I don't think I've ever made a better one. I'm not cut out for children. I realized that when Elena and Clay had the twins. This is right for me."

A moment of silence, then she said, "Make a left up here."

He turned, then said, "You've got my background info. I don't have yours. Ever been married? Any kids?"

"No and no. Too busy for both. I have a niece who lives with me, though. Her mom died of cancer five years ago."

"I'm sorry."

"It was hard, for both of us. My sister was my best friend. Sophie and I had been close since she was born, so that helped. Dawn's death just brought us closer."

"You adopted Sophie?"

She laughed. "No, nothing like that. Dawn was five years older than me, so Sophie was past the age of needing to be adopted. She stayed with her dad until she came out to Boston U and moved in with me."

"You live in Boston?"

"I do."

He found himself mentally calculating the distance. A four-hour drive from the city, but only three from their place.

Vanessa continued. "I know, I don't have the Boston accent. I grew up in Newark. Yes, I'm a Jersey girl. I kept the hair, but I managed to lose the accent, thankfully long before that show started."

"Show?"

"If you don't know it, I'm not mentioning it. Now, you'll want to turn right at the next light. Then we're only a mile away."

He eased back into his seat. "Tell me about Sophie."

She grinned. "Happily."

She did, with as much pride as he'd talked about the boys. By the time she said, "That's it, up there on the left," he was relaxed and ready to handle the situation calmly and rationally.

"Thanks," he said as he pulled into a parking spot.

"Anytime. Now let's scoop Reese up and get him on a plane home. By then, my resources should have a phone number for Malcolm."

23. NICK

They were a couple of blocks from a hotel where he'd stayed with the boys when they visited the Detroit auto show so Noah could choose his first car. Nick figured this had been Reese's last attempt to find him—stop at the hotel and see if he could pick up Nick's scent. When he hadn't, he'd gone for breakfast.

The hotel was actually in a suburb, like most of the city's best. This suburb had been around for decades and had weathered the economic woes gracefully. The road looked like any other well-to-do street, with people bustling about. Or driving about, as the case was. It wasn't a walking neighborhood. Reese must have walked, though, at least from the hotel, because Nick saw no sign of his car. That got his heart speeding up, even if he knew Reese would rather trek a mile than drive it.

"He's fine," Vanessa murmured as they waited to cross the road. "There's absolutely no way that Malcolm . . ."

She trailed off. Nick followed her gaze to see three men getting out of a pickup with Ohio plates. It was the same truck he'd out-maneuvered last night.

"That's not poss—" She cut herself off and reached to grab Nick's arm, but he already had hers, tugging her back between a truck and a van. Nick double-checked the plate number. There was no question. It was the hunters from last night.

"Stay here," he said. "Cover my back while I go inside."

"No. They followed you. They must have. You can't lead them to . . ."

Again she trailed off. This time, Nick didn't need to track her gaze because they were looking at the same thing—the hunters, as they headed straight for the restaurant where Reese waited.

"How the hell?" Vanessa said.

"I'm guessing they hacked my phone. Listened in and heard Reese tell me where he is."

She shook her head. "I'm betting on a supernatural explanation. A clairvoyant on the team or a shaman."

"It doesn't matter," Nick said. "I'm not standing here until I figure out *how* they found him. They did."

She caught the back of his shirt before he could leave.

"Reese is still fine," she said. "They won't touch him in there."

"I'm—"

"—going in after him. I know. And I won't stop you. It's not like I could even if I wanted to. I'm just asking you to take thirty seconds to plan your next move."

"I won't know that until I get in there," he said. "See the layout. See what they're doing."

She nodded. "Fair enough. Swap phones with me, then."

He glanced down at her as she held out her phone.

"Take mine so I can contact you," she said. "I'll take yours so I can call Reese and let him know what's going on before you get in there."

Nick handed her his phone. The hunters headed into the restaurant without a backward glance. He followed.

Nick had told Vanessa he couldn't formulate a plan until he got the lay of the land. Not entirely true. It was only the specifics he needed more data for. The general plan was simple: get Reese the hell out of there.

Reese didn't look up when Nick walked in, meaning Vanessa had indeed warned him. He sat across the restaurant, drinking a Coke and doing something on his phone—or pretending to. The hunters had taken the booth right behind him. Their heads were together as they talked. They didn't look up, either.

Gaze still fixed on his phone, Reese gestured with his free hand. It took a moment for Nick to realize what he was trying to communicate. *Sit down. Wait.*

Nick hesitated and then slid into a booth, positioning himself so he could see Reese but the hunters couldn't see him.

Vanessa's phone pinged. Nick glanced down to see a text from Reese.

They're figuring out how to take me down. Consensus seems to be following me back to my car.

Not surprisingly, the hunters didn't know a lot about werewolves—at least not enough to lower their voices.

Nick texted back. *Head to the restroom. I'll confront them. You slip out.*

Reese looked over and mouthed, "Seriously?"

Nick glowered at him. Apparently he wasn't very good at the expression, because Reese seemed to be stifling a laugh. Reese shook his head and texted.

I'll leave, but only to lure them out. You follow. I'll give them a convenient dark alley to jump me in. We jump them. Find out who they work for.

Nick paused. He could feel Reese watching him.

Another text pinged. *I'm not a kid, Nick. You, me, your spy friend against three of them? Easy odds.*

Nick replied, *It's not them I'm worried about.*

Reese paused, then he sent back, *You saw Malcolm out there?*

No, but he's keeping an eye on the situation. If he's here—

Nick stopped. He didn't send the message. Instead, he flipped to send one to his phone, for Vanessa. A simple, *Everything okay?*

His heart pounded as he waited for a reply. When none came after ten seconds, he called. The phone rang. And rang. And went to voice mail.

Nick scrambled out of the booth. It took him all of five seconds to realize what an idiotic move that was. He scrambled up, the hunters spotted him, and everybody went still.

The three hunters stood frozen, their mental wheels turning as they figured out their next move. Reese was looking at something across the restaurant. Nick started for the men. Reese swung out of his booth, yelling, "Gun!" and grabbing the nearest hunter by the arm—the arm that was under his jacket, holding his weapon.

The gun flew out. People screamed. Reese grappled with his target, the gun hitting the floor. One of the other hunters just stood there, slack-jawed. The other whipped out *his* gun. Nick dove for him as he heard a shout from across the restaurant: "Drop your weapons! Police!"

Two men were on their feet, plainclothes officers with service revolvers trained on the combatants. Reese must have overheard something that told him they were cops.

Reese gave a werewolf-strength heave and threw his target toward the detectives. Nick was still grappling with his. He snapped the hunter's arm. The man yowled. His gun fell. Nick grabbed him by the jacket and threw him to the cops.

Nick and Reese turned on the third hunter. Behind them, the detectives tried to tell everyone to stand down, drop their weapons, get on the ground, but there were only two of them, busy subduing two big men. The third hunter hadn't pulled a gun, and the detectives seemed to decide Reese and Nick could handle him.

Nick took a slow step toward the hunter. He turned and ran for the back door.

"Bring Vanessa around," Reese said to Nick. "I've got this."

Nick shook his head. "Stay with me. I think Malcolm's here. Vanessa's not answering—"

"Then go get her."

"It could be—"

"—a trap. I know. I'll be careful. But if Malcolm sees me *with* you . . ."

Reese was right. As much as Nick wanted Reese at his side, he was safer if he wasn't.

"I'll get what I can from that fuckwit," Reese said. "You find Malcolm."

Nick nodded and took off.

Malcolm had been there. Nick could smell him outside. Put that together with Vanessa clearly not being where she should be—or answering her phone—and Nick wasn't pissing around untangling scents to confirm his suspicions. Vanessa would never chase Malcolm if she spotted him. Not after last night. Malcolm must have taken her. And if Nick was going to get her back, he couldn't be crouching on the sidewalk. He needed a shortcut.

He strode into the first empty service lane, found a spot behind a parked delivery van, and took off his clothing to begin his Change. Was it the safest spot to do it? Nope. Did he give a shit? Nope.

Nick was never speedy at his Changes, even at the best of times. Halfway through, he realized he hadn't thought this through. Would the change in form give him enough advantages to outweigh the delay? He hoped so, because it was too late to go back now.

He finished his Change and struggled up. His legs wobbled, exhausted from the strain, accustomed to a few minutes of rest afterward. He didn't have a few minutes. He gave himself a muzzle-to-tail shake. There was always some adjustment—to being on four legs, to a black-and-white world, to the sounds and scents that assaulted him from all sides. He snorted, exhaling hard and pawing the ground, getting his bearings as fast as he could.

As he turned to go, Vanessa's phone rang from his pocket, now stuffed into a recycling bin, under a layer of shredded paper. He did pause, worrying that it was Vanessa or Reese, needing him. But he couldn't risk Changing back.

The phone stopped ringing. Nick took off.

24. VANESSA

Vanessa listened to her recorded voice, telling the caller to leave a message.

"Nick, it's me. Call back. Please."

She sent the same message by text. There was no reply. It was her own goddamned fault. He'd tried to call her and she'd been running, the phone stuffed in her pocket, unheard.

Now she'd stopped to let Nick know what was going on and discovered she'd had three calls from him. She'd been texting to tell Nick to come after her. Now he was . . . without knowing what the hell was going on.

Damn it. She really had been out of the field too long.

She looked around the shop. Electronics. She was in the accessories section, catching her breath while pretending to check out the vast selection of earbuds. Malcolm was . . . Well, that was the problem. She wasn't exactly sure where Malcolm was.

She'd spotted him as she'd been waiting on the sidewalk, keeping an eye on the restaurant. *One* eye on the restaurant . . . while looking for Malcolm. He was using the hunters, not only for amusement and diversion, but to keep tabs on Nick. He'd set them on Nick with that cell phone trick. Now they apparently had their own methods of tracking Nick, meaning Malcolm could just follow along.

Sure enough, after five minutes, Malcolm had shown up. He'd spotted Vanessa almost immediately. Then he'd begun circling, like a lone wolf with a deer, surveying the situation, determining the best method of attack.

She hadn't waited for him to figure it out. Take control of the situation. That was what she'd been taught, and that was what she did. She didn't run. He wouldn't have bought that, not only because he must know she wasn't some random woman Nick had picked up, but because, let's face it, with the rental car nearby— and Nick within screaming distance—she'd be an idiot to run.

Earlier, they'd decided that the best trap was an obvious one. Let Malcolm see it. Let his ego take over. So she *had* hurried off— after making it very clear through her body language that she was actually luring him away. In other words, she did exactly what she figured Tina had done, and Malcolm went for it.

Vanessa didn't have Tina's overconfidence, though. Nor that desperate desire to impress Nick. Well, yes, she did want to impress him, but not by taking down Malcolm alone—even if she somehow managed it, he'd think her a reckless fool. She'd stuck to the shop-lined road, where Malcolm wouldn't dare strike. Then she would text Nick and tell him what was happening, so he could be in place when she left the shop for a quiet place where Malcolm would pounce.

Except Nick wasn't answering the phone. She tried Reese, too, but it went to voice mail. Was Reese okay? Was Nick with him?

Damn it. She should have looped Nick in right away. She hadn't wanted to worry him while he was dealing with the hunters. She figured she could keep Malcolm on the run until Nick was free. Which was, she supposed, exactly what she needed to do now. Keep texting and keep luring—

"Hello."

She turned to see Malcolm Danvers. Standing right beside her.

He was in his eighties, but looked a quarter century younger. She would not say he was an attractive man—after how he'd killed Tina and Sharon Stokes, there was no way her brain could see anything attractive there—but she could acknowledge that he'd have no trouble with women. Average height, with a powerful build, blue eyes, and dark hair sprinkled with gray. All that passed through her brain as simple data. What she actually noticed were his eyes. Empty and cold even as they sparkled with amusement at her surprise.

"Oh," he said. "Were you texting Nicky? Telling him where you'll lure me so he can take me down? Please, don't let me interrupt. In fact, I can suggest a place about a block over. Have him meet me there in five minutes. You can stay here, or at least pretend to stay here while following me to protect your lover." A pause. "He is your lover, I presume?"

She opened her mouth, but he cut her off. "Oh, you're more than *just* his lover, I'm sure. You're one of Rhys Smith's agents. But you're still sleeping with Nicky. That's a given. You're female and reasonably attractive. A little past your prime, but Nicky isn't as choosy as I am. If he doesn't lose his hard-on looking at it, he'll fuck it."

She tried to give no reaction, but she must have, because he laughed. "Sorry to shatter your illusions, my dear. Sleeping with him doesn't mean you're pretty enough for him. You're merely fuckable. For a night. If nothing better presents itself."

He's trying to throw you off balance. And using what he must think every woman is susceptible to—insulting her appearance. Don't stoop to being exactly what he expects.

"Go ahead," he continued. "Text him. Tell him to meet me in the park. It's empty enough."

When she didn't move, he snatched the phone so fast she didn't see it coming. She grabbed for it. He backpedaled, smiling when another customer looked over, startled.

"My phone," he said to the middle-aged man. "You know how wives are. Always 'borrowing' it so they can see what mischief you've been up to."

The man gave a small laugh and continued on his way.

"Ah, this is *Nicky's* phone." Malcolm whistled as he looked at the screen. "I'm surprised it has enough memory to hold his little black book. So many women . . ." He flipped through. "No notes, though. That's disappointing. Maybe I should forward this list to myself. Rate them for him."

Vanessa grabbed for the phone as he backed up, chuckling.

"One would think you'd appreciate me weeding out the competition." He made a show of flicking down the contact list. "Though even with my appetite, I'm not sure I could make a dent." He looked up. "Such a shame he let you take this, isn't it?"

"A shame?"

"Because it proves he doesn't give a damn about you. If he did, he'd want to spare your feelings."

"Maybe. Or maybe I already knew how big that list would be and I don't give a shit."

Malcolm smiled, shaking his head. "Don't tell me you didn't look. Contacts, e-mail, texts . . . I'm sure there's some interesting tidbits in there."

"You're right. I should have looked. If you see any tips for what he likes, let me know. Now, is there something else we can discuss, while we both stall, waiting for him to track me here? Opinions on Detroit's prospects for a return to economic stability?"

"No, but I do have an informed opinion on Nick Sorrentino's prospects for a continued existence on this earth. Not good, I fear. In fact, I expect him to leave it in"—he checked his watch—"the next thirty minutes. Probably less, but as you may have realized, he's not the brightest bulb. I have to allow some extra time for him to find us. Killing him, though? That will be quick."

When she didn't reply, he looked over. "Did he tell you I wouldn't kill him because I'm too fond of his father? Let me ask you a question, my dear. Does Antonio know where Nick is?"

Before she could answer, he continued, "I don't require a reply. I'm sure he does not. Antonio was always a poor parent. Too soft by far. He felt guilty taking Nicky from his mother, so he coddled the boy and made sure nothing in the big bad world could get him. If he found out Nicky was coming after me, he'd have chained him in the basement to keep him home. Because Antonio has a secret. Do you know why I left the Pack?"

"Your son beat you in the Alpha race."

The amused glitter in Malcolm's eyes evaporated in a maelstrom of hate, so strong and so ugly that Vanessa took an involuntary step back.

"He did not beat me. The coward would never dare challenge me. Not in combat."

"I meant that Jeremy was elected over you. The Pack agreed to vote, and he won."

"And do you know why he won? Because Antonio handed him the Alpha crown on a platter. Antonio could coddle Nicky so well because he had plenty of experience at it. From the time my brat was old enough to toddle, Antonio was there, making sure there was nothing sharp or hard for him to fall on. That's the problem with the Sorrentinos. A strong Pack culls the weak. The Sorrentinos embrace them. Protect them. Look at your Nicky, taking in those young mutts. Joey's boy is a half-wit. The other two aren't much better. Misfits and weaklings."

Vanessa was barely listening now. *Just let him rant. Give Nick time to get here.*

"Speaking of misfits and weaklings . . . So my brat fancied himself Alpha, and what did Antonio do? Double-crossed me to hand him the crown. He promised me his vote. Promised me Dennis and Joey's vote. All I had to do was not take my competition out of the race."

Vanessa had to bite her tongue—hard—to keep from saying, *And you bought it?* Antonio's ploy was so obvious that an agent in training wouldn't have fallen for it. But apparently Malcolm had. Or his ego had.

"Antonio double-crossed me. Dennis ran off to Alaska with Joey, and Antonio didn't stop them. That's when I realized he had no intention of giving me his vote. I fought back, but it was too late. The die was cast. My brat got his crown. And me? Well, let's just say I owe Antonio a debt, one I fully intend to repay any minute now. He's about to regret coddling his son when he should have been turning him into a fighter."

"I think you're underestimating Nick."

Malcolm chuckled. "No, I'm quite certain I'm not. He isn't even here yet. The boy can barely follow a well-laid scent. He's no match for me."

"What if he won't fight you?"

"Oh, he will. Did I mention the Sorrentinos have a weakness for weaklings? That includes women. Especially damsels-in-distress."

She laughed. "I'm hardly—"

"Oh, but you will be, as soon as he walks through that door. I'm going to break your spine. Above the first vertebra. He'll walk in, and you'll be on the floor, paralyzed. For life, I'm afraid. It will cause a commotion, naturally, but it will happen too quickly for anyone to react. Nick will see what I've done. I'll run. He'll follow to repay me for my cruelty. Sorrentinos are terribly predictable."

No one could threaten something that terrible so casually, so confidently, warning her, unconcerned that she might actually be able to stop it. He must be bluffing. Only he wasn't. She had only to glance at his face to see that. To glance at his face and then a split second to remember Tina and the Stokeses.

She took a moment to steady herself. Then she stepped closer, leaning in to whisper, "You're full of shit."

He turned and met her gaze, smiling. "You keep telling yourself that—"

He stopped as she pressed her weapon into his side.

"A gun, my dear? Really?"

"We're going to walk—"

He kicked her. She wasn't prepared for that. She'd been watching his upper body, ready for him to twist, to grab. Instead, he side-kicked her, hard and fast in the calf. As she stumbled, he grabbed for her weapon, only to pull back with a hiss, raising his hand, blood dripping from it.

"Not a gun," she said as she backed away, her knife out.

It took a few moments for customers to figure out what was happening. Even then, it wasn't like pulling out a gun, where everyone screams and panics and dives for cover. They just got the hell out of the way, most making a beeline for the door. When neither she nor Malcolm made any effort to stop those fleeing, the rest followed. And since the woman was the one with the knife, obviously no one felt the need to play hero.

"Did you think that was clever?" Malcolm said, waving at the empty store. "A shame, really. You'd have been a good match for Nicky. Equally stupid. Now I don't need to hurt you quickly." He smiled. "I can take my time."

She went for her gun. That was the plan. Clear the shop with the knife. Then pull the gun. But the moment she went for it, he pounced, anticipating the move. She slashed at him, but she was holding the knife in her left hand now, and it was an awkward, weak slice. It still caught him in the cheek, blade splitting the skin. He didn't even flinch. He hit her knife hand with a chop so hard she heard her wrist snap.

She didn't have time to even process what happened next. That chop to her wrist. Blinding pain. The knife clattering to the floor. And then she was joining it, flat on her stomach. She reacted, her hands slamming down to propel herself up again, but the second she threw her weight on that injured wrist, it buckled and pain ripped through her. Then she felt a foot on her spine and a hand in her hair, ripping it free of the hastily done twist. Malcolm yanked her head back so far she yelped.

"I can snap your neck and kill you," he said. "Or break your spine and paralyze you. Choose."

She reached back with her uninjured hand, her fingers blazing, but he was wise enough to stay clear of her fingers. She had to get her gun—

She couldn't. His foot pinned her to the floor with her gun crushed beneath her.

You were a fool, she thought. *An absolute fool. You knew what he was capable of. You thought you were prepared for it. You weren't.*

"Choose," he said. "You have five seconds, or I'll rip your scalp from your head and crush your spine. Then I'll see how much *more* amusement I can have before Nicky arrives. Do you want to live paralyzed? Or die? Choose."

Choose? How did one choose such a thing?

The answer should be obvious: life. And yet . . .

She swallowed. It didn't matter. Just buy time. Say she chose to live.

Her mouth opened, and then shut. He wasn't going to let her survive this. He just wanted her to beg and then, when she thought her life spared, he'd snap her neck.

"Beg or I—"

A scream sounded from the back rooms. Malcolm tensed, and though she couldn't see him, she knew he was looking over his shoulder. She grabbed her hair, wrenching it from his grip as she rolled from under him. There was a commotion in the back, but he ignored it and knocked her to the floor.

She went for her gun, but in the time it would take her to pull it, he could pin her. She'd lost. There was no way out of this. Nothing to do but her job. Her mission. Finish that and accept whatever came next.

She reached into her pocket and pushed the panic button.

25. NICK

Nick had followed the path easily enough. At first, when it became clear that Vanessa was actually leading Malcolm—their paths had diverged enough that he couldn't be forcing her somewhere—Nick had been confused. She wouldn't run from Malcolm when Nick had been right across the road. Once he realized Vanessa's trail stuck to the sidewalk, he understood her plan: lure Malcolm along an occupied street until he could catch up. She must have been the one who called, to tell him her plan.

So he was no longer barreling down the road, certain she was five seconds from a terrible death. He did lope along the sidewalk, though. As a wolf. In a Detroit suburb. Elena would throttle him. Clay would help.

Under the circumstances, though, there was nothing else he could do. There were no alleys. No maze of side streets and service lanes. This was it—a major suburban thoroughfare in daylight. He could tell himself it wasn't so bad—it was late morning on a weekday, and the shopping district wasn't exactly packed. But even if people would only report seeing a huge black dog, he was still in serious shit.

He made good time, if that helped. And once the trail went into the electronics store, he did keep to the service lane that ran alongside the shop, pacing as he figured out his next move.

Vanessa had Malcolm cornered, so to speak, though he doubted Malcolm would agree. Malcolm was, however, unable to kill her in such a public place. They were at a standoff, as Vanessa waited for Nick. No, as she waited for *human* Nick, with hands that could open the goddamned door.

He could Change back, but that would take too much time. There was only one option: let Vanessa know he was there. That meant letting her see him. He was walking down the service lane, planning to pace in front of the store, when a commotion sounded inside. Sudden chatter, rapid footsteps, the front door opening, then more footsteps as people spilled out.

Nick raced to the sidewalk. The store was emptying fast. People weren't running panicked, though. They were just getting the hell out of there. Meaning Malcolm had made his move.

Nick ran to the front door, but by the time he reached it, everyone was gone and it was closed. He tore around the back. Someone would come out that way, an employee or a customer. But the door stayed closed.

He strained to hear noises from inside. Nothing. He tried to take comfort in that. Vanessa had her gun. If Malcolm did anything, she'd shoot him. Yet his heart hammered as he paced, desperately struggling for an idea.

Break the front window. No, get a look through that window. Evaluate the situation. Break in if needed.

He was turning to start down the lane again when the rear door creaked open. He crouched, waiting and watching as the door slowly opened, and then—

Nick shot forward. A young clerk let out a shriek. Nick knocked him flying and scrambled through. He raced along the narrow back hall, knocking over everything in his path. Finally he saw the half-open door to the shop floor ahead.

Nick smacked the door open with his muzzle and charged through. He saw Vanessa and Malcolm, grappling on the floor. It was no contest. Malcolm was only trying to get a better grip on his prey, and as soon as he found it . . .

As Nick raced over, they both stopped. Vanessa's elbow shot up, slamming Malcolm in the jaw. It was enough to make him fall back. He could have recovered, but Nick was barreling straight at them, and Malcolm wasn't about to ignore a charging wolf. As Vanessa reached for her gun, Malcolm gave her a shove. Then he ran.

Malcolm tore around a display and made a beeline for the rear door. Nick glanced back at Vanessa.

"Go!" she said. "I've called them. They're coming. I'll lead them to you."

He took off after Malcolm.

A healthy ego is a wonderful thing. An overinflated one, though? That gets you into trouble. Antonio had taught Nick that, clamping down whenever he got a little too cocky about the numerous gifts life had bestowed on him.

Malcolm's ego failed him as soon as he got out that rear door. He should have run for the street. Nick might break the rules enough to race along it in wolf form at midday, but he'd never take down Malcolm there.

But running to the safety of humans was more than Malcolm's ego could bear. He tore along the service lane. Then he grabbed a fire escape ladder. He was ten feet up when Nick sprinted and leapt. He'd been aiming to grab Malcolm by the back of the shirt, but that, he realized, had been a bit of ego on his own part. He managed to snag Malcolm's foot. He clamped down hard, though, and when he dropped, Malcolm dropped with him.

They fought. Nick hadn't Changed just so he could better track Malcolm—being in wolf form was the only way he'd get the upper hand in a fight. Malcolm didn't concede easily, though. Nick tore at him with fang and claw, ripping through fabric and flesh, and Malcolm kicked and punched, aiming for Nick's stomach, eyes, muzzle, all the sensitive spots. Soon Nick was fighting through a haze of pain and blood.

He could lose. He hadn't considered that. A match between a wolf and an unarmed man clearly favored the beast. But Malcolm was on a whole other level, and it wasn't just martial superiority. Malcolm was fighting for his life, and that seemed to numb him against every injury.

When Malcolm's fist connected with the side of Nick's skull, the sledgehammer drive knocked Nick unconscious. It was only a second's dip into blackness before he yanked himself out, but it would have been enough for Malcolm to get free. Escape and run. Instead, he grabbed Nick's muzzle to break his neck. And it was then that Nick realized Malcolm wasn't the only one fighting for his life.

Malcolm meant to kill him. The surprise of that realization almost made Nick laugh. Had he really doubted it? After what Malcolm had done to Tina and the Stokeses? Yes, he had, because no matter how hard he tried to convince Vanessa of Malcolm's lethality, he'd considered himself exempt.

He was not exempt. And that was, it turned out, exactly the motivation he needed to dig deeper, fight harder. He clawed and snapped and threw himself into the fight as he never had before, and when he finally got Malcolm pinned, it came almost as a shock. But he was upright and Malcolm was on his back and Nick had his jaws around Malcolm's throat.

One chomp. That's all it would take, and the most dangerous wolf the Pack had ever known would be vanquished. By the omega wolf. Yet Nick didn't think for a moment how sweet that would be. How fittingly ignoble an end. He thought only of his duty. His mission was to find Malcolm. Not to kill him. That right belonged to Clay.

But Nick could not let Malcolm go. Clay wouldn't want that. Yes, Clay would love to kill the bastard himself, but ending Malcolm's life—by any means—was more important.

Nick pulled back for the killing bite. As he swung down, he saw the look in Malcolm's eyes. The rage. The shame. The humiliation. And yes, it was sweet.

Then he heard a shout. Vanessa. That stopped him mid-lunge. Malcolm tried to buck up, but Nick had him firmly pinned. Another shout. A different voice now. Not so much a shout as a snarl of rage.

Clay.

Something hit Nick in the shoulder, and for a moment he thought it was Clay, and confusion flashed through him.

I was doing the right thing. I wasn't stealing your kill. I—

That's when he heard the shot, as if his brain delayed processing it. He heard the shot and then another, and shouts and bellows of rage and fear.

Nick had been shot.

Malcolm reared up again. Nick tried to hold him, but Malcolm managed to chop him in the shoulder, exactly where the bullet had penetrated, and it was too much. Nick staggered enough for Malcolm to scramble out from under him.

Malcolm ran. When Nick tried to follow, his injured shoulder gave way. He glanced back. Clay, Elena, and Reese were running toward him, as Vanessa, Jayne, and Rhys subdued two men with guns—werewolf hunters, he presumed. They were still fifty feet back, not much beyond the shop door. Malcolm was escaping. Nick lurched after him but couldn't manage more than a hobbling lope.

"Stay there!" Elena said, racing up, in the lead. "We've got this. Reese? Stay with Nick. Get that bleeding under control."

Reese slowed. Elena and Clay raced past him, but Nick knew it was too late. Malcolm was gone. They'd lost him.

26. NICK

They were in a hotel room—Nick, Elena, Clay, Reese, Vanessa, and Rhys. Jayne had already departed with backup to recover Tina's body. Rhys had bound Vanessa's wrist at the scene. Then they'd grabbed food, and the werewolves were now ripping through it as if they hadn't eaten in weeks.

Vanessa and Rhys watched them, bemused, as if wondering how anyone could have an appetite after the last few hours. But it was precisely that close call that gave them the appetite. This was a celebration. Yes, as Nick predicted, Malcolm had escaped. But they hadn't lost him. He was right there, a blip on a screen, tracked by the microchip Vanessa had implanted during their fight. It was the best on the market—the black market, that is—the kind of tech the CIA would deny even existed. And the kind of tech Malcolm was never going to find with all his cuts and gouges.

Elena was in charge of the tracking box. Rhys gave it to her as he took Vanessa off to talk shop, leaving the werewolves to finish their meal.

"If you keep checking that, you'll start seeing blips in your sleep," Reese said, as Elena glanced at the device for the hundredth time.

"Just making sure it doesn't stop moving until he's long gone."

"Unless it stops because he's decided to give up," Clay said through a mouthful of burger. "Save us the trouble and off himself, unable to live with the humiliation."

"Of nearly dying at my hands?" Nick said.

"Of nearly dying at the hands of anyone he considers his inferior, which goes for 99.9 percent of the population."

"You don't need to qualify that. Getting killed by me would have been the worst possible fate. I could see it in his eyes. He was pissed."

Clay grinned. "Looked good on him. Too bad those moron bounty hunters interfered. Would have been a fitting end for Malcolm Danvers."

"Oh, I don't know," Elena said, stealing a handful of fries from Clay. "I think living with the humiliation for a while will be even better. He knows Nick had him. He was saved by happenstance. That's going to sting for a long time."

"Right into his afterlife," Clay said. "Which will come soon."

"So what's next?" Reese asked.

"We let him get comfortable," Elena said. "Lower his guard. This little tracker means we don't need to worry about him coming after the Pack. If he sets foot in New York State, we'll take him down. Otherwise, I'll track him until he figures he's safe. Then Clay and I will take a well-deserved vacation."

"Culminating in the death of Malcolm Danvers," Clay said.

"And the hunters?" Reese asked. He'd interrogated the one he'd chased and gotten contact information for the guy setting the bounties.

Elena chewed a fry before answering. The hunters were a nuisance, to be sure. Possibly a deadly one. But she had Malcolm to worry about.

"I can take that," Nick said. "Pay the guy a visit. Convince him it's not a good idea to put out bounties on us."

"I'll run backup," Reese said. "We might even get Morgan to come along. He should be home by then."

Elena looked at Nick. "You sure?"

"I can handle it."

She met his gaze. "I wasn't asking that. Obviously you can handle it. But Karl's up on the duty roster. I can send him if you want a break."

"Nah, I'm on the case already. I might as well stay on it. Compared to hunting Malcolm, this should be a breeze."

"Famous last words," Clay said.

Nick laughed, and they continued plowing through the meal.

Malcolm had indeed vacated the state. Heading west. Far west. Licking his wounds. Clay and Elena had already left, eager to get back before the kids returned that evening.

Nick was riding back with Reese. First, they dropped Rhys and Vanessa off at the airport. Nick hadn't had a moment alone with Vanessa since that morning, so he accompanied her into the terminal, carrying her bag on his uninjured shoulder. Once inside, Rhys went off to buy the tickets.

"You're going to stop at Stonehaven, right?" Vanessa said. "Let Jeremy take a look at your shoulder when he gets home tonight?"

"I am, though I'm sure he'll say that Rhys's first-aid job is all it needs. That and some rest. Werewolves heal fast."

She nodded and hoisted her purse with her good arm. "Okay . . ."

"I'd like to see you again."

She smiled. "To cash that rain check?"

He laughed. "No. Well, yes, but I'd just . . . I'd like to see you again."

"I could come along and help you fix this werewolf bounty mess."

"Ah. Okay. I'll take the hint. You *can* just say no. You wanted a fling. I understand that—"

She cut him off with a kiss, laughing when he started in surprise.

"Sorry," she said. "I couldn't resist. I definitely want to see you again, Nick. But if we make it dinner, then we have to figure out where to meet and who travels, and it becomes this big production, with expectations and pressure and . . ." She made a face. "General awkwardness. I'm too old for that. But I would like to spend more time with you, see what happens. I think the best way we can do that is to work together on another case."

"Sounds reasonable."

"Is that a yes?"

He leaned down and kissed her. "Yes."

CHAOTIC

ONE

"So what kind of stories do you cover?" my date asked, bathing my face in champagne fumes. "Bat Boy Goes to College? Elvis Shrine Found on Mars?" He laughed without waiting for me to answer. "God, I can't believe people actually buy those rags. Obviously, they must, or you wouldn't have a job."

My standard line flew to my lips, something about tabloids functioning as a source of entertainment—quirky pieces of fiction that people could read and chuckle over before facing the horrors of the daily paper. I choked it back and forced myself to smile up at him.

"I did a Hell Spawn feature once," I said, as brightly as I could manage. "That's *True News*' version of Bat Boy. I covered his graduation from kindergarten. He was so cute, up there with a little mortar and board perched on his horns . . ."

I crossed my fingers under my cocktail napkin and prayed for "the look," the curl of the lip, the widening of the eyes as he frantically searched for an escape. Escape would be *so* easy—a crowded museum gala, everyone in evening wear . . . Come on, Douglas, just excuse yourself to go to the bathroom and conveniently forget where you left me.

He threw back his head and laughed. "Hell Spawn's kindergarten graduation? Now that's a fun job. You know what the highlight of my workweek is? Nine holes of golf with the other AVPs and I *hate* golf."

That was the problem with guys like Douglas—they weren't evil. Boring, boorish, and borderline obnoxious, but not so awful that I could justify abandoning them. So I was stuck hoping he'd be the one to declare the date a dud and beg off early.

When my boss gave me tickets to the museum gala, I'd needed a date, and I'd thought of Douglas—my mom had been trying to set us up for months. It seemed like the perfect solution. He'd agreed, and suggested dinner first. That had been a mistake. I should have insisted we meet here, at the party, so if things didn't go well, we'd only have been sentenced to a couple of hours of each other's company. But when he invited me to dinner, even as I'd been thinking *No!* my mouth had done the polite thing, and said, "Sure, that'd be great."

I'd spent forty-five minutes at the table by myself, fending off sympathetic "You've been stood up" looks from the servers, and going through two glasses of water. Then Douglas had arrived . . . and I'd spent the next hour listening to him complain about the cause of his lateness, some corporate calamity too complex for my layperson's brain to comprehend. It wasn't until we arrived here—at the opening of the museum's new wing—that he'd even gotten around to asking what *I* did for a living.

"So what's the weirdest story you've ever covered?" he asked.

"Oh, there are plenty of contenders for that one. Just last week I had this UFO—"

"What about celebrities?" he cut in. "Tabloids cover that, right? Celebrity gossip? What's the best one of those stories you've done?"

"Ummm, none. *True News* includes some celebrity stories, but I'm strictly the 'weird tales' girl, mainly paranormal, although—"

"Paranormal? Like ghosts?" Again, he didn't wait for me to answer. "Our frat house was supposed to be haunted. Frederick and I—your brother-in-law and I were frat brothers, but I guess your mother told you that. Anyway, one night . . ."

My poor mother. Reduced to canvassing my sister's husband's college buddies for potential mates for her youngest child. She'd long since gone through every eligible bachelor she knew personally.

"I don't need you to find me dates, Mom," I said the last time, as I'd said the hundred times before. "I'm not so bad at it myself."

"Dates, yes. Relationships, no. I swear, Hope, you go out of your way to find men you wouldn't want to know for more than a weekend. Yes, you're only twenty-six, hardly an old maid, and I'm not saying you need to settle down, but you could really use some stability in your life, dear. I know you've had a rough go of it, struggling to find your way . . ."

What do you expect? I wanted to say sometimes. *You gave me a demon for a dad.* Of course, that wasn't fair. Mom didn't know what my father was. I'd been born nine months after my parents separated, and grown up assuming—like everyone else—that I was my father's "parting shot" before he'd run off with his nurse.

At eighteen I had begun to suspect otherwise, when I'd realized that my feelings of being "different" were more than adolescent alienation.

Douglas finished his haunted frat house story, then asked, "So what kind of education does a tabloid writer need? Obviously, you don't go to journalism school for that."

"Actually, I did."

He had the grace to flush. "Oh, uh . . . but you wouldn't need to, right? I mean, it's not real reporting or anything."

I searched his face for some sign of condescension. None. He was a jerk, but not a malicious one. Damn. Another excuse lost. I had a half-dozen girlfriends who wouldn't need a justification for ending this date early. They'd cut and run. So why couldn't I? I was a half-demon, for God's sake. I had an excuse for being nasty.

I scanned the room. The gala was being held in the reception hall, which was also—as discreet signs everywhere reminded us—available for weddings, parties, and corporate events. A jazz trio played in the corner, beside a tiny portable parquet dance floor, as if the organizers acknowledged this wasn't a dancing crowd but felt obligated to provide something. The main event here

was schmoozing—fostering contacts while basking in the feel-
good glow of supporting the arts. Large-scale replicas of statues
and urns dotted the room, to remind guests where they were and
why . . . although the pieces seemed to be getting more use as coat-
racks and leaning posts.

"The buffet table looks amazing," I said. "Is that poached salmon?"

"Wild, I hope, but you can't be too careful these days. I had
dinner with a client last week, and he'd been to a five-star restaurant
in New York the week before, and they'd served farm-fed salmon.
Do people just not read the papers? You might as well eat puffer
fish, which reminds me of the time I was in Tokyo—"

"Hold that thought," I said. "I'm going to grab something and
scoot back."

I bolted before he could stop me.

As I crossed the floor to the buffet, I was keenly aware of eyes
turning my way. A wonderful feeling for a woman . . . if those eyes
are sweeping over her in admiration and envy, not glued to her
dress in "What the hell is she wearing?" bemusement.

It was the dress's fault. It had screamed to me from across the
store, a canary yellow beacon in the rack of blacks and olive greens
and navy blues. A ray of sunshine in the night. That's how I'd
pictured myself in it, cutting a swath through the darkness in my
slinky bright yellow dress. Ray of sunshine? No. I looked like a
banana in heels.

Sadly, this wasn't my first fashion disaster. The truly sad part
was that I had no excuse for my lack of dress sense. My mother
routinely showed up in the local society pages as a shining example of the well-bred and well-dressed. My sister had paid her way
through law school by modeling. Even my brothers had both made
the annual "best-dressed bachelor" lists before their marriages dis-
qualified them. It didn't matter. My entire family could have accompanied me to that store and unanimously told me—yet again—that
yellow was the worst possible color for anyone with dark hair and

a dark complexion, and I'd still have walked out with that dress, blinded by my sun-bright delusions.

At least I hadn't spilled anything on it. I paused mid-stride and looked down at myself. Nope, nothing spilled yet. As long as I stuck to white wine and sauce-free food, I'd be fine.

I picked up a plate and surveyed the table. There was a roast duck centerpiece, surrounded by poached salmon, marinated prawns on ice, chocolate-covered strawberries . . .

I wasn't hungry, but there's always room for chocolate-covered strawberries. As I reached for one, my vision clouded.

I tried to force the vision back, concentrate on the present, the buffet table, the smell of perfume circling the room, the soft jazz notes floating past, focus on that, keep myself grounded in the—

Everything went dark. Images, smells, and sounds flickered past, hard and fast, like physical blows. A forest—the shriek of an owl— the loamy smell of wet earth—the thunder of running paws—a flash of black fur—a snarl—teeth flashing—the sharp taste of—

I ricocheted from my vision so fast I had to grab the edge of the table to steady myself. I swallowed and tasted blood, as if I'd bitten my tongue, but I felt nothing.

A deep breath. I opened my eyes. There, in the center of the table, wasn't a roast duck but a newly dead one, ripped apart, bloodied feathers scattered over the ice and prawns and poached salmon, steaming entrails spilling out on the white tablecloth.

I wheeled, smacked into a man behind me, and knocked the plate from his hands. I dove to grab it, but my charm bracelet snagged on his sleeve and I nearly yanked him down with me. The plate hit the floor, shards of glass flying in every direction.

"Oh, I'm *so* sorry," I said.

A soft chuckle. "Quite all right. I'm better off without the added cholesterol. My physician will thank you."

I fumbled to extricate his sleeve from my bracelet. He reached down, hand brushing mine, and, with a deft twist, set us free.

As he did, I got my first glimpse of him, and inwardly groaned. If I had to make a fool of myself, of course it would be in front of someone like this, who looked as if he'd never made a fool of himself in his life. Tall, dark, and handsome, he was elegance personified, marred only by a hawkish cast to his face. Every response to my stammered apologies was witty and charming. Every move as we disentangled was fluid and graceful. The kind of guy you expected to speak with a crisp British accent and order his martinis shaken, not stirred.

As a bevy of serving staff rushed in to clean up, I apologized one last time, and he smiled, his last reassurance as sincere as his first, but his gaze had grown distant, as if he'd mentally already moved on and in five minutes would forget me altogether—which, under the circumstances, I didn't mind at all.

As I walked back to Douglas, the working Big Ben replica clock in the middle of the room chimed the hour. Ten o'clock? Already? No, that made sense—with Douglas being so late for dinner, we hadn't arrived at the gala until past nine.

I hurried over to him. "There's a—"

He cut me short with a discreet nod toward my bodice.

"You have a spot," he whispered.

I looked down to see a dime-size blob of marinara sauce on my left breast. Fallout from the buffet table debacle. Naturally. If food flew, I'd catch some, and in the worst possible place.

I thanked him, and tried to blot it with my napkin. It grew from a dime to a quarter. I stretched my purse strap to cover it.

"I was going to say there's a special behind-the-scenes tour of the new exhibit starting now," I said. "I'd love to see it, and it would be a great way to meet people, mingle . . ." *And save me from another two hours of your corporate war stories.*

"Speaking of mingling, did you see who's here?" He directed my attention to a group of middle-aged couples wedged between a bronze urn and a terra-cotta bull. "Robert Baird," he whispered reverently.

He paused, as if waiting for me to drop and touch my forehead to the floor.

"CEO of Baird Enterprises?" he said.

"Oh, well, if you know him, I guess we could—"

"I don't, but his wife and your mother both serve on the Ryerson Foundation board, so . . ."

"You thought I could introduce you."

"You would? Thanks, Hope. You're such a gem."

"Sure, right after the tour—"

Too late. He was already heading for the Bairds. I sighed, adjusted my purse strap, and followed.

TWO

Thirty minutes later, the tour was over, the attendees were returning gushing over the new exhibit . . . and I was still stuck with Douglas and the Bairds.

I began to wonder whether he'd notice if *I* left. Maybe I could slip away, conduct a little self-guided tour . . .

Douglas put his arm around my waist and leaned into me, as if to take some of the weight off his feet. I bit back a growl of frustration, fixed on my best "Gosh, this is all so interesting" smile, and did what I'm sure every other significant other in the group had done an hour ago . . . turned off and tuned out.

While every other partner's mind slid to mundanities—like juggling the children's schedules, planning next weekend's dinner party, contemplating a report for work—mine went straight to the dark realm of human suffering. I can't help it. The moment I let my mind wander, it turns into a dedicated chaos receiver, picking up every nearby trouble frequency.

Unlike the buffet table vision, these weren't mental blackouts. They were like semi-dozing, that state right before sleep where you're still conscious but the dreamworld starts to encroach on reality. The first thing I saw was a woman sitting at Mrs. Baird's feet, her legs pulled up under her party dress, her makeup running, shoulders heaving with silent sobs.

As the apparition vanished, I felt my gaze slide to the left, and I knew somewhere down a hall I'd find a woman, huddled and sobbing in some quiet place. Maybe someone had called with bad news, or maybe she'd seen her husband's hand snake onto another woman's thigh. I never knew the causes, only the outcomes.

"Tonight," a man's voice hissed at my ear. "He had to do it tonight, while the offices are empty."

I didn't bother looking beside me, instead let my subconscious draw my attention across the room to two men near the door. One was shaking his head, the other's face was taut as he talked quickly.

The voices faded, and others took their place—angry words, accusations, whimpers, sobs, a Babel of voices joined in the common tongue of chaos. Images flashed, superimposed on reality, burning themselves onto my retinas, most meaningless out of context. It didn't matter. I knew the context: chaos, like the voices. An unending parade of negative chaos in every conceivable form, from grief to rage to sorrow to jealousy to hate. I saw, heard, felt, experienced it all.

And the worst of it? Even as my brain rebelled, throwing up every proper reaction—horror, sympathy, and anger—my soul drank it in like the finest champagne, reveling in the sweet taste, the bubbles popping against my tongue, the delicious caress of giddy light-headedness.

Every half-demon has a power, inherited from his or her father. Some can create fire, some can change the weather, some can even move objects with their minds. *This* was mine. My "gift."

For six years, I'd struggled against my growing power, this innate radar for chaos, this thirst for it. I'd fought like the most self-aware junkie, knowing my addiction would destroy me but unable to stop chasing it. Years of dark moods, dark days, and darker thoughts. Then . . . salvation.

Through my growing network of half-demon contacts, someone had found me, someone who could help. I wouldn't say I was surprised. For community support, you can't beat the supernatural world. Most races formed core groups centuries ago, like the witch covens, werewolf packs, sorcerer Cabals . . . When you live in a world that doesn't know you exist—and it seems best to keep it that way—community is a must, for everything from training to medical care.

Half-demons are often considered the least communal of the races, but I'd argue the opposite. We may not have a core group or police our own, but the half-demon regional communities encompass everyone in that region, which is more than I can say for the others. Because we lack the family backup of the hereditary races, half-demons are always on the lookout for others, and once you're found, a world of support opens up to you.

So I was contacted. A meeting was scheduled for lunch, on a sidewalk café, someplace public and private at the same time, which had reassured me from the start. I'd arrived to find only one person at the table, a slight, fair-haired man in his thirties, dressed business casual, like everyone else in the restaurant. Handsome, in a delicate way, well mannered, with an easy smile and warm brown eyes, Tristan Robard had put me at ease from that first handshake. We'd ordered a pitcher of sangria, chatted about ongoing construction in the city core, and spent the first half of the meal getting a sense of one another. Then he'd looked up from his entrée, met my gaze, and said, "Have you ever heard of the interracial council?"

When I hesitated, he laughed. "They really need a better name, don't they? The Sumerian Council, the Grand Guild, or something like that. That's the problem with trying to be understated . . . if you don't give yourself a fancy name, no one remembers who the heck you are. I always tell them that's part of the problem. Get a good name, a clever slogan, a nice logo, and people would remember you and, more importantly, remember you when they need you."

"That's the delegates' council, isn't it? The heads of the various supernatural races—the American ones, at least."

"Exactly. Now, do you know what the council does?"

"Only the vaguest idea, I'm afraid." I smiled. "Like you said, they need a better marketing plan. They're supposed to help supernaturals, right? General policing, resolving conflicts between groups . . ."

"'Protect and serve,' that's the council's motto . . . or it would be, if they had one. The problem is that, for about twenty years, they've been slipping so far under the radar that no one knows they're there, so no one reports problems. They're trying to fix that now, and step one is broadening their reach. Recruiting, so to speak."

"New delegates, you mean?"

He laughed. "No, those positions are filled, and are far loftier than you or I can aspire to . . . for now, at least. What they're doing now is creating a network of 'eyes on the ground,' so to speak, supernaturals willing to join the payroll, help them look for trouble, and, eventually, help them solve it."

My hand clenched around my napkin as I struggled to keep my face neutral. Help look for trouble? Was there anyone out there better suited for such a task? If I could help—use my power for good— Oh, God, please . . .

I don't think I breathed for that next minute, waiting for him to go on.

"In particular, they want people in careers suited to trouble-shooting, like law enforcement officers, social workers, or"—he met my gaze and smiled—"journalists. And the ideal candidate would be someone not only with a suitable job but from a race that could prove equally useful—werewolves or vampires for their tracking skills, or, maybe . . . a half-demon with a nose for trouble."

"You mean . . ." I couldn't say the rest. Couldn't. The words jammed in my throat.

"On behalf of the council, Hope, I'd like to offer you a job."

And so it began. With Tristan as my contact, I'd been working for the council. It'd been eighteen months now. I hadn't been fortunate enough to meet the delegates to thank them personally, but in the meantime, I thanked them with every job I did, putting my all into every task they assigned me.

Tristan had gotten me the job at *True News*. Not exactly a prestigious position for an up-and-coming journalist, but it would help, and that was more important than my professional ego. Tabloids *do* stumble on the truth now and then, and it's usually trouble: a careless vampire, an angry half-demon, a power-hungry sorcerer. I used my job at the paper to sniff out impending supernatural trouble for the council.

I was good at my job. Damn good. So, after the first year, the council had expanded my duties to cover bounty hunting. Supernaturals who cause trouble often flee. If they came near my part of the country, the council set my bloodhound nose on their trail, and I sniffed out the guilty party and then called in the cavalry.

For this, the council paid me—and paid me well—but the best part wasn't the money; it was the guilt-free excuse to quench my thirst for chaos. To help the council, I needed to hone my powers, and to do that, I had to practice. I had a long way to go—I still picked up random visions like that silly one with the duck, which had probably seen its mother ripped apart by a dog or some such nonsense. But I was improving, and while I was, I had every excuse to indulge in the chaos around me.

So when my mind wandered during conversation with the Bairds, that's exactly what I did—practiced. I concentrated on picking out specific audio threads and visual images, pulling them to the forefront and holding them there when they threatened to fade behind stronger signals.

The one I was working on was a very mundane marital spat, a couple trading hissed volleys of "you never listen to me" and "why do you always do this?" The kind of spats every relationship falls into in times of stress . . . or so my siblings and friends told me. Relationships, as my mother pointed out, were not my forte. There was too much in my life I couldn't share, so I concentrated on friends, family, work, my job with the council, and tried to forget what I was missing. When I hear stuff like this meaningless bickering—ruining what should have been a romantic night together—I'm not convinced that I'm missing anything.

The very banality of the fight made it a perfect practice target. Even at a social function like this, there were a half-dozen stronger sources of chaos happening simultaneously, and my mind kept trying to lead me astray, like a puppy straining on the leash in a new park, saying "Hey, what's that smell?", "Wait, did you hear that—", "Whoa, look over there!"

Keeping my focus on the bickering couple was a struggle and—

"You aren't supposed to be back here, sir," said a gruff voice at my ear. "This area is off-limits to guests."

I mentally waved the voice aside like a buzzing mosquito.

Back to the couple. The husband was bitching about the wife ordering fish for dinner when she knew he hated the smell of it.

"Which is why I have it when we're out," she snapped. "So I don't stink up the kitchen cooking it and—"

That gruff voice at my ear interrupted her again, shrill now with alarm. "What the—?"

My head shot up, pulse accelerating, body tense with anticipation, as if my mental hound had just caught the scent of fresh T-bone steak.

"No! Please—!"

The plea slid into a wordless scream. One syllable, one split second, then the scream was cut short, and I was left hanging there, suspended, straining for more—

I turned to pinpoint the source of the chaos. Another jolt, this one too dark, too strong even for me, like that last gulp of champagne when you know you've already had too much and your stomach lurches in rebellion, the sweetness turning acid-sour.

"Hope?" Douglas's hand slipped from my waist, and he leaned toward my ear to whisper, "Are you okay?"

"Bathroom," I managed. "The champagne."

"Here, let me take you."

I brushed him off with a smile. Then I made my way across the room, my legs shaking, hoping I wasn't staggering. By the time I reached the hall, the shock of that mental jolt had passed, replaced by an oddly calm curiosity.

A few more steps, and I wasn't even sure whether what I'd felt had just happened. I often picked up strong residual vibes from events long past, like that dead buffet duck. I'm working on learning to distinguish residuals from current sources, but I'm always second-guessing myself.

When I arrived at the hall T-junction, I could detect traces of the chaos that had bitch-slapped me. That came from the right. But I caught another, fresher source of trouble to the left.

My attention naturally swung left. The chaos-puppy again, far more interested in that squirrel gamboling in plain sight than an old rabbit trail. I headed that way.

THREE

I looked around, then slipped past the sign reminding guests that this area wasn't part of the gala. In other words: keep out, worded nicely to avoid insulting current and future museum benefactors.

As the sounds of the party faded behind me, the clicking of my heels echoed louder. I backed into a recessed doorway and removed them. Then, with the shoe straps threaded through my purse, I leaned from the doorway, looked both ways, crept out, and padded down the hall.

I'd nearly made it to the end when a flashlight beam bounced off the walls. I backpedaled, heart tripping. A security guard's shoes clomped through the next room then receded, and I started out again.

At the end of the hall, I peeked into the next room. The chaos signal was stronger now, a siren's call coming from yet another darkened hallway. As I stepped into the room, the red light of a surveillance camera blinked.

I scooted back, then crouched and shuffled forward, too low for the camera to pick up. I craned my head to look for that light. There it was—a video camera lens fixed on the display cases in the middle of the room.

Squinting, I charted a safe path around the perimeter. Still crouched, face turned from the camera, I edged forward. It wasn't easy, moving in the near darkness through an unfamiliar room dotted with obstacles—*priceless* obstacles—but I reveled in every terrified heart-thump. Part of me wanted to rise above that, to pooh-pooh skulking about dark corridors as an inconvenient and even silly part of my job. I blame growing up in a world that prized detachment and emotional control. But that only made the thrill more precious, the glittering allure of the forbidden . . . or at least the unseemly.

I made it to the next hall. This time I had the foresight to look before I strolled in. I needed more practice at this sort of thing.

As I peered around the corner, I saw, not a room, but another corridor, this one wide and inviting, with a carpeted floor and benches. Paintings and prints decorated the left wall. The right needed no adornment—it was a sloping sheet of glass overlooking the special exhibit gallery below. I had seen Tutankhamen in that gallery, relics from the *Titanic*, peat bog mummies, and, most recently, feathered dinosaurs. Now, if I remembered correctly, it displayed a traveling collection of jewelry.

This second-story viewing hall stretched along two sides of the gallery below. Through the glass, I saw the pale circle of a face. I eased back, but the face stayed where it was, bobbing, as if the owner was cleaning the glass. A janitor? Was my trouble alert on the fritz again? I really needed more practice.

A shard of light reflected off the glass on the other side. Again I moved back, expecting the guard with his bouncing flashlight. But by then my eyes had adjusted enough for me to see the light reflecting off a sheet of glass . . . in a pair of dark-gloved hands.

I bit back a laugh. So that's what I'd picked up—not a janitor or some bored partygoer wandering around off-limits areas, but a robbery-in-progress. My gaze still fixed on the would-be thief, I reached into my purse.

My fingers brushed two objects that Tristan insisted I carry at all times: a gun and a pair of handcuffs. Even tonight, when I was off duty, he'd been so concerned for my safety that he'd had me meet someone from the council security detail so I could pass my gun and cuffs to him and pick them up again inside the gala, circumventing the security at the door. Overkill, but it was sweet of him to care.

I'd rolled my eyes as I'd gone through Tristan's cloak-and-dagger routine, but now I was actually in a position where guns and cuffs could come in handy. *That* would add some excitement to my night. But no. Apprehending a common thief wasn't my job, no matter how tempting. Instead, I pulled out my cell phone to call the police.

Across the way, the thief was climbing over the edge, through the hole he'd cut in the glass. I paused, phone in hand. How would he get down? Rappel? Lower himself like Tom Cruise in *Mission: Impossible*? I'd just see how he did this and then call—

The man jumped.

I gasped. It was a thirty-foot drop. Surely he'd break—

The man landed on his feet as easily as if he'd hopped off a two-foot ledge.

I put my phone away. No human could make such a leap, not like *that*. I knew now why I'd picked up the trouble signal so clearly from so far. A supernatural thief. This was my job after all.

The figure moved across the well-lit gallery. His back was to me as he started working on the security panel.

Knowing his supernatural race would help. The first time I'd followed a paranormal lead from *True News* without council backup, I'd ended up with second-degree burns from a very pissed-off fire half-demon.

I looked down at the man. No clues there. There never were. Half-demons, witches, sorcerers, werewolves, vampires . . . you couldn't tell by looking. Or, with the vampires and werewolves, I'd *heard* you couldn't tell. I've never met one of either race, both being rare and cliquish.

He could be a vampire. Vampires had more than their share of thieves—natural stealth combined with invulnerability made it a good career choice. A vampire could probably have made that jump.

As he continued working on the security panel, I ran through a few other possibilities. My mental databanks overflowed with supernatural data, most for types I had never—and likely would never—meet.

Sometimes, poring over my black market reference books, I felt like an overeager army recruit, digesting ballistics tables for weapons I'd never fire, tactical manuals for situations I'd never encounter. Devouring everything in an effort to "be all that I could be." The council had taken a chance on me and turned my life around. I owed them my best.

Security system disabled, the man walked to the display and, with a few adroit moves, scooped up three pieces as easily as if he'd been swiping loose candy from a store shelf. As he did, something about him looked familiar, the way his hands moved, the way he held himself, the cut of his tuxedo. When he did turn, face glowing in the display lights, I cursed under my breath. It was the man I'd crashed into at the buffet table.

The oath was for me—I'd been inches from a supernatural and hadn't noticed. I could blame that silly "dead duck" vision and the ensuing confusion, but I couldn't rest on excuses. I needed to be better than that.

Jewelry stashed in an inside breast pocket, the man crossed the floor. I pulled the gun from my purse and crept forward, crouched to stay under the glass. When he came through that open window again, I'd—

Wait—how was he going to climb out of it? He hadn't left a rope . . . meaning he didn't plan to exit the way he'd come in. Shit!

I popped my head over the window edge to see him at the door. It was barred on the inside, vertical metal bars, extra security hidden from passersby who would see only a closed door.

The man reached one gloved hand through the bars and pushed the handle. The door opened a crack, any electronic security having been overridden from the panel he'd disabled. So he could open the door. Great, but that still left those metal bars—

He took hold of the nearest bar, flexed his hand, and pulled. As I stared, he pried open a space big enough to slip through and—

Wake up, girl! He's going to get away.

I snapped my hanging jaw shut and broke into a hunched-over jog as I mentally ran through the layout of the museum. At the first junction there'd be back stairs to the main level. Those stairs led to an emergency exit, but the stairwell itself could be used without tripping a fire alarm.

But did it trigger anything else? Maybe a signal in the security station? I couldn't worry about that. When I hit the doorway, I quickly checked for security cameras and then pushed open the door, tore down the steps.

FOUR

Pulse racing, I forced myself to slow enough to peek out the main-level door first. It opened into a dark hallway. No security cameras in sight. I put on my shoes, stuffed my charm bracelet into my purse, and stepped out.

I looked around the next corner to see the thief step into the well-lit main hall leading to the main doors. Cheeky bastard. He wasn't even hurrying.

I *did* hurry. I raced down the hall and called, "Excuse me!"

He didn't slow . . . or speed up, just smiled and tipped his head to a trio of women at the coat check. I picked up my pace. He made it to the door and paused to hold it open for an exiting elderly couple.

I covered the last few paces at a jog. He saw me then—the yellow dress did it, I'm sure. A friendly smile and nod, and he continued on.

"My bracelet," I said, breathing hard, as if I'd chased him from the party. "Charm—my charm bracelet—it snagged—"

"Slow down." His fingers touched my arm, and he frowned in polite concern. "Here, let's step out of the way."

His finger still resting on my arm, he steered me into a side hall, a scant yard or so in, far enough from the door to speak privately but not so far from others as to alarm me. Damned smooth . . . and damned calm for a guy with a pocketful of stolen jewelry.

"My bracelet snagged on your jacket," I said. "In the buffet line—"

"Yes, of course. It isn't broken, is it?" His frown grew.

"It's gone. I noticed it right away, and I've been trying to find you ever since. It must have still been caught on your jacket or—"

"Or, more likely, fell onto the floor. I'm sorry, but if it did catch on me"—he lifted his arms and displayed his sleeves—"it's long since fallen off. It must be on the floor somewhere."

"It isn't. I checked *everywhere*."

Frustration darted behind his eyes. "Then I would suggest, as reprehensible as the thought is, that someone picked it up with no intention of returning it."

Amazing, he could say that with a straight face. Then again, I suspected he could say pretty much anything with a straight face.

"You mean someone stole it?" I said.

"Possibly, although, considering the guest list, I realize that's hard to believe."

"Oh, I believe it," I said, letting my voice harden. "I wanted to give you the benefit of the doubt, but your conclusion just proved me wrong. It didn't *fall* into your pocket, did it?"

He chased away his surprise with a laugh. "I believe someone has had one glass of champagne too many. What on earth would I do with a . . . cheap bauble like that?"

He faltered on "cheap bauble." The man could spin lies with a face sincere enough to fool angels, but lying about his specialty gave him pause. Even in that brief moment of untangling my bracelet, he recognized it for what it was—a valuable heirloom, each charm custom-made. I was surprised he hadn't tried to nick it in the confusion of our collision.

He continued, "And, if I recall correctly, you bumped into me."

"I *tripped* over you . . . and I'm pretty sure that wasn't an accident."

"You think I tripped—?"

A security guard glanced down the hall.

He lowered his voice. "I assure you, I did not steal your bracelet, and I would appreciate it if you didn't accuse me quite so publicly—"

"You think *this* is public?" I strode past him toward the main hall. "Let's make this public. We'll catch up with that guard, you let him search you, and if I'm wrong—"

He grabbed my arm, his grip tight, then loosening as I turned toward him.

He managed a smile. "I would rather not end my evening by being frisked. Why don't I help you search for it, and if we don't find it, I'll willingly submit to the search."

I pretended to think it over and then nodded.

"Last time I saw it was when you freed it from your jacket," I said. "Then I went to the cloakroom, to get my scarf to cover this"— I pointed to the marinara spot—"and I noticed the bracelet was gone. Maybe—" I paused. "When I was looking for the cloakroom, I walked into the wrong room—it was dark, and I brushed against something."

"Perfect. Let's start there, then."

The room I had in mind was a janitorial closet I'd discovered in fourth grade, when my best friend and I had hid after we'd been caught ducking out of the pottery exhibit and sneaking into arms-and-armor. My fault. I'd loved that gallery, even more than mummies and dinosaurs. Even at eight, I could stand in front of those ancient weapons, close my eyes, and hear the clash of metal on metal, smell the blood-streaked sweat, see the rearing horses, feel the hate, the fear, the panic . . . and feel my own soul rise to drink it in.

At the time, perhaps thankfully, I'd seen nothing wrong with my "fixations," nor had anyone around me—at my mother's insistence—chalking it up to a child's bloodthirsty imagination.

As for my second visit to the janitorial closet, that one had no such demonic backstory, only the raging hormones of youth when, on a high school field trip, a cute boy and a dark closet held infinitely more attraction than even the weaponry exhibits.

If the closet door was locked, I had a backup plan, but I really hoped—

"Here," I said.

He waved at the door. "This one?"

I nodded, and he reached for the handle. I slid my hand into my purse, crossed my fingers, and . . .

The door opened.

"Seems to be a janitor's closet," he said. "How far in did you—?"

I pressed the gun barrel against the small of his back. He stiffened, as if recognizing the sensation. At this point, he could call for help, even just cry out, but in my experience, no supernatural likes calling attention to himself. Either that or our powers make us cocky where others would panic. Whatever the reason, he did as I expected—only sighed, then walked into the closet. I flipped on the light and closed the door behind us.

Once the door closed, the man turned to me and smiled. "Nicely done. An excellent trap, and I admit myself caught. My cufflinks are gold, and you're welcome to them, but if you'd prefer cash, there's a few hundred in my wallet. No banking or credit cards, I'm afraid."

"I believe you have something more valuable. Check your inside breast pocket. The left side."

Surprise darted through his blue eyes, but he masked it with a laugh. "Well done again. And again, I surrender and offer my forfeit. Your choice of the bounty."

He started to reach into his pocket.

"Uh-uh. Hands out," I said. "I don't want any of your 'bounty,' but I think the museum does."

"Ah, private security, I presume. I believe you might find my offer more lucrative than the pat on the back the museum will give you."

"Nice try. I'm not—"

"Interested in a bribe? I'm impressed, and I'm sure your superiors will be as well. You see, they hired me to test their security system. They didn't inform your team, naturally, to test your efficiency and, if possible, your integrity. You've exceeded their expectations, and I will personally recommend you for a bonus."

"Oh, stuff it. I'm not museum security."

He only gave a small smile, still unfazed. "So this is a citizen's arrest? Admirable, but police won't appreciate being called for an authorized test of museum security, so I'd suggest you reconsider. And I do hope you have a permit for carrying that gun."

"I'm not calling the police. As I'm sure you already know, our sort have special ways of handling our special problems, problems better dealt with internally."

Normally this was enough, but he only arched his brows, feigning confusion. "Our sort?"

"The sort who can jump thirty feet and bend metal bars with their bare hands."

"Ah, that. I can explain—"

"I'm sure you can. Save it for the council."

"Council?"

The jingle of the handcuffs swallowed his last words.

"You carry handcuffs in your purse?" He chuckled. "Perhaps, when this misunderstanding is cleared up, we can get to know each other better."

I drowned him out by snapping open the cuffs. He only sighed and held his hands in front of him, as helpful as could be. That, too, is typical. I'd only apprehended four supernaturals so far, but three of them had done exactly this: surrendered and let themselves be taken into custody. The council had a reputation for fairness, and even criminals trusted them. As for the fourth arrest, the witch . . . I pushed that thought back. That one had been a lesson to me—not *every* supernatural would come along easily.

"You said council," he said as I fastened the cuffs. "That wouldn't be the interracial council, would it?"

"Had some experience with them, have you? Surprise, surprise."

"And you're a . . . delegate?"

"I'm a bit young, don't you think?" I said as I tested the cuffs.

"No, not really," he murmured. "So you're a . . ."

"Contract agent."

His brows shot up. "I hope you don't really expect me to believe that." He continued, "I'm afraid whoever you're working for has underestimated my knowledge of the interracial council. They don't employ contract workers."

I lifted my scarf.

He looked at it. "I'm already cuffed, and I can assure you, I don't need to be bound in any other way."

"Oh, I think you do."

I jammed it into his mouth. His eyes widened. He looked at me, eyes narrowing, making a noise almost like a snarl.

"Wait here," I said. "I'm going to make a call."

FIVE

One last check to make sure my quarry was secure, and I slipped into the hall. I didn't dare go far, not when I wasn't sure of his powers.

He wasn't a vampire. The Samson routine with the metal bars disproved that theory. Contrary to some legends, vampires don't have superhuman strength. My guess was that he belonged to the most complex of races—my own. I couldn't recall a half-demon type with his particular skill set, but we were a varied lot, with plenty of rare and poorly documented types, like my own.

One thing I *did* know. This meeting had been no accident, and I kicked myself for not seeing a test the moment Tristan offered me tickets to the gala. Granted, he did that kind of thing often—the perks that came with this job were phenomenal, and I sometimes felt guilty accepting them, even telling Tristan and, through him, the council that I didn't need any extras to boost my job satisfaction. But he assured me they were all freebies, like these gala tickets, a gift from a grateful supernatural that would go to waste if I didn't use them. Still, this was the second time Tristan had sent me someplace and I'd "stumbled" onto a supernatural crime in progress.

They were testing me. The council wanted to see how well my chaos nose worked, and I guess I couldn't fault them for that, but when I called Tristan, I couldn't help snapping.

"Okay, okay," he said, laughing. "No more tests. Can you blame us, Hope? An Expisco half-demon? We're like kids with a new toy, dying to see what it can do. And you outdid yourself, as always. Karl Marsten, caught by a half-demon rookie agent."

"So the council's been after this guy for a while?"

"They have, which is why I should stop my backslapping and remind you that you really shouldn't take down targets on your own. That's why we provide backup. You're too valuable."

"It wasn't much of a risk. He did as he was told. Superhuman strength or not, he didn't even try to fight." I paused. "Those handcuffs *will* hold him, won't they? You said they're specially made to hold anything supernatural."

A moment's hesitation. "You cuffed him?"

"So they *won't* hold?"

"He can't break the cuffs, Hope. That's not the problem. I thought you knew. You usually know what kind of supernatural you're dealing with."

"This time, I didn't get a vision—"

Oh, yes, I had. Standing in line at the buffet, with him behind me, a vision of forest and fur and fangs and blood.

"He's a werewolf," I said.

"Yes, an extremely dangerous one. You need to subdue him now."

"If he's dangerous, don't you want me to wait—"

"No time. As charming as Marsten seems, he's a werewolf—the most brutal and unpredictable kind of supernatural—and now he's cornered, which makes him ten times as dangerous. If he knows it's the council who captured him, he'll do anything to get away—kill anyone in his path."

I swallowed. "Okay, so how do I subdue a werewolf?"

"Knock him unconscious. Shoot him if you have to. You don't need silver bullets."

"I know."

"Don't kill him, just—"

"Disable him. Got it."

I was already hanging up as Tristan promised me a backup team was on the way.

I made it as far as the broom closet door, one hand on the knob, the other on my gun, still hidden in my purse. I turned the handle and—

"You there!"

I dropped the gun into my purse and wheeled as a white-haired security guard strode toward me.

"What are you doing in that room?" he said.

I let go of the knob and stepped away. Inside, a broom clattered to the floor. The guard's eyes narrowed.

"Let me guess," I said. "This isn't the coatroom."

Something clanged against a metal bucket. Then a clacking, like nails against linoleum. Marsten had changed into a wolf. Of course he'd changed into a wolf. What else would a cornered were-wolf do?

The guard reached for the handle. I envisioned him pulling open the door, and a wolf leaping at his throat.

I grabbed the knob and held it. "It's jammed, see?" I made a show of jangling it. "I heard something inside. That's why I was trying to open it. But it's jammed."

"Probably locked. The janitor has the keys."

"Good," I said. "Why don't you go find him. I'll wait here."

The guard started to leave. Then he paused. "First, let me try the door. It might just be sticking."

I backed into the door so fast my head cracked against it. The guard reached to steady me.

"Heels," I mumbled. "I'm always tripping in them."

I stepped forward, and let my knee give way. The guard grabbed my arm as I grimaced.

"My ankle. Damn. I think I twisted it."

"Just sit down, miss. I'll find a doctor. Let me try the door."

Now what? Short of falling to my knees and howling in agony, I was out of stalling tactics. He reached for the handle. Okay, one pratfall coming up—

The knob turned on its own. The door opened. Karl Marsten stepped out, fully dressed.

"Well, that was embarrassing," he said with a self-deprecating half smile. "I could've sworn this was the bathroom, and then the door jammed shut behind me. Thank you. I really didn't want to call for help."

He shook the security guard's hand. Then he turned to me and, with a murmured thank-you, a tip of his head, and a smile, he strolled off down the hall. I took a step after him.

"Miss?" the guard said. "Do you want me to call a doctor?"

"Doctor? Oh, right. My ankle. No, my . . . my date is a doctor. I'll just—"

I looked up and down the hall. The guard pointed toward the party . . . in the opposite direction to Marsten's retreating back. Damn. I managed a weak smile and a thank-you, and fake-hobbled back to the gala.

When I reached the party, Douglas was still with the Bairds. I tried making a beeline for the opposite door, to go after Marsten, but Douglas hailed me.

"Sorry," I said as I returned to him. "I saw an old friend over there. I'll just go say hi."

"Friend?" He perked up. "What company does he work for?"

"She's a musician. Classical. With the symphony."

His face fell. "Ah, well, you go on, then." He nodded toward the Bairds. "I'm fine here."

*

Marsten was gone. I switched on my mental tracking radar to find him before he escaped. I wasn't giving up that easily. Maybe I was being naive, but Marsten hadn't *acted* like a cornered wild beast. He'd barely even exuded any chaos signals.

Tristan could be something of a mother hen. Expisco half-demons were rare, and one willing to work on the side of the white hats was rarer still. So I understood when Tristan didn't want me in on take-downs or kept me sequestered from other agents. I knew my limita-tions, which were many, and I was careful.

I cleared my mind, and pulled up the images I'd seen at the buffet table: forest, running, fur, fangs. After about a minute of mental scanning, I picked up Marsten's frequency. It was faint and flat—meaning he wasn't causing any trouble. Not yet.

I focused on the signal and followed. I reached the T-junction again. Marsten's trail went left. Heading for the back exit.

I hurried down the next corridor, turned the corner—and reeled back, smacked by a wave of chaos.

The voice came again, just like before, a gruff voice telling some-one he shouldn't be back here. The plea. Then the scream.

I closed my eyes and pivoted, trying to find the exact location—

There, around that next corner. I walked into a wall of darkness and braced myself as visions flashed.

Metal glinted. A blade winked in a flashlight beam. The flash-light clattered to the floor. A plea. *No! Please—!* The blade sheered down. Hands flew up. Blood sprayed.

I froze the vision there as I panted, my heart racing.

I fumbled in my purse, took out my key-chain penlight, and waved the weak beam over the walls. There. Blood droplets, invis-ible in the near darkness.

SIX

Were the blood drops still wet? I almost reached up to one before snatching my hand back. Look, don't touch. Standing on my tip-toes, I moved the light closer to the specks. They glistened. Still wet, but drying. Recent.

I swung the beam to the floor and found faint smears of blood.

The trail stopped at a door. Tissue over my hand, I turned the knob. The door opened into an office. I shone my flashlight around. Nothing.

As the door closed behind me, I grabbed it and checked to make sure it wouldn't lock me inside. Reassured, I eased the door shut and moved toward the center of the room.

As I walked, I picked up a twinge of trouble. This had to be the right place, but I couldn't see anything out of . . .

A booted toe protruded from behind the desk. I hurried to it. The desk faced the wall, with a wide gap for computer cord access behind it, and that's where the killer had stuffed the body. The desk was wedged between the adjoining wall and a huge metal filing cabinet, so I had to crawl onto the desk to peer behind it.

I shone the flashlight beam into the gap.

A man lay faceup in the gap. His eyes stared up in a final flash of "I don't believe this is happening" horror. His security uniform shirt was a mess of gaping holes, the edges torn. Shredded. The flesh beneath the holes looked . . . mangled. Chewed.

A hand clamped over my mouth.

I kicked backward. My foot connected, but a second arm clinched around my neck and yanked me off the desk. My attacker spun me around, his hand slapping over my mouth again, and I found myself looking into blue eyes so cold and hard that my heart skipped.

"Did you think I wouldn't smell the body when I walked by?" Marsten's voice was as cold and hard as his eyes, all traces of smooth charm gone. "You would have been wiser to let me leave through the front door."

I pulled back my fist and plowed it toward his gut. He caught my hand easily and squeezed. Tears of pain sprang to my eyes. He brought his face down to mine.

"I'm going to let go," he said, his voice calm. "If you scream, I will crush your fingers. Do you understand?"

I blinked back tears and nodded. He took one hand from my mouth and relaxed the other one just enough to stop the throbbing pain.

"I will only ask you this once," he said. "Who do you work for?"

"I told you. The—"

"Interracial council? Then tell me, which delegate hired you?"

"I was approached by a representative—"

"Which delegate?"

"He's not a delegate. He works for the council."

He exhaled, as if in frustration. "All right, then. Which delegates have you met?"

"None. I only work through my contact."

He cut me off with a humorless laugh. "Oh, you're well trained, aren't you? I'm sure this story has worked for you in the past, but it falls a little flat when dealing with someone who actually knows the interracial council, knows most of the delegates, and knows—beyond any doubt—that they do not employ 'agents'—"

Voices sounded in the hall. Marsten half turned, his attention diverted just long enough for me to ram my spiked heel into his shin.

I wrenched my hand free. He grabbed for me. I kicked and lashed out, knee driving into his stomach as my nails clawed his face. He fell back. I ran for the door, threw it open, and raced into the hall.

Running toward those voices might have seemed safer, but I couldn't—wouldn't—endanger others. I'd already underestimated Marsten once.

I tore down the halls. Marsten's soles squeaked behind me, a reminder that he was in flat dress shoes . . . and I was in heels—giving me no hope of outrunning him.

I grabbed the first doorknob I came to. Locked.

I dove for the one across the hall. As my fingers closed around it, I saw Marsten running toward me. The handle turned. The door opened. I darted through and slammed it.

Even as I turned the lock, I knew I might as well not have bothered. It was a flimsy household privacy lock, easily snapped by even a strong human.

I reached for my purse and . . . my fingers closed on nothing. It must have fallen when Marsten yanked me off the desk. No purse. No gun.

Marsten's footsteps slowed to a walk. He didn't need to hurry. I'd trapped myself in an office with no second door, no windows, no way to escape.

Blockade the door.

The council backup team was on the way. I just had to slow Marsten down.

The footsteps stopped outside the door. The knob turned.

Someone laughed, the sound close by, and the knob stopped turning. A drunken giggle. A voice, growing closer.

I grabbed the sides of the metal filing cabinet. It wouldn't budge.

"Oh," someone said near the door. "Didn't see you there."

"Unless you're staff, this hall is off-limits," Marsten said.

"Oh, right, we were just—"

"Lost," the woman giggled.

"Then I suggest you turn around. Follow the sounds of the party."

I looked for something to block the door, but anything big enough was too heavy for me to move. Outside, the man was telling Marsten to mind his own business, but his companion's voice was already moving away as she called to him to just drop it.

My gaze rose to the ventilation shaft over the desk.

Oh, please. You've seen too many movies.

I silenced that inner voice and climbed onto the desk while Marsten threatened to call security. As much as I appreciated the distraction the couple was providing, I prayed they would move on before Marsten gave up trying to handle them discreetly.

As the woman tried to cajole her partner away, I grabbed a coin from a bowl on the desk and quickly unscrewed the ventilation cover.

"I'm coming, I'm coming," the man slurred before muttering a parting obscenity at Marsten.

I yanked on the cover. One side came free. I tugged again, but the other side caught.

The footsteps were receding fast. Any second now, a very pissed-off werewolf was coming through that door. Palms sweating, I fumbled for a better hold. The cover popped off with a ping that I was sure could be heard throughout the museum. I shoved the cover into the shaft, grabbed the edges, heaved, and managed to get inside . . . right up to my breasts. I stuck there, upper torso in, butt hanging out, legs flailing, arms trembling with the strain of just holding myself up.

Goddamn it! Three evenings a week at the gym, and I couldn't do better than this?

The door handle turned.

Shit, shit, shit!

"And another thing, asshole," the man's voice boomed from the end of the hall.

One last push, boosted by a wave of relief, and I heaved in up to my waist.

"Come on, Rick!" the woman called. "Do you want me to go back to the party alone?"

I wriggled, getting my legs in and then twisting around so I was facing the shaft opening. I tugged the cover from under me, hooked my fingers through the slats, and pulled it into place just as the door lock snapped.

Marsten threw open the door fast—as if expecting me to be standing there armed with a heavy stapler. He paused in the opening, his gaze tripping across the room, nostrils flaring.

Nostrils flaring . . . Werewolf . . .

He could smell me.

Damn it! I tried to turn around. My shoulder knocked against the metal. A dull thump, but he heard it. Of course he heard it.

Heightened smell, heightened hearing, heightened strength . . .

I was out of my league. Way out of it, and I would pay for my hubris—

"Let's make this easy," he said. "You don't want to play hide-and-seek with me. I have all the advantages, and a low tolerance for frustration. So we'll skip the games. If you feel safer in your hidey-hole"—he scanned the room—"you're welcome to stay there. You can hear me, and that's all that matters."

I shifted my shoulders, testing my space limits again. Too tight. I'd been able to turn around with the vent open, but without that added space, I was stuck. No, not stuck. I could move backward. Awkward, slow, and probably loud, but if it came to that, I would.

"Whoever you are, you're of no interest to me," he continued. "That means I have no particular desire to hurt you. So you have a choice. Tell me who you're working for, and I'll step aside and let you out this door. Refuse, and I'll use you for leverage. That's not a position you want to be in."

I stayed still and quiet.

"I don't have all night," he said. "Nor do you. When I hear your associates approach—which I'm sure will be soon—I'll sniff you out, and the choice will be made. After that, whether you walk out of here depends on how willing your employer is to negotiate."

I said nothing. As he moved, his nostrils flared, searching. Then his gaze lifted to the ventilation shaft.

A quick leap, and he was on the desk. As he pulled off the cover, I scrambled backward. I got about five feet before my shoulders hit the sides, stopping me. While I struggled to back up, he peered into the shaft and smiled, his teeth glinting in the dark.

"I do believe you've backed yourself into a corner."

I wriggled, but the shaft had narrowed, and the more I moved, the tighter I wedged myself in.

"Are you going to tell me who you work for?" he said.

"I already did."

"And I already told *you* that I know better." His voice was calm, conversational, no trace of the cold fury from earlier. "You're obviously a bright young woman, so why you insist on sticking to this story—"

"I know who I work for, and nothing you say is going to make me second-guess that—or betray them."

He lifted his hand to his mouth and rubbed it, his gaze searching mine.

"You didn't kill that security guard, did you?" he said.

"Kill—?" I gritted my teeth. "We both know who killed him, so don't try pinning that on me."

"That spot on your dress. I suppose you'll tell me it isn't blood."

I snorted. "It's marinara sauce from the damn mussels you threw at me in the buffet line."

"I *threw*—?"

He rubbed his mouth and growled. Or I thought it was a growl, until I saw his eyes dancing and realized he was laughing.

"All right. Here." He reached into the shaft. "Come on out of there. I believe we both have a problem, and we'd best set about resolving it before your associates arrive."

"You really think I'm a fool, don't you?"

He tilted his head, as if considering it. "Young, yes. Reckless, yes. Naive, probably. But foolish? No. Not foolish. You—"

A sound from the hall. A door opening, then closing. He swiveled, his eyes narrowing as if tracking something I couldn't hear. His gaze shot to the door, and he mouthed a silent oath.

"Couldn't lock it, could you?" I said. "That's the problem with breaking things. They tend to stay broken."

He shushed me, grabbed the vent cover, and knocked it back into place. Then he peered through the slats and whispered, "If you want to find out whether I'm lying—and I think you do—stay there and be quiet."

SEVEN

Marsten jumped off the desk and was halfway to the door when it opened. Two men strode in, guns in hand. Part of the council security force. I recognized both of them from other operations.

I crawled forward, ready to push open the vent and . . . I stopped, palms against the cover. I didn't need to eavesdrop to know Karl Marsten was full of shit. I heard the web of lies he'd spun when I'd first confronted him with the theft. He'd say anything to get out of this. Yet there was a reason to stay up here, hidden and silent, the perfect position from which to watch Marsten and make sure he didn't try anything.

A man strolled in then. Mid-thirties, average height, and reedy, with light brown hair and a delicate, almost feminine face. Tristan, my council contact.

"Ah, Karl," he said. "I didn't know you were a patron of the arts."

"Tristan Robard," Marsten said. "I'd say I should have known, but I'd be lying. After the last time, I thought you'd have the sense to leave me alone. I guess I overestimated you."

Tristan's eyes narrowed.

"I should give you credit, though," Marsten continued. "You have quite a clever setup here. And your young agent? Well done. A beautiful young woman always lays the most irresistible traps, and it seems even I'm not immune." He paused. "Aren't you going to ask where she is?"

"I'm not terribly worried."

Marsten smiled. "Oh, but you should be. The one problem with using beautiful young women as bait? They make equally irresistible hostages."

"So you have her."

As Marsten nodded, I opened my mouth to call out and let Tristan know I was safe—

Tristan smiled. "As I said, I'm not terribly worried."

I blinked but shook it off. Of course Tristan would say that. He was a skilled negotiator. He wouldn't let Marsten know he had leverage.

"I don't think your superiors will approve of that attitude," Marsten said. "Oh, but your superiors have nothing to do with this, do they? This is personal. A little boy lashing out because the big bad wolf embarrassed him."

Tristan's jaw set.

"I didn't embarrass you, Tristan," Marsten continued. "You did it to yourself. You offered me a job, and I turned it down—respectfully and politely. But that wasn't good enough, because you'd already promised your bosses I'd do it, and you had the whole job ready to go. If I refused, you'd need to explain that you'd overreached, and there was no way you were doing that, so you came after me. I was happy to let the matter rest. A rejected business proposition is no cause for animosity. But you came after me. *That* was your mistake."

Tristan give a tight laugh. "My mistake? You're the one being held at gunpoint. Delusional to the end."

"If you say so."

Marsten stepped forward, as if ready to go with them. Then he stopped.

"I suppose you'll want me to tell you where I hid that security guard you had killed. A backup plan, I presume?"

Tristan only reached for his cell phone. Marsten's gaze flicked to the vent shaft, and then back to Tristan.

"So you didn't trust your girl to do the job. If she failed, you'd still have a mauled security guard, found at the scene of a jewel theft, a little tale you could take to the interracial council."

Tristan only smiled, gaze still down as he checked messages on the phone. "I think the Pack would be more interested in that story."

"Ah, of course. The werewolf Pack. A clever plan, and one that might have worked . . . if I hadn't been part of the Pack myself for the past two years."

Tristan looked up.

"Not very good at homework, are you?" Marsten said. "That's obvious from that preposterous story you told the girl. Working as an agent for the interracial council? I'm sure Aaron, Paige, Adam, and the other delegates will be thrilled to know they have a team of secret agents working on their behalf."

Marsten caught Tristan's look. "Your story probably works much better on those who don't know the delegates personally. I could toss a few more names at you, including the werewolves' delegates, but I doubt you'd recognize them, and they wouldn't appreciate me filling that void for you."

He paused, head tilted, feigning deep thought. "Oh, but I do have another name, one you might find infinitely more interesting. You know who Paige Winterbourne's husband is, I presume. You can't possibly be that out of touch."

Tristan stiffened.

"Ah, you *do* know. A very nice young man. I did some work for him last year. Quite pleasant." Marsten frowned. "I hear his father isn't always so pleasant, though. A decent employer, I'm sure . . . unless he finds out one of his employees has been building his own little spy network behind his back."

"I haven't been doing anything behind Benicio's back. He knows all about my initiative. And he's very impressed."

"Oh? So this is a Cabal-sanctioned hit? Funny, I could've sworn it smelled like personal revenge. Well, what do I know. A Cabal killing a Pack werewolf shouldn't cause too much trouble."

Tristan waved to the guards. "Get him out of here."

He turned, and Marsten started to follow.

One of the guards spoke up. "Sir? What about the girl?"

"Oh, I wouldn't worry about her," Marsten said. "She's quite resourceful. I'm sure she'll get herself free, if she hasn't already. But the security guard? Now that's a problem."

Tristan turned sharply. "Hope's still alive?"

"Is that her name? Of course she's alive. You didn't think I'd—" Marsten shook his head. "I suppose, considering who I'm talking to, I shouldn't need to ask. Oddly enough, I find the best hostages are the live ones. Yes, Hope is fine and, as I said, will almost certainly free herself, so there's no need to worry."

"Where is she?"

"The question is: where's the dead guard? The girl can take care of herself. That guard, sadly, is beyond assistance."

"Where is she?"

Marsten paused and rubbed his chin, as if realizing he wasn't going to talk his way out of handing me over. I'm sure he had some self-interested reason for not wanting to do so, but I was grateful for the effort nonetheless. I didn't know how I'd face Tristan, knowing the truth.

The truth.

My stomach heaved.

"She's in a janitor's closet," Marsten said. "Restrained with her own handcuffs, which I thought was appropriate. I can take you there, if you'd like."

"You'll wait here. I'll come back for you when I'm finished with her."

Finished with me?

As Marsten gave Tristan directions to the closet I'd used to hold him earlier, I scrambled for an escape plan. Yes, escape. Marsten's life was in danger. And I'd put it there.

Tristan left with one guard. When he was gone, the second one backed onto the desk, gun still trained on Marsten.

I eased the vent cover out. Marsten looked away and flicked his fingers, telling me to stay where I was.

As quietly as I could, I moved the cover into the shaft and laid it down under me. Marsten's gaze met mine and he shook his head.

When I grabbed the edge of the vent, he threw me one last glare. Then he cleared his throat.

"You do work for the Cortez Cabal, I presume," he said to the guard, his voice loud in the small room, covering me as I eased forward.

"I've heard the Cabals frown on employees taking outside jobs," Marsten continued in that same too-loud voice. "Yes, I know, Tristan is a Cabal associate vice-president, so one could argue it's not truly moonlighting, but I suspect Mr. Cortez wouldn't be so quick to see the distinction."

I braced myself at the edge of the opening.

Marsten continued. "An AVP using Cabal resources for a personal vendetta? I'll wager Mr. Cortez would richly reward—"

I pushed from the ventilation shaft and hit the guard in the back. An *oomph* as he fell forward. Marsten snatched the gun. Then he tossed it to me. The move caught me off guard, as I was awkwardly trying to right myself. I scrambled for it, but my hand knocked it flying, and the gun ricocheted onto the desk, tumbling down behind it.

Marsten grabbed the guard around the neck. The man flailed. Marsten swung him off his feet and bashed his head against the filing cabinet. As the guard's body went slack, Marsten looked over at me, still crouched on the desk, staring.

"Don't worry," he said. "I didn't kill him."

The last licks of chaos rippled through me. I shuddered, eyes rolling in rapture. Marsten's brows arched. I turned the shudder into a more appropriate shiver of fear.

"Are you sure?" I said. "He looks—"

"He's fine." Marsten knelt beside the guard as he pulled my handcuffs from his pocket. "Though I do hate to waste these on him." Another dig into his pocket and he tossed me my scarf. We secured the guard. Then Marsten waved me to the door as he double-checked my knot. My fingers brushed the knob, but Marsten yanked me back.

"I was going to look first," I said.

"You don't need to. I can hear them coming." He looked around. "You take the vent." He grabbed my arm and propelled me to the desk. "Go headfirst this time, and you'll be able to squeeze through."

"After you," I said.

"No time. Go."

"*After you.*"

He gave me a look, as if contemplating the chances of stuffing me in the shaft himself. Then, with a soft growl, he hopped onto the desk. He grabbed the edge of the shaft and easily swung himself up and in, then paused in the opening, his rear sticking out.

"It's very narrow," he said. "I'm not sure I can—"

"Try," I said, and gave him a shove.

He wriggled through as I climbed up. The door clicked. No time to replace the cover. I pulled my legs in, and followed him.

EIGHT

In the movies, ventilation shafts are the escape route of choice for heroes trapped in industrial buildings. They're clean and roomy and soundproof, and will take you anywhere you want to go, like a Habitrail system for the beleaguered protagonist on the run. I don't know where Hollywood buys their ventilation shafts, but they don't use the same supplier as that museum.

We crept along. The passage widened enough to crawl, but our sound reverberated through the shaft. I could feel skin sloughing off my knees as I scraped over the rivets, and imagined a snail's trail of blood ribboning behind me. And the dust? I sneezed at least five times, and managed to whack my head against the top with each one.

"Breathe through your mouth," Marsten whispered, his voice echoing down the dark tunnel.

Sure, that helped the sneezing, but then I was tasting dust. Would it kill the museum to spring for duct cleaning now and then?

I smacked face-first into Marsten's ass.

"Warn me when you stop," I muttered. "Please."

A low chuckle. "At the next branch you can take the lead, so you won't have that problem. I will . . . but I suspect *I* won't complain about it."

"You won't bump into me. Werewolves have enhanced night vision."

"Mine's been a little rusty lately."

I head-butted him in the rear. "Move."

The first vent we hit, *he* hit, driving his fist into it and knocking it clattering to the floor. Apparently I wasn't the only one getting claustrophobic.

Marsten crawled out. I started to, then my dress snagged on a rivet, and I tumbled out headfirst, floor flying up to meet me—

Marsten grabbed me and swung me onto my feet. I regained my balance and took a deep breath of clean air.

"Well, there goes two thousand dollars," he muttered, looking down at himself.

Both elbows of his jacket were torn, and the front of his shirt was streaked with dirt, as were his face, hands, and pretty much every exposed inch of skin. Cobwebs added gray streaks to his dark hair. His shoes were scuffed, as were his pant knees. While he surveyed the damage, he looked so mournful that I had to stifle a laugh. Well, I tried to stifle it. Kind of.

"Don't snicker," he said. "You're just as bad."

"The difference? I don't care."

As he brushed himself off, I looked around. We were in some kind of laboratory, with microscopes and steel tables and what looked like pots of bones in the midst of de-fleshing. At any other time, curiosity would have compelled me to take a closer look. Tonight, only one thing caught my attention: the exit door.

As I strode to it, Marsten grabbed my arm.

"You can't go out like that," he said.

"Oh, please. My life may be in danger. You really think I care how I look? You stay here and pretty up if you like, but I'm bolting for the nearest exit."

His grip tightened as I tried to pull away. I yanked harder. He squeezed harder.

I glared at him. "That—"

"Hurts. Yes, I know. But you'll hurt a lot worse if Tristan catches you. He wasn't heading to that closet to congratulate you on a job well done, Hope. He wants me dead, and to do it safely—without risking his own life on the repercussions—he needs to clip off his loose ends. That includes you and, later, those guards."

"Kill four people because you *embarrassed* him?"

"There's more to it than that."

"What did—?"

"Whatever I did, it came after *he* retaliated because I turned down his job offer. But that doesn't matter. To a man like Tristan Robard, killing four people to avenge his ego is perfectly reasonable."

He studied my face and then shook his head. "At least give me the benefit of the doubt by not strolling out that door and testing my theory."

"There are plenty of exits. I know my way around."

"Good. But wandering the halls looking like this, we're going to raise alarms."

"All right. Let's pretty up, then."

Marsten declared his tux jacket a write-off. That was fine—it was nearing midnight, and jackets and ties would be coming off anyway as the party wore down. Under it, his shirt only needed a brisk wipe-down. My dress had actually fared quite well, with only a rip under the arm and a smear of blood on the skirt. Take off my nylons, wipe down my dusty shoes and bloody knees with a damp paper towel, and I was fine . . . below the neck, anyway. There were no mirrors, and my distorted reflection in the stainless steel table wasn't very helpful.

"Here," Marsten said, "I'll get your face if you can clean mine."

He wet a fresh paper towel in the lab sink. I lifted my face. He raised the cloth to my cheek and then paused to brush cobwebs from my hair. When he finished, he smiled, took a stray strand, and wrapped it around his finger. Out of the corner of my eye, I saw it was more than a "stray strand." It was a huge hunk of hair, which thirty minutes ago had been battened down in an upswept twist.

I groaned. "How bad is it?"

"It's a bit . . . tousled. Very sexy."

I lifted my hand to my hair and swore. At least half of it had come free. Beyond repair without a brush, a mirror, and a half hour of styling time. I yanked out a handful of pins and gave my hair a shake, letting it fall down my back.

"Mmmm . . . very sexy."

"Down, boy. We're fleeing for our lives, remember." I raked my fingers through my hair. "Any better?"

A wolfish grin. "Much. You look like you just crawled out of bed."

"*Not* the look I'm aiming for. Damn it."

He caught my hands as I tried to smooth out the damage. "It's fine. Tousled, yes, but it looks intentional."

He put his hand under my chin and lifted the wet cloth again. Then he paused again.

"What now?" I said.

A low chuckle. "I was just thinking I've never seen a woman who looked so beautiful in dirt and cobwebs. Trouble suits you."

"You have no idea," I muttered.

"I'm sure I don't, but I certainly hope I get the chance to find out." He brushed his finger over my cheek.

"Fleeing for our lives, remember? Let's save the flattery and soulful gazing until *after* we escape."

"Is that a date?"

"Date!" I jumped so fast I knocked the paper towel from his hand. "Sorry. My date. Douglas. He'll be looking for me. I need to tell him—"

"Tell him what? *Don't worry, I was held captive by a werewolf, but I'm okay now . . . except for the deranged Cabal sorcerer on my tail?*"

I glared up at him. "I'm serious. He'll be worried."

"Let him worry. From what I saw, it's only, what, a first, maybe second date? You didn't seem very enamored."

"He's a nice guy. Kind of. He's not evil."

Marsten's brow shot up. "That's your dating criteria?"

"You know what I mean. He was worried, and I can't just walk out on him. Plus, if my mother finds out I abandoned the guy she set me up with—"

"Your mother sets you up on blind dates? With guys like that?" The corners of his mouth twitched. "She doesn't like you very much, does she?"

"My mother—" I bit back the rest, and started again. "My mother is just fine, which is why I won't embarrass her like this. Believe me, I embarrass her enough . . . as much as she tries to pretend otherwise."

His face softened. "All right. But while I *do* understand, you're forgetting—"

"The whole 'fleeing for our lives' part?" I took a deep breath. "You're right. I'll work something out later. Apologize to my mother. Make it up to Douglas . . ."

"I don't think you owe Douglas anything, but if we need to go past the party, you can tell him. Make an excuse to leave, and call it even."

I was picking cobwebs out of Marsten's hair when I remembered something else.

"The gun," I said. "I should've grabbed the gun."

"I wouldn't worry about it. In my experience, guns are only good for threatening. In combat, I'm as likely to shoot my own foot. Best to avoid them altogether."

"Easy to say when you have super-strength, super-senses, fangs, claws . . ."

He glanced up at me as I plucked out another cobweb. "You *are* a—what's the word they use?—a supernatural, aren't you?"

"Sure, but not all of us come with built-in defense mechanisms. Why do you think I carry a gun?"

"So what is your—"

"Speaking of my gun, it's also still back there, in my purse, with my bracelet. Damn it."

"The charm bracelet is an heirloom, I presume."

"So you didn't mistake it for a 'cheap bauble' after all. And you still didn't try to nick it?"

He glowered as he got to his feet.

"What?" I said. "I've offended you? I should be ashamed of myself. Those pieces in your pocket just fell in there, didn't they? Damn museum displays. Stuff just drops off them—"

"Point taken," he said as he stood and smoothed his hair. "But no, your bracelet isn't at risk. Valuable or not, it's worth more to you than to me. These"—he reached into his jacket pocket and transferred the jewels to his trouser pocket—"are worth something only to an insurance company. Which I realize is no excuse, but—" He shrugged. "As for your bracelet, considering it's with your gun, and you'd probably feel safer carrying that, I suggest we make that office our first stop, presuming Tristan has moved on."

I shook my head. "Yes, I want it back, but we need to go. I have to trust my purse will still be there when all this is done."

"I'll make sure I get it for you later."

Later? I hoped that didn't mean he planned to come back and steal something else.

No, he'd been leaving when I'd first stopped him. So why . . .?

He took my elbow and propelled me toward the door. "Let's go before they find us."

*

It took a few minutes to get my bearings. The laboratories weren't part of a typical museum tour and were woefully lacking in directional signs. The lack of windows didn't help. Great for security and artifact preservation; not so great for those needing to end their visit in a hurry.

"There," I whispered to Marsten. "That's the media room. I was there last month for a story."

"You're a journalist?"

I nodded, not mentioning I'd been covering the story of an "ancient curse" that a former worker swore was responsible for his herpes outbreak.

Did all this mean I'd never cover another silly curse story? An unexpected pang of panic raced through me. I liked what I did. Once I'd worked past the "I'm too good for this" phase, I'd genuinely enjoyed tracking down UFOs and Hell Spawn sightings, far more than I'd ever liked covering drive-by shootings and political scandals. But if I wasn't working for the council plugging supernatural leaks . . .

Had I ever been suppressing leaks? Or had I just been covering up a Cabal's messes?

My gut twisted.

Not now. Time for that later.

I looked up at Marsten. "We're in the northeast quadrant, closest to the main doors, which I know we can't use, but there must be an emergency exit."

"There's one along the west side, probably fifty feet from the front."

"Perfect."

We found the exit. As Marsten strode toward it, I called, "It might trigger an alarm."

"A chance I'm willing to take."

I stayed at his heels, eager to be out of this place—

Every hair on my body leapt to attention, my lips parting in an involuntary hiss. I grabbed Marsten by the back of the shirt.

"It's trapped," I said.

"I said—"

"Not alarm-trapped. *Trap*-trapped. Magically. They must have a witch or a sorcerer—" I stopped myself. "Earlier, you said something about a Cabal sorcerer. You meant Tristan, didn't you?"

As Marsten nodded, I winced. Another unforgivable faux pas. Tristan had let on he was a half-demon, but I'd never seen a display of his powers. If I'd known he was a sorcerer, I would have been suspicious of his "working for the council" story.

Witches led the interracial council, and witches and sorcerers had as little as possible to do with one another. The Cabals were the great sorcerer achievement—powerful corporations staffed by supernaturals and run by sorcerers. I knew little about Cabals—every half-demon I knew stayed away from them and had warned me to do the same—but if I'd realized what Tristan was, I'd have suspected who I'd really been working for.

"What kind of trap is it?" Marsten asked.

I shook my head. "No idea. I can just tell that it's there, and it's dangerous."

When I caught his frown, I said, "That's my so-called power. Chaos detection. Primarily negative chaos. Like you said, trouble suits me."

"So you're a half-demon?"

When I nodded, his frown grew. "Admittedly, my knowledge of demons is next to nothing, but I was under the impression that they were all chaotic. They feed off chaos or some such thing."

"Demons, yes. Half-demons inherit their father's special power without his affinity for chaos. Lucky me, I'm the one type that gets the reverse."

I walked toward the door and peered at it. "All I can tell you about this is that someone cast a spell on it, and I know as much about spells as you do about demons. It might just alert Tristan . . . or it could immolate us instantaneously."

"Having no great desire to end the evening in flames, I say we don't test it."

"Agreed." I paused. "I'm sure he'll have the other unguarded exits trapped, too, and the main one well guarded. So now what?"

"We'll revert to the second mode of passive defense: hiding. We'll start by getting that gun for you, then find a safe place and try to outlast them. When the party ends, we'll exit the floor and slip past his guards."

When we neared the offices with my purse, Marsten made me wait while he scouted. When he came back, I could tell the news wasn't good.

"Tristan's gone, but he left a guard behind," he whispered.

"Maybe they're getting rid of the guard's body."

He shook his head. "Tristan will want it found eventually. That's his backup plan."

"But you said—" I stopped. "That was a lie, wasn't it? About being part of the werewolf Pack."

"It's . . . complicated. But the Alpha knows I'm not a man-eater. My reputation in that respect is spotless. However, I've done things, in the past, to the Pack, and while I've had a change of heart in that regard . . ."

"The ink on your reprieve is still wet, and you can't afford to test it yet."

"Exactly."

"Which is why you tried persuading Tristan to take care of the body."

"No, I was trying to divert his attention from you. But yes, admittedly, I had a secondary goal in mind."

"Okay, why don't we look after it now? Take out Tristan's guard, and move the body someplace safer, to dispose of it later. That will give me back my gun, and we'll have one fewer guard to worry about."

One corner of his mouth twitched. "For an amateur, you're remarkably good at this sort of thing."

"It's in my genes."

NINE

I leaned against the wall, closed my eyes, and focused. The guard was a supernatural, probably half-demon, and after a moment I picked up his vibe, too far away to be in the office with the body.

"He's in the second office, isn't he?" I whispered as Marsten returned. "The room we escaped from."

Marsten's brows shot up.

"Supernatural radar comes with my package."

"But you didn't detect me earlier. Not even when you ran right into me."

"I did. That's *why* I ran into you." I shook off the urge to explain. "I'm still practicing. The package doesn't come with a user's manual."

"Yes, he *is* in the second office. Tidying up, it seems."

"Good, then let's go."

"I'll look after him. You stay—"

He caught my expression and exhaled the softest sigh. "Just stay clear. As you said, I'm better equipped for this. Provide backup if you want, but—"

"Don't turn this into a hostage situation."

"Exactly."

Marsten started to leave, then wheeled back to me. "He's coming."

He held his finger to my lips before I could answer. His eyes narrowed as he tracked the footsteps. A moment passed. Then he shoved me in the opposite direction, prodding me around the corner just as the guard stepped into the hall we'd vacated.

Marsten pressed me against the wall, still listening, his body against mine as if he expected the guard to veer around the corner and open fire.

The footfalls grew softer.

Marsten started to pull away from me. Then he froze.

"Was it okay?" a muffled woman's voice asked. She giggled. "I'm kind of tipsy."

"It was great, babe."

Marsten winced as we recognized the privacy-seeking couple from earlier. Guess they'd found what they were looking for.

A door opened less than ten feet away. Marsten swore and looked toward the corner, but it was too late to run, and we'd risk being seen by the departing guard. If we stayed here, though, the couple would recognize him, and if the man got belligerent again, the guard would overhear the argument and—

Marsten's mouth dropped to mine, and he pushed me up against the wall, his hands wrapping in my hair and pulling it up to shield the sides of our faces. As he kissed me, I felt a stab of disappointment. His kissing was excellent, of course. Polished and perfect, just like the rest of him. For most people, finding an excellent kisser is cause for celebration. But I prefer the ardent gropes and kisses of an enthusiastic—if less experienced—lover.

Behind us, the man laughed. "Looks like we aren't the only ones looking for a little diversion. There's an empty office right over there, guys."

Marsten raised his hand in thanks. The couple moved on. I let the kiss continue for five more seconds, then pulled away.

"They're gone," I said.

Marsten frowned, as if surprised—and disappointed—that I'd noticed. I tugged my hair from his hands.

"Okay, coast clear," I said. "Let's go."

He let out a small laugh. "I see I need to brush up on my kissing skills."

"No, you have that down pat."

"She says with all the enthusiasm of a teacher grading a math quiz . . ."

"A-plus. Now let's move go. Before someone else comes along."

We reached the office safely. The door was locked, but Tristan hadn't trigger-spelled it.

Marsten gave the handle a sharp twist, and it snapped open.

"I'll find my purse," I said as we hurried inside. "You pull the body out."

"Yes, ma'am."

I flipped on the light and looked around. No obvious sign of my purse. It must have fallen—

"It's gone," Marsten said.

"No, I'm sure it just fell—" I glanced up to see him leaning over the desk. "You meant the body?"

A grim nod, and he pulled the desk farther from the wall. "Find your purse. I'll find the body."

He leapt onto the desk, hopped into the gap behind it, bent, and disappeared. I resumed my purse search. I looked under the desk, beside it, between the desk and filing cabinet, under a stack of papers—every place my purse could have fallen and a few it couldn't.

Marsten popped back over the desk, started to crouch, and then noticed me watching.

"What?" I said when he paused.

"I have to sniff the floor."

"Then sniff the floor."

Again he paused, as if trying to think of a dignified way to do it. I sighed and turned my back to give him privacy.

A moment later he said, "Nothing. They must've carried him out."

"Meaning you can't pick up the trail. Not of the museum guard, at least. But what about Tristan's guard?"

"Questionable. I can try, but it's difficult to do in human form."

He motioned for me to keep looking for my purse as he pitched in, checking the other side of the room.

"I'll still try tracking," he said as we searched. "I know a few tricks."

"Ah, so you *did* get the user's manual."

"Most werewolves do."

"Right. Most of you are hereditary. So your father . . . ?"

"Raised me and taught me everything I needed to know about following a scent." A quick smile. "Although there was usually a diamond or two at the other end."

"Your father raised you to be a thief?"

The smile vanished. "My father raised me to have a career suitable for a non-Pack werewolf who can't stay in one place without being rousted by the Pack or his fellow 'mutts.'"

"The Pack doesn't let—?"

He cut me off with a wave. "It's not like that anymore. Not entirely. But in my father's day, a nomadic life was a must, and thieving skills helped."

"Tell you what, then. You don't slam my mom for setting me up on blind dates, and I won't slam your dad for teaching you to steal."

The smile returned. "Fair enough. No jabs against well-meaning— if occasionally misguided—parents. As for your purse . . ."

"It's gone, isn't it? Tristan or his guard found it when they were cleaning up."

"Most likely. As for the body, though—"

"Billy?"

The voice echoed down the hall. We both froze and turned toward the closed door.

"Billy? You down here?" Then, softer, "Damn kid."

It was another security guard, looking for his dead colleague. The only place to hide was the same spot the body had been, behind that desk wedged between the wall and the filing cabinet. Marsten waved for me to get behind the desk, and we both climbed onto it just as the door opened.

A flashlight beam pinged off our backs. Marsten slipped his arm around me in an awkward, interrupted embrace. We looked over our shoulders to see the same older security guard who'd "helped" me open the janitor's closet. He speared Marsten with a glower.

"Get lost on your way to the bathroom again, *sir*?" he said. "This is bigger than that storage closet, but I'm sure the young lady would be more comfortable in a hotel. There are two right down the road."

"Uh, oh, yes, of course," Marsten stammered. "We weren't—that is to say, we wanted to look around the museum, see the sights."

"Oh, I know what sights you wanted to see, *sir*." He waved us off the desk. "You're a long way from the dinosaur exhibits."

We complied, getting off the desk and pretending to straighten up. The guard continued to glare at Marsten, as if disgusted that a man wealthy enough to afford tickets to this gala couldn't spring for a bed.

"There's a Holiday Inn three doors down," he said as we walked past. "But I'm sure the lady would prefer the Embassy, which is—"

One of Tristan's guards strode in. He didn't notice the security guard against the front wall. His attention—and his gun—were on us. The security guard stepped up behind him, surprisingly silent for a man of his size.

"I thought I heard voices," Tristan's man said to us. "Good thing I came back. Tristan will—"

The security guard pressed the barrel of his gun between the younger man's shoulder blades.

"Didn't see me, huh?" the old guard chortled as the other man stiffened. "A word of advice, boy? Always check the room before you walk into it. Now, lower that gun or—"

The younger man spun, his gun flying up. The security guard's eyes widened and he froze, whatever ex-cop reflexes he had buried under years of chasing kids off dinosaur displays and foiling amateur thieves. Marsten threw himself at Tristan's man. I wish I could say I did the same. God, how I wish I could. But the truth is that I just stood there, as shocked into impotence as the old guard.

Tristan's guard fired.

Marsten hit him in the side, knocking him away even as the silencer's *pffttt* still hung in the air, even as the museum guard was still falling, bloody hole through his chest, even as I reeled backward from the chaos explosion.

I hit the floor and, for a moment, could only lie there, system shocked by the high-voltage jolt. If there was any pleasure in that shock, I didn't feel it. I lay there, gasping, my mind blank. Then another silenced shot snapped me from my shock, and I leapt up. Marsten was crouched over Tristan's guard, who lay in a heap, neck twisted, eyes open and staring.

"The shot," I said. "Did he hit—?"

Marsten waved to a bullet hole in the wall but didn't speak, just stayed crouched with his back to me, his breath coming in sharp pants.

I ran to the old security guard. Even as my fingers went to his neck, I knew he was dead. The bloody spot on his breast now covered half his shirt.

As I looked down at the man, I remembered him sneaking up behind Tristan's guard, his eyes dancing as he imagined himself retelling the story, how he'd single-handedly apprehended an armed man. I heard his "See, I've still got it" chortle as he put his gun to the young man's back. I rubbed my arms, trying to chase away the chill, unable to pull my gaze from his body.

My first murder. My first witness to death.

What had Marsten said when I'd asked if he thought me a fool? Naive, probably, but not a fool. *Probably* naive? Could I have been any *more* naive? I'd pulled a gun on a werewolf thief. I was lucky Marsten hadn't snapped my neck.

"I need to hide the bodies," he said, his voice soft. "You can wait in the next room if you'd like."

"No, I'll help clean—" I took a deep breath. "I'll help clean up."

That's what I did. Cleaned the crime scene as he hid the corpses. When I realized—really *realized*—what I was doing, my blood went cold.

All this time playing secret agent, and now that you're actually doing something illegal, you get scared.

As I wiped away evidence of a crime, all I could think about was what would happen to my family if I was caught. The shame, the embarrassment, the humiliation, but most of all the "why didn't we do more to help" bewilderment and grief.

What would I say? *No, no, you got it all wrong. See, I thought I was helping supernaturals with this interracial council, but really I was working for this sorcerer corporation, and then this werewolf. . .*

I loved my family way too much to inflict *that* explanation on them.

"It's clean," Marsten murmured behind my head. When I tried to give the tile one last rub, he caught my hand. "It's clean, Hope."

"Out damned spot," I said, trying to smile.

"There's no blood on your hands."

"I wouldn't be so sure of that," I said softly.

I thought of all the cases I'd solved, the "criminal" supernaturals I'd turned in. I could see that one witch, so terrified she couldn't cast a spell, begging me—*begging* me—not to hand her over, swearing it wasn't the council who wanted her but a Cabal.

"Hope?" Marsten grasped my shoulder, his grip hard enough to push back the memory.

"Sorry," I murmured. "Just . . . ghosts."

"Whatever you did, you thought you were helping supernaturals."

"Doesn't matter, does it? It's actions that count, not intentions. Ignorance isn't an excuse. That's what my ethics prof always said. Ignorance isn't—"

I chomped down on my lip hard enough to draw blood and then pushed myself to my feet. "So what's next? Resume the plan and find a place to hide?"

He nodded. "We'll try that."

That didn't sound very optimistic, but considering our luck so far, I can't say I blamed him.

TEN

We discussed options and settled on hiding out in one of the less "sexy" exhibits—those displaying artifacts unlikely to interest a bored partygoer conducting his own off-limits tour. The ceramics or textiles galleries seemed like the safest bets.

Both required going up the back stairs and passing the party, but we'd take the back hall around it. Seeing two people die had convinced me this wasn't the time to worry about my abandoned date.

We hurried into the hall skirting the gala and then veered left. We jogged through the looming skeletons of the dinosaur exhibit, and were crossing to the Graeco-Roman wing when I picked up the twang of a supernatural vibe.

I told Marsten. He listened for footsteps and then inhaled for scents.

"Tristan and the other guard," he said. "Coming right where we're headed. Is there another—?"

He stopped and answered his question by looking at the open doors down the hall. A quartet of men lounged in the doorway, ties and jackets off. Beyond them stood more gaggles of partygoers.

"We could go back," I said.

"Too late," he said, and steered me toward the party.

"We'll cut straight across to the main exit," I said as we moved. "From there, the first left will take us to ceramics."

We squeezed past the drunken quartet, who were ill-inclined to move out of our way. Once inside, I motioned to the door across the room.

From there, we could slip into the ceramics exhibit. We were passing the buffet table when I caught sight of Douglas, still talking to the Bairds. Douglas saw me and then looked beside him. Figures. Here I was, worrying that he'd been worrying, and he probably hadn't even noticed I'd been gone. Douglas only lifted his brows in polite question. When I gestured to the buffet table, he smiled, nodded, and turned back to the Bairds.

"Don't mind me," I muttered. "I'm just passing through, killers in hot pursuit. No, no, it's okay. You just go back to networking. I'm fine."

Beside me, Marsten chuckled. "Your mother knows how to pick them, doesn't she?"

As I rolled my eyes, Marsten's gaze shot to the door we'd come through, and I saw Tristan and the other guard brush past the drunken quartet. Douglas lifted a finger and motioned me over. Probably wanted me to grab him something from the buffet.

When I hesitated, Marsten tugged the back of my dress and nearly yanked me off my feet. I backpedaled as fast as I could to keep from tripping, as Marsten dragged me into a large group of people and out of Douglas's sight. I spouted apologies to the party-goers whose circle we'd invaded—and whose toes we were crushing as we scrambled to get to the other door.

When I glanced back, Tristan's guard was striding around the back of the buffet table, moving as fast as he dared without calling attention to himself.

Marsten gave me a shove, none too gently, toward the door. I hurried out it and turned left, toward the ceramics exhibit.

When I rounded the first corner, Marsten caught up and pushed something at me. A tuxedo jacket. Not his, which we'd discarded back in the lab, but presumably one he grabbed from a chair in the gala.

"Take it," he said when I made no move to do so. "Put it on."

I almost said, "But I'm not cold," an automatic response that, under the circumstances, would have made me look like an idiot. Instead, I settled for an equally idiotic "Huh?" stare.

"Your dress," he said.

My . . .? Oh, shit. My canary yellow dress. When I'd bought it, I pictured myself as a glowing beacon in the black night. Now, I had my wish. I might as well be wearing a flashing neon sign.

Marsten steered me around the next corner.

"The ceramics are the other—" I began.

"I know. We're circling back. He won't expect that. Now put this on."

I took the jacket as we jogged into a room of Grecian urns. It fell past my short skirt, and could have wrapped around me twice. The sleeves hung past my fingertips.

"A bit big," I whispered.

"No, you're just a bit small. Now move—"

He grabbed my arm and *stopped* me from moving. I caught the distant sound of footsteps—running footsteps, growing steadily louder. Marsten pushed me into a gap between two stelae, and squeezed in with me.

When only one set of footfalls entered the room, Marsten's eyes narrowed, and his fingers flexed against my sides. As he tracked the steps, his face went taut.

What had Tristan said about a cornered werewolf? Looking up at Marsten's face, I knew he'd been right, not because a cornered werewolf panics and lashes out, but because no predator willingly accepts the position of prey.

When Marsten's lips moved to my ear, I knew what he was going to say.

"Wait here."

One look at Marsten's expression and my protest dried up. He was right. Things had changed since he'd halfheartedly tried to keep me from following him into danger. Two men had died, and I'd learned this wasn't some movie jewel-heist caper, where the most I stood to lose was my dignity.

I nodded and let him slip off into the darkness alone.

The footsteps had stopped, as if our pursuer had paused. Was it Tristan or his guard? I trusted Marsten's nose could tell. It would make a difference, facing a sorcerer versus a half-demon.

With the other man standing still, the room had gone silent, but Marsten managed to move without breaking that silence. I could see his white shirt gliding—

His white shirt? I should have offered him the jacket.

I eased forward enough to glance out. About fifteen feet away, beside a gilt statue of Athena, stood the guard we'd knocked out and handcuffed. He faced the other side of the room, with his back to Marsten.

Marsten crept forward, his gaze fixed on the guard, managing to skirt obstacles as if by instinct. His feet rolled from heel to toe, soundless. The guard's gaze swept a hundred and eighty degrees, and I fell back, but Marsten only froze in place.

The guard took three steps and then peered around another statue. Marsten kept pace less than five feet behind, so close I half expected the guard to feel Marsten's breath on his neck.

Marsten took one last step, tensed, and sprang. At the last second the guard turned, too late to fire his gun but fast enough to throw Marsten off his trajectory.

Marsten checked his leap at the last second and smacked the guard's gun arm back hard and fast. The guard let out a hiss—part pain, part rage—and dove for the gun.

Marsten knocked the guard flying. The guard crashed into a vase stuffed with replica scrolls. As he reached up, sparks flew from his fingertips, and I knew his half-demon power. Fire.

The guard's hand closed around a scroll. Even as my lips parted to shout a warning to Marsten, the paper burst into flame. The guard swung the fiery torch at Marsten, who was already in mid-leap, coming straight at him.

The scroll caught Marsten in the side of the face, and he fell back. The guard dropped the paper, now nearly ash, and dove for Marsten, his good hand going to Marsten's throat. Marsten drilled his fist into the guard's stomach. As the guard fell, he grabbed Marsten's arm, and Marsten yanked away, but I could see the guard's scorched handprint on his white sleeve.

As the two men launched into a full supernatural power brawl, I finally snapped out of my "mmm, chaos" intoxication, and realized that I too had a weapon—the guard's gun lying less than twenty feet away.

I crept along the shadows, moving from exhibit to exhibit. Yes, I was worried about the guard spotting me and deciding I made an easier target, but I was even more worried about distracting Marsten.

Whether Marsten *could* be distracted was another question. He fought with the single-minded purpose of someone who's done a lot of it. Not what I would have expected. But was I surprised? No. I had seen that look in his eyes, and I hoped never to be on the receiving end of it again.

The gun had slid under a scale model of Pompeii. I managed to get behind the low table. Then I stretched out on my stomach. I reached into the narrow opening until my shoulder jammed against it and swept my hand back and forth, feeling nothing but gum wrappers and dust bunnies.

I peered under the display table. In the dim emergency light-ing, I could see the gun still inches from my fingertips. I wriggled and stretched and twisted and finally brushed the barrel. Another wiggle, and I got my index finger into the lip. Not the safest thing to do with a loaded gun, but I managed to tug it forward enough to grab it from a safer angle.

I crouched, steadied the gun, and then jumped up—

Marsten was sitting beside the guard's prone body, surveying the burn damage to his shirt. He looked over at me, poised Dirty Harry style, gun drawn, hair wild, still drowning in the oversized tux jacket. His lips twitched.

"I, uh, have the gun," I said.

"So I see."

"And I see you have the situation, uh, under control. So I'll just . . ."

I let the sentence trail off as I lowered the gun and moved from behind a table, ignoring his barely stifled laughter.

"If you can stand guard, I'll hide this one," he said as I approached.

As I looked down at the dead guard, I pushed back a stab of regret. This had long passed "just knock him out" solutions. We already *had* knocked this guard out—and handcuffed him—and he'd still come after us. Still, if I had managed to leap up from behind that table, could I have pulled the trigger?

You've been carrying a gun for a year, and you don't know whether you could have fired it? What did you think it was? A fashion accessory?

"Hope?"

Still crouched beside the body, Marsten touched my leg, gently prodding me back to reality.

"If you are not up to it—" he began.

"Guard duty. Got it."

ELEVEN

The burning scroll hadn't triggered any fire alarms, nor had the grunts and punches of combat been loud enough to bring party-goers running. As Marsten stowed the dead guard, I concentrated on both exits, looking, sensing, and listening. I caught a super-natural vibe just as Marsten said, "Footsteps. Supernatural?"

I nodded. "Are they coming—?"

"This way," he said. "From the direction we did."

I glanced toward the other doorway but knew without asking that Marsten had no intention of fleeing. When Tristan realized he'd lost both his guards, he wouldn't walk away. He'd call in rein-forcements, presumably the guys watching the main doors.

Marsten turned to track the approaching footsteps. "More than one set. Probably partygoers. Can you tell?"

I concentrated, but my heart was pounding, reminding me with each rib-jangling beat that I didn't have time to dawdle. My powers caved under the pressure, and I couldn't even pick up that one vibe anymore.

"It doesn't matter," Marsten whispered when I told him. "We'll see them soon enough."

The last word was leaving his lips as Tristan came into view, flanked by what could only be two more Cabal men. Marsten let out an oath and propelled me back to our original hiding spot between the stelae.

As they passed, I saw Tristan take his cell phone from his ear and scowl.

"Russell still not answering?" one of the guards said.

Tristan shook his head. "I'll try Mike. See if he can go look for Russell."

Marsten and I glanced at one another and then at the spot where Marsten had hidden the body—less than three feet from us. As Tristan finished dialing, Marsten tensed and I tugged the gun from my pocket, waiting for the dead guard's phone to ring. Then I leaned out to see Tristan as he kept walking, phone to his ear. Seconds ticked past. He stabbed the Disconnect button.

"Set to vibrate," Marsten whispered.

That made sense. Nothing blows your cover faster than the chords of "Ride of the Valkyries" resounding through a supposedly off-limits hall.

When the three were gone, we headed back the other way, across the main hall and into the biodiversity wing, a.k.a. the stuffed animal gallery. On the other side was the ceramics exhibit. Halfway across the biodiversity room, we caught the strains of a lively monologue coming from the ceramics gallery. The midnight behind-the-scenes tour.

I debated joining them and taking refuge in numbers. The wisdom of that depended on how likely he thought Tristan was to avoid public confrontation. After a moment I shook my head, and Marsten prodded me toward the narrow opening between a pillar and the African savanna diorama.

He backed in first and crouched to sit on a fan box. Then he motioned for me to back onto his lap.

We settled in for what could be a long wait. Or he settled. My brain was racing, struggling to hold back all the regrets and self-recriminations I'd have to deal with later. To distract myself, I indulged instead in replays of the running and fighting—those delicious spurts of chaos that only sent my heart tripping.

Soon other visions crept in: a vulture circling overhead, an ocean of long dry grass whispering as I moved through it, a breeze bringing the heavenly scent of musk, my stomach growling, tail twitching in anticipation—

As Marsten adjusted his hands, his fingers grazed my hardened nipples and I let out an involuntary moan, my breath coming faster.

He chuckled. "Not immune to me after all, I see."

"Hmmm?"

He cupped his hand under my left breast, and pressed it there as my heart raced beneath his fingers. When those fingers climbed to my nipple again, I moaned again.

"Sorry," I said. "It's not you."

Another chuckle. "If you want to tell yourself that . . ."

I closed my eyes and saw the lioness crouch, hindquarters twitching, mouth watering in anticipation. I could feel her excitement, pulse racing, and my own raced to match it. Marsten's hand slid up to my shoulder and I sucked in breath.

He hesitated. "Either half-demons have some strange erogenous zones, or you're right. It's not me, is it?"

I opened my eyes. "It's—" I waved at the display. "I pick things up, from the past . . . chaos."

Another brush against my hard nipples. "And this is what happens?"

"Mmm, yes." My eyes closed again. "Strange, I know . . ."

"Actually, no. Not to me, at least. Should I stop?"

"Not unless you want to."

A soft chuckle. He unzipped my dress and tugged it off my shoulder, pulling the bra down with it. A wave of cool air rushed over my bare breast and I shivered, backing against him as his hand went to my breast, lips to my neck, tongue sliding over the sensitive spot behind my ear, raising more shivers. I shifted again and he put his free hand around my waist and repositioned me on his lap. I felt his erection, hard against my rear, and pushed against it, thrusting softly. He let out a low growl and moved his lips to my ear.

"Tell me what you see," he whispered.

When I hesitated, his free hand moved to my leg, pushing up my skirt, fingers tickling up the inside of my thigh. He traced the edges of my panties and then slid a finger under them. I parted my legs to let him in, but he only teased me with his finger.

"Tell me," he said.

"It's . . . a hunt."

"Mmmm." A growling chuckle. "Nothing like a good hunt. What do you see?"

I told him, the words coming hesitant at first, then flowing faster as his finger slid in, moving expertly, egging me on when I slowed, my excitement feeding his. As the lioness sprang for the kill, I felt the first wave of climax—

Then he stopped.

"It's still not me, is it?"

"Wh—wha—?"

His lips moved down my neck. "Yes, it's insufferably vain of me, but if I'm going to seduce you, I want to be the cause of your arousal, not the passive recipient."

"You don't seem all that passive to me."

He laughed but shook his head, fingers still on my thigh.

I craned around to look at him. "So that's it, you're just going to leave me hanging?"

He hesitated, then shook his head. "That wouldn't be very gentlemanly of me, would it?"

"Not at all."

"Hmmm."

He still hesitated, toying with the edge of my panties.

"Well . . .?" I said.

"I'm trying to decide . . ."

"I say yes."

He laughed. "I doubt it, and I doubt we're thinking of the same question."

"Which is . . .?"

"Control. As in, can I help you without wanting to help myself to you?"

I turned around and repositioned myself on his lap, facing him, squarely straddling him, hands around his neck. "What if I'm offering?"

He growled deep in his throat, and reached for me, pulling me against him, hands tugging up my skirt as I unbuttoned his trousers—

An alarm rang, so fast and sudden I almost toppled backward off him.

I looked around. Smoke wafted from the hall. I pictured the fire demon again, reaching for the vase of scrolls, sparks raining from his fingertips. A few must have fallen into the vase, smoldered there, and caught fire.

From the next room came the shrieks of people hearing alarms, smelling smoke, and reacting as if the building had transformed into the Towering Inferno. I caught the first lick of chaos and shivered.

Marsten's arms went around me, pulling me back against him with a hard thrust and a soft growl. I rotated to face him, my hands going around his neck, mouth finding his, drinking in the chaos arising around us. It was just a burning building. I had a more urgent fire to put out.

Marsten growled again, this one harsher as he pulled his lips from mine.

"I hate to be the one to bring this up, but . . ."

"The building's on fire?" I said.

"Unfortunately."

I slipped my hands under his shirt. "How fast can it burn?"

A low, growling chuckle as he pressed against me. "You have no idea how badly I'm tempted to test that. But I have to remind myself that you're acting under the influence of something."

"Something *other* than you, you mean."

"There's that, too."

"Vain," I said, poking him in the chest.

He caught me up in a hard, deep, tongue-diving, groin-grinding kiss, then put me back on my feet.

"Time to go," he said, and started across the room.

"Tease."

"Just giving you something to remember, once all this is out of the way."

We reached the main hall to find it logjammed with people. Marsten led me straight into the heart of the mob. The crowd buoyed us along, and before I knew it, the cool night breeze was rippling through my hair. I looked up, and only then, seeing the stars winking against the city's glow, could I truly believe it.

We were out. Free.

If Tristan and his guards were here, they'd be watching with dismay as the museum expelled a steady river of white shirts and black jackets and nary a yellow dress to be found.

As fire engines and taxis competed for curb space, sirens and blaring horns rose above the din of partygoers yelling for their lost spouses and friends. A few taxis managed a passenger snatch-and-grab before the police cordoned off the area.

We let the crowd carry us across the road, where the taxis were regrouping. Marsten's grip suddenly tightened, and he ducked sideways, nearly plowing me into a white-haired woman with a walker. As I glared at him, a voice cut through the din.

"Hope? Hope!"

"Don't look," Marsten muttered by my ear as he steered us into another pocket of people. "Just pretend you don't—"

"Hope?"

Douglas cut between a couple. He smiled at me. There I was, bedraggled and dirty, hair flying everywhere, wearing a tux jacket, running from a burning building, and he only smiled, as if I'd just popped back from the buffet line.

"The Bairds have invited us for drinks," he said.

I stared, certain somehow the din around us had turned "Oh my God, are you okay?" into an invitation for post-inferno cocktails.

"I—I have to go," I said finally. "The—the paper. The fire. I need to—"

"Oh, you'll need to write it up, won't you?" He smiled and winked. "For a cause, I'd go with spontaneous human combustion."

"I was thinking more of fire demons," I muttered.

"Sure. That's different. I'll let you go, then. Have fun, and don't work too hard."

Marsten yanked me backward again, as Douglas slipped off through the crowd. When we reached the sidewalk, Marsten body-checked a young man and shoved me through an open cab door, crawled in after me, and slammed it.

He looked over. "Your address?"

I gave it.

To the driver, though, Marsten just said, "Head east."

"Riverside is beside the river," I said. "Which is north."

Marsten just shut the panel between the front and rear seats and buckled up.

"To be safe, you should spend the evening someplace else. Is your mother in the city?"

"Yes, but if I'm in danger, I'm certainly not taking it to her."

"Friend, sibling, cousin . . ."

"Same issue. We should find a hotel or motel and get some rest before we figure out how to resolve this, because I'm assuming Tristan won't just give up and go away."

"He won't. All right, then. We'll find a hotel, and I'll make sure it's safe. Then, when I come back—"

"Back?"

He patted the trouser pocket with the jewels. "I need to take care of these tonight. I shouldn't be more than an hour or so."

"Just long enough to hunt down and kill Tristan?"

When Marsten looked over, I said, "I may be foolish, but I'm not stupid and, after tonight, not nearly so naive. The only way to end this is to kill Tristan, so that's what you're going to do. That is why you said you'd retrieve my bracelet 'later'—you meant once I was out of the building and you went back for Tristan."

He studied my expression and then nodded. "I've tried walking away twice, and he refuses to leave it at that. I can't walk away again."

"That's why you asked for my address, isn't it? Because you think that's where he'll go. Right now, I'm the more urgent threat, the one who could let his Cabal know about his extracurricular activities."

"Yes."

"Then you know I'm not going to a hotel." I held up a hand against his protest. "Have I interfered yet?"

"No, but—"

"And I won't. I am so far out of my league—" I shook my head. "Let's just say I won't embarrass myself further or endanger you by interfering. But Tristan wants me, and if you show up alone at my townhouse, he'll know it's a trap."

Marsten hesitated. Then he pulled back the panel and gave the driver my address.

TWELVE

I live in a brownstone backing onto the river and surrounding parkland. Not your typical twenty-something tabloid journalist digs.

My mother had bought the place while I was in J-school. She called it an investment, but when I graduated, she'd wanted to give it to me. College had been a struggle—not academically but personally, as I'd dealt with my demon powers, which my family presumed were mental health issues. I think the brownstone was Mom's graduation gift . . . and hopefully a source of stability for a daughter sorely in need of it.

I love the townhouse, love the area, love my beautiful riverfront "backyard" with its winding forest trails, an escape whenever I need it, which seems to be often. So I'd agreed to keep living there, as a property manager of sorts, maintaining the building and protecting Mom's investment. But I refused to take the deed, and insisted on paying all expenses and upkeep—though the property taxes alone were nearly enough to bankrupt me. Thank God I had two jobs—

Two jobs?

As the taxi disgorged us on the front lawn, I stared up at my beloved brownstone and realized I no longer had two jobs. Probably not even one.

Of course, my mother could—and would—step in and pay the bills, and do so happily, without ever mentioning it. I so desperately didn't want that.

I'd given my mother enough sleepless nights to last a lifetime. I often wondered whether, at some level, she knew my problems were rooted in something she'd done, that brief post-separation encounter that no one could blame her for. Even though she didn't understand the true nature of my trouble, I think she blamed herself, and I didn't want that. I wanted to be strong and independent and stable, to be able to take her for lunches on my dime and say, "See, Mom, I'm doing fine." And I *had* reached that point, stuffed with the newfound confidence my job had given me—

"We'd better get inside," Marsten whispered as the cab pulled away.

He looked around, nostrils flaring, body tense, ready for trouble. Not the time to worry about my life's recent crash and burn. When this was over, I should just be thankful I still had a life to repair.

"Good security," Marsten whispered as I undid the dual dead-bolt. "Are the other doors and windows—?"

"All armed. Motion detectors in every room, too. My mom worries."

I hurried in to disarm the system. It was still active. If Tristan had beat us here, he'd backed off when he saw my security. This wasn't the kind of neighborhood that ignored screaming sirens.

"What now?" I said as Marsten relocked the front door.

"Turn on a couple of lights, and stay away from the windows. Is that open land out back?"

"A park," I said. "Mostly forest."

"Good. That's where I'll try to get him, then. Away from the houses. We'll stay here for a bit, give him time to arrive and stake out the house. Then I'll Change and lead him into the forest."

"Change?" The words *But I don't have anything for you to wear* were on my lips when I realized what he meant. "Into a wolf."

He nodded. "By far the preferred way for dealing with these things. It's easier to track, easier to fight, and"—a quick smile—"a built-in disguise if anyone sees me."

I flipped on the living room and hall lights.

"What about the television?" I said. "Should I turn that on, too?"

A brow arch. "We escape death, flee to the safety of your town-house . . . and watch television?"

"So what would Tristan expect—?" I followed his gaze to the stairs leading to the second level. "Ah, of course. You'd want a good night's rest."

"And that's probably all I'd get," he muttered. "Unless I set the place on fire first. From Tristan's point of view, though, we just had a harrowing evening, I saved your life—"

"You did?"

"Play along. You take me upstairs—"

"Oh, reward sex." I paused. "But for proper reward sex, we probably wouldn't even make it past the front door. I just push you against the wall, get down on my knees—"

He cut me off with a growl. "I'd suggest you stop there unless you plan to follow through."

"I might follow through . . . if you'd saved my life." I swung around the banister onto the stairs. "Not that you'd *let* me follow through, though. No sex unless it's *you* I want, remember? No chaos sex. No reward sex. That's your rule."

He muttered something and followed me up the stairs.

At Marsten's suggestion, the first thing I did was remove my dress . . . which sounds a whole lot more interesting than it was. As he pointed out, heels and a slinky yellow dress didn't make good late night commando gear. While he cleaned up, I put on jeans, a T-shirt, and sneakers. Then we headed for my bedroom. Yes, I have a separate dressing room. It's a three-bedroom townhouse—I'm just trying to make efficient use of space. Really.

I walked into my darkened bedroom, flicked on the light, then made a face.

"Sorry," I said. "It's a mess. I wasn't expecting company."

"Poor Doug." Marsten walked to the unmade bed, plunked down on it, and gave it a test bounce. "Doesn't get a lot of use, I'll bet."

"I'm picky. Sorry."

A wolfish grin. "Don't be. I like picky." He pushed to his feet. "Well, no, usually I don't like picky, but this time I think I do."

With a sidelong glance through the window, he put his arms around my waist, leaned down, and kissed me. It was a slow kiss, easy and relaxed, with none of the practiced attention to art of his first kiss.

"Setting the scene?" I murmured with a nod toward the window.

"A good excuse." He kissed me again and then sighed. "You really *are* immune, aren't you?"

"To what?" I caught his look and rolled my eyes. "Oh please. You really *are* vain, aren't you?"

"I already admitted that. I can't help it. I'm accustomed to having my attentions returned."

"Hmm."

"Not even going to bite for that, are you?"

I stepped back and sat on the edge of the bed. "What? If you find me attractive, I'm honor bound to return the compliment? Fine, yes, you have your charms."

A twist of his lips.

"That's not good enough? Okay, let me try again. I think you're the most gorgeous thing I've ever seen and I can barely keep my hands off you . . . Well, not when there's a decent source of chaos around."

He growled and scooped me up off the bed, kissing me again.

"Enough already," I said, squirming free. "I admitted you were—"

"Charming."

"I said you had your charms."

"Which means you find me charming."

"No, well, yes, you *are* charming, but I don't find that charming."

He laughed and shook his head. "All right, you find me physically attractive, then."

"Yes, you are, but no, I don't find that particularly attractive."

He bared his teeth in a quick grin and stepped closer. "My wit?"

I moved back and shrugged. "Witty enough, though not as witty as you think you are."

"Ouch." He gave an almost self-mocking grin. "Then it must be my undeniable sense of style."

"Because you can pick out a decent tux?" I snorted. "There's, what, one color option, two or three styles?"

A feigned look of shock. "You mean you don't find me irresistibly suave, debonair—"

"Where I grew up, guys learn suave from the cradle."

His grin only grew. "Then whatever you find attractive about me has nothing to do with any of this—" He waved his hands over himself. "—this infinitely polished package?"

"Nope. Sorry."

"Good."

"Good?"

"Very good."

He caught me up in a kiss. As he did, a distant vibe twanged through me.

"They're here," I whispered.

Marsten glanced out the window, his body blocking mine, gaze scanning the dark street.

"They're across the road," he murmured as he turned back to me. "They must have just arrived. On the count of three, I'm swinging you past the window and onto the bed."

He did. As soon as I hit the mattress, I rolled to the far side and dropped onto the floor. Marsten followed. We crawled into the hall, down the stairs, and to the back door. We reached it in time to duck behind the kitchen cabinets before we heard footsteps. The guard tested the door, peered in, and then moved on.

"Quickly," Marsten murmured. "They'll be back. This is the safest place to break in."

As we slipped onto the rear deck, I started pushing the handle in, to relock it when it closed. Marsten caught my hand.

"We want them to know we came out this way," he whispered.

Hunched over, darting from bush to tree to garden shed, I led him across my tiny yard, and down the small hill to the woodland beyond. Marsten found a place for me to hide. He made sure I had my gun and warned me, whatever happened, to stay where I was. Then he gave me a card from his wallet and told me, if he didn't return in an hour, I was to get to a public place, call the hand-written number on the back, and explain everything.

A moment later, he was gone.

I did as Marsten instructed. I had no choice. As impotent as I felt cowering in those bushes, I knew, if I tried to help, I'd more likely get us both killed.

I listened as the soft lullaby of cricket and frog calls went silent under the heavy footfalls and guttural muttering of Tristan and his guards. I listened as those mutters gave way to orders and oaths. I listened as those trudging footsteps divided and turned into running feet. I listened as a shot shattered the night. Then a scream, cut short by flashing fangs.

That wasn't my imagination working overtime. I *saw* those fangs flash, smelled bowels give way, felt hot blood spatter my face, and the visions brought not a split second of chaos bliss. With every cry, every scream, every silenced pistol shot, I was certain Marsten had been hit.

The death vision came twice, and still I heard multiple running feet and voices. My God, how many were there? How would he ever—

Another shot. Then a piercing canine yelp of pain.

THIRTEEN

I gripped my gun and slunk through the shadows until I was close enough to see a flashlight beam cutting a swath through the dark forest. The beam stopped, and my gaze followed its path through the trees.

A black mound of fur lay motionless at the end of that flashlight beam. A guard stood beside the mound, his gun pointed down.

Something flashed near the top of the heap, a blue eye reflected in Tristan's flashlight beam. The eye rolled, following Tristan. I took another three steps, until that dark mound became a massive wolf, lying on his belly, his head lowered but not down, ears and lips drawn back as he watched Tristan's approach. The fur on Marsten's shoulder was matted with blood. The guard had his gun pointed at Marsten's head, and I couldn't tell whether he was staying down because of that gun or because he was too badly injured to rise.

"Hope!"

Tristan's voice rang out so loud that I jumped. Only the barest rustle of dead leaves gave me away, but Marsten's ears swiveled in my direction. His black nostrils flared. Then he let out a low growl, and I knew that growl was for me. As clear a *Get the hell out of here* as if he'd shouted the words.

"Hope!" Tristan yelled again. "I know you're there."

Marsten's muzzle turned sharply as bushes crackled. The top of a head bobbed from the darkness. Tristan waved for the guard to stand near Marsten.

"Hope! Don't you think you've caused enough trouble tonight? Three men dead and another to follow? All because you couldn't do your job and catch one man—a thief, no less. Isn't that what you'd signed on to do? Help us put away scum like Karl Marsten?"

When Marsten had found us hiding spots, he'd emphasized protecting our backs. So where could I safely . . .?

I looked up into the trees.

While Tristan shouted for me, I scurried to the nearest candidate, grabbed the lowest branch, and channeled my inner tomboy. In minutes I was lying on my stomach on a thick branch.

"Hope! You have thirty seconds to show yourself, or I put a bullet in this mutt's head."

I ignored him. He wasn't about to kill the only way he had to get to me.

My sight line into the clearing was less than ideal. I could make out heads and torsos, but nothing below waist level, which included Marsten. I wriggled farther along the branch and spotted him, still on the ground at the guard's feet, his head raised as he glowered at Tristan.

"Hope? Last chance."

Tristan's finger moved to the trigger. Was I so sure he wouldn't shoot? Tristan wanted Marsten dead, wouldn't leave this forest until he was dead. He had him dead to rights. Getting me was secondary.

"Wait!" The word flew out before I could stop it.

Tristan smiled and lowered his gun. "That's my girl."

"I want to negotiate," I said. "I made a mistake."

"Yes, Hope, you did."

Tristan hand-signaled for one guard to search in the direction of my voice.

"Uh-uh," I said. "I'm not coming out. Not yet."

Tristan jerked his chin, motioning for the guard to circle around from behind.

"Don't tell him to sneak up on me, either," I called, my voice ringing in the stillness. "I can sense supernaturals, remember? He comes anywhere near me, and I'll do what you threatened to do to Karl—put a bullet in his head."

"Ah, a bullet." He pulled my pistol from his pocket. "From this gun, maybe?"

I unscrewed the silencer and fired the gun into the ground below. "No, *this* gun."

"So you have a weapon. Wonderful. It would be even better if you knew how to use it. But they don't teach marksmanship in debutante classes, do they?"

"Do you really think I'd let you go to all the trouble of getting me a gun and not even learn how to use it? I'm a keener, Tristan, remember? I was at the gun club an hour after you handed it to me. Oh, and yes, the West Hills Country Club *does* have marksmanship facilities. Excellent facilities. You'd like it . . . if they'd ever let you in."

Tristan stiffened.

"I made a mistake," I said. "Marsten tricked me."

Tristan smiled. "Charmed you, more like."

"No, he lied to me," I said as I looked around, babbling while I searched for a way to help Marsten. "He said I'm working for a Cabal, not the interracial council."

One of the guards shot Tristan a confused look, mouthing, "Council?"

So they didn't know?

The other two guards had been in on Tristan's scheme, but these ones apparently had no idea what I was talking about. Marsten said Tristan was working on personal revenge, that the Cabal would never have sanctioned his death. The other two guards had known that. They must have been moonlighting outside the Cabal with Tristan. But these two weren't? Interesting . . .

"I don't know what you hope to gain by killing me, Tristan." I pulled out the business card Marsten had given me. "We've already called—"

Earlier, I'd glanced at it just long enough to register the last name—Cortez—and I'd remembered Marsten saying he'd done work for Benicio Cortez's son, Lucas, the one who wasn't part of the Cabal. So that's the name I expected. When I saw what was really printed there, my heart thudded.

I turned it over. A handwritten phone number. Oh God, was that real? What if it wasn't?

"Yes, Hope? You were saying?"

I'd been about to say that I'd called the person on the card and told him everything. But that wouldn't work now. If I had already called, these guards wouldn't be here.

"Who am I really working for, Tristan?" I said. "Who sanctioned this job?"

He snuck a look at the guards. "The Cortez Cabal, Hope. You already said that."

"Yes, but I . . . I'm confused. You two down there. When you were called in, what did Mr. Cortez say Karl's crime was?"

The guards looked at one another.

"Wait," I said. "Mr. Cortez didn't give the order, did he? So what did *Tristan* say Karl's crime was?"

"He's a thief," Tristan said, surveying the forest as if trying to pinpoint my voice.

"Okay . . . but—well, he's been a thief all his life, right? And his father before him. But now, out of the blue, Mr. Cortez decides he deserves to die for it? Right after Karl joined the Pack. Right after the Pack joins the interracial council. Wouldn't killing a Pack werewolf cause a serious diplomatic crisis? I thought Mr. Cortez was pretty careful about stuff like that."

The guards turned to Tristan.

"I don't question my orders," Tristan said.

"Maybe, but I do. I'm going to call Mr. Cortez. Got his card right here." I read off the Cabal office phone number, so they'd know I was telling the truth. "And while I'm sure that would get me through to some flunky, I can save time by using the number on the back. Benicio Cortez's personal number."

"How'd she get—?" one of the guards began.

"She didn't, you—" Tristan clipped off the insult. "It's a stalling tactic. You really are a naive little girl, aren't you, Hope? Where did you get Benicio Cortez's number? Dialing 411?"

The second guard snickered, but the first took out his cell phone.

"Here," he said. "Give me the number and I'll call."

Tristan smiled. "Yes, Hope. Give him the number."

I stammered it out instead, as if I was making it up . . . which I really hoped I wasn't. What if someone had given it to Marsten as a joke?

As I read the number, I looked down at him, trying to gauge his reaction, but his eyelids were flagging, as if he was struggling to stay conscious.

My hesitant delivery made Tristan smile, and he made no attempt to stop the guard from dialing, just leaned back against a tree and awaited my downfall.

Ten seconds after the guard finished dialing, his head jerked up. "Mr. Cortez?"

Tristan chuckled and shook his head.

"This is Bryan Trau," the guard said. "SA Unit 17. I'm sorry to disturb you, sir, but we have a situation here."

Tristan jumped so fast he nearly tripped. He motioned for the guard to hand over the phone, but the guard stepped away. Tristan started to lift his gun but stopped as the second guard raised his.

The guard explained the situation. When he was finished, he listened and said, "Yes, sir," then held out the phone.

"Mr. Cortez would like to speak to you."

Tristan stepped back and looked ready to bolt. Then he caught sight of Marsten and must have, in that second, seen a possible way out: the elimination of the only person who could confirm the entire story. He lifted his gun.

A shot.

I didn't think. I jumped from the tree. The second I started falling, my brain screamed, *Idiot!*

I hit the ground hard, but scrambled up. As I ran to the clearing, I heard, "Yes, sir." Pause. "No, sir. He's gone."

I flew into the clearing to see the guard on the phone, kneeling beside a body. Tristan's body.

"Yes, sir, I did. You said if he made a move—" A pause, then the guard nodded and glanced over at me. "She's here now."

The guard held out the phone. I hesitated, then took it.

"Is this the young woman who was with Karl?" a voice asked. A pleasant voice. Calm and alert, as if he hadn't been woken in the middle of the night.

He asked whether I was hurt and what had happened, his tone mild but concerned, avuncular, not what I'd expect from the head of the most powerful Cabal in the country. After a few quick questions, he said, "You've had a very long night, and I'm sorry you had to go through this, but I can assure you, Mr. Robard was acting outside his jurisdiction. Since he is an employee, though, I take full responsibility for his actions, and will do everything I can to put things right, starting with looking after Karl. Is he badly hurt?"

I'd been so shocked I hadn't even checked. I raced to Marsten's side. The second guard was already there, tending to Marsten, who was unconscious. He'd been shot through the shoulder, and his entire side was wet and sticky. Blood must have been pumping out the whole time he'd been lying there.

Mr. Cortez assured me a doctor was on the way from a nearby satellite office.

FOURTEEN

The guards carried Marsten back to my house and returned to clear the scene. They weren't even out of the backyard when the doctor arrived. He did a double take when he saw his patient in wolf form, but got Marsten's wound cleaned and covered, left antibiotics and painkillers, and told me to call if his condition worsened.

The two guards stopped back at the house to let me know everything was cleaned up. They brought something for me, too: my purse, left by Tristan in the van. My bracelet was still in there, as was my wallet. Everything back in order, just as Mr. Cortez had promised.

Marsten was in the living room, on a blanket. I found a second blanket and laid it over him. Yes, he looked kind of ridiculous, a huge wolf on my living room floor with a pink and white knit afghan tucked in around his muzzle. At least I didn't get him a pillow . . . though I did consider it.

I stretched out on the sofa above him, intending to keep watch until he woke, but within minutes I was asleep.

I awoke to the sound of running water. I looked down at the floor. Marsten was gone.

"Up here," he said when I called for him.

I climbed the stairs. He was in the bathroom, with the door open a crack.

I stopped a few paces from the door. "Let me grab your clothes."

"Found and on. What's left of them, anyway. Now, if I can just—" He growled. "This bandage fit me better as a wolf."

"Here, I can—"

I started pushing the door open and stopped, realizing he might not want the help. He kicked it open the rest of the way as he quickly shrugged on his shirt.

"Didn't peg you as the shy type." I gestured at the shirt. "I can't fix your shoulder like that."

He hesitated, and let the shirt fall off. His chest and upper arms were a loose patchwork of scars. He tensed, as if waiting for me to comment. I grabbed bandages and iodine from the closet and set to work.

"The Cabal sent a doctor over," I said. "I'm not sure he did a very good job. He didn't seem to know much about werewolves."

"No matter. I know someone who does." He glanced at me. "So I didn't imagine that, then. You contacted Benicio Cortez."

I nodded. "That's all it took. Tristan's dead, you're alive, the mess is cleaned up, and Mr. Cortez has promised to look after any fall-out. Which, of course, led me to wonder, if you had that number, why didn't you use it right away. I think I know the answer, but I'm hoping I'm wrong."

"Probably not," he murmured.

I looked up at him. "As nice as Mr. Cortez was, I'm guessing he didn't get where he is by playing Santa Claus. Cleaning this up for us wasn't a free gift, was it?"

"We owe him. He wouldn't say that, because it would have been crass, but it's a chit." He rubbed his shoulder and adjusted the bandage. "When I turned down Tristan's offer, Benicio came to me and made one personally. *He* was much more persuasive—"

"He threatened you?"

Marsten smiled. "Benicio Cortez does not threaten. He knows a lollipop is a better motivator than a swat on the behind. He made me a lucrative offer, and when I respectfully declined, he let it go but gave me that card, in case I ever 'needed help.'"

"And now I've accepted it on your behalf, putting you in his debt."

"If I hadn't wanted you to use it, I wouldn't have told you to. Given the choice between being dead and owing Benicio Cortez, I'll take the latter, as uncomfortable as it may be. He will eventually call in the chit, but in the meantime, you can go back to your life, including your job at the paper, assuming that's what you want."

"It is." I sat on the edge of the counter. "I'd like to—well, maybe I'm kidding myself thinking I could do anything on my own."

"You could still monitor and report problems. To the real council this time. They have someone doing something similar, another journalist, and I know she'd love the help."

When I hesitated, Marsten stepped in front of me, a hand on each side, balancing against the counter. "Take it slow and start there. The only drawback, I'm afraid, would be the pay . . . or lack of it. The real council isn't a group of white-haired supernatural philanthropists. Most of the delegates aren't much older than you, meaning it's a no-budget operation."

"That doesn't matter. I never even wanted Tristan to pay me. I get paid well enough." I stopped and shrugged. "Well, you know . . ."

"In chaos dollars."

My cheeks heated. "I know that sounds awful, helping others because I get something out of it."

He put his hands on my hips. "You need an outlet. Do you think I don't understand that?" He reached into his pocket and took out the jewels. "This is mine. A way to get a regular adrenaline shot without ripping apart strangers in alleyways. And with you, it isn't all about the chaos. You have balance. The good impulses with the bad. Me?" He smiled. "A little more inclined to the latter." His eyes glinted. "Though not irredeemably so."

I laughed. "Something tells me that would be a fun but futile challenge."

"Challenge is good."

I shook my head. "If you're happy with what you are, then anyone who wants you would need to accept that."

He ran his fingertips along my jawline. "Wouldn't be easy, I'm sure."

"No, but if you look hard enough, I'm sure you'd find someone willing to try. You know, my mom's great at finding dates—"

He growled and kissed me. When he pulled back, he ran the tip of his tongue over his lips, as if sampling the kiss.

"The immunity is breaking down," he murmured. "But still has a ways to go." He leaned toward me again. "I'd ask if I should stay, but I suspect the answer would be no. So instead I'll ask whether I can come back."

I smiled. "Yes, you can come back."

"Good. Better, actually."

"Better?"

"Much."

I laughed and shook my head.

Marsten stepped back. "I should go. I have a doctor to visit and goods to dispose of . . . not necessarily in that order. And I will make those calls for you, ensure the termination from your old job and the start of your new one proceed smoothly."

"Thanks. I appreciate that." I caught his hand and met his gaze. "I really do, Karl."

He leaned over for a kiss, little more than a brushing of the lips, but very . . . nice. He backed up to the door and then stopped.

"I'm too old for you."

"Too old for what? To come back for a visit?"

A dramatic sigh. He shook his head, and walked out of the bathroom. From the hall I heard a murmured, "I'm going to make a fool of myself."

"It'll look good on you," I called after him.

He chuckled. I smiled and listened to his footsteps recede down the stairs, across the floor, and finally disappear out the back door. Then I took a deep breath. One life gone. Time to reinvent myself—again. Was I up for it?

God, I hoped so.

AMITYVILLE HORRIBLE

ONE

"You know how you said you'd never do another reality ghost show?" Mike's voice bounced off my dressing room walls.

"Yep, I did." I turned the speaker sound down on my cell phone and pulled a tendril of loose hair from my twist. "And it still stands. Never, ever, ever—"

"It's for charity."

"Doesn't matter. Not after the last time."

"*Charity*, Jaime. Using your good fortune to raise the fortunes of others. I know that's important to you."

I tried to force out another "no," but it stuck in my throat. Damn it. I took a deep breath. "What's the cause?"

"Cotard's syndrome."

"Never heard of it." I picked up the phone, switched to the browser, and typed in a search.

"It's a neurological disorder," he said. "That means it affects the brain."

I bit back a retort. That's the price I pay for playing ditzy minor celebrity for thirty years. Not that I'm a brain surgeon, but I do know the word for it is "neurosurgeon."

"Cotard's is very debilitating," Mike continued. "It's a rare but terrible—"

"'Walking corpse syndrome'?" I read from the screen. "Hell, no."

"It's a real condition, Jaime," Mike hurried on. "Sure, there's a promotional tie-in. Ghosts, zombies, walking corpses. But that's just the hook. We'll be raising real money for actual victims. Think of the children."

"It says here Cotard's only affects adults."

"Think of the children *of* those adults. Can you imagine what that's like, having your parents believe they've been zombified? Absolutely tragic. But you can help. See, the idea is—"

I hung up. As I was turning off the phone, a knock sounded at my dressing room door.

"Ms. Vegas? Ten minutes."

I shoved the phone in a drawer, checked my hair one last time, and headed out.

Live shows are hell for performers. At the end, you feel like you've run a marathon, shouting the whole way. It's not just a physical toll. It's mental and emotional, too. A live show means your audience is right there, waiting to be entertained, and you sure as hell better deliver, because if you don't, they'll let you know. It's not just heckling. I've learned to deal with that. I actually prefer heckling to that most insidious critique—boredom. I swear, I can be on my catwalk in front of five hundred people, talking a mile a minute, half blinded by the lights, and still hear every yawn, notice every pair of closed eyes.

My professional reputation is good enough that I could earn more giving private sessions. I could certainly earn more with a TV show. There was a time when I dreamed of that. Then, after doing a TV special, *Death of Innocence*, I got my offer, and I realized I didn't want it. I was happy where I was, and sometimes that's more important.

So what gets me out on that stage? The audience. Yes, there are jeers and there are eye rolls. I'm a spiritualist. There's always part of the audience that comes to mock the crazy lady who thinks she talks to the dead. There are also yawns and even snores on a really bad night. But that's five people out of five hundred. For the rest, I deliver what I promise. Not just entertainment. Happiness. Peace. Closure. Even if it isn't real, it does something. Something magical.

Tonight's show was in an old theater. With this kind of performance, the older the venue, the better. It was a traditional setup with a proscenium stage at the front, but my crew had added a portable catwalk to allow me to walk down the middle aisle, elevated so everyone could see me. As I walked, I talked.

"There's a spirit trying to come through. It's a woman. The name . . ." I lifted my hand for quiet as I strained to listen. "Margaret? Marg? Meg? Megan? Do we have anyone hoping to contact a loved one—"

Two dozen hands shot up before I even finished.

"Wait . . ." I said. "I can see her now. Marg? Meg? I know this isn't easy, but if you can just come a little . . ." I smiled. "Yes, that's better. Thank you. Take a moment now. Rest." I turned back to the audience. "She's partially through the veil. I'm still not hearing her clearly, but we're going to give her a moment before I ask her to complete the journey. We had a few people who'd lost someone named Margaret or Megan . . ."

The hands shot up again. Another dozen joined them, those who had, in the last few minutes, sifted through their memories and remembered Great-aunt Marguerite, who died when they were five.

"I can see enough to give a partial d—————— I said, my gaze fixed on the stage. "She's dark-haired.

Several hands lowered. A few more

"She's not tall," I said. "Five-two?

More lowering. More wavering.

"Average weight? Maybe slightly

We were back to a dozen hands and headed down the aisle to one

first question.

"I feel a pull in this direction,"

The woman—gray-haired, mid-sixties—stood. "Nancy. Nancy Masters."

"And who are you looking for today, Nancy?"

"My sister Margie. She passed last winter. Stroke."

I looked toward the stage. "The woman I'm seeing is young, but spirits often choose their materialized form from a time when they were happiest. Margie was a brunette? Petite?"

Nancy nodded.

I backed up to where I could see both Nancy and the stage. "She's coming through a little better now. She's wearing her hair . . ."

I squinted at the stage, while watching Nancy's reaction out of the corner of my eye.

"Down?" I said.

No reaction.

"Short?"

A slight dropping of her jaw. Disappointment.

"No, actually it appears to be up."

Nancy's gaze returned to mine. Getting warmer . . .

"Yes, that's why it looked short. It seems to be pinned up. In a bun?"

A faint droop to her eyelids. Cooler . . .

"Wait, is that a twist?"

Nancy's eyes gleamed, crow's feet wrinkling as she struggled not to smile.

"Yes, definitely a twist. Like mine tonight. She has excellent taste."

A laugh tittered through the audience. Relief and approval. The whole rapid-fire exchange had taken a matter of seconds as I [look]ed at the distant figure, as if trying to get a better look.

[There w]as no figure. No ghost. In fact, there was vervain burn-[ing . . . a]nd in the lobby. If anyone asks, my staff will explain [. . . tr]oubled spirits. It's actually to keep them away.

I'm a necromancer, which is an old word for those who can speak to and raise the dead. Like most, I stick to the "speaking" part and do as little even of that as possible. One place I won't do it? A show, because if I snuff out that vervain, the room will fill with the dearly departed of audience members.

Wouldn't that make me more credible? No. Because if Nancy's sister Margie really did appear, she'd have a message. She might ask Nancy to get Margie's favorite necklace back from her divorced daughter-in-law. Or to tell Margie's husband not to flirt with that fifty-year-old hussy down the road. Or to make sure Margie's grandson didn't buy that motorcycle he was eyeing.

Nancy didn't want—or need—to hear such petty concerns. She needed to hear that her sister was happy. That Margie was in a good place and looking forward to the day when they'd be reunited.

Unless Margie loathed Nancy—or had been a closet ax murderer—she really *was* happy and missing her sister. That just wasn't the first message she'd impart. So I did it for her.

Was that wrong? Probably. I've long since stopped worrying. I make people happy. I give them closure. It's as close to a money-back guarantee as you can get—in this world or the next.

After the show ended, I held a press conference. Normally, that would be a waste of time. You want the media coverage while folks can still buy tickets. But this had been my first show in Oklahoma City in a decade, so advance media hadn't been necessary. With proper outreach from my team, tonight's show had sold out a month ago.

However, as long as I was in Oklahoma, I might as well do a few stops. That's where this press conference came in handy, letting people know that if they missed tonight's show, they could catch the ones in Tulsa and Lawton later this week, but they'd better move, because seats were filling fast. Doing the press conference postshow meant the cameras could catch the happy audience members as they departed.

While my audience members had sold the show for me, I'd been resting backstage. Then I swanned out, apologizing profusely for my disheveled appearance, explaining the mental and physical toll a summoning took on me, joking about aging ten years in two hours. I looked fine. Or as fine as I can look at forty-eight without the help of needles or scalpels. Of course, I'd spent the last twenty minutes touching up backstage—I'd rather dive into a pit of putrefying zombies than appear on camera without at least a mirror check. It's not about vanity. It's about image. Okay, maybe a little vanity, too.

When I came out, cameras clicked and mics turned my way. I mingled with the crowd, asking after everyone's health as if we were at a cocktail party. There were even cocktails. Bloody Marys and Zombies. When you do this schtick, you either embrace it or try to dignify it. I've learned long ago that I'll get a lot more laughs—and a lot less ridicule—if I play it up.

I was making my way through the crowd when a pert blonde rattled off a TV station call sign so fast I didn't catch it. I focused on her name instead, which I've always found to be more important. It was Brittany. I'm guessing at the spelling, though I'm quite sure there was really an extra *i* or silent *h* in there somewhere. There always is.

"Ms. Vegas!" she squeaked. "Is it true you've signed on for the Amityville show?"

"Amityville?"

She raised her voice. After you reach a certain age, everyone mistakes confusion for hearing loss. In showbiz, that age is about thirty.

"The charity event?" she said. "For Cotard's syndrome?"

I opened my mouth to give a gracious response, something about my schedule. But she kept going.

"I heard you signed on. That is so amazing. It's a great cause. My father has Cotard's. It's such a tragic disease that no one ever hears of, but that's going to change." She put out her hand. "Thank you. Really. On behalf of the families of Cotard's sufferers everywhere." Her eyes brimmed with tears. "Thank you."

All around us, camera bulbs flashed, and I knew I was screwed.

TWO

"I'm going to kill you," I said when Mike finally answered his phone. "I'm going to murder you, then summon your spirit and stick you in a very small, very dark box. No, wait. I'll stick you in front of a television, where you are forced to watch reality TV reruns for eternity. Reruns of your own shows."

"I—"

"I did *Death of Innocence* as a favor because I owed you for my first Keni Bales appearance. So I signed on to help raise the ghost of Marilyn Monroe. And when it all went to hell, was it my fault?"

"No, but—"

"Your first big show was about to be canceled. But then one of your performers discovered a child's body in the garden. Who did that?"

"You, but—"

"I found that poor girl, and soon no one gave a crap about Marilyn, because you had something even juicier. *Death of Innocence: Satanism in Brentwood.* A smash hit. Who gave you that?"

"Well, it was a joint—"

"Joint effort, my ass. It was me. I even went along with the wildly inaccurate satanic cult angle for you. I put up with Todd Simon and Bradford Grady, and I turned a train wreck into a ratings smash hit. Five years later, the video is still selling enough to send you to Venice every spring. And how do you repay me?"

"By giving you another smash," he blurted. "Star billing in a brand-new special. At double the rate I paid you for *Death*."

"I am not—"

"With a cut of video sales."

I paused. "Net or gross?"

"Net, of course. I can't—"

I hung up. I counted to three. My phone rang.

"Okay, gross, but it will be a much, much smaller percentage than you'd get for net—"

"A smaller percentage of something is better than a huge cut of nothing. I know how your accounting works. I'll take gross—*if* I agree to do it, and we're a long way from that. Setting me up with that fake reporter tonight—"

"Fake?" he sputtered. "I don't know what you're—"

"Cut the crap and this will go much smoother. You sent her. She nailed me on camera. That means I have to at least listen to what you have to say or I'm the diva bitch who couldn't spare a few minutes to raise public awareness of zombie-itus."

"We'd prefer to call it—"

"Whatever. Yes, Cotard's is a real condition. Yes, people suffer from it. But that's not why you're using it, so let's cut the crap and stop pretending you care. You know that if I do this, I'll treat it seriously, even if I'm the only one who does."

I let him sputter. Then I cut in with, "So what's the gig?"

. . .

"Yes, *that* Amityville."

I was lying on a hotel bed with my feet propped against the wall. I'm sure I looked like a sixteen-year-old on the phone with her boyfriend. Which was pretty much accurate. I was on the phone. With my boyfriend. I may be a long way from sixteen, but there's something about Jeremy Danvers that makes me feel like a teenager even after five years together.

I've had friends look at our long-distance arrangement and question just how committed I am to Jeremy—and he to me. After all, we *aren't* kids. To them, we should be living together by now, if not married. Which goes to prove, I guess, that those people aren't actually friends, or they'd know there's no question about what I feel for Jeremy.

Yes, we *aren't* kids. That's the point. I have my career, which keeps me on the road. He has his, as werewolf Alpha, which keeps him in New York State. I suppose, to some of them, if I was truly in love, I'd give up my job for him. Which again proves how little they understand me. I love Jeremy. I love my job. I can have both. He's already planning to step down as Alpha, and when he does, he'll join me on the road more often, but neither of us is talking about a permanent move. Maybe someday, when I do retire, we'll grow old together at Stonehaven. Until then, I'm ecstatically happy with exactly what I have.

"It's not actually being filmed at *the* Amityville house," I said to Jeremy. "Mike couldn't get that. So he's renting a similar-looking place and renovating it to match the movie set. He won't claim it's the Amityville house . . . but he won't try to avoid confusion, either."

"I see."

"Yes, totally cheesy. But the charity angle helps. Also, I'm the only spiritualist, which means no ego clashes like we had in Brentwood. The other pros are parapsychologists. Then there are the extras. They'll start casting those slots after the press release goes out tomorrow."

"So the extras will be actors?"

"Mmm, not exactly. They're supposed to be just regular folks who dare to spend a night in a haunted house. It's an old routine. I'll send you links to some YouTube clips. They're good for a laugh. Basically, a bunch of people running around in the dark, hearing pipes creak and mice skitter, and scaring themselves silly."

"I see."

I lowered my feet. "It's *too* cheesy, isn't it." I swore under my breath. "I should have—"

"You should have done exactly what you wanted to do. Or, in this case, felt compelled to do. I was assimilating, not judging."

"Sorry. Just . . ." I inhaled. "I know it's not exactly a brilliant career move. For respectability, it's two steps down from the Marilyn show, and that wasn't exactly the highlight of my career."

"It didn't damage it. In fact, it raised your profile, didn't it? Boosted attendance at your shows?"

As he spoke, a shadow flickered off to the side.

"Jaime?" he said when I went silent.

"Just a sec. I may have a visitor."

Most people who know I'm a necromancer would ask questions. *Has a ghost been bothering you? Is Eve being a pain in the ass?* Jeremy knew that the best response was silence while I puzzled it out.

The natural thing would be to call, "Who's there?" but with ghosts, that's like rolling out the welcome mat. It's better to wait and let the ghosts make contact . . . then send them packing as quickly as possible.

That sounds cruel. It *is* cruel. It's also self-preservation. I help when I can, but if I opened myself up to every spirit who asked, I'd be plagued by ghosts every moment of the day. Luckily, I have a very effective watchdog—my ghostly bodyguard, Eve Levine. Dark witch, half-demon, and ascended angel. Yes, angel, which might be the scariest of the three. She has only to show up, Sword of Judgment in hand, and most spirits decide they really don't want to talk to me after all.

Unfortunately, being an angel means there are long stretches when Eve isn't available. Like now. She's out of contact, and I'm on my own, relying on her reputation to protect me.

When I looked around now, though, I saw no sign of a ghost. A trick of the light. That happens, even with necromancers.

"False alarm." I lay down on the bed and propped my feet up again. "You're right about the show. I'm just . . . I feel like I was railroaded into this, and now I'm scrambling to convince myself it's not as bad as it seems."

"It won't be as bad as it seems. Because you're in it."

I smiled. "Thanks."

"When does it film?"

"In two months."

"Would you like company on set?"

My smile widened. "I would."

Promo work on the show began a few weeks before the cameras rolled. Jeremy wasn't joining me for that part. Promotion is hell, and if he's around, I do silly things like arrive at interviews at the last possible moment, almost hoping they'll cancel so I can hang out with Jeremy instead. I know that's unprofessional, but when it comes to Jeremy, I really do revert to a sixteen-year-old girl, ignoring her assignments and bouncing around shrieking, "He's here! He's here!"

Most of the promo was done in New York City—there aren't many major media outlets in Amityville. I did morning shows. I did talk shows. I summoned spirit after spirit. A few of them were even real.

Then, two days before filming started, it was time to go to Amityville to meet my fellow ghost hunters. And time to meet the house where we'd be ghost-hunting.

The show had hired a sedan service to take me to Amityville. That sounds fancy, until you realize the town is only an hour east of New York City. A taxi probably would have cost more.

The main crew was supposed to meet at the house for a big "getting to know you" party. Then, at the last minute, we were texted directions to a local inn with a curt "change of plans" note.

"Change of plans, my ass," I muttered on my cell to Jeremy as the car entered Amityville. "They never planned for us to meet at the house."

"They want to film your first look at it. For part of the special."

"Exactly. They did that in Brentwood, but it was such a mess they cut it. No one wants to see jet-lagged spiritualists stumbling in, muttering about their crappy flight. They want a big reveal this time. And the party isn't for the real people anyway."

"Just the fake ones?"

I laughed. "Close. Pros only. They'll hold off on introducing us to the regular folks who 'won' slots. They'll want to film that, too. Get my reaction when I realize I'm about to spend the night with people who'll probably make me look like Mensa material."

His silence worked better than any verbal rebuke.

"Sorry," I said. "Hey, I've *almost* stopped doing that."

"Around me."

He meant that I still mocked myself around others. Getting the jokes and insults in before they could. Which he hated.

He changed the subject with, "So it's just the parapsychologists today. Did Mike provide you with a list of names yet?"

"He doesn't dare. I'm sure he looked back through my career and hired everyone I've ever had friction with, to make for better TV. I'll handle it. I just . . . I wish, for once, I could tell myself it'll all work out fine."

"It will," he said. "You'll make sure of it."

THREE

The driver dropped me off at the inn's front gate. Apparently, his fee didn't cover actually pulling into the lane. I could have bitched—normally I would have, oh so politely, as I've learned from Jeremy—but the traffic in New York meant I'd spent two hours in the car and I was happy for the excuse to walk, if only up the drive.

The inn was on the outskirts of Amityville. It was your typical New England inn, a big white Colonial with rose gardens just coming into bloom. I meandered up the drive, stopping to smell the roses, literally.

As I was straightening, I felt a ghost behind me. It's not an icy draft running down my spine or anything so dramatic. It's like sensing a person there, because that's what ghosts look like to a necromancer. Regular people. It's only when you see them walk through objects that you realize otherwise.

When I turned, I caught the flicker of a spirit and I sighed. A disappointing reaction for anyone who'd be watching the upcoming show. I should shriek. Turn pale. At least tremble in my boots. But given that I was wearing designer boots with five-inch spike heels, trembling really wasn't wise.

The truth, as much as it would dismay every horror fan, is that your average spook isn't all that spooky. In fact, they'd be kind of offended if I ran screaming.

So I sighed. Then I waited. But my phantom was a shy one. Finally, I said, grudgingly, "If you want to talk to me, wait until

I'm in my hotel room." As much as I hate to invite ghostly encounters, it was better than having one show up on camera. Nothing ruins a fake séance like an actual spirit.

"If you contact me *before* I'm alone, I'm not listening—"

"Jaime? You're early."

I looked up as Mike bounced down the front steps.

"What are you doing here?" I said.

He flashed a thousand-dollar smile. "Helping bring my baby to life, of course."

Mike never showed up on set. Hmm. This did not bode well.

"Did I hear you talking to someone?" he asked.

"Just a ghost."

He laughed and hugged me.

"You'll be pleased to know I took your advice about our afflicted guests," he said.

"It wasn't advice. If you parade people with Cotard's in front of the camera, I will walk off the set."

"I've invited relatives instead. They'll tell their stories in brief clips to be played throughout the special."

"Tastefully and respectfully."

A mournful, "Yes." Then, "I think you're overreacting and doing a disservice to the sufferers—"

"It's a mental illness where people think they've died. They believe they're in hell or zombified, missing limbs or internal organs."

His eyes glittered. "I know."

"They've been known to stop eating and die of starvation. Or test their death theory by committing suicide."

"Oh, well, we wouldn't show *that*."

I gave him a look as we walked up the front steps.

He sighed. "Yes, yes. There will be no Cotard's sufferers on set."

"Couldn't find any who'd agree, could you? It's hard to get excited about being on TV when you think you're dead."

As we walked through the inn's front doors, Mike tried to persuade me to go to my room—take some time, fix my hair, freshen up. Ten years ago I'd have hurried off, certain I looked like hell. I knew better now. Mike just didn't want me going to the party yet.

I was significantly earlier than Mike had instructed—intentionally, because I knew he wanted me to swan in thirty minutes late and start establishing my diva-hood as soon as possible. So I turned my suitcase over to the bellhop and insisted on joining the party.

We walked into the party. There were no decorations that looked as if they'd been hauled out of a musty Halloween box. No decorations at all, which told me this part was not going to be filmed. I could relax a little.

Mike steered me straight to a tall gray-haired man. "Jaime, I believe you know Oliver Black."

I tried to hide my surprise. I certainly did know the producer. He was supposed to helm the Marilyn show, and I'd been thrilled about that, not just because Oliver seemed to be a genuine fan of my work, but because I was a genuine fan of his. At the last minute he'd been pulled and I got stuck with Todd Simon, beer-commercial producer extraordinaire. When Mike had said Oliver would be producing this show, I'd expected the same switcheroo.

Mike's up to something, I thought as I air-kissed Oliver's cheek and told him how thrilled I was to have him here. Before we could chat, though, Mike led me to the next surprise.

"And your director," he said. "I believe you two have worked together before?"

"Becky!" I said.

It was Becky Cheung, who'd directed *Death of Innocence*. At the end of that show, I wouldn't have been nearly so thrilled to work with her again. She hadn't been bad, simply inexperienced. When her star ascended postshow, her first act had been to cut ties with Todd Simon, which had proved she was brighter than I'd thought.

Becky had never forgotten that I'd contributed to her big break.

Anytime we were due to be in the same city, she'd invite me out for dinner. I could have chalked that up to simple networking, but she continued asking even after I withdrew from Hollywood.

The gifts kept coming after that. For the parapsychology pros, Mike had hired Ted Robson, the EVP expert from *Death*, and Bruce Wong, who'd handled spirit photography. Both ranked high on my list of "pros I'd like to work with again."

I chatted with the two parapsychologists and was introduced to a third, whom I'd never worked with but had heard great things about. We talked about their plans for the show as I enjoyed a glass of champagne, and I began to relax.

If I saw anything nefarious about the too-good-to-be-true casting, I was being paranoid. With something like this—a group of strangers shoved together in a "haunted" house—there was no need for the interpersonal drama so essential to other reality shows. It was a different audience with different expectations. They wanted to see ghosts and ghouls, not meltdowns and catfights.

"Jaime?" Mike said. "There's someone else I want you to meet."

Mike led me into a small room adjacent to the party. Inside, a man sat on a couch, checking his e-mail. He was in his thirties, slender, with slightly shaggy blond hair and horn-rimmed glasses. I didn't recognize him.

"Jaime, I'd like to introduce you to Gregor Baronova."

The name meant nothing. When Mike spoke, though, the man noticed us and leapt up.

"This is most unprofessional," he said, speaking with a thick Russian accent. "I am so sorry. My wife had asked me to tell her when I arrived safely, so I came in here to send her an e-mail message."

He extended a hand and then realized he was still holding his phone and fumbled to get it into his suit pocket. "It is a great honor, Ms. Vegas. I have followed your career with much interest.

When I was told I might work with you, I thought someone was making a joke."

"No joke," I said, flashing a smile. "Though you might start to wish otherwise after a few hours on the set with me."

"She's kidding," Mike said quickly. "Jaime is a dream to work with."

Gregor nodded. "I am certain she is."

"So you're joining us on set?" I said. "What's your specialty?"

Gregor looked anxiously at Mike. "She does not know?"

My smile froze a little. "Know what?"

"I was assured that my participation had been approved by you." Gregor turned to Mike. "Quite assured."

"Er, yes," Mike said. "We . . . seemed to have a communication gap on that. The producer was very clear about wanting everyone to meet at the same time. Otherwise, I would have been *more* than happy—"

"He didn't tell me," I cut in. "But that only means that I haven't had the chance to get to know your work better. Your name sounds familiar . . ."

It didn't, but never tell someone in showbiz that you haven't heard of him.

"I am new to this line of occupation," Gregor said. "I have only performed in Russia."

"Performed?" I looked at Mike. Sweat was trickling down his face.

"Yes," Gregor said. "I am a . . . what do they call it here? A spiritualist. Like you."

FOUR

There was only one clause that I absolutely insisted on in my contract: no other spiritualists. That might sound like ego. And sure, part of it is. I like to be the star. My last experience, however, had taught me that the risks of working with other spiritualists outweigh the advantages. Namely, that I can—inadvertently—cost them their careers. Or their lives.

On *Death*, I'd been haunted by the ghosts of children buried in the garden. With Jeremy's help, I'd investigated and unmasked those responsible. But my young spiritualist colleague, Angelique, had been convinced I was doing something show-related behind her back. She'd tried to insert herself into the investigation . . . and wound up being the killers' final victim.

Then there was Bradford Grady, famed British spiritualist with a long-running hit series. While I was investigating the deaths, I'd gotten some advice from a eudemon who'd possessed Grady. Somehow—perhaps proving he did have psychic ability—Grady recalled elements of his possession and became convinced that Satan himself had taken over his body. He quit his show and moved from ghost hunting to demon busting, destroying his career in the process.

Did I feel guilty for what happened to my colleagues? Yes. Especially Angelique. People had noticed, too, and bloggers and tabloids still talked about the "*Death of Innocence* curse." There were also plenty of tasteless jokes accusing me of some "satanic" sacrifices of my own, offering up one coworker's life and another's career to advance my own.

So, I had good reason for making sure that clause went into my contract. I continued chatting with Gregor—it wasn't his fault—but didn't delay long before suggesting we shouldn't hold him captive. Mike wanted to show Gregor around, but I gave him a "talk to me or I walk" look that he couldn't ignore. We returned to the small room.

"There is a clause in my contract—" I began.

"We haven't violated it," he said as he closed the door.

"What?"

"The clause specifies an American or internationally known spiritualist. Gregor is neither."

I stared at him. "You set me up."

"It wasn't me. The studio insisted—"

"Why the hell am I surprised? You've done nothing except set me up since—"

"Hold on. That's not fair, Jaime."

"You didn't set that fake reporter on me after my show?"

"Er, yes. But the rest—"

"*One* thing. I only insisted on one thing."

"And I couldn't give it. You know how it is. I have a helluva lot of clout, but I still answer to the studio. They hold the purse strings. Without them, there is no show. If they want another spiritualist, I can argue, but ultimately all I can do is make this as easy on you as possible. Find someone American viewers have never heard of, meaning he won't compete with you on the marquee but might boost international sales. And I can make sure I don't hire an asshole, which I think you can agree Gregor is not."

"I reserve judgment."

"I tried to cushion the blow. I built you a dream team to minimize conflict. Focus on real entertainment. I even gave in on the Cotard victims."

"Because you couldn't find any."

He sighed. "I know you're not happy, but . . . this is what we have to work with."

I left the party as soon as I could exit gracefully.

"Seven o'clock pickup," Mike called as I was leaving. "Is Jeremy coming?"

I nodded and continued toward the door.

"I'll see you at the house, then," Mike called. "When all will be revealed . . . on camera."

Normally, I'd have found a joke in that. Something about not being paid enough to reveal all. That's why he said it, and my lack of response said he was still in the doghouse.

"Have you met Jaime's boyfriend?" he was saying, loudly, as I left. "Jeremy Danvers. He's an artist. I bought one of his older works at auction last year. Let's just say it was an investment. Of course, it's worth it. Gorgeous work. We'll be lucky to have him here. He's very reclusive, as all the best artists are . . ."

I picked up my pace so I didn't need to listen to him brag, as if getting Jeremy here was a personal triumph. Jeremy wouldn't appreciate everyone knowing who he was. He's not quite so reclusive these days—I give him a reason to leave the Pack and Stonehaven. But he does value his privacy more than anyone I know.

He'd texted me before the party to say he'd begun the trip. Another text an hour ago told me he'd stopped at Antonio's for a coffee break. I'd insisted on that. It was a six-hour drive, and I knew it was hard to pass within ten miles of his best friend's place without stopping. Another text thirty minutes later said he was back on the road. So, allowing for New York traffic, he should be here—I checked my watch—in about half an hour.

I stopped at the front desk to get my room number. I had the top-floor corner room. The best in the house, the innkeeper informed me. Mike had insisted on it.

I should have ignored the clerk's advice to take the far stairs. There were too many directions involved in getting there—down this corridor, make a left, take a right, another left, you can't miss it.

I missed it.

I ended up in the service hall, by the kitchens. The inn didn't serve lunch, and it was only mid-afternoon, so there was no one around to ask for directions. I'd feel a little foolish doing that, anyway. *That Vegas woman? She got lost looking for the stairs. We were all worried that, once she found her room, she'd be trapped inside, searching for the door out.*

I was backtracking when I caught a flicker down a side hall. I turned to see a woman standing there. Unless the inn was hosting a Roaring Twenties event, I'd just spotted my first spook. I pretended not to see her, as if I was just a regular person.

"Help me. Please help me."

Damn. The "regular person" shtick would work so much better if I could douse the spirit-world glow that marks me as a necromancer.

The woman—about twenty, with a blond bob and beaded dress—stood partway down the hall. As I moved closer, I saw tears streaming down her face and blood on her dress, more spattered on her bare arms.

"You aren't real, are you?" I murmured. "You're a residual."

"Please, help me."

Her gaze seemed to be fixed on mine. A trick of perspective. She was just the psychic replay of a traumatic past event. A ghostly hologram, the real victim long since passed over to the other side, living a happy afterlife.

Still, I took another step.

"I need help," she said. "He's coming. Please—"

She let out a shriek, her eyes going huge as she stared at something over my shoulder. Then she ran through a door.

I looked behind me. There was nothing there.

It's a residual. You know it's a residual.

But she'd looked straight at me.

A trick of the light. Real ghosts don't run down halls in blood-spattered clothes fleeing invisible killers.

Still . . .

I looked each way, took a deep breath, and went after her.

FIVE

That door the girl had run through? Clearly marked Do Not Enter. Of course, I did. Of course, it opened to reveal stairs leading down into a pitch-black basement.

I tugged off my heels and flipped on the lights. Before I closed the door behind me, I made sure it would reopen. I've had ghosts prank me before.

I started down. Given the amount of dust, I was sure no one had been down there in years. It certainly smelled that way.

The stairs ended in a small room. Four doorways branched off it. Two were closed, two open. The girl stood just inside one of the open ones.

"Quick!" she said. "Follow me! He's coming!"

"Are you talking to me?" I said. "Can you see me?"

Too late. She'd taken off. I looked back at the stairs and then at the dark room the girl had run into. She had to be a residual, but I was down here now. The worst thing that could happen was that I'd witness the replay of a crime I'd really rather not witness.

I raced after her.

"If you're really a ghost, this isn't happening," I called after her as she ran through a second doorway. "It can't be happening. No one can hurt you now."

"He's coming! Please! Save me!"

Was she responding to my words? Or was the timing coincidental? Damn it. Everything in my experience insisted this had to be a residual. Chasing it was an amateur move, the kind of thing necromancers joke about— *Hey, remember the time you called 911 when you saw a residual jump off a bridge?*

But this felt different. So, against all logic, I kept chasing the girl, flipping on lights as I went.

"He's coming!" she said as we came out in a hallway. "Quick! We have to hide!"

"There's no one coming. You're—" I paused. It's never fun to tell a ghost she's dead. Normally, though, that only happens if you have the misfortune of meeting one at the moment of death. From this girl's outfit, she'd been dead nearly a century.

"You can't be hurt," I said instead. "Tell me what you see, and I'll—"

"He's coming! Hide!"

She darted through a closed door. I ran to it and turned the knob. It wouldn't open. I threw my shoulder against it, a move I'd seen Jeremy and other werewolves perform all the time, one that works far better if you have super-strength.

Pain slammed through my shoulder. The door didn't budge.

On the other side, the girl screamed. I twisted the knob again and shoved the door. It flew open so suddenly I stumbled through, my heels flying from my hand and clattering to the cement floor.

The girl screamed again. I looked up to see her crouching in the shadows, the room lit only by the light from the hall. I patted the wall for a light switch but couldn't find one.

I started forward. "It's okay. Whatever you're seeing, it isn't real. You're—"

She screamed and fell back as blood blossomed on her beaded dress. A jagged hole appeared, blood seeping through. Then another one, as if an invisible knife was stabbing her. I raced over, but there was nothing I could do. I couldn't see what was attacking her. I couldn't fight it. I couldn't drag her to safety.

I tried reaching out, but of course my hands just passed through her. All I could do was stand there, babbling that it wasn't real, she would be okay. The knife kept plunging in until the whole front of her dress was shredded and bloody. Then, finally, she dropped to the floor, and the blows stopped.

I stood there, breathing hard, shaking as I stared at her crumpled body, waiting for it to fade. Instead, her arms twitched. Then one reached out, clawing at the concrete.

"Help . . . me . . ." she whispered.

"If you can hear me, it's okay," I said. "Just hold on. It'll all be over in a second."

She lifted her blood-freckled face. Her dark eyes met mine. "Why didn't you help me?"

"I can't," I said, crouching. "I'm so sorry. I don't know what's going on, but you're . . . you're out of your time. Whatever happened to you, it was a very long time—"

She reached for my foot, hand passing through it. Then she looked up at me with her tear- and blood-streaked face. "Stop him. Please stop him."

She disappeared. I took a deep breath. Then I felt a draft behind me, a sudden whoosh of air, and I spun to see the door closing. I raced toward it, but it slammed shut, plunging the room into darkness.

I didn't give up on the door for a while. It hadn't wanted to open earlier, so I told myself it was just stuck again. As for how it slammed shut, well, I'd felt a draft, hadn't I? I told myself that a crooked foundation made the door swing shut. When it comes to anything potentially paranormal in origin, I'm the worst skeptic, always searching for natural answers. That may seem perverse, but knowing the supernatural exists makes it too easy to jump on paranormal explanations. It's like people who religiously watch ghost shows and interpret every groaning pipe as a sign that the dead walk among us.

So I kept yanking on the door. The handle refused to even turn. Next I searched for that missing light switch. The room was pitch-dark, without even a sliver of light coming under the door. I systematically felt my way along all the walls. Still no switch.

Finally, I did what some might argue I should have done when the door first shut: I took out my cell phone. I used the glowing screen for another round of the tiny room. Still no light switch.

As for using the phone to actually call someone, that might seem the obvious solution to my predicament, but I wanted to be absolutely certain I couldn't free myself first. Getting locked in an inn basement was not going to help my reputation at all.

But the door wasn't opening, and the light was staying off, so I hit my speed-dial for Jeremy. A recording came on immediately, telling me my call couldn't be completed. I looked at my screen.

No service.

How was that possible? I'd had a couple of bars upstairs.

I lifted the phone overhead as high as I could. Still no—?

"Run," a man's voice whispered behind me.

I spun so fast I almost dropped my phone, fumbling to catch it as I backed into the corner. I lifted the screen to shine it in front of me.

"Who's there?" I asked.

No one, you fool. It's a small, empty room.

No, it *had* been empty. I'd had my back to the door when it slammed shut. Meaning someone could have come in and closed it behind him.

I pressed my back against the wall and waved the phone around. Nothing. I could see nothing.

"If someone's there—"

"Help me," whispered a voice from below.

I swung the cell phone light down to see the girl on the floor. She was rising, bloodstained hand reaching for me.

"Help . . ."

See, it's a residual. It's replaying.

But she hadn't reached up before. She'd reached out for my foot. "Why didn't you help me?" she said. "Why won't you stop him?"

"Can you hear me?" I said. "If you can—"

"You need to stop him."

"Run," the man's voice whispered.

I wheeled, back slamming into the adjoining wall. My cell phone flickered. The light went out. I banged it against my thigh. I hit buttons. I held down the power switch. Nothing worked.

It had a full battery when I left New York. There's no way—

The light. It drained because you were keeping the screen on at full brightness.

That was silly, of course. I had enough power. I knew I did.

A click sounded, like the door opening. When I looked over, though, I couldn't see any light shining through it. With my back against the wall, I sidestepped to the door and ran my fingers along the edge. It was shut tight. I tried the handle. It still wouldn't—

Another click, as if the door had closed. I yanked my hands back. I hadn't pushed it shut. I knew I hadn't—

A whimper sounded behind me. I turned, instinctively lifting my dead phone. All I saw was darkness, but I could hear someone there, sniveling and crying softly. Then, slowly, I began to make out the edges of a faintly glowing figure. It was pressed against the far wall, as if hiding behind some invisible object. The figure came clearer. It was a girl—a young woman, maybe in her early twenties—dark-haired, with a chiffon head scarf and polka-dot fifties-style dress.

Tears streamed down her face as she hid there, breathing so hard I could hear it. When I took a step toward her, she jumped and then looked up, her eyes meeting mine.

"Hide!" she said. "Quick! He's coming!"

"Who's coming?" I asked.

She struggled for breath as her eyes filled with panic.

I walked closer. "Who's coming?"

"He's going to find me. I know he's going to—"

She let out a shriek, head jerking up, eyes rounding. Then she fell back against the wall, hands up. Blood spread across her dress as she screamed. The knife plunged in again.

"Help! Please help!"

I did. Not by running to shield her or pull her away. I couldn't do that. Instead, I focused on whoever was stabbing her, to see him, to pull him through the ether. I tried every trick I knew to summon the ghost attacking her, and I didn't see so much as a flicker. An invisible force just kept stabbing her with an invisible knife until she lay there, heaped by the foot of the wall, eyes closed.

I knelt down to her and said, "Can you hear me? I don't understand what's—"

Her eyes flew open. "Help us. Stop him."

Before I could say a word, she disappeared.

SIX

A third victim came after that, this one in a cleaning uniform and ponytail, the exact period difficult to guess but seemingly more modern. She ran in, she saw me, she entreated me to help her, then "he" came and she died. Again I tried with all my power to pull her attacker through—to no avail.

Then it started anew, with the first victim. This time, I concentrated on trying to make contact with the attacker, to get him to speak to me. Still nothing. She died, and the second girl returned. I asked her questions, begged her to reply. She didn't. She looked right at me. She tried to get me to hide with her. But she wouldn't— or couldn't—answer my questions.

"I need you to talk to me!" I said as she faded. "I can't help unless—"

"You can't help." It was a man's voice behind me.

I turned. "Show yourself."

His laughter fluttered around me.

"Who are you?" I said.

No answer.

"What am I seeing?" I said. "What did you do down here?"

Silence.

"Are you showing me this? What do you want?"

"Run," his whisper snaked past, raising goose bumps on my arms.

"You're a ghost," I said. "I don't run from ghosts."

His voice, right at my ear: "You will."

I stumbled back in spite of myself.

"Help me . . ."

I looked down to see the first girl, on the floor, lifting her hand.

"Help me . . ." The girl from the fifties appeared beside me, both hands reaching for me.

As I backed away, the cleaning girl whispered behind me, "Help me . . ."

"Help us," all three said, all reaching for me, their hands covered in blood. "Help us or join—"

The doorknob rattled. I staggered away from the dead girls. A crack. The door flew open, light flooding through, and all I saw was a figure silhouetted there, and I pushed back into the corner—

"Jaime?"

I ran into Jeremy's arms.

The natural first question, on finding your girlfriend locked in a basement room, would be, "How'd you get in here?" or at least, "What happened?" Jeremy just held me until I got myself together. Then I told him the whole story.

When I finished, I walked to the door and looked at it. "It was just jammed, wasn't it?"

"We should go upstairs," he said after a moment.

"The door. It wasn't locked, was it? And don't lie to make me feel better. There *is* no lock. I can see that."

"Then the knob was jammed, because I had to break *something* to get in here." He walked over and put his arms around me. "You were trapped, Jaime. Don't tell yourself you made a mistake. And don't tell yourself those were residuals, either."

I nodded but said nothing.

"Residuals don't talk to you," he said.

"They didn't talk *to* me. They talked *at* me." I paused and shook my head. "I don't know what they were. Maybe they were residuals, and I'm just under a lot of stress and—"

"No."

"It's a new show, and I—"

"No." He took my chin in his hand and tilted my face up to his. "You have never hallucinated in your life. I don't have an explanation for what you saw, but you saw something."

"Can we stay somewhere else tonight?"

He chuckled. "We can absolutely stay somewhere else tonight. In fact, I insist."

I paused.

"No," he said.

"I was just—"

"There's nothing here for you to do, and you won't feel guilty about leaving."

"Maybe I should try to contact any spirits—"

"I'll have Elena research past crimes connected to this inn. If we find anything, we can come back after the show and you can attempt a proper summoning. *After* the show. You saw three victims spanning almost a century?"

I nodded.

"I'm not even sure how that's possible, but it means we aren't dealing with a serial killer who'll strike in the next few days. You can walk away." He met my gaze. "Guilt free."

I kissed him. "Thank you."

"Is it haunted?" Mike asked as he followed us down the inn's front steps.

I threw a look over my shoulder.

"Okay, okay," he said. "There's no such thing as ghosts. But that *could* be why you're checking out. We could *say* that's the reason."

"I don't think the inn would appreciate that," Jeremy said as he steered me toward the parking lot.

"Then you'd be dead wrong, my friend. Pun intended. Being haunted is a marketing bonus with places like this. The trick is to only have a room or two with ghosts, so guests have the option." He paused. "Which room were you in?"

"My room was not—"

"Of course it wasn't. But imagine the publicity. Oh! Hold on. We need to *film* you guys leaving. I'll call Brad. We'll use digital. Make it seem very spur-of-the-moment. You're freaked out and fleeing—"

"Michael?" Jeremy said.

It may have been the use of his full name that stopped Mike mid-spiel, but I think it was the tone, one that's been known to stop Clay mid–temper tantrum. It worked for Mike.

"Are you certain this wouldn't actually detract from the feature?" Jeremy said. "If Jaime flees from an inn twenty miles from the set location, it's clearly unrelated. That might dilute her reactions at the real house."

"How do I explain you leaving, though?"

"Don't," Jeremy said. "There's nothing wrong with a little mystery, particularly if you make it very clear that the inn did nothing to make her leave. Let people draw their own conclusions."

We walked down the corridor to our new hotel room. I turned to say something to Jeremy and for a second I forgot what. I just stared at him, that moment of "hot damn" that never seems to go away. I remember when we first got together, thinking, "Well, at least now I'll stop gaping at him like a love-struck teen." Nope. Never happened. Never will.

Jeremy is fifteen years older than me. With a werewolf's slow aging, he doesn't look it. Not that it matters. When he's ninety, I'll still be thinking, *Hot damn*. He has the kind of face that catches your attention and holds it. Arresting. Dark eyes, dark hair, sharp cheekbones, sharp chin. A face more fox than wolf, which isn't surprising. He's also a *kitsunegari*, meaning he has Japanese kitsune—fox spirit—blood.

Jeremy gestured down the hall. "Not exactly what you're accustomed to."

"I'll live," I said. "Amityville isn't exactly booming with five-star hotels."

We'd ended up in a Best Western or Days Inn or something like that. I hadn't paid much attention. We'd driven past a few mid-range chains before I chose one that seemed a little less run-down than its brethren.

"There was the Hollywood Motel in Farmingdale," I said. "Though it would have been a tough call, deciding between the Cheetah Room and the Arabian Room."

"Arabian," Jeremy said as he unlocked our door. "I'm not keen on cats."

I laughed and let him usher me in. "The Web site also mentioned an exotic dancer room. Complete with stripper pole."

He paused in the open doorway. "Stripper pole?"

"And stage."

"How far did you say Farmingdale was?"

I grinned. "I think we'd better pretend it's *too* far for now. Considering I'm in town officially . . ."

"*Jaime Vegas Checks into Stripper Room with Lover* isn't quite the headline you're looking for?"

"No, sorry. Especially since, by the time it got through the rumor mill, I'd have checked in with three guys, all half my age, and invited the rest of the motel to watch the show."

"I would defend your honor. In fact, I would go so far as to provide photographs proving that I was, indeed, the only person in the audience."

I put my arms around his waist. "That's very chivalrous of you."

"I would, however, for the sake of discretion, refrain from posting videos. Although I've heard such things can make people quite famous, even if they lack any other discernible talents. For someone with your proven abilities, it could be quite a marketing coup."

"Twenty years ago, maybe. I think my body's a little past that."

"Not unless it's changed drastically since I last saw you." He slid his hands down my thighs and pushed the hem of my dress up to my hips, hands cupping my rear as he leaned over my shoulder. "Mmm, no, this half looks photo ready. As for the rest . . ."

One hand moved to unzip my dress. He tugged it off my shoulders and let it pool around my feet. His thumbs traced down my sides, sliding over my breasts before stopping to rest on my hips. Then, still holding me, he stepped back a bit for a better look.

"Definitely camera ready. And I have been told that my new phone takes excellent pictures."

"You are more than welcome to take photos anytime you want. Provided your phone is password locked and kept out of the reach of everyone at Stonehaven."

I slid from his grasp and circled around him, feeling his gaze on me as I walked across the room. I ran my fingers over the short post at the end of the bed.

"Not exactly a stripper pole," I said. "And I don't have much to strip."

"You have enough. Those heels go very nicely with those stockings."

I grinned over my shoulder. "I thought you'd approve."

The heels were last year's, but the rest of the "outfit" was new—a black and teal lace demi-bra with matching garter belt and stockings and a very tiny pair of panties.

I reached up and pulled out the pins in my hair, letting it sweep down over my shoulders.

Jeremy let out a soft growl and started toward me.

"Uh-uh," I said. "Not yet." I reached one hand over to caress the bed knob. "I still need to figure out what I can do with this. Since we missed out on the stripper pole." I moved closer, still rubbing it. "Umm, I don't know. Any ideas . . . ?"

"I have plenty of ideas. None of them involve that bedpost."

"Too bad." I moved closer and rubbed the front of my panties against it. "Hmm, let's see. What could I do . . ."

I lifted onto my tiptoes and straddled the post, then leaned forward, hands on top of the footboard, to give him the best view as I rubbed myself against the pole.

"Oh . . . Now that is a good . . ." I exhaled through my teeth. "Damn, I didn't realize quite how much I missed you. That feels . . ." I shuddered. "Damn . . ."

I glanced back at him. He was watching intently, one hand gripping a chair against the wall.

"You can sit if you want," I said. "Just relax and enjoy the show."

"I am definitely enjoying. But I can't help feeling a little jealous, too."

"Hmm."

I rolled onto the bed and popped the clasp on my bra. I slid it out from under me and flipped it across the room. My panties followed. Then I reclined on the pillows and slipped my hand between my legs, arching back and groaning.

"Better?" I asked.

"Same problem. While I can't argue with the view . . ."

I eased to the edge of the bed and knelt on it, flipping my hair over my shoulder as I looked back at him.

"You'd prefer this one . . .?"

"That one will do nicely." He undid his pants as he crossed the room, gaze fixed on me. "Thank you."

"Oh, you're very . . ." I gasped as he slid into me. "Very welcome."

SEVEN

I stretched out in bed, Jeremy warm against my back, sheets tangled around us. I idly pulled my knee up and fingered the protection rune tattooed on my ankle.

"Yes, it does appear to be defective," Jeremy said. "The artist should give you your money back."

I laughed softly and flipped over, curling up under his arm. "If it brought you to me in that basement, then it's working just fine."

"Actually, you left a scent trail."

"Ah. Right. But if I hadn't, you'd still have found me."

"Perhaps. The tattoo, however, is only tangentially related to that."

Both came from the same place—his *kitsunegari* blood—but they were separate powers. Powers he'd never comfortably rely on, having spent most of his life not knowing where they came from, only that he was different from other werewolves. Uncomfortably different.

He rose on his elbow and looked down at the tattoo.

"It works just fine," I said. "The runes add protection; they don't protect absolutely. Nothing can. Whatever I saw in the basement didn't hurt me, just scared the crap out of me, and that only bothers me because it hasn't happened in a very long time. I think I'm long past the point where a ghost can send me shrieking into the night, and then . . ." I shrugged. "It happens. It seems there's always something new lurking around the corner."

I glanced up at him as he settled back on the bed. "Did Elena say she'd have time to check the inn?"

Elena was a Pack werewolf, the Alpha-elect, to succeed when Jeremy stepped down. She was mated to his foster son, Clayton. Along with their five-year-old twins, they lived at Stonehaven with Jeremy.

As a freelance journalist, Elena had access to online media databases. If there was a story on my dead girls, she'd have found it.

"She texted back while you were dozing," he said. "There's nothing."

Now it was my turn to rise, hair tickling as it fell over my shoulder. "Nothing?"

He pushed the hair back. "No murders at the inn. No hauntings at the inn. No crimes matching that description in Amityville or the surrounding area. Which means you were *not* seeing a residual."

"So I was hallucinating."

He met my gaze. "No, you were seeing ghosts. *Real* ghosts."

"But how? Why? What reason would ghosts have—"

He cut me off with a kiss. "Questions for another time, though I strongly suspect I already know the answer."

"Which is?"

"They were doing what ghosts always do. Trying to make contact. With added drama to get your attention. They've piqued your interest. Now, when they come with their message, you'll be so curious that you'll listen."

I stood in the Amityville front yard looking up at the house. It really was a ringer for the famous one. I wondered how much of that was original and how much had been cosmetically altered. That may seem like a lot of wasted money for a single TV special, but it would still be a damned sight cheaper than the expenses incurred by a scripted show. Afterward, they could likely sell it for a profit. All the creeptastic allure of living in the Amityville Horror home, without that icky tragedy.

As I met the cast—the "real" folks who'd be joining us—Mike waved to tell me to detail that tragedy from the second-story balcony.

Inside, it looked like a typical family home. That was, I suppose, the point. *Look at this house. So nice, so normal. Just like yours. But this house holds a secret. A dark, bloody secret— Oh, wait. Not this house. The one three miles away that looks just like it. Close enough.*

They set me up on the balcony as the cast and crew gathered below. An even bigger crowd—curious onlookers—waited beyond the security tape. I felt like I was about to deliver the Gettysburg Address. Or start quoting Juliet. My Romeo was indeed below, off to the side, watching me, a faint smile on his lips. I returned it, before fixing on a proper look of gravitas.

"Many of us have heard the story of the house in Amityville," I began, addressing the crowd as the camera rolled. "How the horror truly began, on an autumn night in 1974, when Ronald DeFeo Jr. murdered his entire family, urged on by voices no one else could hear. A year later, the Lutz family moved into what they thought would be their dream home. Instead, it turned out to be a nightmare few of us could imagine . . ."

Actually, "dream home" was a better description, if your dream included exploiting tragedy for profit. Amityville was a hoax. Oh, sure, the Lutzs still claimed it was "mostly true," but when they sued and were countersued, scrabbling for the profits, a judge decided—based on the evidence—that their book was a work of fiction. Maybe something did happen in that house, but there were no demon pigs and secret satanic rooms.

Of course, I was forbidden to mention that. Forbidden by contract. Also by contract, I had refused to say anything to suggest I believed it. So the script was worded like a campfire tale. *They say that deep within that house there is a room, painted red, not found on any blueprint . . .*

I recited my spiel. Then I joined the crew on the lawn, and it was Gregor's turn. He'd been assigned the far less exciting task of telling other tales from Amityville's past. Because we weren't, you know, actually at *the* house, so we weren't going to see *that* haunting. But who knew what other deep, dark secrets this sleepy New England town might hold . . .

No one. Because there weren't any. Put haunting and Amityville together, and you got a certain Dutch Colonial home by the water. That was it. So Gregor's script had to stretch. A lot. He mentioned a massacre of Native Americans in 1644 and a suicide cult in 1931. There were even Hollywood connections. Maurice Barrymore died in the Amityville Asylum and Jim Morrison's Wiccan high priestess wife, Patricia Kennealy-Morrison, grew up in the township. The researchers had found another so-called satanic connection—a teen named Ricky Kasso, who'd held some kind of ceremony on the Amityville Horror house front lawn and later convinced friends to help him kill another teen as part of a ritual. Not surprisingly, Kasso was also an alumnus of the Amityville Asylum.

It should have sounded like a desperate attempt to find scandal in a quiet town. Yet Gregor managed to make it sound as if the Amityville region was a hotbed of horror. Part of it was just him— his bookish looks, his Russian accent, his slightly stilted diction, all giving the ludicrous script an air of academia.

I was making a mental note to congratulate Mike on finding Gregor—give credit where it's due—when Gregor said, "Yet there is one more tale, perhaps the most tragic, an untold story of Amityville: the disappearance of three young women, from three different eras, connected only by the mystery of their vanishing. Or, perhaps, by their killer."

I glanced over my shoulder at Jeremy, staying off camera. He caught my eye, and I caught his message.

Don't jump to conclusions. Listen to the story. Everything is all right.

Except it wasn't all right, because Gregor went on to tell the story of those three young women, one from 1924, one from 1952, and one from 1988. Clara Davis, the first girl, left a wedding reception and was never seen again. Polly Watson, the second girl, had been last spotted leaving a church dance with a young man. And Dawn Alvarez had disappeared while walking home from her job as a chambermaid.

And what had I seen in that basement room? A young woman from the twenties in a formal dress, a girl from the fifties in a party outfit, and a more recent one in a maid's uniform.

I glanced back at Jeremy. He stood poised, watching me. I waved for him to stay put. I didn't need to; he knew better than to rush to my side on camera, not unless I was convulsing on the ground. He nodded and texted me with, *I'll have Elena look into it.*

Gregor continued. "These three young women all disappeared, never to be seen again. It would appear they are unconnected cases. How could they not be, spanning nearly seventy years? Yet it would seem there is indeed a connection, for after each, the local newspaper received a letter from a man claiming responsibility. Claiming to have killed these pretty girls. Claiming to have stabbed each one to death."

I swallowed and struggled not to look at Jeremy again.

"Three murders. Decades apart. It could not possibly be the same killer. Yet all signs pointed exactly to this conclusion. Each letter provided details only the killer could know. How is this possible?" Gregor paused and glanced surreptitiously to the side, where his script was displayed on a hidden screen. "That is what we hope to discover tomorrow. When we enter this house—the home of Polly Watson—the second young woman to vanish. We will enter this house, haunted by the spirits of these girls. We will speak to them. We will help them find peace. We will help them find their killer."

EIGHT

When the cameras turned off, I tracked down Mike. He saw me coming and tried to evade, but I cornered him outside the makeup trailer. Well, actually, Jeremy cornered him, coming out the other side.

"I need to talk to you," I said.

Mike lifted his hands. "I know, I know. You're not happy with our cast of regular folks."

"It's a reality show that doesn't even have a prize attached. You risk public humiliation for sub-SAG rates. Of course they're stupid and self-centered. Who else would apply?"

"Well, actually, we did have some—"

"Strike that. Others may apply, but you're sure as hell not going to cast them. For a haunted house show, you don't want anyone who'll stop worrying about their close-up long enough to notice the effects are all faked."

"We are not going to fake . . ." He shook his head and waved us into the trailer.

"Can't even finish that sentence, can you?"

He muttered under his breath. When we were inside, he shooed the one remaining makeup artist out, then collapsed on a chair and motioned for us to do the same. I took the one beside him; Jeremy opted for the one nearest the door.

"All right, so what *do* you want to talk about?" Mike asked.

"The girls we're supposed to summon—"

He cringed. "Of course. Yes, murdered young women is a blatant ratings grab and feeds a disturbing cultural psychosexual interest. The beautiful victims, brutally murdered and violated. The stabbing only makes it worse, with the obvious sexual overtones. I knew you wouldn't be happy. I remember the lecture I got after *Death*."

It wasn't a lecture. Just a forcefully stated opinion, when we'd met to celebrate the success of *Death of Innocence*. He'd lamented the fact that the victims were children. It helped the pity factor but also hurt sales, turning off those who found children's deaths too disturbing. If only they'd been young women, he'd said. That would have sold much better. Particularly if they were young and attractive. That's when he got the "forcefully stated opinion."

A few years ago I'd have kept my mouth shut. Hell, I've made a career out of using my femininity—and, yes, sexuality—to my advantage. There's no law that says you can't be a feminist and embrace your femininity. Or if there is, I missed the memo.

So I let Mike blather on about how they were going to keep this tasteful, no graphic reenactments of the alleged murders. When he was done, I said, "Good. And I'll hold you to that. But it isn't actually what I wanted to talk about."

He cursed under his breath as he realized he might have sacrificed viewers, jumping the gun to placate his star. That dismay lasted about five seconds—as long as it probably took him to realize he'd only promised no reenactments on the *show*. DVD extras were a whole other matter.

"I've checked all our correspondence," I said. "And there was no mention of these girls or their murders. There was certainly no suggestion that we were focusing on a specific crime connected to this house."

"That's the idea. You and Gregor knew nothing about the crimes until today, which means you had no time to prepare. Anything you say, then, will be an honest communication with their spirits."

He winked. "Or with your Internet connection in the next twelve hours."

"Which brings me to point number two. Obviously I did my research on the house as soon as I got the address this morning. I only found a domestic disturbance call in the seventies. If Polly Watson was living here when she went missing, I'd have seen it."

"Er, well, she wasn't actually living here at the time . . ."

"When did she live there?"

"The summer she was seventeen. She had some disagreements with her parents and went to stay with her aunt and uncle for a few weeks."

I sighed. "Fine. Gregor's script said these girls vanished, never to be found. So what's this about them being murdered? And three letters? I did a Google search ten minutes ago and there was *nothing* online about any letters."

He leaned back with a smug smile. "Because it's a closely guarded town secret. One that we are about to expose."

"Uh-huh." I beckoned for details.

He sat forward. "When we were planning the show, we were looking for some crime or scandal at any of the properties we were considering. We sent e-mails to local historians, reporters, bloggers. Finally, we got the Polly Watson link. That seemed the best we could do, so we bought the house, got things under way, and then, a month ago, we get an anonymous tip from someone who used to work at the *Amityville Record*. He said a journalist there received a letter after each of those three girls went missing. A letter from their killer, confessing to the deed."

"And what does the *Record* say?"

"It denies all knowledge of the letters. Threatens legal action if we mention them on air." He rolled his eyes. "Our lawyers are already on it. We just need to be careful what we say before we can prove a cover-up. Until then, the story is that we've been told someone at the paper received them—we don't claim it went beyond that person."

"What does your informant say?"

"Nothing. He sent us copies of the letters and then disappeared into cyberspace."

"Maybe because he's the one who received one of the letters. Or he's a relative."

Mike's eyes gleamed. "You're right. Driven by a conscience plagued with guilt—"

"Save it for the voice-over. Tell me more about the letters."

As Gregor's script said, they contained details about the victims only their killer could know—birthmarks and so on. A handwriting analyst confirmed all three were penned by the same person. Given the time span, that opened a whole lot of questions, none of which Mike could answer. So I got everything he did know and left.

We were walking from the trailer when a ghost dashed over. It was a middle-aged man dressed in modern garb, and I'd never have guessed he was a ghost if he hadn't run right through two set workers.

"Ms. Vegas," he said. "I need a message sent to my business partner."

I kept walking. Jeremy glanced over at the ghost. He'd say he was just responding to my reaction, however slight, but his kitsune blood gives him a few psychic powers. He can't see them or hear spirits, but he seems to know they're there.

"Necromancers do not appreciate being approached in public," Jeremy said, his voice conversational, as if chatting to me. "If you wish to speak to her, you'll need to contact Eve Levine."

"It's just a message. And it's urgent. He's going to sell my shares to my son, and that lazy good-for-nothing will ruin everything I built—"

I lifted a hand to silence him.

"You'll need to speak to Eve," Jeremy said.

"Bitch," the ghost snarled, and stalked off.

Out of the corner of my eye I noticed someone else had turned from a conversation and was gaping at us. Gregor stared at the spot where the ghost had been . . . and he looked confused.

"Well, that's interesting," Jeremy murmured.

"He saw something," I said.

"Necromancer blood?" Jeremy said.

"It's possible." I paused. "Either way, we are cohosting a show together and I haven't said more than a few words to him. Do you mind if I ask him to join us for a drink?"

"Not at all."

Gregor seemed pleased by the invitation. Relieved, too, as if he'd been unsure of his welcome. It wasn't his fault I'd been duped. He wasn't Bradford Grady, and he wasn't Angelique. I shouldn't shut him out because of what happened to them.

As for whether Gregor had necromancer blood, it was hard to tell. He'd seemed to react to the ghost earlier. It's also possible that I'd reacted to it myself, and he'd been looking confused about that. He didn't mention it and there was no easy way to broach the subject.

There was no easy way to broach the subject of his "gift," either. You'd think there would be. After all, we're professional spiritualists. I should be able to say, "So, how did you start seeing ghosts?" But it's a tricky topic, because most spiritualists *don't* see them. Of course, no one admits that openly. Some wouldn't even confess it to their therapist. Most will do a little "nudge, nudge, wink, wink" with colleagues. There are some, though, who genuinely believe they have "the sight." And they might.

I know a few spiritualists who seem to have necromancer blood. That's still no guarantee of actual powers, and even then, it comes in varying degrees, from "I catch glimpses" to "I hear voices" to my full-on "I see dead people." Real necromancers usually know what they are, from their families, and wouldn't dream of entering the business professionally. That's just crazy . . . as I've heard many, many times.

Then there are the people who are, well, crazy. Or, more likely, had a breakdown at some point and saw ghosts. Non-supernaturals can detect spirits when the barrier between reality and fantasy is thin, like a mental break. In those cases, I think spiritualists honestly did see the dead once and have never stopped believing they have the power, lying dormant within them.

As for figuring out which type Gregor was, it wasn't as hard to get him on that subject as I feared. He started it, asking me point-blank about my own powers, when they started and so on, as if it was a normal topic of conversation.

I gave him my usual story, about first spotting a ghost when I was twelve. It's a funny little anecdote, one that suits my persona— more "stumbling over my powers" than having the finger of God show me the way. It's mostly true, even. Embellished, of course, particularly the "stumbling" part. I come from a family where most inherit the power. My father killed himself when I was little, but I was close to my paternal grandmother, who'd prepared me for the day when I might start seeing people who weren't there.

That doesn't mean it was a breeze. There's nothing that can truly prepare you for a lifetime of pleading and demanding ghosts. Most of my tales were nowhere near as funny as the ones I told. But the horror stories are mine; the world gets the slapstick versions.

Once I shared that backstory with Gregor, it left an obvious opening for me to ask his, which wasn't nearly so cheery.

"My wife and I lost a child," he said. "Our oldest daughter. She was three. She became very ill and did not recover."

Jeremy and I offered sincere regrets for his loss, which he accepted with a nod before continuing.

"After Liliya passed, it was . . . not a good time for me. I was with her when she became ill. I worked from our apartment, as a tutor. My wife taught at a school. So I was with Liliya, and I was the one who did not think her illness was serious. I told my wife it was just a childhood ailment. When it became more . . ." He fingered the side of his glass. "The doctors said it would not have made a difference if she was brought to them sooner, but I did not believe that. I blamed myself. That is when I started to see ghosts."

"Her ghost," I murmured.

"No, that is what was odd. I did not see her. I saw others. Glimpses, mostly. Never her. I spoke of it to no one. I knew what they would say: 'Gregor is mad with grief.' I tried to make the ghosts go away. When they would not, I went to doctors. It did not help. They said I was punishing myself. I was imagining other ghosts to tell myself I was not worthy of seeing my Liliya."

He drained his drink and then shook his head. "That is the start of a very long story. It was five years ago that my daughter died. It is only a year ago that I began to offer my help to others who are grieving. In the middle, I told my wife, and she was the one who said I was not going mad, not imagining it. She asked me to stop seeing the doctors and instead speak to others like me, like you. To help me understand. So I did, and now . . ." He spread his hands. "I am here."

NINE

By the time we returned from drinks, I had e-mails from Elena with links and attachments, along with a note to call her to discuss it. The kids hadn't gone to bed easily, so she and Clay were still up.

I checked a few of the links and then called before they headed off to bed. Elena ran me through the cases. In the background, I could hear the faint pop of the fire and the occasional clink of a glass or the murmur of Clay's voice as he commented. I could picture them, on the sofa in the study, Clay sitting at one end, reading journals or research books, Elena stretched out, her back against him, fingers tapping on her laptop. It was a scene I'd witnessed many times on my visits to Stonehaven.

Elena hadn't found much more to the cases than I'd heard. Three young women had vanished from Amityville over the years. They'd been going someplace and they never arrived and no one ever saw them again. No notes. No witnesses. Nothing.

She did find photos. Were they the girls I'd seen? That should have been easy to answer. But the pictures were old newspaper shots, whatever the family could grab at the time, rendered in black-and-white.

All three were over eighteen, with seemingly good family relationships and solid jobs. So they didn't appear to be teen runaways. There were no angry ex-boyfriends or wannabe boyfriends. The second girl, Polly Watson, had been seen leaving her dance with a guy, but he was later found and exonerated. As for where Polly had gone . . . that's where the connection between the girls and my ghosts fell into place.

Polly hadn't left with a "boy." She'd left with a man—a thirty-five-year-old chaperone at the dance. He said he was driving her home, but the investigation found they'd made a pit stop at the inn where I'd seen her ghost. He admitted they'd stopped there, but only because she needed to use "the facilities." Which didn't explain the witnesses who'd heard them arguing because Polly changed her mind about getting a room. They fought. She took off. She was never seen again. Her "date" was questioned, but it seems that after the fight he'd gone straight to the inn's lounge, gotten plastered, and passed out. A half-dozen witnesses attested to it.

That was Polly's connection to the inn. The other two girls had one, too. The first, Clara Davis, had been attending a wedding reception there. The third, Dawn Alvarez, had worked as a chambermaid in the inn, and had vanished on her way home.

Little had been made of the connection. Given the decades between the disappearances, that isn't surprising. Two of the three had left the inn before they vanished. Maybe money changed hands to ensure the connection was left out of media accounts. People might like to stay in a haunted inn, but "resident serial killer" really doesn't have the same marketing hook.

"Which is why the cases didn't turn up the first time I searched," Elena said. "When the place is mentioned in the accounts, it's just called 'a local inn.'"

"Plus, they aren't crimes," I said. "Just disappearances."

She made a noise in her throat, as if this didn't excuse her oversight. "Multiple missing young women is usually the first sign of a serial killer at work. Or a man-killing mutt."

"Could that be what we have? That would explain the time frame. Werewolves live longer."

I glanced at Jeremy for his input. He was on the bed but didn't hear me. He was too busy sketching. Which meant he was worried.

He doesn't only sketch when he's stressed—that would be a hard way for an artist to make a living—but if he is, it settles his mind. It also takes him someplace not quite reachable, which is why he'd missed the werewolf comment.

I turned my attention back to Elena as she said, "It's possible. A werewolf killer would explain the lack of bodies—he took them away to eat. But I can't recall ever seeing a mutt kill with a knife. It wouldn't satisfy the hunting instinct. And a mutt sure as hell wouldn't be sending notes to the papers. Again, that's classic serial killer."

"So what do you make of the notes?"

She paused. Clay rumbled something in the background.

"What's his verdict?" I asked.

"He thinks they're fakes. We only have one anonymous tipster claiming any knowledge of them, so that makes it suspicious."

"You disagree?"

Another pause. "Those ghosts *weren't* fake, which makes it hard to reconcile with phony notes."

"How does Clay reconcile it?"

"He doesn't." A low rumble, and Elena's voice faded as she moved the phone to speak to him. "Well, you don't. You just say the notes are obviously fake."

He said something, again too low for me to hear.

"Yeah, yeah," Elena said. "Get back to us when you have an actual theory."

"Do *you* have a theory?" I asked.

"Nothing but the obvious. The killer sends the note. The guy who gets it is a young reporter, who decides it's a crank and files it away. Second note comes thirty years later, and he does an 'oh, shit.' He can hand over both notes and take his lumps. Or he can just hide the second. He picks option B. The third note comes thirty years later again, which means our guy is long retired. Still alive? Maybe. He gets it, hides it, and after his death a family member finds it. When the call goes out for stories on Amityville, whoever has the letters decides it's time to bring them out, maybe make some cash."

Clay muttered something.

She spoke to him again. "Like I said, get back to us when you have a theory. Until then—"

A clatter, phone falling. Elena retrieved it.

"Sorry," she said.

"Flying pillow?"

"Yeah. I'll pay him back later." The sound of footsteps, as if she was crossing the room. A creak as she settled into Jeremy's chair. "That's all I've got. As for the killer, you have a sixty-year span between three murders. Not impossible if he started young and ended old, but that would be unusual. Real-world explanation? Father-son team, son killing the last and getting Pops to write the note—or forging it himself. Supernatural explanation? More possibilities there, none of them very plausible."

"Vampires," Clay said, raising his voice loud enough to be heard this time.

Elena made a rude noise in response.

"Could be," Clay said. "Explains the timeline."

"But not the stabbing. Beyond that? Demons, spirits, magic . . . the list goes on."

It did. That was the problem.

When I got off the phone, Jeremy was still engrossed in his sketch. I watched him off to the side, so he wouldn't notice. I've dated plenty of guys who, if they caught me looking, would flex and primp like a cover model. Jeremy is not one of them. He isn't particularly shy; he's just not good with direct attention.

He'd started undressing for bed. His shirt was off, but he'd stopped there. He was lying on the covers, which meant I had a very nice view of a very nice body. There's nothing quite like werewolves for drool-worthy physiques. They have the kind of metabolism for which I'd seriously consider sacrificing virgins.

I slipped out of my dress and crawled into bed on his other side, being careful not to disturb him. He seemed to have frozen there, only the scratch of his pencil giving him away.

I resisted the urge to reach up and brush the hair from his neck. There wasn't much to brush anyway. Normally, haircuts are one of those annoying necessities Jeremy skips as long as possible, but he'd gotten it done for my shoot. He always did, since a reporter once noticed him at one of my shows and used "bohemian" in her description. Jeremy decided he was getting a little old for the shaggy look. I disagree. I love it when his hair gets a little long, dark locks threaded with silver, hanging boyishly in his eyes and over his collar. Sexy as hell. But if it makes him self-conscious on a shoot, I keep my mouth shut and wait for it to grow out again.

The stylist—or, more likely, the local barber—had left a bit in the back, just a small lock that curled up, as if trying to hide. I wanted so badly to tug it out. But I kept still, resting there, until the pencil scratches stopped. He lifted his head, looked around, and then craned over his shoulder to see me.

"When did you finish with . . .?" He sighed. "I'm sorry."

"Don't be." I shifted up and leaned over him. "Can I see?"

He handed me the sketchbook without hesitation. I remember shortly after I met him, catching him drawing and asking to see it. He'd deflected me and slid the book back into his bag before I could ask again. I'd been hurt by that. I'd come to realize, though, that I'd been rude to ask—it was a work-in-progress. He shared those raw beginnings only with his Pack, and only if they expressed an interest.

This new sketch was of the twins watching a hole in a hillside. Logan lay stretched on his stomach in the long grass. Kate was perched over the hole, balanced precariously as she bent to look upside-down into the dark.

I smiled. "It's adorable. Even if we know why they're really look-ing in there. Sussing out a potential meal."

"Actually, potential predatory competition. It's a fox hole."

I noticed the faintest outline of a snout deep in the dark hollow. "Seriously?"

"Yes. They found it when we were hiking upstate. A fox kit was in there. Cowering in terror, I think."

I laughed. That only made the picture even more ironic, with Jeremy being part kitsune. I imagine there were times, growing up surrounded by boisterous werewolves, when he felt like that fox kit, shrinking back into his hole before he got trampled.

The twins knew that Jeremy and their parents were werewolves. Elena and Clay decided to tell them last winter, when it became obvious Kate and Logan weren't going to make it to teen-hood before realizing their family wasn't quite like the other kids'.

Were they werewolves themselves? It was hard to say. Unlike Jeremy, Clay and Elena were both bitten, not hereditary werewolves. But having two werewolf parents wasn't exactly normal, either, and it was clear the kids had inherited at least some secondary charac-teristics. Even before they knew, they'd have been watching that fox hole, not quite sure why they found it so fascinating.

"You will do a painting of it, right?" I said.

"I will."

"Personal or for sale?"

"I'd say personal, but Kate has started asking why I don't sell any of my paintings of her and Logan. She's starting to feel slighted."

"I can see that."

"Then you'll have to talk to her, because Mom and Dad cannot fathom why she'd ever want her picture hanging in a gallery." He picked up the sketch. "But this would be a good one. It doesn't show their faces, which is a must if I sell it."

"It'll amuse Elena, I'm sure. An adorable painting of her innocent little naturalists."

He smiled. "Yes, she'll like that. Perhaps I'll use it for shows, put an exorbitant price on it, so it will never sell."

"Oh, it will, and Kate will be thrilled that she's worth so much."

"She will." He put the sketchbook on the table. "Now, if we're done talking about the children . . ."

"You're exhausted and want to sleep."

His hand snaked over my waist, pulling me closer. "Not exactly."

"Good."

I slid into his arms.

TEN

I slept until almost noon. Considering I'd be up all night shooting the show, that was perfectly reasonable, but I'm not an early riser at the best of times. This just gave me a good excuse.

Jeremy was reading when I woke. He'd likely been up for hours already—quietly dressing, slipping out, and grabbing breakfast before settling in to read.

I placed a quick call before my shower.

"Cortez Winterbourne Investigations," a voice sang. "When dead loved ones twitch, it's time for a witch."

"One of these days, you're going to do that accidentally. To someone who really shouldn't know what you guys investigate."

Savannah made a rude noise. She was the receptionist at the agency where her former guardians—Lucas Cortez and Paige Winterbourne—worked. Savannah is Eve's twenty-one-year-old daughter. We met a couple of years after her mom died, when I'd helped Lucas and Paige on a case. That's how I met Eve and got my guardian angel.

"So, what's up?" she said.

"I had a weird experience that I'd like Paige to cross-reference in the files."

"Weird? Huh. Let me guess. You've managed to go several years now without being kidnapped, and you suspect it's a sign of the apocalypse."

"Hey, you've tied my record."

"No, I believe I'm still one kidnapping behind. So what's so weird?"

I told her.

"Huh. You know who you should ask about that? The necromancer council delegate. She's the expert. I'm sure she'd know . . . Oh, wait."

"Do you still want that delegate to take you shopping in Paris this fall? I could ask Elena to take my place. You know she loves fashion almost as much as she loves shopping."

"No need for threats. I'll get on this right away."

"Thank you."

When I came out of the shower, there was a fresh, steaming cup of coffee waiting. Jeremy was at the tiny desk, on Skype with the twins. I got him to tilt the screen so I wasn't flashing five-year-olds as I dressed. Once I was decent, I sat on the bed behind him so I could talk to the kids.

In public, Jeremy refers to the twins as his grandchildren. That's easiest, though it does lead to some confusion from those who are quite certain he can't be old enough for them. To the kids, he's just Jeremy. More parent than grandparent, a part of their everyday lives, just as likely as Elena and Clay to be fixing their breakfast or driving them to school.

What does that make me? I'm not sure. When I'm there, I'm part of the family circle. When I'm not, I'll talk to them a few times a week. Maybe I'm like an aunt. Maybe a grandmother. Maybe, as with Jeremy, the label isn't important. What matters is that I am *something* to them, more than the family friends who pass in and out of their days.

I like that. It fills something in my life. I won't say it fills a maternal hole, because I'm not sure I ever had one. I suppose, if we wanted, Jeremy and I could still have children, but the subject has never come up, because it's moot for both of us. We're past that stage in our lives, and we're okay with that.

After the Skype call, we headed out for lunch and then onto the set. It was still hours until showtime, but there were plenty of taped bits to be filmed and spliced in through the show. For me, that consisted mostly of relaying past ghostly encounters, which they could insert when the action on-screen proved underwhelming.

The afternoon and early evening sped by. Finally, it was time to head into the house for a few last-minute things before the cameras rolled. They wouldn't film us actually entering. That had been done last night—a staged clip of us meeting for the first time and then streaming into the dark house.

I left Jeremy in one of the trailers, where he'd watch the taping. Naturally, I'd told him he didn't need to stay. *Go have a nice dinner. Return to the hotel. Read. Sketch. Relax. At the very least, you don't need to stay all night*. He would, of course, no matter how boring it got.

Gregor and I headed to the house together. We were talking about a case he'd had in Russia, where he kept seeing a ghost who wouldn't make contact. I gave him some advice. It was honest advice, more like I'd give to a fellow necromancer than a fellow spiritualist. I still wasn't sure if he was the real deal, but he was earnest and sincere enough, and that prodded me to be the same in return.

"Hey!" someone called as we climbed the steps. "You can't go in there. Cast only."

A blond girl was coming up behind us. I recognized her as one of the "ordinary folks" who'd be joining us.

"Melinda, right?" I said with a big smile. "We met yesterday. I'm Jaime."

"You can't go in there, Janey. It's a closed set."

"I'm one of the cast. Jaime Vegas."

She stared vacantly at me.

"I'm a spiritualist," I said. "I contact the dead. We met last night." I waved to the side of the house. "Remember, I was up on that balcony?"

"Were you the one who talked about the dead girls?"

"No," Gregor said. "That was me."

She still looked confused.

"It's okay," I said. "We're part of the show."

I climbed the steps. Gregor held the door for me.

"Hey, what about him?" Melinda called. "No one told me we could bring a date."

She stalked off to speak to someone about that oversight. Gregor stared after her.

"I do not understand," he said.

"Don't even try."

I won't mock poor Melinda for not remembering me. I can't, considering that I'm not even sure I was talking to Melinda. Apparently, we had identical twins in our cast. I'd probably been introduced to them separately and never figured out they were two people. So, yes, I can't mock Melinda. Or Belinda, as the case may be.

We went inside and chatted with the parapsychology guys. I was supposed to explain their equipment in a few pretaped clips. I was running through my notes with them when the cast—the regular folks—filed in.

Becky had stopped by earlier and taken Gregor. He'd be taping the bits about Cotard's and "throwing to" the victims' families.

"All right," Becky said, walking into the now-crowded parlor. "Jaime? Let's get you upstairs. We'll start with the EVP equipment."

"What's she doing?" asked Melinda—or Belinda.

They wore identical pink sweat suits and had their blond hair pulled back in ponytails. If they weren't wearing a half-inch of makeup, I'd have thought they were ready to go jogging. There was no way to tell them apart. If I had to address one, I'd mumble the name.

"She'll be taping segments explaining how the equipment works," Becky said. "We can splice those in at the appropriate times, so the action on camera is otherwise seamless."

B/Melinda just stared at her.

A girl to my left sighed. It was Rory, the token Goth chick, a tiny girl with a shock of blue and black hair, wearing a tight black Poe tee. "Imagine the machine starts blipping because there's a ghost. Are you going to stop screaming and running away so Jaime can tell the audience what the machine does?"

"You mean she gets extra screen time?" the other twin squawked.

"Um, yeah. 'Cause she's the star."

"What?" Wade, the token jock, woke up from a standing nap. "Who's the star?"

"Why can't we do it?" the twins asked.

"Can either of you even spell EVP?"

"Why do we need to spell it? We can just say it."

Cameron, the token geek, snickered.

"Maybe we should get one of the cast to help me," I said. "That way, I'm explaining to a person, not the camera." I turned to Rory. "You know what an EVP is, I take it?"

"Electronic Voice Phenomena. It occurs when white noise—such as static or interference—sounds like a voice. Parapsychologists study the possibility that it's the spirit world trying to communicate."

"Show-off," B/Melinda muttered.

Becky waved for us both to come along. When we reached the foot of the stairs, Rory said, "We should invite one of the guys, too, so it doesn't look as if only the girls need explanations. I'd suggest

Ricardo. He's very pretty. And he barely knows any English, so he won't say anything dumb."

"He doesn't speak English?" I said.

"The networks were getting flak for only picking English speakers for reality shows. Apparently, it's better to have non-English speakers standing there, lost and confused."

"I see."

"At least he's pretty."

I turned to Becky. "Get someone to grab Ricardo."

ELEVEN

The final preshow step was splitting the cast into two groups, one to be led by me, the other by Gregor. It was supposed to be a random draw, but I'd texted my picks to Mike, who'd asked for them. Another concession to keep his star happy.

I chose Rory, Cameron, and Ricardo. Yes, Ricardo was pretty. Or I suppose he was, but I've reached that age where I see a hot twenty-year-old and a mental barrier leaps up in my brain, substituting "cute" for "hot." As Rory said, though, he didn't speak much English and seemed content to follow us around, listening intently. Kind of like a puppy. A cute puppy.

Cameron was a student at MIT, which gave him his token geek status. He didn't know much about ghost hunting, but he obviously had a brain, and he was as quiet as Ricardo, so he seemed a safe choice.

Rory had pulled off the science clips with aplomb and seemed shockingly normal for someone who'd sign up for a reality show. Yes, I suppose it's ironic that the Goth girl was the most normal one of the bunch, but in my experience they often are, which just might suggest that my *normal* is a little skewed.

I did feel kind of bad leaving Gregor with the twins and the jock, whose combined IQ wouldn't hit triple digits. But I figured, if they asked stupid questions, he could always fake a language barrier and ignore them.

It wasn't yet dark when the show began. It would have been smarter to tape in the winter, when night stretches longer, so they'd get more footage. That's why they'd pretaped us meeting and entering the house last night. Now, they'd have us start in the basement and the attic, with the windows blocked out so we could pretend the sun wasn't shining.

The twins had a little trouble with that concept. "But it's still light out," they wailed. "Ghosts won't come out when it's light."

Gregor made the mistake of trying to explain that real ghosts don't care if it's day or night. That only made them start grumbling that he must not be a real ghost whisperer. Which made me feel even worse about pawning them off on him. But not enough to offer to take them myself.

My team got the basement.

"Good," Cameron said as we headed toward the stairs. "The attic is bound to be dusty, and I have asthma."

"Of course you do," Rory muttered.

"What's that supposed to mean?" Cameron said.

"Only that I really wish they'd make their tokens a little less token." She plucked at her shirt. "I don't even like Poe. Dude was a druggie boozer who married his thirteen-year-old cousin. I came dressed in a Scooby-Doo T-shirt, but they thought that was too cute for Goth Girl."

"Well, I do have asthma," Cameron said. "These glasses aren't prescription, though. They gave them to me."

"I rest my case." She looked back at Ricardo. "If you do speak English, go ahead. We'll just keep it off camera."

"¿Cómo dice?" he said.

She sighed and looked at me. "It was worth a shot."

Our cameraman, Frank, waited downstairs to film our descent into the gloomy, musty basement. With him was Sal, our assigned crew guy. As we went down, I could see signs that it hadn't been so gloomy or so musty before they'd gotten to it. Judging by the fine scattering of drywall dust, it'd been a nicely finished basement. Reverse renovation. Because a basement with a big-screen TV and a pool table just isn't all that chilling. Unless you add teenagers and a full liquor cabinet.

They'd gotten rid of most of the lighting, too, leaving us sickly yellow bulbs with dangling pull cords. I didn't even know they made those anymore. Quite impressive, really. It did add to the atmosphere. Even Rory shivered a little.

Ricardo pulled a light cord for us. It only made things worse, bringing the shadows to life. Then the light flickered and, with a pop, went out.

"Okay, that's not creepy," Cameron muttered.

Rory opened her mouth, doubtless to say they'd rigged it. My look silenced her. I nodded, though. Yes, it was rigged, but pointing that out would only get her on the fast boat off the island.

"It's rumored this is where the killer brought his victims," I said, shining my flashlight around the empty room. "Into the basement. Through one of those doors." I pointed out each with my beam.

Yes, it was a basement, I thought. *But not this one.*

I mentally flashed back to the inn. To that room. The girl racing in. The blood. Her screams. Her pleas. The door slamming. The voice behind me.

Run.

"Ms. Vegas?" Cameron said.

I found a smile. "Sorry. I was just thinking about those girls. The tragedy of their passing. I hope we'll be able to make contact tonight and assure ourselves they're safe and happy in—"

A scream cut me short. Cameron jumped back into the wall. I followed the noise overhead, where it had now been joined by the thump of running footsteps.

"Already?" Rory muttered.

I motioned for her to keep it under her breath. The cameras were still running.

I started up the stairs. The door at the top flew open and Wade thundered down, the twins behind him.

"He saw something," Wade said. "That ghost dude. He saw something in the attic."

"It was right there," one of the twins said. "That—" She looked at her companions. "That . . . whatever it was. Right there. With us."

I glanced up to see Gregor coming down.

"It was nothing," he said. "I did not mean to startle them. I thought I saw someone, but I was mistaken."

"You talked to it, dude," Wade said. "You, like, had a whole conversation with thin air."

"No," Gregor said carefully. "I heard a creak. I saw a flicker. I believed it was one of the crew. I said, 'Yes?' I turned. I was mistaken, and I apologized for that mistake." He looked to me for help.

I laughed softly. "Okay, I think we're all just a little nervous. This place is definitely creepy." I cast an apprehensive look around for the cameras. "Maybe we should stick together for now. We'll explore the basement."

I shone my weak flashlight beam toward the doors. "As I was saying, it's rumored that the killer brought the girls down to one of these rooms. We're going to check each one tonight. Later, we'll bring in the equipment. For now, though, we simply want to open ourselves up to the spirit world, let the girls know, if they are here, that we mean them no harm. Clear your mind and radiate peace and calm. Can we all do that?"

They all nodded. Rory arched her brows.

"Work with me," I mouthed off camera.

She sighed.

There was nothing in the basement. Not surprising, since I'd conducted a little ritual out back earlier, warning any spirit bystanders that, if they bugged me during the taping, they'd be on my blacklist.

And on Eve's track-you-down-and-kick-your-ass list, which was much worse. I'd noticed a few outside already, hanging around. I assured them that, post-filming, they'd get an hour of my time if they made sure no other ghosts joined in. That was all the incentive they needed to play spook security for me. So, my haunted house was ghost free. Just the way I like them.

I timed it so we'd come upstairs after the sun had dropped. That gave us a few good shots of "kids being spooked by their own reflections in the darkened windows." Most of it came from the twins. Even after we explained what they were seeing, they'd shriek with every flicker. Finally, Becky stopped the taping and had the crew close the blinds.

Becky wanted us to split up again. Eight people had been fine in the basement, where they'd followed me about like a tour group. Up here, we were all just crowded into small rooms, jostling for elbow space.

"I would suggest that Jaime take her group to the attic," Gregor said. "I was unable to make contact there. I am hoping she will be more fortunate. We will return to the basement."

"We've already seen the basement," Wade said.

"It's boring," one of the twins said.

"And dirty," her sister added with a shudder.

"Gregor's right," Becky said. "Let's mix things up."

I stepped toward Gregor. "Maybe check out that front corner room again. The one with the old carpet rolled up in the corner. I felt something in there. A sadness." I lowered my voice to a stage whisper. "I didn't want to spook the kids, but I thought I saw spots on the carpet. They could be . . ." I dropped my voice a little more. "Bloodstains."

"Blood?" Wade perked up. He looked at Gregor. "She's right. That room did have a vibe."

Gregor smiled conspiratorially at me. "I think you are right. I felt something myself, but I did not want to startle anyone again."

He turned to the others. "All right. We will return to the basement. If those young women were murdered in this house, we will find the place and put their spirits to rest."

As they trooped off, Becky said, "You guys? Attic."

"Yes, ma'am." I shuttled my troops from the room, then slipped back to Becky. "Um, Gregor has the script for the attic. What's the story?"

"Beats me. Wing it."

TWELVE

It was a walk-up attic, one that had, at some point, been finished into a third floor. The current owners had let it revert to storage, all that stuffed into one room now for the taping. Following Becky's instructions, the kids, Sal, Frank, and I headed through the first door, into the room she'd deemed "most attic-like." In other words, it was claustrophobic and dark, just bare walls, no dormer window, with a second door on the other side, leading to another room.

"Okay," I said as we stepped into our room. "We've tried the lights, but they still don't work. Gregor said they came on for a few seconds and then went out."

"Just like the basement," Rory said.

"Yes. We'll try not to read anything into that. These old places have electrical—"

A light in the next room flicked on.

"I think someone heard you." Cameron laughed, but there was a nervous edge to it.

"Well," I said, "as long as that light's working, we might as well move into—"

The light turned off. I motioned to Sal to tell Becky to cut the theatrics. It was too obvious.

"Seems we aren't welcome in that room after all," I said. "Let's go this way, then." I started toward the next doorway. "It's rumored that—"

The other light turned on again. I shot an off-camera glare at Sal, who gestured that the crew wasn't doing it. Right. That's the problem with these shows. Because I'm also part of the cast, they're hoping to get a few startles out of me, too.

"Is that light a message from the spirits?" I said, looking up. "Telling me they'd like me in that room?"

No answer.

"Okay, but if the light goes off again, we stay out. No one likes a tease."

Cameron gave a nervous giggle.

"We'll move in there," I said. "But be aware that if this is a manifestation, it may not be a friendly one. As I've been trying to say—"

"Run," a voice whispered behind me.

I jumped, stumbling in my heels. Ricardo leapt forward to catch me.

"Okay?" he said.

"I just . . ." I took a deep breath. "I think I'm spooking myself." I managed a smile. "Which is really not the point."

"At least we didn't all run screaming downstairs like *some* people," Rory said.

I motioned Frank to cut the camera. Once it was off, I took a deep breath and rubbed my arms. The boys watched me, looking concerned. Rory's gaze bore into me, her expression guarded.

"You okay?" she said. "Or is this part of the show?"

Cameron snapped, "If it was part of the show, the cameras would still be rolling."

"I just got spooked," I said. "It happens, even to spiritualists."

I wanted to take a moment. Figure out whether I'd really heard that voice. But the cast and crew were waiting with growing impatience.

"Roll on," I said.

When the camera began filming, I headed toward the lit room. "It is rumored that the man who murdered Clara, Polly, and Dawn has joined them in the spirit world, and that he departed from this very attic. After killing Dawn, he came up here and hanged himself from the rafters. Perhaps . . ." I stepped into the lit room and motioned up. "These very rafters."

It was all bullshit, of course. But Becky *had* told me to wing it.

"The family who lived in this house never realized they had a dead monster in their attic. Years later, it's said that someone working on the house found his mummified remains, lying on the floor, rope still around his neck. The worker raced out and called for help, but when he returned with his supervisor, the body was gone. Worried that they'd be implicated in murder, they didn't notify the homeowners or the authorities. But they told someone. Maybe a friend, maybe a spouse. And so the story was born. But without a body, it remains just that. A story."

As stories went, this one straddled the border between ridiculous and ludicrous. I'm a performer, not a writer. As long as I framed it as rumor, though, I'd spare the studio from lawsuits, which was really all that mattered.

"If it's true, then what we have here is a very dangerous situation," I said. "In the basement, the ghosts of the victims, searching for peace. In the attic, the spirit of their killer. Searching for mercy? For forgiveness? Or endlessly hunting for his victims—"

The door slammed shut. Everyone jumped.

"Th-that's not funny," Cameron said, his voice wavering. "Who's out there?"

"Um, no one," Frank said. "There was no one outside the—"

Another slam. Then another. Two more in quick succession. In the basement, one of the twins started to scream.

"What the hell?" Rory crossed the room and yanked on the door. It didn't budge.

Frank laughed nervously. "Well, you kids wanted a haunted house."

Rory strode back to him. "Bullshit. You say no one was at the door? Show me the tape."

She seemed startled when he lifted the camera without argument. Cameron and Ricardo edged in to watch, along with Sal, who'd been standing off camera.

I walked to the door and tried the handle. No luck. I tried the other one, across the room. It had been closed when we came in. Closed and locked, as I now discovered.

I glanced at the others. They were watching the tape, saying, "Look!" and "Seriously?" and "Play that again," and I knew what they were seeing. A door slamming with no one behind it.

"Must be a draft," Rory said. "Old houses are full of them."

"A draft slammed *all* the doors?" Frank said.

Now, both twins were screaming in the basement.

"They must be locked in, too," Frank said.

By this point, I was pretty sure I heard Wade's screams joining the girls'. My team, though, stayed calm.

"It is . . . ghost?" Ricardo said finally, his accent thick.

"No," Rory said. "It's a house built on SFX. Flickering lights? Fine. But locking doors?" She took out her cell. "That violates my civil liberties. I didn't sign anything that lets them do that."

She hit speed-dial, then lifted the phone to her ear. After a moment she pulled it down, frowning, and looked at the screen. I knew what she'd see, but just stood there, blank-faced, bracing.

"Motherfucker! They're blocking the cell signal."

The others checked their cells. I did, too, for show, but I knew it'd be blocked. I glanced slowly around the room.

Ghosts can't block a cell signal, Jaime.

And they shouldn't be able to slam and lock doors. But they had. At the inn and now here.

"Um, our phones have been blocked since we got here," Cameron said. "I checked. Our contracts say no tweeting or anything, and they're obviously using a blocker to be sure."

Great, but that doesn't explain the door, does it?

As the others bickered, it was almost surreal. We were in a

supposedly haunted house and, except for the cameraman, not one of them seemed to consider that this could be an actual haunting. That's what I got for choosing the smartest of the bunch.

Rory wheeled on Sal. "You've got an earpiece. Tell that Becky chick—"

"I can't tell her anything. It's dead." He took it out and handed it over. "Been dead since the door slammed."

"Okay," I said. "I don't know what's going on—"

"Of course you do," Rory said. "It's a setup to scare us silly. Only, unlike the morons in the basement"—she raised her voice to a shout—"*we aren't scared*. Just very, very pissed off."

The lights flickered and went out.

"Yep," Rory said. "Just what we needed."

"Flashlights on, everyone," I said. "We'll just hang tight and wait. Frank isn't filming, so there's no footage coming."

"Sure there is," Rory said as we turned on our phone lights. "Hidden cameras."

"Which work so well in the dark," Cameron muttered.

"Infrared cameras."

"Everyone, just stop arguing. Even if Rory's right, no one is panicking, so we still aren't giving them *useful* footage. If it's staged, they'll give up—"

A yelp sounded, muffled, as if from another room.

I shone my light around. "Where's Ricardo?"

A panicked babbling in Spanish answered from behind the second door . . . which was now cracked open. We all raced through.

THIRTEEN

Our flashlight beams bounced around the dark room, then all settled on Ricardo. He sat on the floor, clutching his side. Blood dripped through his fingers.

I made it to him first. I dropped and tugged his hand away. There was a slice through his shirt.

"Run," a voice whispered in my ear.

I jumped, but before anyone could ask what happened, I gritted my teeth.

Yep, it's a ghost. Admit it. Accept it. Deal with it.

I raised Ricardo's shirt. The wound wasn't more than a shallow slice, but blood had soaked his shirt and his hand. More smeared the floor.

"How the hell did that happen?" Rory said, her voice rising an octave. "There's nothing in here to cut him."

She was right. The room was empty.

"Does anyone have a tissue or—"

Frank passed me a handkerchief. I pressed it against Ricardo's side. Ricardo took over holding it. I rocked back into a crouch. When my heels threatened to give way, I yanked them off and tossed them aside. I turned to Ricardo, who stared numbly as he held the cloth against the wound.

"Can you tell me what happened?" I said, speaking slowly, keeping eye contact.

He stared at me.

I fumbled in Spanish, asking roughly the same thing. I got a rapid-fire response far beyond anything I could interpret with two years of high school Spanish—failed high school Spanish.

"He says he doesn't know what happened," Cameron said. "He heard a noise and came in here. It was dark. He thought the sound was coming from the other side. He walked across the room and something slashed his side. When he turned, no one was there."

"Okay, that's it," Rory said. "We're getting out of here. I don't care if they rip up my contract." She strode to a door behind Ricardo. "If the front way is blocked, there's got to be a back—"

As she yanked on the handle, the door we'd come through slammed. Sal raced over to it as fast as his thick legs would take him. The door wouldn't budge. Neither door would.

"Okay, everyone—" I began.

"Help me," whispered a voice to my left.

I looked over. It was Polly Watson, dressed in her party sweater and skirt. She was pressed against the wall, her wide eyes fixed on mine.

"He's coming," she whispered. "Please, help—"

She let out a shriek. The first knife blow struck, and blood welled up on her sweater front.

"What do you see?" Frank asked.

I yanked my gaze away and turned to see every flashlight beam and eye focused on me.

"You saw something," Frank said. "What was it?"

"Nothing. I was thinking. Now, we need to just stay calm. We're in a house full of people. We're just fine—"

"No, we aren't." Frank gestured at Ricardo, still on the floor, eyes wide with shock. "Something is going on here. I don't think any of us"—a pointed look at Rory— "can deny that now. This isn't staged."

"Then the plan is the same. We sit tight and wait—"

"And wait for this *thing* to attack someone else?" Frank stepped toward me. "You see ghosts. I've followed your career for years. You're the real deal, and you see something in this room."

I glanced toward Polly, now on the floor, dying. I swallowed and reminded myself she wasn't dying, she was long dead, and I had no idea why I was seeing this, but there was nothing—

"What are you seeing?" Frank whispered.

"Nothing." I paused as I felt their gazes, skeptical, even a little angry, as if I was keeping vital information from them. "I keep thinking I see something, but if it's a spirit, he or she isn't coming through."

Ricardo let out a stream of panicked Spanish and jabbed his finger toward the wall, right behind where Polly's body was fading. I lifted my flashlight. There was blood on the wall. I'd seen it there earlier, when her ghost had been attacked. It was just like in the basement. Spectral blood spattering the walls and—

"Is that blood?" Cameron whispered.

They could see it?

I looked again. The blood was different now. Earlier, I'd seen spatters. This was thin lines trickling down, as if the drywall was sweating blood. I walked over and touched it.

"Jesus!" Rory said.

I turned. They were all staring at me.

"Guess you've seen this kind of thing before, huh?" Cameron said, trying for a laugh.

"Never." I lifted my fingers to my flashlight. The red was faint. Without a werewolf nose, I couldn't smell anything, and I sure as hell wasn't going to taste it. "I can't tell if it's really blood."

"I'm going to vote yes," Frank said.

"Jaime?" Rory said. "Can you get us out of here? Please?"

I looked at them. Ricardo was still on the floor, but the other four were huddled close enough to touch shoulders, all watching me, faces pale, gazes shooting to the blood-sweating wall then back to me. Waiting for me to save them.

Well, that's a twist.

I laughed softly under my breath.

"I'm glad you find this funny," Rory muttered.

"I wasn't laughing. I was—"

"Hide!" a voice said behind me.

It was Clara, the first victim. She raced past and "hid" in the corner, gesturing for me to join her. I struggled to keep my breathing even. Struggled not to think of what was coming.

"You *do* see something," Frank said. "Damn it, Jaime. I know you do. It's them, isn't it? The girls."

I took a moment to compose myself and to turn away from Clara. Turn my back on her. That's what it felt like. A girl was about to be killed behind me, and I was turning my back on her.

"I don't know what I'm seeing," I said. "I'm catching flickers—"

"Bullshit," Frank said.

My head shot up. "Excuse me?"

"You're seeing them. I can tell by your face. You're seeing those girls."

Cameron answered before I could. "Then why would she lie about it? She's a spiritualist. She's not going to pretend she *doesn't* see ghosts."

"She's scared," Frank said. "This isn't some stage act. She's seeing real murdered girls and—"

"Frank?" Rory said. "Shut it."

"I do see something," I said. "It might be the girls. It might be the killer. It might be a completely separate entity. Or it might be nothing at all. But I'm going to suggest—"

"A séance," Frank said. "If these ghosts aren't making contact on their own, they need help. Talk to them. See who they are and what they want."

I argued against that, of course. But I was the only one who did.

Even Ricardo chimed in, translated by Cameron, who apparently hadn't failed *his* high school Spanish. Ricardo wanted to find out what had happened to him. Conversing with the spirits seemed the best way to do that. It wasn't as if anyone was coming to our rescue anytime soon.

We could hear the occasional faint voice below, as if someone was on the attic steps, but they sure as hell weren't banging down the door to get to us. Hell, no. We were trapped in a room by super-natural forces. Real supernatural forces. I almost hoped there *were* hidden cameras, or I feared Frank would lose his job when they realized he'd stopped filming.

I didn't like summoning real ghosts in front of non-supernaturals. What bothered me more, though, was summoning ghosts who weren't acting like ghosts. Doors slamming and people getting injured suggested a telekinetic half-demon spirit, the only kind that could manipulate objects in the real world. But locking doors with-out obvious locks? Cutting someone without an apparent weapon? That made no sense, and I was reluctant to open the lines of com-munication when I wasn't sure what I was dealing with. But that also seemed like the only way to find out what I was dealing with. So, with trepidation, I agreed.

"Séance" implies a lot of things to a lot of people. To most, it con-jures up images of people sitting on the floor, holding hands, burn-ing candles and incense, maybe playing with a Ouija board. None of that is necessary. To talk to the dead, I simply . . . well, talk. I focus on opening my mind and making contact. I did have every-one sit and join hands, though. It would make them feel better. Frank resumed taping, too.

When I started the séance, Clara's ghost had faded and Dawn's hadn't yet arrived. So the room was spook-free. It remained that way as I entreated and cajoled any spirits to appear.

"Why are you doing that?" Frank said finally, as he paused the filming. "You know who they are, so why aren't you summoning them specifically?"

"That's not how it's done. You risk offending the ghost if you call it by the wrong name. Instead, you must remain open to all possibilities."

"*What* other possibilities?"

Rory turned on him. "What the hell difference does it make to you? Is the studio paying you extra if she conjures a specific spirit?"

"Course not. But this seems silly."

"The whole thing seems silly," Rory said. "But we're stuck with it. So, once again, shut—"

The light overhead turned on. Then it flickered out.

"What the hell is with that?" Rory muttered.

"I think—" Frank began.

"No one cares what you think," Rory said.

I lifted my hands for quiet. "I'll go ahead and call the girls by name. It can't hurt."

When everyone settled down, I said, "I'm trying to contact the ghost of Clara Davis. If she's—"

"*Run.*"

I didn't jump this time. I'd heard that disembodied voice often enough. But it did stop me mid-sentence. And it stopped everyone else, too.

"Did you hear that?" Cameron whispered.

I looked around. They'd heard it.

What the hell?

"Keep going," Frank said.

I took a deep breath. "I want to speak to the spirit of Clara Davis. If she can hear—"

"*Help me.*"

Ricardo leapt up. "*¿Que eseco?*"

"It's a woman's voice," Cameron said. "The first was a man's. I think it was the killer."

Frank motioned for me to keep going. Ricardo cursed in Spanish and pointed. The wall was sweating blood again.

"You need to talk to those girls," Frank whispered. "They have a story to tell. Help them."

I looked around. To my left, a shape flickered. It was Polly. Her mouth was working, but I couldn't hear anything.

"If you're trying to talk to me, then talk," I said.

"Who is it?" Frank whispered.

I ignored him. "I want to know what happened to you. I want you to find peace—"

"He killed me," she said.

I looked around the small circle. Everyone was watching intently, giving no sign they'd heard her.

"Who killed you?" I asked.

Frank leaned from behind his camera, mouthing for me to say who I was talking to. I ignored him. I tried to get Polly to give me any details on her killer, but she started getting frantic, insisting she didn't know. That wasn't surprising. Violent death usually wipes the last minutes from a ghost's memory. Merciful for the ghost; terribly unhelpful for crime solving.

"What's she saying?" Cameron asked. "It's a she, right?"

Frank switched off the camera. "We need more, Jaime. The studio will kill us if you actually made contact with a spirit and this is all we get. Let's back up. Tell us who she is and what she's said so far."

I looked over at Polly. She was kneeling in the center of our circle, skirt pulled demurely over her knees. When she heard Frank, she started to nod.

"I want to tell my story," she said. "The whole story." She met my gaze. "Only you can do that."

Yes, only I could do that. I thought of her terrible death. She deserved peace and justice.

And yet . . .

My gut said there was more here. Given the choice between following my head and following my gut, there's never any contest.

I motioned for Frank to roll the camera. "I've made contact with the ghost of a young woman." I described Polly. "She says she was murdered. I've been unable to get details of her killer, which isn't surprising, given that she probably can't remember those final traumatic moments. What I'm doing now is trying to take her back—"

"You haven't told them my name," she cut in.

I turned to her. I said nothing, just turned and looked.

Her face tightened with anger. "I'm Polly Watson. You know that. *Tell* them that."

"What is your connection to this house?" I asked.

"I came to live with my aunt and uncle the summer I was seventeen."

"Why?"

"What?"

"Why did you come to live with them? What happened?"

"I had a fight—"

"About what?"

She floundered, mouth opening and closing as she glared at me. "A boy," she snapped finally. "It was about a boy."

"Did your aunt and uncle have any pets?"

"What?" Her face screwed up. "Are you interrogating me?"

Frank flicked off the camera again. "What's going on here, Jaime?"

"She's making sure the spook is who she says she is," Rory said. "Like asking for ID. Nothing wrong with that."

Cameron nodded. "I looked up Polly Watson last night, after the show. Ask her—"

"*Get out!*" a man's voice boomed through the room.

The door behind Ricardo flew open with a bang.

"*Get out now!*"

Ricardo scrambled up and raced through the door. It slammed shut behind him. Everyone else was still sitting in the circle. Rory and I got to our feet. Cameron followed. We ran to the door. It was locked.

FOURTEEN

"Ricardo!" I said, banging on the door. "Are you okay? Can you hear me?"

"*¡No!*" Ricardo shouted. "*¡Alto!*"

"He's saying stop," Cameron said. "Something's happening in there."

Cameron tried to body-slam the door while Sal ran to the other one, shouting at the top of his lungs, "We need help! Hey! Help!"

"Fire!" Rory screamed. "Fire!"

That worked. I heard the distant sound of footsteps on the attic stairs. In the next room, Ricardo was still babbling for his attacker to stop.

"Serves him right," Polly muttered. "Serves you all right."

I turned to see the ghost standing there, her arms crossed.

"He's going to kill him," she said, smirking. "And it'll be all your fault for not believing me."

Ricardo screamed. Mid-scream, he was cut short, with an *oomph*. Then, "Who the hell are you?" and, "Hey! Put me down!"

Rory and Cameron both turned from the door to look at me.

"Is that . . . Ricardo?" Rory said.

I could hear someone working on the attic door now, yelling for tools. Then there was a sharp crack at the door Ricardo had run through. It flew open. Jeremy stood there, holding Ricardo aloft by the back of his hoodie.

Cameron looked from Jeremy to the broken door. "How'd you get that open?"

"I work out."

"That's . . . your boyfriend," Rory said, turning to me. "What's going on here?"

"Make him put me down!" Ricardo yelled—in perfect English. "He's assaulting me."

"No." Jeremy kicked a switchblade through the open door. "I saved you from an assault. Self-inflicted." Jeremy walked through, still holding Ricardo. "I found him screaming and getting ready to cut himself with that."

"He's possessed!" Frank said. "Quick! Pin him down before he attacks someone."

I gave Frank a withering look. Jeremy lowered Ricardo to the floor but kept a grip on his hoodie. Rory slipped behind Jeremy and retrieved something from the next room.

"Ricardo's cell phone." She looked at him. "It seems to be voice-recording. Do you want me to stop it?"

Ricardo scowled at her.

She checked out the phone. "Oh, look. E-mails. From your editor. About the exposé you're running here." She turned to me. "We've got ourselves an undercover reporter."

"He stabbed himself?" Cameron said. "Seriously? That's fucked up, dude."

"I suspect he did more than that," Jeremy said. "There's sound equipment back there, too, which I'll wager explains the voice I heard when I was coming through into the attic."

"I had nothing to do with that. It was—" Ricardo's gaze shot toward us then away. He squared his shoulders. "I'm still going to expose this fraud. I know the truth. There were no 'letters.' There are no dead girls."

"Sure there are," Cameron said. "I found them online."

"*Missing* girls. Not dead ones. That was all faked to see if you'd fall for it." He gestured at me.

"But she didn't," Jeremy said. "I heard her. Jaime never said she saw the missing girls. No matter how strongly she was urged to do so."

I slowly turned toward the guy who'd been *urging* me so strongly. Frank edged backward. Rory strode past me.

"Hey!" he said as she reached into his pockets. "You can't—"

She pulled out a remote. When she hit a button, a voice boomed, "Get out!"

She looked up at him. "Okay, you can say it now."

"Wh-what?"

She glanced over at Ricardo. "You, too. Repeat after me. *I would have gotten away with it, too . . .*"

Cameron grinned. "*If it wasn't for you meddling kids.*"

We'd been scammed. It seemed, though, that our enterprising young journalist hadn't orchestrated the scheme. Frank had discovered what Ricardo was doing and offered him a real scoop, in return for a little extra role-play.

The house had been rigged by Frank before we arrived. He'd put in a sound system with the "ghosts" heard by everyone. He'd added remote-activated locks to mechanically operate doors. He'd even gotten a special effects buddy to set up the blood-sweating wall.

Yet there were things Frank couldn't have done. Namely, the ghosts.

Even more importantly, Frank lacked something else. A motive. He hadn't been hired by Ricardo. Even if he was lying about that, rigging this house took some serious cash. No journalist would have that kind of expense account—and no newspaper or magazine would knowingly pay for a false exposé.

So who masterminded this? I had an idea. As for motive, well, that wasn't quite so clear. But as soon as we got out of that room,

I had Jeremy slip off to call Savannah with a few questions for Paige's database.

I let the kids handle the fallout . . . I mean, take credit for unmasking the villains. I figured it was a reasonable trade-off. I trusted they wouldn't make me look like an idiot, and I'd get my share of the limelight later. For now, I had to find the real man behind the mask.

As one might expect, the aftermath was chaotic. It was easy enough for me to tear Gregor away from the questions and the cameras.

With Jeremy accompanying us, I led Gregor to a second-level bedroom.

"I thought you might need a break," I said.

"Yes, thank you. It is . . . overwhelming." He sat on the edge of the bed and exhaled. "I am still trying to understand everything. There were no dead girls?"

"No, there were. That's what I came to tell you. I talked to Polly Watson."

"I thought—"

"No, it *was* her. I'm sure of it." I told him how I'd seen the girls at the inn and now here.

"That is terrible," he said, getting to his feet. "You must tell those reporters downstairs."

"Actually, that's why I called you in here. I want you to tell them." I beamed at him. "You have a gift, Gregor. A true gift, and your story really touched me. I've had my fifteen minutes of fame. Now, it's your turn."

He shook his head. "No, this is yours. You saw them—"

"I'll tell you everything you need to know." I took his arm. "Come on. I've already seeded the story."

"Seeded . . ."

"Oh, I'm sure you know what that means. Your English is a lot better than you let on, which is what I'd expect from someone who lived in the States for most of his childhood."

"Wh-what? I did not live . . ."

When he trailed off, I released his arm. "Not sure you want to finish that, considering it's a matter of public record? So is your real last name. Demidov. I don't know why you changed it. It's such a great name. Did you know there's a family of Russian necromancers by that name? Quite famous. They say one even worked for the czars, back in the day."

"I don't know—"

"Well, I do. I know you're a necromancer. You came on this show hoping to make your name by crushing mine. You found Polly Watson's link to the house and invented a story, which you leaked to Mike. Then you convinced—or bullied—ghosts who looked like the missing girls to put on a show for me, complete with period costume and tragic death scenes. You hired Frank to help with the scheme. What is he? Half-demon? Minor telekinesis? Good at slamming doors? Doesn't matter, really. His main role was to persuade me to say on camera that I was seeing the dead girls and the killer. Then you'd refute my claims. When the truth came out, that the letters were fake, it would be obvious I was a con artist and you were the real deal."

Gregor edged toward the door. "You're crazy," he said, dropping most of his accent. "I don't know what—"

He bumped into Jeremy.

"Hello," Jeremy said. When Gregor tried to duck past, Jeremy tugged him back. "Not yet."

Gregor struggled, but Jeremy just stood there, casually holding him fast.

"You know," I said, "you really need to do more research on the people you try to scam. Do you know who Jeremy is?"

"I don't care," Gregor said, backing into the room as Jeremy released his hold. "You can't prove any of this, and I'll fight you if you try. I know people and—"

Something shimmered in the corner. Gregor noticed it. I did, too. Jeremy frowned slightly, sensing a ghost.

Light flashed, bright enough to make Gregor stumble back. A figure strode through. She was about forty, with long dark hair, and was dressed in jeans, boots, and a white blouse. In her right hand she held a four-foot-long sword, glowing with a blue light.

"Goddamn it," Eve said, striding toward us. "I did not need this. I really did not need this."

Gregor backed up until he hit the bed. "Is . . . is that—?"

"An angel," I said. "A very pissed-off one, apparently. Let me introduce you to my spirit guide, Eve Levine. I'm sure you've heard of her."

"What?" Eve said, turning her scowl on Gregor. "He's a necromancer?" She squinted at his spirit glow and then swore under her breath and shook her sword at him. "You breathe one word of this—"

"I-I won't say anything."

"You know what this is?" She waved the sword as he backed into the corner.

"Sword of Judgment," I said. "Used to send souls to purgatory." I paused. "Is that blood on it?"

"Yeah, I'm racking up bonus points today." She swung the sword at Gregor. "Don't make me add to—"

"I-I won't. I-I'm not going to say a word. I'm just . . . I'm leaving now." He turned to me. "I'll go back to Russia. You won't hear from me again."

"Good."

Gregor stumbled out the door. I shut it behind him.

"Damn," Eve said. "I've met some nervous necros in my day, but that guy's a mess. Did he really think I'd run him through if he told anyone he saw an angel?" She shook her head. "Exactly how bad is my reputation these days?"

I sputtered a laugh. "That's what you were warning him about?"

She plunked onto the bed. "I missed something, didn't I?" She glanced at Jeremy. "Hey, Jer."

"Eve says hi," I said.

He returned the greeting and offered to make sure Gregor fulfilled his promise to leave quietly.

"Where the hell are we?" she said, looking around after Jeremy left.

"Amityville."

"Of course." She pulled her legs up to sit cross-legged. "I have a problem and I need your help. Leah O'Donnell has escaped from her hell dimension."

"Leah . . ." I paused. "*The* Leah O'Donnell?"

Leah—a half-demon—had befriended, betrayed, and then kidnapped Savannah as a child. She'd tried to kill Paige, and ended up being killed by her.

"Savannah's home, isn't she?" Eve said. "In Portland? Same with Paige?"

I nodded. "Jeremy spoke to both of them about twenty minutes ago."

"Good. Leah's apparently over here, on the east coast. If she wants to remain out of hell, she'll stay far away from Savannah and Paige. She knows that's the first place I'd look. So we aren't going to tell them she's out."

"Are you sure that's—?"

"They'd only worry and want to help. I want you to keep in contact with them. If they start reporting flying objects, we know our Volo has made her way west. For now, though, I have a bead on her and, with your help, I'm going to get her back to hell before Paige and Savannah ever know she was out."

One case ending, another starting. Feast or famine, that's the way it seems to go in this life. The show was over. Mike had flown to LA to meet with the studio execs and figure out their next move. I was sure they'd find a way to salvage this wreck, as they had with *Death of Innocence*. At least now maybe they'd believe I really was a reality-show curse. Unless, once again, they ended up making more money with the revised version than they'd hoped for with the planned one. Damn it. I might have to lie low for a while.

Lying low wouldn't work with Eve. She needed my help. Our relationship went both ways, with me doing tasks in the human world that her non-corporeal form wouldn't allow. Luckily, a lot of that involved computers and telephones, which kept me out of any actual action. This time, considering who was involved, staying out of the action might not be so easy.

"I think I need more of these." I sat on our hotel bed, fingering my rune tattoo. "Do you have one for protection from TV reality shows? And guardian angels?"

Jeremy smiled and rubbed my foot. "Sorry. I'll help with Leah, though. You know that. I can get Clay and Elena involved if it comes to that."

"I don't want that bitch anywhere near the kids." I paused. "I mean Leah. Not Eve."

He laughed and leaned over to kiss me. "She's still tracking Leah, isn't she? You don't need to rush off yet?"

"I said unless she needs me, I could use a few days to wrap up the show stuff." I looked at him. "In other words, I lied."

"So we have a few days?"

"We do. And the stripper room at that motel is booked for one of them."

SORRY SEEMS TO BE
THE HARDEST WORD

"Looks like someone made a wrong turn on her way to Yorkville," Rudy grunted as his bar door swung open, a blast of October air rushing in.

"Close the fucking—" someone began.

The complainer stopped and murmured an apology that almost sounded genuine. That's what made me twist on my stool to look. The newcomer did indeed look as if she'd gotten lost on her way to the fashionable shopping district. She was in her early forties, long designer coat pulled tight, knee-high boots under it, short copper hair perfectly coiffed, as if the gusts outside didn't dare disturb it.

As her gaze swept Miller's, I swear every guy sat up straighter, even the ones so drunk they needed to prop themselves on their elbows to do it. Part of that was because she was an attractive woman. Mostly, though, it was for the same reason one had apologized—because something about her said they damn well better. A bar filled with supernaturals—half of whom look like they'd rob their grandma for beer money—but when she walked in, they straightened and squirmed like errant schoolboys.

She strode across the hardwood floor, heels clicking. I was impressed. I've never been able to manage that sound effect in here, where the sheer amount of old booze and vomit underfoot sticks to my boots with every step.

"If you're looking for the wine bar—" Rudy began.

"I would love the wine bar," she said. Her accent was French. France, not Quebec. Old, aristocratic French. Very old. Very aristocratic.

"In fact, I'm quite certain I would prefer to chug boxed wine in the alley next door. However, the person I am meeting seems to be quite comfortable here. Which does not surprise me one bit."

I lifted my beer. "Hey, Cass. Found the place okay, I see?"

"No, I do not find the place 'okay,' Zoe, as I'm sure you knew when you told me to meet you here."

"Rudy? Meet Cass. Cassandra DuCharme."

Up until this moment, Rudy had been the guy in the bar who didn't quail under Cass's haughty stare. When she'd been insulting his bar, he'd looked about ready to toss her out on her ass. Now he stopped, bar towel hanging from his fingers. It took him a moment to close his mouth.

"Ms. DuCharme." He hurried from behind the bar and extended a beefy hand. "Rudy. Sorry about the, uh . . ." He waved around the bar. "The mess. We had a party last night, and I haven't quite finished cleaning the place up."

I peered about. Miller's looked exactly as it has every day for the last fifteen years. In all that time, I'd never heard Rudy apologize for it. Now he was wiping off a stool and offering Cass some Cristal he "kept in the back." He kept Cristal in the back?

I could say he was tripping over himself to be nice because Cassandra DuCharme is a vampire. But so am I. The difference, as I'm sure he'd point out, is that Cass is a real vampire—the kind that other supernaturals imagine when you say the V word. Hell, even other vampires aspire to be Cassandra DuCharme. She embodies the romantic sophistication of the stereotype with none of the broody angst. Also, she's a stone-cold bitch. Who doesn't want to be a bitch? Well, me, for one. But that's why the joke in Miller's is that there are no vampires in Toronto, because Zoe Takano doesn't count.

"I don't believe we're staying," Cass said when Rudy offered the Cristal.

I opened my mouth.

"No," she said. "We aren't staying." She started for the door.

"I haven't finished my beer."

"Bring it."

"Haven't paid for it, either."

She growled under her breath, stalked back to the bar, and slapped down an American twenty. I mouthed for Rudy to apply the rest to my tab, but he was too busy gaping at Cass to even pick up the money—another first for Rudy. He didn't even give me shit for absconding with his glass.

"There *is* a wine bar up the road," I said as we stepped out. "And a fetish bar the other way. I'm fond of the fetish one myself."

"I'm sure you are. As I believe I tried to indicate on the phone, this is a private conversation, Zoe. We're going to your apartment."

She swept off, coat fluttering behind her. I let her get twenty feet before calling, "Wrong way!"

She glowered, spun on her heel, and headed back as I went to hail us a cab.

If I was still using oxygen, I'm sure I'd have been holding my breath as we walked into my apartment. I'm very proud of my place. I spent two decades in Toronto before I found just the right apartment, high above the city, with an amazing view. Then I'd set about decorating it just as slowly, each piece chosen with exquisite care.

With anyone else I'd have rested easy, knowing they'd be impressed. But Cass makes her unliving dealing in art and antiques. I consider myself something of an expert in old stuff, too—I'm a thief, specializing in artifacts. Both are excellent occupations for people who've been around a few hundred years. But as confident as I am in my expertise, I'm not on Cass's level, and I watched her walking around my apartment, waiting for her to snark.

"Nice," she said, sounding surprised.

"Thank you." I should have left it there, but I couldn't. "Any suggestions?"

She took a slow look around. "The sake jug doesn't fit. It's a very nice piece of folk art, though. Meiji period?"

I nodded.

"I would suggest a teakettle from the same period. I saw a beautiful *tetsubin* one last week. Octangular. Silver inlaid handle. I could provide you with the seller's information."

I said I'd take it. She was right about the sake jug. As much as I liked it, I'd known it didn't quite fit.

"Also," she said, "I'd get rid of the human hiding in your bathroom."

"I'm not hiding," said a voice from the hall. "I was using the toilet. Do you want to check?"

A young woman walked out. I'd say "a teenage girl," but she hates being called that, even if, at nineteen, Brittany technically still is one. I'd forgotten she'd be here—she often used my place as a crash pad following afternoon classes.

"Who's the vamp?" she asked as she strolled in.

"What makes you think I'm a vampire?" Cass said.

"Because I wasn't making any noise," Brittany replied. "You sensed me. Ergo, a vampire."

"Brittany's an ex-slayer," I said.

Cass turned to me, as if she'd misheard. "A what?"

"Former vampire slayer. Well, she never actually got around to slaying one, but that was her plan. I dissuaded her."

Brittany gave me a look that said she might be un-dissuaded if I kept introducing her that way. It was like having your mom tell people you wanted to grow up to be a rock star.

"She wants to work for the council someday," I said. "I'm training her to fight."

I braced myself for Cass to make some sly remark about Brittany's chances improving if she found a new trainer. Yet she resisted, which only made me more anxious. Cass was being nice. Cass wanted something. Shit.

"Speaking of the council . . ." Cass made herself comfortable, while managing not to inflict a single wrinkle on her outfit. "I need to speak to you about an opportunity there. Perhaps your young friend should be on her way?"

"The council?" Brittany plopped into the chair nearest Cass. "Hell, no. What's your connect—" She stopped and her eyes rounded. "You're Cassandra DuCharme. Holy fucking shit."

"Language," I murmured.

"But this is *Cassandra DuCharme*," Brittany said. "A real . . ." She didn't finish that. Even managed to look guilty for thinking it. "You know what I mean. She's, like, the Queen of the Vampires."

"I wouldn't say that," Cass murmured.

"You are," Brittany said. "You're the oldest one around, right?"

Cass stiffened. Brittany didn't notice and barreled on. "You must have the most amazing stories."

"I'm sure Zoe does, too."

"Sure, but none she'll tell me."

Cass hesitated, and then seemed to remember why I might not be eager to share my past with Brittany. Might not be willing to share it with anyone I actually want to stay friends with. Cass knows what I was like in the early days. It's just been so long that she forgets.

"Well, maybe they weren't that interesting," Cass said. "You know Zoe. She has two modes: stealing things and partying. Both terribly exciting in the short term, but after a hundred and fifty years? Quite dull, I'm sure. The settings may change, but Zoe Takano does not."

Brittany tensed at the insult and looked over, waiting for me to react. When I didn't, her annoyance shifted my way. Even when I was insulted in my own home, I didn't rouse myself to fight back. But Cass was actually saving my ass with her insults—giving an excuse for me not telling those old stories.

"What do you need, Cass?" *Now that you've finished buttering me up.*

"I don't need anything. However, the council will eventually be in need of a new delegate. My term won't last much longer, as I'm sure you're aware."

"I thought delegates served for as long as they wanted," Brittany said.

Cass meant her life term was ending. Our immortality comes with an expiry date, and by all accounts Cassandra DuCharme's had passed years ago.

"Are you asking me . . .?" I said.

"Of course not." Her words came out clipped. "The *council* is asking you. I thought it would be better if Aaron came, but he insisted I do it."

She muttered something uncomplimentary about Aaron. She didn't mean it. If there's one person in this world that Cassandra DuCharme cares about, it's Aaron. They were lovers for over a hundred years before she betrayed him, leaving him to a Romanian mob while she fled. He'd spent the next century avoiding her, but rumor had it they were back together. Did he forgive her? Probably. If Cass is the bitchiest vampire you'll ever meet, Aaron is the nicest.

But if Aaron sent Cass to ask me to sign up as his co-delegate, that could mean only one thing.

"Britt?" I said. "I think you should leave."

"Hell, no. This is just getting—"

She stopped as she saw my look.

"I'll catch up with you tomorrow," I said. "We'll get some training in."

She hauled herself off the chair, managing to sigh the entire time. She made it to the hall and then turned to Cass.

"Are you staying long?" she asked. "In Toronto?"

"No." Cassandra paused. "But if you are interested in the council, perhaps we can speak tomorrow. Briefly. My plane leaves at noon."

"Sounds good. Sorry you aren't staying, but that's probably just as well. It's a bad time to be a vampire in Toronto. Zoe's been having trouble with some immortality questers." She looked at me. "You were going to warn Cassandra about that, right?"

"Of course."

Brittany's look called me a liar, but she only shook her head and left.

When she was gone, Cass said, "Immortality questers?"

"Wild and crazy supernaturals who want to live forever and think we can help them do it. Preferably by decapitating us, carving us up, and seeing what makes us tick—and keep on ticking."

"Obviously, I know what an immortality quester is, Zoe. If you're having problems with them—"

"Nah. There are always a few in town. Every now and then they get annoying. I haven't lost my head over it yet. So, Aaron sent you here to ask me about the delegate post. He wants you to apologize, doesn't he?"

"For what?"

"Ha-ha."

She sighed. "If you mean that business back in the twenties . . ."

"Thirties. Nineteen thirty-four, to be exact. Spring in Venice. A perfect time for love."

"She was human, Zoe."

"No law against that. Which didn't stop you from interfering."

"I misunderstood the situation."

"Bullshit. You didn't trust me."

She straightened. "Which was understandable, given your past—"

"Ten years. I fucked up for ten years. Then I got my head on straight, and I hadn't caused one speck of trouble in decades."

"Given your line of work, I'd hardly say you don't cause trouble."

I glowered at her. For a vampire, stealing was about as serious as jaywalking. "I'm as clean as they come, in every way that counts. Yet you interfered. You cost me someone I cared about. Someone I loved."

"I didn't *kill* her."

"No, you just drove her away and made sure she'd never want to speak to me again."

"It wouldn't have worked out."

"Then it wouldn't have worked out. She wasn't in danger. You know how I was turned."

Silence. A look passed over Cass's face. It seemed almost like compassion, but I'm sure it was a trick of the light. They say it's impossible to make someone a vampire against her will. It's not. That's what my first lover did to me, when I refused her "gift." It was a hell beyond imagining.

"Then you know I would never, *ever* do that to someone else," I said, my voice low. "I would not have told her what I was. I would never have asked her to join me. She was safe. And you interfered."

"That was a very long time ago, Zoe."

"So no apology?"

"I don't believe I owe—"

I stood. "Then find yourself another delegate. Tell Aaron I'm sorry. He'll understand."

"This isn't about me, Zoe. The council—"

"—will be fine with one delegate. Aaron can handle it. Now, if you'll excuse me . . ."

I escorted her out the door.

Cass was right. Agreeing to replace her on the council didn't help her. It helped Aaron, whom I liked. It helped the werewolf delegates, whom I also liked. Hell, I knew most of the council. Good people doing good work. I wasn't much of a joiner, but I wasn't exactly antisocial. I could help. I probably should. And I would, just as soon as I got something from Cass.

Aaron had sent Cass here to make amends. Put her affairs in order. One could argue that Cassandra DuCharme didn't give a shit who she'd mowed down in the last four hundred years. A cast of thousands, I was sure. But if she truly didn't care, Aaron wouldn't have sent her on this quest for forgiveness. So I'd get my apology, for her own good.

"Five hundred," Rudy said when I told him my plan.

I snorted a laugh.

"Six hundred, then," he said. "You keep arguing, the price keeps rising. I need my cut, Zoe."

"If I pay you six hundred, then your cut will be the whole six hundred, because whoever you hire will work for a bottle of booze. Cheap booze, which you'll write off as spoilage. I'll give you what you'd get with the standard fifty percent cut of five hundred. Two hundred and fifty."

"Three."

"Three and you wipe my tab." I counted out the money on the bar before he could argue.

Next I called up Cass, said I felt bad about the way we left things, and asked if she'd accompany me to the opera that night. She jumped at the chance, certain it meant I was waffling. Aaron would be so much happier if she secured my agreement. And she'd be so much happier if she could secure it without all that apologizing nonsense.

It was a lovely performance of *Fidelio*. Afterward, I took Cass to a wine bar—a very nice one, I might add. Together with the tickets, the evening cost me as much as I'd paid Rudy for his performance artists. But Cass was impressed. Also a little tipsy, as we made our way along the darkened streets. Tipsy enough that she let me steer her into a "shortcut" through a churchyard. She didn't even pick up the life signs of the guy at the other end until he stepped into the moonlit gap.

"Hello, Zoe," he said. "You're a hard girl to find these days. Been thinking hard on our offer, I hope."

I wheeled. Another man slid from the shadows, blocking our retreat. When Cass turned to see him, he lifted a machete and grinned.

"Oh God," I whispered to Cass. "I am so sorry. Don't worry. I'll get us out of this."

"I'm sure you will," she said, her tone as dry as the Chardonnay we'd just finished. "But I think I can handle it."

"No, don't—!"

She was already striding toward the guy with the machete. "And what do you think you're going to do with that?"

"What should be done to all bloodsuckers. Off with 'er head." He grinned and waved the machete, blade glinting in the moonlight. "You'll be a lot more useful when you're dead, parasite. You'll help someone for a change. A lot of someones. Once we discover the secret—"

"Oh, stuff it," she said as she stopped in front of him. "Do you really expect me to believe you're going to lop off my head *here*? In downtown Toronto? And then what? Drag my decapitated corpse to your lair?" She turned to me. "Really, Zoe? I thought you were smarter than this."

"Cass! Watch—!"

She grabbed the guy's arm as he swung the machete. She didn't even turn around to do it. Just reached back, grabbed his arm, and yanked. He may have been almost twice her size, but she caught him off guard and he stumbled. She was on him in a second, teeth sinking into his neck.

"No!" the other man cried.

He raced toward his companion as Cass let the man fall to the ground.

"Oh please," she said. "Save the drama. I'm sure you know enough about vampires to realize I've merely sedated him with my saliva. I'm hardly going to drink from a man reeking of cheap whiskey.

God knows what kind of hangover I'd get." She stepped toward the second man. "Now, unless you'd like the same . . ."

He turned and ran. Cass looked at me, shook her head, and resumed walking.

I had to jog to keep up with Cass. Even at four hundred years old, the woman can move damn fast.

"I did not set that up," I said. "I swear it. There's no way I could have told Brittany to warn you about fake immortality questers."

"No? The girl can't receive text messages on her phone?"

"You think I texted her to say that? When? You didn't mention the delegate offer until she was in the same room with us."

"Elena forewarned you. No, not Elena. It was Clayton, wasn't it? The man has a grudge against me. I have no idea why."

"Um, because you hit on him . . . while Elena was being held captive, fighting for her life."

She wheeled, boots scraping the pavement. "Who told you that?"

"Everyone knows. But Clay wouldn't call me with tips. He doesn't much like me, either. Probably because I hit on Elena."

She rolled her eyes and resumed walking.

"Okay," I said. "Clearly those two were not real immortality questers. I'm guessing someone from Rudy's is playing a prank on me. They know I've been having trouble with questers and that you're in town. Making me look bad with a *real* vampire. Ha-ha. I'll get them back. But I did think, at first, those two were the real deal, because I have been having problems."

"I'm sure you have. Your ruse has failed. Don't compound the damage by insulting my intelligence."

"But—"

"Go home, Zoe. Our evening is at an end."

*

I'd been following Cass for five blocks, reasoning that if she really wanted to get rid of me, she'd have hopped in a cab by now. She knew I was there, keeping pace fifty feet back, working out a strategy. Also, I was calling directions when she'd pause on a corner and try to figure out which way to turn.

We were cutting across a quiet residential street of townhouses when I noticed the car. It was black, all the lights off as it inched along the road toward us. Then it stopped.

I broke into a run and caught up to Cass.

"That car," I whispered. "I've seen it before."

She fixed me with a look. "Really, Zoe?"

"No, I'm serious. It's them. The immortality questers."

She sighed. "I cannot believe you'd honestly try this again after—"

The car shot forward, motor gunning. I grabbed the back of her coat.

"Come on! There's a walkway right—"

She pulled away and turned to continue down the sidewalk as the car raced toward us.

"You'd better warn your friends," she said. "If they lay a hand on me, they will lose it. I am not in the mood for games."

The car's rear door flew open as it slowed.

"Cass!" I yelled. "I'm serious! This isn't me!"

A man leapt from the car. Cass ducked him easily, but a second man had swung out from the other side. He caught her from behind, wrenching her arms back.

"Zoe!" she snarled. "This isn't funny. Tell these men to unhand me or—"

The first man grabbed her legs and they threw her into the backseat. As he wrestled her in, the second man took a step toward me.

"Little Zoe Takano," he said. "What are you going to do now? Try to stop us? Or be happy we have a prize in your stead?"

I took a slow step back.

He laughed. "That's what I thought."

I could see Cass in the backseat, fighting two men as they restrained her. She looked over at me, her eyes blazing.

"I'm sorry," I mouthed. Then I turned and ran.

I watched from my hiding place as the car made a right turn, sticking to the residential roads tucked deep in the heart of downtown. I knew a shortcut, and the roads here were narrow, plagued with stop signs that would keep their progress slow.

I calculated where they'd go, coming out onto a busier street to make a speedy escape. Sure enough, the car appeared as I waited, hidden, near a stoplight. They were on a side street, meaning at this time of night the light wouldn't change until it needed to. As they idled at the red, I snuck out, used a pick to carefully pop the trunk, and slipped inside.

They took Cass clear out of the city to what looked like an abandoned farmhouse, on a chunk of property with signs warning that condos would be coming soon. Sneaking out of the trunk and into the house was a breeze. Hey, I'm a thief. It's what I do.

Cass was being held in the basement with only one guard on duty, the others upstairs, on a phone conference. I snuck past the guard and found Cass, huddled dejectedly in a room, resigned to her fate . . . Yeah, not in this lifetime. She was on her feet, pacing as she waited for that life sign that would tell her someone was coming. Although the door made barely a whisper as I opened it, she spun, fangs out, eyes glittering.

She saw me and stopped. For at least five seconds, she just stared.

"It's okay," I whispered. "I had nothing to do with this."

"Yes, I know," she said. "But . . . you came back."

I knew why she was so shocked. If the situation had been reversed, she would not have come for me. She would have gotten help—she's not a monster—but she wouldn't have rescued me herself.

"I had to," I whispered. "As nice as Aaron is, he'd have hunted me to the ends of the earth if I let you die before your time. Now, there's only one guard on this level. I didn't want to disable him, in case someone noticed. I'll go do that now. Count to ten and follow."

Before I could go, she laid her hand on my arm, stopping me.

"Thank you," she said.

"Hold that thought. We're not out of here yet."

The guard was easily dispatched, and the way was still clear. The only problem was the hike to civilization after we escaped, but we stayed away from the roads, so it was merely long and cold, until finally we saw lights that suggested a place where we might find a cab.

As we headed across a field to reach the lights, Cass said, "You have my apology, Zoe. I know that's important to you, so I'll give it."

"Even though you still don't think you did anything wrong?"

She glanced over, green eyes shimmering in the dark. "No, I do not. The relationship wouldn't have lasted." She turned forward again. "They say that, for vampires, this is our afterlife. If so, then *that* is our hell—everyone we care about will die. If it happens often enough, you learn that the only way to protect yourself is not to get too attached to anyone or anything."

"Even other vampires?"

"Perhaps. Everything can die."

That's why she'd betrayed Aaron. To drive him away. Obviously, it hadn't worked. Sometimes the pain of forced separation—knowing your beloved is still out there—is worse than death. I could understand her reasoning, but I didn't agree with it. Attachments are all we have. Yes, a vampire will watch their world crumble over and over, but there's always something that follows, something new and filled with promise. And the memories remain, sweet and bittersweet.

"I did what I thought was right," she said. "But you are correct that I interfered, when I should not have. I didn't trust you to handle the situation. For that, I will apologize. Sincerely."

"Thank you."

We continued on in silence. Her mission was accomplished. Both of them. She'd been forgiven and the council would have a new delegate.

Mine had been accomplished, too. I got my apology, and it only cost me three hundred bucks. Rudy's guys had done well. I'd need to buy them a round the next time they were at Miller's.

OFF-DUTY ANGEL

Getting an audience with the Fates is like getting an invitation to tea with the Queen. Most people in the afterlife never receive one. To actually wrangle one yourself? Damn near impossible. Unless you're me: Eve Levine—dark witch, half-demon, part-time ghost, part-time angel. I'm in their throne room so often, they might as well install a revolving door. Most times, I'm getting hauled in and chewed out—a fake chewing-out, as the Fates pretend to upbraid me for breaking some rule or other on a mission, while they're really just relieved that someone got the job done.

Today, though, I'd requested the audience. So they were making me wait in their reception room, watching the mosaics subtly changing as the story of life and death played out on the walls. Finally, the floor turned and deposited me in the throne room, at the foot of the Fates' dais.

"I have a deal for you," I said to the oldest Fate, as she snipped a length of life-yarn.

"We're honored," she said, peering down with a withering look. "The answer is no. We've had quite enough of your deals, Eve."

"Really? Huh. Then how about you undo the one that makes me a halo-slave for six months a year? If you're regretting that, we can renegotiate. Or just forget the whole thing."

She morphed into her sister, a middle-aged woman with long, graying blond hair. "You wouldn't want that, Eve. No more than we would. While I'm quite certain any offer of yours is not to our advantage, we'll hear you out."

"Good." I reached back to pull off my Sword of Judgment, so I could lean on it, as I usually did in the throne room—if only to make the eldest Fate sputter. But I didn't have it. I was off duty. Which was the problem. "I'd like to offer you seven extra days of my time. I'll voluntarily go back into the angel corps for the next week. In return, you give me a week off during my regular shift. You can schedule my downtime whenever you want it. Anytime things get slow, you give me shore leave. Totally at your convenience."

"Kristof's still in court, I presume?" The middle Fate had returned.

"Sure, but that's not why—"

"It is exactly why." The oldest Fate now. "Your lover is busy. You are bored. You want us to entertain you. Absolutely—"

"Not so hasty, sister." The middle one came back. "I believe her angel partner would be very happy for her assistance right now."

I perked up. "Trsiel's hunting? Who? Or what?"

"It's a what. He's hunting for answers, deep in the bowels of the Great Library. We've asked him to research the political ramifications of a proposed treaty between two djinn factions. We expected it to take a few weeks, but with your help . . ."

"Right. Um, now that you mention it . . ."

"You've suddenly remembered another pressing obligation?"

"Yeah. Sorry. Thanks for your time. And if anything—"

"—more exciting comes up?" The Fate smiled. "We'll call you."

I flopped onto the front-porch swing of my Southern manor. The Fates were right, of course. Kris had been tied up in afterlife court for the past week, and it didn't look as if the trial would end anytime soon. I should point out he was the defense attorney, not the defendant. Kristof Nast would never be found in a defendant's seat. He always bribed, threatened, or manipulated his way out of trouble long before it reached that point.

So he was busy and I was bored. That sounds bad, as if I rely on him so much that I don't know what to do with myself when he's gone. But I'd spent most of my mortal life by myself—or with our daughter, Savannah. Even now that Kris and I had been reunited after death, we were often apart, for my angel gig and his job. We've even kept our own afterlife homes—my manor and his houseboat—though if we're in the same plane, we rarely sleep in separate beds.

I was bored because I was nearing the end of my latest shore leave. Whenever I first returned from angel duty, I had a long list of things to do. Check on my mortal guide, Jaime Vegas. Check on Savannah. Check on Kris's boys, Sean and Bryce. Check on my afterlife contacts, see if they had anything interesting for me. Call in some chits. Chase down new contacts. Explain to them why it's really a good idea to have Eve Levine in their Rolodex. Just maintaining my contact network is a job in itself.

But that work was long done. This was the time when I truly would be enjoying a little R&R with Kris. Even after nine years here, there are endless nooks and crannies and planes and dimensions we haven't explored. I suppose I could go on my own, but it really wasn't the same.

A figure turned onto my block. A man. A couple of inches taller than my six feet. Late forties. Thinning blond hair. Broad shoulders. Carrying some extra weight, but his big frame hid it, as did his expertly tailored suit.

I flew off the swing, sending it rocking as I raced down the steps. Along the front path, through the gate, down the road, like a war bride spotting her discharged husband.

Kris caught me up in a hug and kiss.

"I thought you didn't get a break until tonight," I said.

"I wrangled a recess," he said. "It's a brief one, but I wanted to come by. I may have a job for you."

"Seriously?" I paused. "It's not research, is it?"

He laughed. "Never. It's a real celestial-bounty-hunter-worthy mission."

I threw my arms around his neck and kissed him. "I love you."

"Uh-huh." He leaned back. "Did I just get a bigger kiss for giving you a job than I did for the surprise visit?"

"Maybe. So what's the mission?"

"I need you to follow someone. I don't know the what, the where, the how, or even the why. Just the who."

"Intriguing. Is it connected to your court case?"

"I don't know. Someone came in to speak to the prosecutor during the trial. It was important enough to earn her a five-minute recess. As I was using the opportunity to stretch my legs, I caught a name and enough of the context to know that the owner of that name is very important to the prosecution. Even if it *isn't* my case, finding out more could be useful."

"A mystery," I said. "Exactly what I'm in the mood for. And—if you're in the mood and have time—I'd be happy to make up for that kiss." I waved at my house.

That was one offer Kris never refused.

Even if Lewis Stranz wasn't up to something, he was certainly keeping me on my toes, which was a pleasant surprise. Tailing people usually involves long periods of sitting in one place, trying not to let my attention wander.

Stranz didn't seem to be doing anything of import. He was just very, very busy. Going here, going there, meeting this person, meeting that one. With every encounter, I had to get close to figure out what was going on. Easy enough for a witch who's also an Aspicio half-demon.

My father is Lord Demon Balaam, which makes life as an angel just a little more interesting. It does help in stalking, though, because the power he confers on his offspring is vision enhancement. If I can get on the other side of a wall, I can clear a "peephole." If I can't, then that's when my witch powers come in handy, with blur spells for getting close and cover spells for staying there.

After all that work, I'd discovered that Stranz was simply socializing. Getting together with friends for a walk, a chat, a drink. While we may not need sustenance, we still partake in the rituals of human social life.

As for Stranz himself, my research hadn't given me any hints to explain the prosecution's interest. He was a shaman, which meant in the mortal world he'd had a spirit guide, could astral-project, and had healing abilities. Stranz still had his ayami—his spirit guide—except now the guide inhabited the same plane and had truly become his life partner, as often happens. As for healing and spirit travel, those are absolutely useless in the afterlife. As if to compensate for this loss of powers, ghost shamans get special access to the teleport system, and what Stranz seemed to do with that access was make himself a wide and varied circle of friends. Which was a fun challenge for me, chasing him across the globe. But it wasn't all that interesting. Until he went to London.

Stranz's first stop in London was the British Museum, which operates a little differently in the afterlife. In the mortal realm, if you visit a museum exhibit on, say, cave paintings, you'll get photos of faint-colored lines on dimly lit cave walls, with artist reconstructions of what they might have looked like and theoretical crap about the artist, the purpose, blah, blah, blah. But in the afterlife, if you're interested in cave paintings, you get yourself over to our version of France and hike out to the caves at Lascaux, and there they are, the colors just as vivid—and the animals just as misshapen—as they were when first painted. If you want to know how or why they were done, you ask one of the painters himself, who lives there, happily telling visitors about his life's work.

Same goes for pretty much everything you'd find in the British Museum. If you want to explore the past, you just travel. So what *is* in the afterlife British Museum? Artifacts, pretty much as you'd find in the mortal-world version, complete with temporary exhibits. But each artifact is actually a touch portal, which can take you to its natural environment. Access is available to any afterlife resident who hasn't had his basic teleportation privileges revoked.

Stranz's access was fine. From my background check, he didn't seem like the kind of guy who'd even need to worry about revocation. A real straight arrow. Born during the Depression, died in the eighties, worked as a family doctor, never had more than a parking ticket in his life. In other words, the sort of person I usually had zero contact with, which made the prosecution's interest all the more intriguing.

My guess? Stranz was an unwilling—and probably unwitting—pawn in some scheme. A patsy. His squeaky-clean background made him perfect for it, as did his vast number of acquaintances. It was a good bet that one of those "friends" had set Stranz up, either to unknowingly transport goods or to take the fall for something.

Which meant, if I was right, that I'd not only be helping Kris, but I'd be helping an innocent guy. That would win me brownie points with the Fates. They get excited when I do good deeds off duty, as if the whole angel gig is finally rubbing off. I might be able to parlay this one into an extra vacation week.

As Stranz climbed the museum's massive front steps, I lurked in a crowd of the recently dead. You can tell by the dresses and suits—they hadn't yet learned how to change out of their grave clothes. I skirted them and hurried on, earning catcalls and whistles from a group of toga-clad young guys lounging on the stairs. I told them where they could shove it—in ancient Latin. That stopped them. One of the gifts that comes with ascended angelhood is a permanent universal translator in my brain. The Fates can't rescind that when I'm off duty. They've warned me that I should avoid using it for frivolous reasons. My definition of frivolous just doesn't always match theirs.

I spotted Stranz as soon as I entered the museum. He took a left at the Rosetta stone—which, by the way, I can fully translate—then headed through the wing to the room containing pieces of the Greek Parthenon. From there, he teleported to the Acropolis itself. I waited behind Assyrians sighing over friezes as they lamented the late great sport of lion hunting. Then I cast a blur spell, hurried to the next room, and crossed over into ancient Athens.

Like every other place that has passed its heyday, Athens is stuck in its glory years—the good old days of Ancient Greece, before the Romans took over and renamed all their gods. And long before the Ottomans used the Parthenon as an ammo dump and a stray flame reduced it to pretty chunks of marble. Because irreplaceable historic buildings make great places to store gunpowder.

In the afterlife, the Parthenon still stands, its marble buildings shimmering blindingly white under the midday sun. The grounds were covered with picnickers in garb from across the globe and the centuries. Tourists wound their way through the Acropolis. There were a few guards, but only to make sure no one tried to set up residence.

Most tourists flocked to the Parthenon—the most famous temple on the Acropolis, the one with the forty-foot-tall ivory and gold statue of Athene. When Stranz exited the portal, he headed down the sloping road to the Erechtheion on the Acropolis's north side. It's a smaller temple, dedicated to yet another aspect of Athene. Don't ask me what aspect. I've been here; I've explored; I've never taken the tour.

Stranz headed straight into the temple, meaning he wasn't touring, either. He was meeting someone. Sure enough, as he made his way through the Erechtheion, a woman broke from the gaggle of gawking ghosts and slid after him. I could see they were both heading to the south porch, and I was about to go around outside to eavesdrop when the woman . . . pulsed.

One second she was a solid, fully materialized form, then she faded a little, becoming slightly translucent, before "firming up" again. No one else noticed. I only did because the ability to spot glamours is yet another part of my angel package.

I concentrated on the woman, trying to see what lay beneath her glamour. For a moment, she was just a woman. Late twenties, dark hair, pale skin. Then her skin went as white as the surrounding marble. Her dark hair began to writhe, snakes slithering through it. Two more snakes encircled her arms and a third acted as a belt. Her short skirt and boots stayed the same, but she accessorized with wings. Put the wings together with the snakes and the huntress costume and there was no doubt what I was seeing. An Erinys. Better known as a Fury.

I zipped out of the temple and around to the south, where I cloaked myself in a cover spell and hid under the row of Caryatids—the marble maidens that stand watch over the porch. I could hear three people above speaking in ancient Sumerian, which sounded like they were waxing poetic on the beauty and majesty of their surroundings . . . until I realized they were just trying to figure out where to grab lunch. I presumed Stranz and the Erinys were up there, waiting for the others to move on.

Erinyes are, technically, demi-demons. But that's a catch-all term that basically means "not a ghost or celestial spirit." Within it, the actual degree of demonic varies wildly. You have creatures like Nix, whose sole purpose is to convince mortals to act on their darkest desires. Clearly demonic. Then you get entities like djinn, who take advantage of human greed and offer a deal that usually won't go in your favor. More mischievous than evil.

Further along are the Erinyes, who were known by the Greeks as goddesses of vengeance. You call on them to avenge yourself on someone who has wronged you, and by "wronged" I don't mean "cut off in traffic." It has to be a serious offense, like murdering a loved one. Erinyes have ethics. Strict ones. However, they aren't going to talk you into turning the other cheek. That's why they're classified as demons. They may intend to mete out justice, but they can wreak serious havoc doing it.

Finally, the Sumerians moved on. And the Erinys moved in.

"Do you have what I need?" she whispered to Stranz.

His voice quavered as he said he did. He passed her what sounded like a piece of paper. I managed to clear a peephole through the porch, but there was no way in hell I could see what was written on the paper the Erinys was now reading.

When she finished, she crushed the paper. Light flashed. She opened her hand, and fine ash drifted to the floor. Great.

"That's what you needed, isn't it?" Stranz asked.

"It is. I will do as we discussed."

Which is . . . ? Come on, guys. Give me something.

Light footsteps crossed the porch, heading back inside. One set of footprints, as the Erinys walked away.

Shit!

I hurried around the building under the cover of a blur spell. I reached the entrance just in time to see the Erinys striding across the main room. She passed behind the three Sumerians, still discussing lunch. I saw her walk behind them . . . and I didn't see her come out again. She'd crossed over to another dimension. Which one? I had no idea.

I followed Stranz instead, though I didn't know what good that would do. Clearly the Erinys was the one to stalk. Her mission of revenge was almost certainly what Kristof was looking for.

As Stranz crossed back into the museum, I tailed him on autopilot as I flipped through my mental Rolodex. There were two Erinyes I could speak to—one was a contact, one owed me a favor. Neither would inform on her sister, but I might be able to get some information about this particular Erinys. I could also dig deeper into Stranz's afterlife and figure out why he'd need one of the Furies.

Yet in the afterlife, it's hard to wrong someone so grievously that they could invoke an Erinys. Murder is out of the question, obviously. Possessions are easy enough to come by, and Erinyes don't avenge mere theft. And what punishment could the demi-demon inflict on a ghost anyway?

Damn. It had to be a wrong committed in the mortal realm. But I couldn't imagine Stranz had waited thirty years to take revenge for something from his lifetime. Maybe he'd just discovered that someone he cared about had been hurt or killed. But why would that interest an afterlife prosecutor?

My brain was still spinning when I realized that Stranz wasn't heading for the exit. I probably should have figured that out as soon as I found myself climbing stairs to the second floor, but I'm so accustomed to following people that I don't need to engage much of my brain to do it. Once up there, Stranz didn't seem to be sightseeing or heading to a specific destination. He was just wandering—quickly.

Had he spotted me? I saw no evidence of that. He didn't glance back or duck down rear hallways or try to lose himself in a crowd. He just kept walking. Through Egypt, then over to Iran and Mesopotamia and across Europe.

Between Europe and Ancient Greece, there was a space for temporary exhibits. Today, it was empty. Well, empty of exhibits. Filled with people. A massive tour group milled about like a herd of lost sheep. Stranz could have gone through them or turned back. Instead, he veered into a back hall, moving faster now. He turned, then turned again, getting deeper into the warren of halls. Another turn and . . .

Silence. One second his shoes had been tap-tapping along. Then nothing. I cast a quick cover spell.

Shoes squeaked on linoleum. Stranz stumbled around the corner, as if he'd been shoved out. He glanced back, face tight with annoyance, and muttered something under his breath as he resumed walking.

I let him round the next corner and then hurried to where he'd been. It was a short hall, maybe ten feet long, ending at a door marked Private, and Please Use Other Entrance.

I tried the door. It was locked, and an unlock spell didn't fix that. When I cleared a peephole, I saw a dark storage room with a massive box blocking the door.

What had Stranz wanted in that room?

I'd come back later. For now, I needed to catch up with—

The hall vanished. There was a moment of darkness, no longer than an eye blink, then I was staring at a wall. I turned slowly.

I was in a small, empty room.

The Fates have been known to reach out and grab me. Very inconvenient. But this wasn't their waiting room, and I hadn't done anything wrong.

Another flicker of darkness, and I landed back in the museum hall.

Huh. Apparently I'd walked into a dimensional slip—just as Stranz must have. Step on the right spot and in you go. Like a magical version of those bookcases that spin into a secret room.

I put my hands out, ready to start looking for that doorway again. Then I stopped. Stranz. He was on the move. This dimensional pocket wasn't going anywhere. I hurried off to find my target.

I caught up with Stranz on the far side of the second floor, where he met his former ayami—now his wife. A blur spell got me close enough to hear him apologizing for being late.

"So what do you want to see?" he asked her.

"Vikings." She smiled up at him. "I want to see Vikings."

"Then you shall." He looped his arm through hers. "When do we need to meet Ted and Anna?"

"In two hours, at Seven Dials. There's a lovely little pastry shop near there . . ."

They wandered off. Two hours of Vikings followed by a visit with friends just a few blocks away. Time to check out that dimensional pocket.

I found the spot I needed to step on to activate the dimensional slip. It teleported me to the pocket, which was still an empty room.

I walked over each inch of floor and peered through the walls, but it was like looking out into a black hole. Same with the floor. Yet whenever I passed one section of wall, I felt a buzz like a low-grade shock. A magical, *Hey, there's something here.*

It took some work, but I found the source. A hand-sized section of wall just above the floor. I put my hand against it and—voilà!—a dimensional door popped me into . . . another empty room.

At first, I thought it was the same one, but when I paced it off, I realized this one was a couple of feet smaller. Some searching located the door back to where I'd come in. I also found a door into yet another, slightly smaller room.

"Seriously?" I muttered as I paced the new one, bending slightly to keep from hitting my head on the ceiling. "What is this? The Russian nesting doll of dimensional pockets?"

I found another door, into a smaller room, then another, this last one taking me into a long crawl space, so narrow my claustrophobia kicked in. I crept along on all fours, ignoring the jabs of panic, reminding myself that I knew the way out. Then the crawl space ended. I crouched there, hitting the walls and . . .

The floor gave way, and I tumbled down into darkness.

*

As soon as my feet hit the floor, I leapt up and cast a light-ball spell.

"What is it?" a voice whispered in the darkness.

"A shade," another hissed. "A mortal shade."

"No, it is more. Much more."

I conjured my sword then. Yes, technically against the rules when I'm not on angel duty, but those whispers weren't in any human language. They were demonic.

A four-foot glowing blue blade materialized in my hand. I swung it up, and all around me tiny forms skittered back, hissing and growling. I strode to the nearest one and impaled it on the end of my sword as the others shrieked curses. They didn't interfere, though—they were just happy I'd skewered someone else.

I lifted the squirming demon. It was an imp—a type known as an oni. Ugly little beggar. In Japanese folklore, oni are big, hulking, ogre-like beasts. Personally, I think they just got themselves some good PR. They're actually about two feet tall, humanoid, with blue skin, red hair, three eyes, and long claws on their feet and hands, which I could hear as they scurried about, gibbering among themselves.

Oni are usually thought of as a form of ghost, because the name is derived from the Japanese word for "hidden" or "conceal." Another misunderstanding. They don't hide themselves—they hide things. Items of value. Usually behind a secret demon gate, which they guard.

I lifted the oni on my sword and peered at it, and when I did, it let out an ear-piercing shriek.

"Balaam!" it cried. "Lord Balaam!"

The imp tried to prostrate itself, which is really hard to do while dangling from a blade. Around it, the others began to whisper, their voices swirling through the darkness.

"Yes, yes! So I said. More than a shade. Much more!"

"Balaam's daughter."

"The angel."

"Yet not an angel . . ."

They moved forward now, sniffing and peering at me. I held my ground and listened.

"Not an angel now. Balaam's now."

"She comes on his behalf. Her lord father's."

"It is said that she works for him."

"Balaam is clever. Balaam is wise."

Actually, Balaam is neither. He's a conniving bully who threatens and schemes and fights to get what he wants. Which explains a few things about his daughter, I guess.

I stay as far from Balaam as I can, but I do understand him. I also understand that a whole lot of demons—and angels—think I'm a double agent for him. Pisses me off—I'm many things, but I'm not a traitor. Still, the rumor can be useful.

So I just kept listening as they chattered.

"He wants the book."

"Yes, he does. He's heard of it. Someone has spoken."

"Someone will pay for his betrayal."

"But Balaam . . ."

"Yes, Balaam . . ."

Their voices came faster now, panicking and thinking as fast as their little brains could think, struggling for a way to get out of this encounter without offending a very powerful demon.

"Yes," I said finally. "I've come for the book. It's a very important one, because it has been . . ." I took a guess. "Hidden for so long."

"Yes, yes. Hidden. Lost. But we found it. Yes, we did."

"Of course you did. The oni themselves are very wise, very clever. I'm not surprised they found this lost book of . . ."

"Moses," one helpfully supplied.

"Right. The lost Book of Moses." Seriously? Moses? What the hell?

Yet it did twinge some buried memory. One about spells, which made absolutely no sense in the context of the dude who led the Israelites out of Egypt. I suppose I should know more about that—with a last name like Levine, I probably had ancestors making that trek with old Mo. But I hadn't been raised in the faith. Or any faith, really.

Still, if my brain wasn't misfiring . . .

A long-lost spell book? Hell and damn, now *those* were words to get my dead heart pumping.

I tossed the oni off my sword tip and swung the blade, blue light crackling through the dark.

"I want that book."

Silence. Then manic gibbering. Finally, one voice, as the others fell still.

"We respect Lord Balaam. We respect the daughter of Lord Balaam. But the book is ours."

I skewered the speaker and tossed him up, and he shrieked as the others scampered back again.

"Mmm, try again," I said.

"We—we are willing to speak to Balaam on this matter." The oni struggled to keep his shrill voice calm. "Negotiate. Yes, yes. We know Balaam is fair. Balaam is powerful but fair. We will negotiate and let him see the book."

I considered. I could push the matter, but there were a lot of oni here, and mass slaughter didn't seem to be the way to handle this. At least, not until I knew more.

"I'll be back," I said. "Have the book ready."

Human lore tells us that hell is guarded by a three-headed dog. Not true. It's three giant dogs—the Cerberi. But they do guard hell. Or my own personal version of it: the Great Library.

The Great Library exists only in the afterlife dimensions, the real one having been set aflame when Caesar torched the Egyptian fleets. Yes, further proof that war and historic buildings are not compatible.

I said hello to the girls—Cerberus One, Two, and Three. Boring names. Also insulting, I think. I call them Polly, Molly, and Rue. I think they like it. They also appreciate that I stop to pet them, where most hurry past, spurred on by the sight of those foot-long fangs. But the girls really are very sweet and they're good to me, letting me by even when I'm not on angel duty. As the presence of massive guard dogs may suggest, the Great Library isn't open to the afterlife public.

I passed the dogs and headed in to find Trsiel. I joke about the Great Library being my version of hell. It's more of a love/hate relationship. If I'm looking for lost spells or rituals, it's like a giant candy store where everything is free. If I've been sent here to do research, it really is a living nightmare. Chasing people with answers is more my kind of research.

I wandered through the collections. I could say I was looking for Trsiel, but really I was just waiting. Sure enough, it took about ten minutes before a gray-haired scholar spotted me and raced off to find my far more angelic partner before I got myself into trouble.

I slouched into a chair and waited. Two minutes later, a figure rounded the shelves. He looked as much like an angel as I did—just a regular guy, about thirty, dark-haired and olive-skinned, dressed in jeans and a pullover. Trsiel is the real deal, though. A full-blood. Or close enough. There are rumors of full-bloods with a shot of human DNA, to help them better understand the people they're sworn to help. Other full-bloods say that explains Trsiel's "lowbrow" tastes. I say they can go to hell. Maybe he has human blood or maybe his more human tastes started the rumors. Doesn't matter. Whatever it is, it *does* make him a better angel than most of the ineffective snobs who populate the angel dimensions.

Despite his very human appearance, there's a faint glow to Trsiel's skin that gives him away to those who know angels. And for those who don't, his cover is blown once he opens his mouth—his voice is so richly compelling that every shade in hearing distance will stop to listen.

"Eve," he said, striding to meet me. "What do you need?"

"Good to see you, too. Been a few months. How are things?"

He fixed me with a look. He knew I'd come for something, and he knew I wouldn't want to endure twenty minutes of chitchat to get to it. We'd been partners for six years. I spent about as much time with him as I did with Kristof, and we knew each other as well as most couples. It was good to see him after almost three months apart. I wouldn't say that, but he knew it.

"Lost Book of Moses," I said.

"Hmmm." He turned and peered down the hall. "Room twelve, shelf three, right beside—"

"Unless you're going to tell me the actual book is there, you can save the directions."

"If the book was there, it wouldn't be lost."

I snorted. "I bet half the lost books of the world are in here somewhere. Just mis-shelved."

"Probably. So if you start looking for that one now—"

"I'd rather fight through a legion of oni. Tell me about the book." I paused. "Please."

He waved me into an alcove with more comfortable chairs. Also, soundproof walls.

"You're talking about the Sixth and Seventh Books of Moses. Purportedly a lost text following the Five Books of Moses, also known as the Pentateuch—the first five books in the Hebrew bible. As often happens with sacred texts, a rumor started that parts were removed because they contained so-called dangerous knowledge."

"Like spells."

He nodded. "The Sixth and Seventh Books are believed to be a grimoire, containing incantations to replicate the miracles in the bible."

"Seriously?"

He made a face. "Depends on your definition of serious. Yes, the book is supposed to exist. Yes, it contains spells that roughly duplicate some of the miracles. Was it actually part of the Books of Moses? Probably not. It just makes a good story, one that has influenced several religious movements. Spiritualism, hoodooism, Rastafarianism . . ."

"Influenced by a *lost* book? How does that work?"

"The original text is lost, but there have been copies for several centuries. Of course, the problem with reproduced grimoires . . ."

"Is that someone always screws up—a typo, a bad translation—and the spells don't work."

"Exactly."

"Well, I may have found the originals. Through a secret passage in the British Museum, guarded by oni."

A *Huh?* passed over his face, then a blink of comprehension, quickly doused, as he got comfortable again, saying as casually as he could manage, "And what led you there?"

"A job for Kristof. I was tracking a shaman who is apparently up to no good. Something to do with a Fury and these texts. I have no idea how the two connect, but I'll figure it out."

"Sounds like a challenge."

"It is."

A flicker of a smile. "Good."

I pulled my legs up, pretending to get comfortable myself as I studied his face.

What are you up to, Trsiel?

My angelic partner is not well versed in the art of deception. It might seem that's just part of the angel package, but I've met full-bloods who rival arch-demons for duplicity. Trsiel is just good by nature. That's why the Fates paired him with me, hoping he'd rub off. Any transfer, much to their chagrin, has gone in the other direction.

Trsiel is genuinely good, not sanctimoniously or self-righteously good. That means he's willing to accept the need to get his hands dirty in the pursuit of justice. Under my tutelage, he's become an adequate liar, but he'll never be good enough to fool me. Even when he's merely "up to something," he tips his hand. Today he was waving it wildly.

"So," I said. "Should I bother trying to trick these oni into giving me the book? Or should I just tell them the game's up and Kristof wants it back?"

"Wh-what?"

"Oh, wait. No. If this is a setup, there is no book." I sighed. "Damn. It would have been better with a book." A pause, during which Trsiel couldn't seem to get a word out. I looked at him. "Or did Kris actually find the book? Because that would be kind of awesome."

Trsiel's mouth worked. He leaned forward. "I don't know what . . ." One look in my eyes and he slumped. "Shit."

"Uh-huh."

"It's not his fault. It was my idea."

"Right."

"No, it was. I went to see him a few days ago. I needed advice on a complex demon contract, and he's the expert. We were talking about you—his case running into overtime, you getting bored—and I suggested he give you a mission. A mystery to solve."

I stared at him. "*You* suggested he send me on a wild-goose chase? Lie about a mission?"

"It's not a wild-goose chase. It's practice. A challenge, like you said. He balked at first, but I said it was like other guys giving their wives a weekend in a spa. You're just a little different from most wives. But it was my idea, so if you're angry, blame me."

Was I angry? I felt as if I should be, but Trsiel was right. I'd had fun. I'd been challenged. For me, this *was* the equivalent of a week-end at the spa. A break from the everyday to calm my restlessness.

A mental puzzle with a physical chase. And it was, admittedly, a good puzzle.

"So there is no book?" I said.

"I don't know. Being Kristof . . ." He shrugged. "I suspect there is a prize at the end. He wouldn't get your hopes up like that. It might be a spell or a magical whatnot. I'm just trying to figure out how he got the oni involved."

"He helped some of them out of a bad contract last year. They owe him." I got to my feet. "So, presuming the oni really do have a prize for me, let's go get it."

"Me? No, I'm supposed to be doing research—"

"Which you hate almost as much as I do. You just don't complain. But I've gotten myself into a potentially dangerous situation, trying to rescue potentially sacred texts from oni. You're honor bound to help me. So come on."

Before we left, Trsiel had to go put away his books. God forbid he should leave a mess. Then I took him back to the museum. It wasn't hard for him to mingle among mortal shades. He just needs to employ a bit of voice modulation, so he only sounds like a guy who should be doing radio. As for the faint glow, ghosts don't notice that. Even in the supernatural realms, angels are such mysterious entities that most people expect them to come with halos and harps.

I took Trsiel through the first two dimensional pockets, then I went ahead through the smaller ones. This time, I avoided the fall into the final room, dropping instead. When I hit the ground, I conjured my sword as the oni skittered and whispered all around me.

"I've come for the book," I said.

"No, no," one said. "You must bring Balaam."

"Balaam would not come," another replied. "He is a lord."

"Yes, his daughter comes in Balaam's stead. She bears his words. She—"

"Enough," I said. "The gig is up, guys, but it's not your fault. I'll tell Kristof you did great. Slate wiped clean. Now hand over—"

One of the oni screamed. Another joined in and they began scrabbling about like kernels in a defective hot-air popper.

"Sorry I'm late," Trsiel said behind me.

I turned. "You really know how to make an entrance, don't you?"

I whistled, trying to be heard over the shrieking. Forget the popcorn analogy. It was more like a tenth-grade booze-fest when the cops show up.

I whistled again. "Hey! Knock it off! He's with me!"

"You have tricked us," one oni hissed as the noise level dropped. "Yes, tricked us. You brought an angel. A true angel."

"Yeah, yeah. Did I mention the game's over? I caught on. Now, just give me—"

"We give you nothing."

"Fine," I said. "How did Kristof want this to play out? Was I supposed to sneak back here? Trick you? Fight you?"

"We do not know this Kristof." An oni walked out. He was taller than his brethren, with wild orange hair. "You will leave now, witch. Take your angel and leave. Out of respect for your sire, we will allow you to leave—"

"Allow?" I waved my sword. "I'll leave when I want to. And I'm not leaving without the damned—"

Trsiel nudged me to silence and stepped forward, his own sword conjured but lowered. Respectful. When he spoke, it was with the full-on vocal treatment. "You say you do not know Kristof Nast?"

"Nast?" The oni's ugly face crinkled. "I know that name. It is a Cabal. But this Kristof . . .?"

"He is hers." Another oni pointed a bony finger at me. "I have heard of him. He helped oni."

"But the oni he helped weren't you," Trsiel said. "He didn't ask you to play a game with Eve, did he?"

More face scrunching from the leader. "The oni do not play games."

"Sure they do," I said. "Hide-and-seek. And now you're hiding—"

Another wave from Trsiel. He continued questioning them, and it didn't take long to realize that they weren't just trying to prolong the game. A full-blood angel's voice truly is compelling—it makes you want to listen and to obey. For demons, it's like a truth serum. These oni weren't part of Kristof's scheme. Stranz really had just stumbled into the dimensional pocket by accident, probably as he'd been heading for that Private door, adding a little spice to the chase.

But if Kristof didn't set this up, then the oni really were guarding the Sixth and Seventh Books of Moses.

"Fine," I said when Trsiel stopped. "It's a misunderstanding. But we are going to need that book. So just hand it over and we'll go. We won't tell anyone you took it."

The oni laughed now, cackling and yipping.

"We took nothing," the leader said. "We found it." He pulled himself up tall. "And so we keep it."

"I'm afraid not," Trsiel said. "The Sixth and Seventh Books of Moses are believed to be lost scriptures. As such, they would belong to the Almighty. As an agent of the Almighty, I need to ask you to relinquish them."

Trsiel had said he didn't believe they were real sacred texts, so he worded it carefully, to avoid lying. The oni didn't care. They began gnashing their teeth and moving closer, claws raised, fangs bared. Trsiel subtly motioned behind them—into the dark recesses of whatever dimensional pocket we were in. Presumably the book lay on the other side.

We could hack our way through the oni, but that wouldn't be fair. They had every right to guard what they'd found, and wholesale slaughter would land us in deep shit with the Fates. Contrary to popular belief, the war between the celestial and the demonic isn't an endless bloody battle. It's more like a cold war. Has been for eons. An uneasy stalemate, reinforced by endless treaties, including the kind that say two angels can't massacre oni to get a book, even a sacred one.

We waited, swords drawn, until they charged. Then we sliced through the first couple—self-defense—and barreled into the darkness. Realizing our goal, the oni leapt in from all sides. I swung behind Trsiel, covering his back as he pushed through the seething mass of imps. Tiny teeth dug into my arms and legs, and hands pummeled me. I shoved them off when I could and cut a swath with the glowing blue blade when I had to. The blade worked better. They saw it and dove out of the way.

We kept going, the blackness so complete now that our swords didn't do more than illuminate their own metal, blue light sabers cutting through blackness. Then . . .

"Shit!" Trsiel said. "Watch . . . !"

His voice trailed off. Falling. I hit the edge of the floor and teetered for a second. Then two oni jumped me and over I went.

It wasn't a long drop. It helped that I landed on Trsiel. Above, we could hear the oni chittering and giggling.

"Trapped!" one chortled. "Yes, the angels are trapped."

"Oni didn't do it," another said. "They trapped themselves."

"Yes, trapped themselves."

"Yeah, yeah," I muttered, pushing off Trsiel. I lit a light ball and waved it around.

"Huh, not much of a trap," I said.

We were at one end of a tunnel that—like the room above—stretched into darkness. A long black tunnel, presumably with the book at the end.

"Find the book and teleport out," I murmured. I turned to Trsiel. "It's not an empty dimension, is it?"

We can't teleport out of empty dimensions. They're off the grid. I had to ask the question again, though. He was looking around, hand tight on his sword.

"No," he said finally. "It's not empty."

I didn't like his tone. "Is something here?"

"I'm . . . not sure."

"Well, hopefully it won't mind us taking the book."

I swung the light ball in front of us, to illuminate the way, then I started down the corridor. Trsiel followed, walking backward, covering me now. I didn't see the need for it. We were in a narrow corridor with nothing in sight. Just—

A growl reverberated through the hall. Trsiel swung in beside me, sword raised.

"It didn't come from down there," I said. "Or behind us. It seemed to come from . . ." I turned to the wall. Then I leaned over and cleared a peephole. "Nothing. Black—"

The wall crumbled. Just crumbled. So did the ceiling. And the wall behind us. We were left standing in darkness. Endless black on every side. I threw my light ball, but all I could see was the glowing sphere itself, going and going and going until it disappeared.

The growl came again. Then the flapping of wings. Leathery, bat-like wings, beating currents of hot air all around us.

"That sounds like . . ."

"Yes. That's what it sounds like."

"But it can't be. Hell-beasts are only found in—"

An ear-shattering shriek as the creature dove at my head. I ducked and swung my sword. It made contact, fluorescent green blood spraying my face. The blood burned as it struck my skin, and I let out a yelp, so shocked at the sensation. Ghosts don't feel pain. Angels don't, either. Not unless they're in . . .

"Hell dimension!" I shouted.

"Which explains the hell-beast." Trsiel grabbed my arm and

yanked me as he stumbled backward over the uneven ground. "Hide your sword."

I unconjured it and cast a privacy spell so we could speak without our voices being heard. "It can't be a hell dimension. We didn't step through a hell-gate."

"No, we *fell* through one. I thought I felt it, but it happened too fast."

"Shit!"

"Exactly," he muttered.

We'd been in hell dimensions before. Very, very rarely, and only when we absolutely couldn't avoid it. We got in and we got out fast, before anything found us.

"Hold on," I said. "I'll cast . . . Shit!"

Hell dimensions also negated teleport spells. Meaning we were trapped here, in the dark, with a hell-beast. A very pissed-off, injured hell-beast.

"Just stay still," Trsiel murmured.

Right. Like sharks, hell-beasts sensed movement, in this case in air rather than water. We stayed still and listened to the flap of its wings as it circled the cavern. Trsiel had found us a spot behind what felt like stalagmites, cold and wet stones soaring up all around us.

The hell-beast swung past a couple of times. I tried to gauge its size, but all I had to go on was the sound of those wings, which really didn't help at all.

"The exit," Trsiel whispered. "We need to find the exit."

I paused. "Right."

"We can't look for that book, Eve. Not here. Not now."

"I know."

"We'll get to the exit, climb out, and teleport from the top, before the oni attack."

"Good plan."

It *was* good. I just would have preferred if it had included finding the book. But Trsiel was right—we couldn't see anything, meaning there was no way to find the book, not while that hell-beast guarded it.

"Maybe if we kill it . . ." I began.

As if in answer, we heard claws scrabbling to our left. Then more to our right.

"Oni?" I whispered.

"I don't think so."

"Damn." Oni were a threat I could handle.

The claws clicked closer on both sides.

"Any idea where we'd find the exit?" I whispered.

Trsiel paused. Presumably it was back the way we'd come. Since there was no longer a corridor, though . . . Also, the exit was a hole in the ceiling, which wouldn't make things easy.

"I can guess the general direction," he said.

Something leapt at me, something small and furry, teeth digging into my arm. Pain ripped through it. I conjured my sword and caught a glimpse of a mole-like snout as I threw the beast off and brandished my sword, Trsiel doing the same.

We'd been down here long enough for our eyes to adjust, and I could make out a little beyond the glow of our swords. We were surrounded by what looked like a dozen moles, each the size of a fox, blind things, with no obvious eyes but lots of sharp teeth and equally sharp claws. I had no idea what they were—there was no afterlife Darwin willing to brave the hell dimensions and name all the inhabitants.

They were dangerous. They were guarding the book. They'd shred us with those teeth if they got the chance. That was all we needed to know.

Another one leapt at me. Before I could swing my blade, Trsiel had sliced the creature in two, both halves falling, twitching, to the rocky floor. Two more shrieked as if in shared pain. They jumped.

I skewered one. Trsiel lopped the head off the other. Then we heard the beating of massive wings as hot air swirled around us.

"Incoming!" I yelled.

"Run!"

"Where?"

Trsiel gave me a shove. Another mole-fox sprang. I swung, but it was too close to hit. Its teeth sank into my arm. Trsiel yanked it off and threw it aside.

As we started to run, I heard the beat of the hell-beast's wings. Then silence. I knew what that silence meant, and wheeled just in time to see a massive scaled creature diving at Trsiel. I yelled. He dove to the side, but the beast only changed course, talons outstretched. I ran, swinging my sword at those huge talons. The beast yanked them up just in time, and I staggered, spinning with the force of my empty swing.

Trsiel shouted. Something grabbed my sword arm, wrapping around it. Talons caught my shoulder, digging in like daggers, making me gasp, pain blinding me. The ground disappeared under my feet. I looked up to see scales and feathers.

I cast a binding spell, but the beast just kept winging its way up. Then it stopped, and I thought it was just a delayed reaction to the spell—was shocked that it had actually worked. Then the hell-beast screamed. I let out a yelp, too, as acid blood rained down. I heard Trsiel shout something from below, but I didn't catch it, just focused on launching a fireball. As I threw it up against the hell-beast's underbelly, I saw Trsiel's sword there, embedded nearly to the hilt. Then the sword vanished as he unconjured it. I threw a fireball straight at the gaping wound. The beast let out an unearthly howl and dropped me.

I hit the hard ground. Which hurt. Trsiel yanked me to my feet as the hell-beast swooped. I saw its head this time—a massive furred skull with giant fangs. Trsiel yanked his sword arm back and I was going to tell him it wouldn't do any good—the beast was still too high to reach. But he didn't swing the blade. He threw it, like a javelin, straight up at the beast's throat. It pierced it, and I covered my head as acid blood spattered us.

"Nice trick," I said. "You've got to teach me that one."

A growl came from deep in the cavern, like the one we'd heard before. Not the hell-beast, then, and too loud to be the mole-foxes.

Above our heads, the hell-beast let out a gurgling shriek. It wasn't dead, obviously. Maybe not even mortally wounded.

"Let's go!" Trsiel said, hand on my elbow.

We ran. We could hear the hell-beast's wings flapping as it retreated. Surrendering? Or simply pulling back for another attack?

We continued through the darkness, our swords and a light ball illuminating the way. Then I saw a faint glow across the cavern. I blinked, kicking in my extra vision. It helped just enough for me to see what looked like a box, with a glow shimmering through the cracks.

"The book," I whispered as I skidded to a stop.

"No," Trsiel said. "We can't—"

The hell-beast shrieked deep in the cavern, followed by a growl to our left. Something was stalking us, not willing to attack unless we tried for the prize it was guarding.

I tried to judge the creature's size from its growl. I also tried to judge how injured the hell-beast was. The book was only a couple of hundred feet away. If I could just—

If I went after it, Trsiel would follow. I could tell him to continue on, find the exit, forget about me, and there wasn't a chance in hell he'd actually do it, no more than I would if the situation were reversed. We were partners. If I took a risk, I took it for both of us.

I yanked my gaze away from the box. "Okay," I said, and let him continue leading me.

*

As we jogged, there were a couple of times when I swore I heard something moving in the cavern. I tried not to dwell on it—there were probably lots of things in this cavern, all of them ready to make a meal of us. By the time we reached the wall, I could hear only the growling creature, but it stayed too far away to be seen.

We felt along the walls for an exit. I cast my light ball up, searching the ceiling, but even if I found a hole, we'd never get to it. The growling came closer now, and I could make out a huge dark form slinking toward us. Then I caught the scrabble of claws on rock. Lots of claws. The mole-foxes, with reinforcements.

We frantically searched for an exit, casting teleport spells with every step, praying for a weak spot. A snarl sounded behind us, and I turned to see white fangs, as big as my forearm, flashing in the darkness.

"Here!" a voice called. "Over here!"

A light ball sparked thirty feet away, illuminating Kristof's face. He gestured wildly, and we ran toward him. As we drew close, the wall shimmered. The exit—not a hole but a portal. He pushed us through. We tumbled again, falling into a heap in the darkness.

"They return," a voice hissed.

"How do they return?"

"They have. No!"

The oni started to shriek. Claws scraped at me. Then Kristof murmured, "Hold on," and he teleported us out.

We landed on our asses in the middle of a jungle, surrounded by ferns the size of trees. Overhead, a tiny prehistoric primate peered down at us, then raced off, chattering.

Kristof looked around, frowning. "Not quite what I was aiming for."

I laughed and threw my hands around his neck. "It never is."

As I hugged him, I felt something like a breastplate under his suit jacket. When I backed up to take a look, he flipped open a button and pulled out a faintly glowing book.

"I believe you wanted this," he said.

I stared down at it. "How . . .?"

He pushed the book into my hands. "Consider it my apology, for a somewhat misguided attempt to cure your boredom."

"Oh, you cured it all right."

I took the book and flipped through it. It was indeed a grimoire, filled with spells I'd never seen before. I turned to Trsiel.

"Is this . . .?"

"Seems to be." He looked at Kristof. "Thank you for the rescue."

"But how?" I said, waving the book.

"Trsiel came to warn me that you'd uncovered my plot and might be annoyed with me."

"When?" I answered my own question. "Ah, while you were 'cleaning up' your books."

Trsiel nodded.

Kristof continued. "I was in session, so he left a message. When I got it, I realized that, in following my fake adventure, you'd stumbled into a real one. So I went after you."

I didn't ask how he'd found us. Ask Kris to teleport us to the beach and we'd invariably end up in the desert. His sense of direction is hopeless . . . with one exception. Ask him to find me, and he can do it with the precision of a bloodhound.

"I arrived as you were fighting the hell-beast. You conquered it before I could be of any assistance, so while every creature in that place was tracking you two, I found the book."

"And they didn't notice you stealing it?"

A lift of his brows. "Of course not. I was careful. And I replaced it with a spell that emitted a similar light long enough for us to escape." He paused. "So, am I forgiven?"

"You brought me a secret spell book," I said. "You are absolutely forgiven."

Trsiel cleared his throat. "That grimoire . . ."

I sighed. "It may be a sacred text, which you must return to the Fates."

"No, I think you can," he said. "I have research to do. Just make sure you return it in a reasonably timely fashion."

I grinned. "Thank you."

We said our goodbyes, and Trsiel teleported back to the Great Library. I looked around. In the distance, something roared. Something very large.

"Where are we, anyway?" I asked.

"I have no idea. But it does seem interesting."

He pulled back a frond. The little simian from earlier was there, spying on us. Seeing Kristof, it raced off again.

"While I'm very tempted to explore," he said, "you do have that book on a limited loan."

"Mmm . . ." I looked around. "I think we can do both. A little exploring. A little spell-casting." I paused. "Unless you need to get back to court."

"I wrangled a twenty-four-hour recess to pursue something very important." He gestured to the jungle and then at the book. "Those look important." He leaned over to kiss me. "That could be important, too."

"All right, then. Twenty-four hours alone together, in a prehistoric jungle, with a secret spell book. I do believe my boredom has officially been cured."

"Good. So where shall we begin?"

The creature roared again.

"I want to know what that is," I said.

He smiled. "Of course," he said, and off we went.

THE PUPPY PLAN

Curiosity may have killed the cat, but it causes serious problems for werewolves, too. Logan had been wandering the forest behind Stonehaven, goofing off, tramping through the newly fallen snow. At nine, he was a little old for playing like that. Or he considered himself too old for it. But his twin sister, Kate, had gone into the city with their parents to buy Christmas gifts, which meant there was no one to see him. And it *was* new snow. So he wandered about, breaking fresh paths, startling mice, and maybe even scooping up a few, like he and Kate used to do when they were kids. Little kids, that is.

As he neared the edge of the property, he noticed the sun just starting to drop over the open road. Time to head back. He was supposed to be in before dark, and while there was at least an hour left, he hated even skirting the edges of irresponsibility.

It was then, as he turned, that he caught the scent. He stopped in his tracks, lifted his nose, and inhaled.

It smelled like a dog, which was weird. With the Pack roaming these woods, other canines steered clear. Once, he and Kate had spotted a fox ambling across the road, and when it caught their scent, it practically went into spasms before it tore back to its own side.

This definitely smelled like dog, though. That made Logan curious. Okay, *most* things made Logan curious. He liked learning and discovering. He also liked testing boundaries, though not in the same way his sister did. Kate pushed the ones that would get her into trouble. With Logan, boundaries were about knowledge and exploration. Lately, he'd been testing how close he could get to domestic animals before he startled them.

He walked toward the scent, but it remained faint. Then it was gone. He looked around. He saw the road, and trees and snow. *Lots* of snow. When he backed up, the smell wafted by on the breeze.

Had a dog passed this way earlier, its tracks now covered in snow?

No. His gut told him that whatever caused this smell was still here, and he paused, analyzing that. Gut feelings were for Kate; Logan preferred fact. He decided that it was the strength of the scent. As faint as it was, it was more than the detritus shed by a passing dog.

That still didn't answer the question of where the dog could possibly be, when all he saw was snow. The forest started ten feet back from the road, the edge too sparse to hide anything bigger than a rabbit.

Maybe the dog *wasn't* bigger than a rabbit. Like the one they saw when Uncle Nick took them to visit Vanessa, and they'd been out walking on a busy street and passed a woman with a tiny dog in her purse. The dog had smelled werewolf, freaked, escaped, and ran into traffic, followed by Kate, who'd nearly gotten hit catching it. Uncle Nick had decided it was a story their parents really didn't need to hear. Logan agreed. He'd also pointed out to Kate that, while rescuing the dog had been a fine impulse, she'd nearly given the tiny beast a heart attack when she scooped it up, which would have rather undone the point of saving it.

It could be a small dog, then, cowering behind a tree, waiting for Logan to pass. Which meant he should just move along. Except that, well . . . curiosity. He had to see if his theory was correct.

As he started through the ditch, snow billowed over the top of his boots. He should have worn snow pants, but this winter he'd declared he was too old for them. The price for maturity, apparently, was wet jeans and snow sliding down the insides of his boots.

His foot hit something. A rock or a root. When he went around it, the smell faded. That's when he decided curiosity wasn't always such a good thing.

He had a good idea what he'd just kicked in the snow. A dog. Or the body of one that had been struck by a car and made it into the ditch before dying. He scowled at the thought. Sometimes you can't avoid hitting an animal on the road, and it isn't safe to try, however much Kate would protest otherwise. But if you did hit a dog, you should at least stop. Help it if you can, and find the owner if it's too late.

He didn't need to see a dead dog. But when the snow melted, Kate would see it, and that would upset her. A lot. She'd been trying for the past year to convince their parents to let them get a puppy. Reese had dogs growing up, and he said, if you raised them from pups, they were fine with the werewolf smell. But werewolves and pets were two things that didn't normally go together, and with Malcolm being back, this was one time when their normally indulgent parents held fast. Maybe in a year or so, they'd said. Not now.

Logan would move the dog deep into the woods on the other side of the road. It wasn't something he *wanted* to do—at all—but it was something he should and could do for Kate.

He peered up into the sky. The sun had not miraculously stopped dropping. He still had plenty of time, but he ought to leave this task until morning, when he could bring a bag. First he'd check and see how big a one he needed, and if he should bring the toboggan, too.

He returned to the spot where he'd kicked the poor thing, and he bent to scoop out snow. Soon he saw a bag. A canvas one, like the kind potatoes came in. Which meant this wasn't a dog hit by a car. As for what it was . . .

Let me be wrong. Please let me be wrong.

He undid the tie at the top and opened it to see . . .

Logan's stomach clenched so hard he doubled over. Tears prickled as he squeezed his eyes shut, but the image stayed emblazoned there. Two puppies, one on top of the other, the top one's eyes open, pink tongue sticking out between its tiny teeth.

Logan dropped the bag and scrambled to the road and started pacing, heaving deep breaths, trying to get himself under control. Get his *temper* under control. Everyone said Kate was the one with the temper. Not completely true. His didn't come out nearly as often as hers, but when it did, it was like a fire in his head and his stomach, burning through everything.

How could people do this? No, really, *how*? If they couldn't keep the puppies, they could damned well find someone who could or leave them at the goddamned shelter, because this, *this* was unforgivable. Someone should put *them* in a bag. Toss them by the roadside like garbage. That's what he'd like to do if he found them, and he didn't care if it was wrong. It was fair.

He paced until he stopped raging. And stopped cursing. Then he rubbed his hands over his face, took a deep breath, and . . .

Harsh bass boomed from his pocket, making him jump. The opening chords of Bikini Kill's "Rebel Girl." Kate's ring tone. She set up everyone's ring tones, an idea she got from Savannah, though his sister's taste in music was somewhat more eclectic.

Logan answered quickly.

"I thought you were staying in the city for dinner," he blurted.

"Dad and I got tired of being out. Mom did, too. She just wouldn't admit it."

He turned his back on the bag.

"You okay?" she asked.

"Sure. Just out walking."

There was a pause, Kate trying to emotion-read him through the phone. That was not, he was aware, the technical term for what she did. There probably wasn't a technical term, because her ability to interpret mood and emotion bordered on the preternatural. But after a moment she gave up and said, "I'll join you."

"It's getting dark."

"Which is fine as long as we are together and have our phones. I know the rules, Lo. I even kinda follow them. Oh, and I'll bring your hot chocolate. We picked it up in town. The good stuff from the new coffee place. I'll have to reheat it and put it into a thermos. There was whipped cream, but it melted. I could say I ate it, but that would be gross."

"Uh-huh . . ."

"Does it help if I say I used a spoon?"

"Did you?"

"Where are you? I'll be there in ten."

Logan started to tell her. Then he spun back toward the bag. "No! I'll . . . I'll come there. I was just heading in."

"Then you can go out again. With me."

"My jeans are wet."

"Because you won't wear snow pants." She sighed. "For such a smart kid, you can do some really dumb things, Lo."

"Because I'm still a kid. It's allowed. Give me ten and I'll be there."

"Fine. But if I drink your hot chocolate, it's your own fault."

"How would it be—? Never mind. Ten minutes."

He set the timer on his phone, knowing if he wasn't within sight of the house by the time it went off, his sister would come looking for him. Patience was not one of her virtues. He was still fussing with his phone when he bent distractedly over the bag and caught the smell and stopped short at the reminder of exactly what he was doing.

He couldn't think about it. Just couldn't. Sometimes doing the right thing meant doing stuff you really didn't want to. He might have a bad dream or two after this, but finding the dead puppies would give Kate screaming nightmares, wondering if they'd been alive when—

Nope, he wasn't thinking about that. Wasn't.

He picked up the bag . . . and it seemed to move. Which he was clearly imagining, because he'd just been thinking about the puppies being alive.

So he was going to presume they were dead without checking? *That* would give him nightmares. He steeled himself and peered inside, recoiling as he saw the puppy with its eyes open. There was no doubt it was dead. No doubt at all.

The one underneath it had its eyes shut, but its lip was curled back as if in a final snarl of defiance. He saw that, and he wanted to cry. Not rage and curse, but cry, because, when he looked at that puppy, he felt what it must have.

He'd planned to leave them in the bag, but now that seemed as wrong as if he'd put them there himself. He reached in and took out the body of the first puppy, cold and stiff. Then the other . . .

The other was not cold and stiff.

Logan nearly dropped the first puppy in his rush to get the second one out. He scooped it up with both hands.

It was warm. Warm and pliant, its head lolling. He put one hand under its muzzle to support it while he pushed his fingers deep into the thick fur around its heart, searching for a beat.

The puppy lay on his hands, a deadweight.

Deadweight.

He blinked back tears. Tears of frustration and disappointment now, and maybe a little of anger, as if he'd been tricked, some cruel joke making him think that the puppy lived.

No, the joke was worse than that. The puppy was still warm, meaning that maybe, if he'd gotten to it faster . . .

He swallowed and wrapped his hands around the puppy.

"I'm sorry," he whispered. "If I wasn't fast enough, I'm sorry."

The puppy whimpered.

Logan froze. His heart pounded, and he was sure that the whine was just an echo of his own voice. His fingers dug into that thick fur again, checking in case, just maybe . . .

There was a heartbeat.

A faint heartbeat.

Logan sat down fast, put the puppy on his lap, and examined it for injuries. No obvious broken bones. No soft spots on its small skull. As he looked down at the puppy, he swore he heard his sister's voice in his ear.

It's cold, you dope. It's been lying in the snow. Stop playing doctor and start playing nurse.

Right. Yes. Of course. Hypothermia. He unzipped his coat fast and put the puppy inside. Before he could zip it back up, he took the puppy out again and put it under his shirt, too, right against him. Then, being careful to leave the zipper undone enough so the dog wouldn't smother, he wrapped his arms around it and started to run.

Get to the house. Get Jeremy's help. He was the Pack medic. He'd know what to do. As for what he'd do about Logan bringing a puppy home? They'd deal with that later.

He was under no illusion that his parents would say, "You found a puppy? All right, then, you can keep it." And when they *didn't* say that, when Kate had a puppy in the house only to see it sent to the shelter? When she blamed their parents? Let's just say it wasn't going to be a very merry Christmas.

But he couldn't think about that. The important thing was the puppy. Maybe he could convince Mom and Dad to set a timeline for Kate. To tell her, "Not this puppy, but another. In a year."

He was halfway to the house when the puppy woke up. Fast. Like he'd dropped it into a frozen pond. All four tiny limbs shot out and sixteen tiny—and remarkably sharp—claws ripped at his chest.

"Whoa!" Logan said as he skidded to a halt, snow flying. "Hold on!" With one hand, he rubbed the puppy, trying to calm it—and keep from being totally shredded—as he got his coat open and pulled it out.

Once free, the puppy froze, motionless, as if trapped in the jaws of some massive predator. Logan tried to pet it, but it started trembling, like a rabbit under a wolf's paw. Logan's own heart pounded along with the puppy's. What if he did exactly what he'd warned Kate about with that purse dog? If he rescued it, only to give it a heart attack from his scent?

"It's okay," he said. "Everything's okay."

He kept his voice low and soothing, but the puppy whimpered, as if his talking only made things worse. It twisted in his arms, wriggling and struggling. He couldn't let it go—it wasn't old enough to survive out here—but if he scared it to death . . .

He growled with frustration. The puppy stopped wiggling. It went still. Then, slowly, it looked up at him, confused. He growled again, and it tilted its head but stayed motionless, watching him. Its nostrils flared as it sorted out his scents—canine and human—and he wondered if it *wasn't* the canine one that had made it freak out.

He growled, keeping the noise low, the kind of reassuring growl a parent might give. The puppy gave a yip of joy and started wriggling madly, in excitement now, small tongue bathing his face.

"Okay, okay," he said. "We're good. Now just . . . Can you—" The tongue slid into his mouth. "Ugh. No, stop—" He held the puppy at arm's length. When it stopped, he settled it, firmly, in his arms. "You're obviously fine. Which is great. But . . ."

But it was also a problem, because as much as he'd tried to remain sensible and mature about the whole thing, a part of him had still been shouting, *I found a puppy!* The part that hoped maybe, if he brought home an injured and abandoned dog, and it had to stay with them to recover, their parents would see it wasn't a big deal and let them keep it. Now, though, he had a perfectly healthy abandoned dog, which would be easy to just whisk off to the shelter. That was, he had to admit, not what he wanted. Not at all.

He looked down at the puppy. It was black and white with medium-length fur. Border collie was the breed that sprang to mind. Border collie mingled with something else, because it was already an armful, meaning there was a larger dog mixed in there. German shepherd, maybe?

Kate had researched the various breeds, trying to find the right one. He'd helped, allegedly just because he enjoyed research but admittedly because, well, because he wanted to dream a little, too. Border collies and other shepherds were at the top of their list. Intelligent and loyal working dogs. German shepherds appealed more to Logan, but Kate had her heart set on a border collie or Australian shepherd, like Reese used to have. Something loyal and intelligent but also cuddly.

Logan looked down at the ball of fur in his arms. This was her dog. There was no other answer. He'd found exactly the perfect dog for her, three days before Christmas. That meant *something*. It had to.

His sister was supposed to have this dog.

His phone jangled, the alarm sounding.

Shit! Er, crap.

He hit speed-dial as fast as he could, juggling the phone with the puppy. It rang. Rang again.

Come on, Mom. You haven't put your phone in a drawer yet. I'm out in the forest, which means you'll keep it in your pocket—

"Hey," came the answer.

He exhaled. "Mom. Good. You're there."

"Not sure where else I'd be, but, yep, I'm here. Your sister's on her way out to find—"

"No!"

"Hmm?"

"That's what I'm calling about. Can you stop her? Keep her there? Distract her or something?"

The puppy wriggled, and he adjusted his grip on it.

"Is everything okay?" Mom asked. "You sound—"

"I'm feeling a little off. Restless."

"Is it your Change? It's only been a week."

"No, no. Just restless, like Kate gets. Anyway, it's nice and quiet out here and . . ."

Mom chuckled. "And your sister will shatter that silence?"

"I just need time by myself to walk it off. I'll be in before it's totally dark. I promise."

"I know you will. And you are, as always, entitled to time on your own. I'll keep your sister at bay."

"Thanks, Mom."

He hung up. That should do the trick. Even for twins, Logan and his sister were close. Best friends who understood each other in a way no human playmate ever could. But Mom worried that they might need time to themselves now and again, especially as they got older. She'd keep Kate away. Now he had to figure out what to do.

Three days until Christmas. Three days to figure out how to tell his parents that he planned to give his sister a puppy.

His stomach twisted at the thought, because it felt disloyal and a little underhanded. No, a *lot* underhanded. They weren't saying "No pets" without good reason. If he said he wanted to give this puppy to Kate, it would kill them to refuse.

What he needed was a defense. Not an impassioned plea, but a reasonable argument. Which meant he had three days to come up with a way to convince his parents, while not making them feel they'd been tricked into agreeing . . . or like they were monsters if they refused.

What to do with the puppy until then . . .

The playhouse.

He and Kate had a fort in the forest. Uncle Nick, Reese, and Noah had built it for them a couple of years ago. Or they'd tried. When it failed to actually stand upright, they'd recruited Morgan, who had more experience with construction. The result was a perfect shelter from the elements. Also, the perfect place to hide a puppy.

Putting the puppy in the fort was a fine idea . . . except that it required the cooperation of the other party, and the puppy was having none of it. After trying several times to leave the dog—only to have it start howling—Logan decided the answer was the same one his parents had used when *their* "puppies" wouldn't go to sleep.

He brought the dog into the snow and played with it, keeping an eye on the sun as it dropped below the trees, and while he told himself he was just trying to wear the puppy out, he was a little disappointed when it did finally collapse, exhausted. He scooped it up and took it into the fort, where he'd made a nest with his hoodie, and the puppy fell into snoring slumber.

"I'll bring you food later," he whispered as he filled an old Frisbee with snow and mashed it for drinking water.

Bringing food would mean sneaking out at night, and he hated that, but if the alternative was letting a puppy starve, it really was no question at all. The rules had to be broken. Just this once.

Next, he had a much less pleasant task: burying the dead puppy. He did that quickly, burying both the bag and the puppy deep in the snow across the road. The sun had almost set. He started jogging back to the house, deep in thought, until the smell of deer made him pause, instinctively lifting his face to inhale the scent.

Scent.

Oh, no.

He stank of dog.

He looked up. Pine needles? Would that smell be strong enough? Maybe if he rubbed them on his clothes and then made a beeline for the shower. But how would he explain to Mom and Dad that he really needed to wash his clothing? By himself?

Well, I have to learn sometime, right?

Dad might let it pass, but Mom had a keenly tuned sense for when something wasn't quite right with her kids, and she'd sniff out answers like a hound on a trail.

What he needed was a dead animal. Gross, yes, but it would cover up the dog scent. When he sniffed the air, though, he picked up a smell that would do that job even better. Except . . .

He ran to the source of the scent, looked down, and shuddered.

Kate had really better appreciate this Christmas gift.

"Oh my God," Kate said as Logan walked in the door. Her hand flew over her nose. "What the hell happened to you?"

"Kate!" Mom called. "Language."

"You said there's a time for cursing," Kate yelled back. "I think this is it. Logan's covered in deer poop."

Mom sighed, probably just relieved Kate had said "poop." Then she rounded the corner and stopped short, her hand flying up to her nose in a matching pose. "Oh my God, Logan."

"Language, Mom," Kate said.

Logan lifted his hand. "Don't come any closer."

"Don't worry," Kate said. "We're not. What happened?"

"Ice."

Kate's lips twitched. Then she burst out laughing. Mom tried, somewhat unsuccessfully, to stifle hers, snorting half-choked laughs.

"Thanks, Mom," Logan said.

"Sorry, baby. It's just . . ." She struggled to swallow more laughter.

Dad's footsteps thudded down the stairs. He poked his head

into the mudroom. "What's . . ." His nostrils flared, and then he drawled, "Well, that's unfortunate. Ice?"

Logan nodded. He turned and pulled off his boots.

"On your back, too?" Mom said. "How'd you manage that?"

"Ice. It's slippery. Very slippery if it's covered in snow."

"So you fell on your face in deer poop," Kate said, "got up, and fell in backward?"

"My face is fine."

"Uh, no, actually there's a little . . . Eww. Sorry, Lo. You really stink. I'll go watch Jeremy make dinner."

"You could help Jeremy," Mom called after her as she left.

Kate laughed and kept going. Dad followed. Mom turned to Logan.

"Okay, baby, strip down and I'll get your clothes into the laundry."

"I can handle it. It's my mess, so it's my cleanup."

"You don't have to—"

"I've got it." He gave her a wan smile. "It's not something you want to do before dinner."

"Just toss your clothes in the washer, and I'll run it after we eat."

Dad reappeared with a wet washcloth.

"Please tell me Kate was kidding about my face," Logan said.

Dad shook his head and walked toward him, as if to wipe it off, but Logan took the cloth and backed up. "Got it. I've got the laundry, too, Mom. I want to learn. I've been thinking I need to take on more responsibilities."

"All right," Mom said. "I'll show you how to run it. I *am* sorry about laughing."

"But it was funny," Dad said. "And it'll get funnier each time your sister retells it."

Logan sighed.

Mom gingerly reached out and squeezed his shoulder. "You just need to find something to hold over her so she doesn't tell everyone at Christmas. Not that I'd recommend blackmailing your sister . . ."

"Yeah, we absolutely recommend it," Dad said. "It's the only defense."

Logan smiled, and they left him to strip down and run upstairs to the shower.

Kate spent the meal regaling Logan and Jeremy with stories of the "strange behavior of humans"—all the weird things she'd witnessed while out Christmas shopping. Mom's eye rolls said Kate was exaggerating. Dad's smirks said she wasn't exaggerating very much.

That was part of growing up in a werewolf Pack. Humans sometimes seemed a foreign species to Logan and Kate, the way they did to Dad, who'd been bitten when he was a kid. Mom had grown up human, so she didn't pay any attention when humans did things like let their kids wander off in a mall, or yell at them in public, or cuff them upside the head. Logan got the feeling none of that was weird—or foreign—to his mother. He wondered what her childhood had been like, but she never talked about it, and if he or Kate asked, she'd just tell them a funny story from her school days.

With Kate entertaining at dinner, no one noticed he was quiet. Quiet and deep in thought, his brain racing to come up with all the necessary facets of "the puppy plan."

He had to get his parents onside. Jeremy didn't count. No, that sounded wrong. Jeremy definitely counted—it was his house, and he was Dad's foster father and also the former Alpha. He always counted. When it came to raising Logan and Kate, though, Jeremy kept out. He was like . . .

Logan wasn't really sure what Jeremy was like, because he had no frame of reference other than what he could glean from other families. Jeremy seemed more involved than a grandparent. He wasn't like a parent, either, because he left all the decisions to their mom and dad. One of Logan and Kate's school friends had a stepdad, who did everything a dad did except when it came to discipline and decisions about raising him. That's what Jeremy was like. As close as you could get to a parent without actually being one.

When it came to having a dog, Jeremy's position was simply "whatever your parents say," as it was on everything else. He wouldn't even be here for Christmas. He was leaving tomorrow to spend a few days with his girlfriend, Jaime, and then they'd both come back for the big Pack holiday Meet on the twenty-sixth.

The two people Logan had to convince, then, were his parents. He'd considered going straight for Dad. His father might be the most feared werewolf in the country, but his kids saw a very different side of him. Last summer was the first time he'd really raised his voice to them—getting into a shouting match with Kate long after their mother had lost all patience with her acting out. But Kate had had a reason for her bad behavior—signaling her first Change—and they'd sorted it out, and Dad went back to being his usual self, which meant if Logan had to pick who he could more easily woo to his side, it was definitely Dad.

That was a problem. The rest of the werewolf world might think Dad was the scary one, but he wasn't Alpha. Mom was. That meant that Logan *shouldn't* go around her to his father to ask for something. Yes, Mom wouldn't want him saying that. She wanted to be his mom, not his Alpha. But she *was* his Alpha, and he felt that.

Even if she wasn't Alpha, he shouldn't go around her to his dad. He'd never heard his parents disagree on something to do with him and Kate. Either they never disagreed or they just didn't do it in front of the kids. He shouldn't pit them against each other. Which meant he had to ask them together. That did not, however, mean he couldn't work on Dad first.

The next problem was getting Dad away from Mom. Like Kate and Logan, they weren't *always* together, but it seemed like it.

Luckily, this was Christmas, which meant routines had changed. Last night, they'd all gone out to cut down a tree. Tonight, they'd trim it. After dinner, Dad's job was getting the decorations out of the attic while Mom and the twins made cookies.

"I don't think three of us need to do this anymore," Logan said as Kate stirred chopped chocolate into the dough.

Mom got out the cookie sheets. "Someone needs to make sure all that chocolate goes into the pan."

"I'm not five, Mom," Kate said . . . and tossed a chunk of chocolate his way before eating a piece herself.

"I thought I'd help Dad this year," Logan said.

"Why?" Kate said. "You liked the smell of deer poop on your clothes so much that you want to see if mouse poop smells just as good?"

He flicked the back of her head and dodged as she kicked backward.

"Go on," Mom said. "Just ignore the cursing."

Dad was definitely cursing. He was snarling, too, as he stomped around in the dark attic.

"Where the hell did she move everything?" he was muttering to himself as Logan climbed up. "Goddamn it."

"Language, Dad."

His father only looked over and snorted. Logan got the feeling the "no swearing" rule came from Mom. Logan understood it, though—if they were allowed to curse at home, then they'd slip up at school, and Mom didn't need more calls from the teacher.

"Mom didn't move the decorations. You just toss them up here after the holidays and then forget where you put them."

A grunt, but no argument. Logan picked up a flashlight and scanned the boxes, saying as casually as he could, "I meant what

I said earlier about wanting to do more chores . . . taking on more responsibility."

Another grunt.

"We're old enough, and I think it's a good idea."

Dad walked deeper into the attic. "I asked Jeremy for more responsibility when I was about your age." He shone the light on a box and heaved it up, placing it by the ladder. "Because I wanted something."

"What? No, I don't—"

"I wanted to go camping with the Sorrentinos. Jeremy said no."

Logan picked up a box marked *Xmas* and moved it to the ladder. "Why?"

"Something about me being responsible once for us getting asked to leave a campground."

"You got kicked out?"

"Asked to leave. It's different."

"Uh-huh." Logan plunked down on a box as his dad kept hunting.

"I just wanted to sleep," Dad said. "That's the idea of camping, right? You hike and swim and go for a run, and then you sleep at night. Except we couldn't, because the people next to us sat around the campfire all night talking. Loudly. So I decided, if we were going to have a quiet night, I needed to move their beer."

"Steal it?"

"Move it."

"But how would that help? They could still have a fire and talk."

"Not without the beer."

"That doesn't make any sense."

Dad shrugged. "Some people . . ." His gaze went distant. Then he shook it off. "That's how it works with some people. The point of the campfire is the beer. Now, do I get to finish the story?"

"About how you stole their beer and got kicked out of the campground?"

"Moved. Asked to leave."

"Because there's a difference."

"There is." Dad caught Logan's grin and gave him a mock glare. "I *moved* the beer to another site, where there happened to be a bunch of teenagers. If those kids chose not to track down the rightful owners, that wasn't my fault."

"Did you get to sleep?"

"We did. It was very quiet . . . until the next day, when the people next door saw the kids with their empties. One of the girls had seen me with the case and ratted me out. Then we were asked to leave. So the moral of the story is . . ."

"Don't let anyone catch you when you move the beer?"

"Exactly. But the *point* is that I decided I'd show Jeremy I could go camping again by proving I was more responsible. I did more chores, and he let me go."

"It worked, then."

"Sure. After I broke a bunch of dishes, threw a red shirt in the white laundry, and doubled the salt in the stew, Jeremy was just happy to get rid of me for the weekend."

"You're not really making your case here, Dad."

His father laid down the last of the boxes. "I'm kidding. Well, not entirely. I tried, though, and that was the main thing. The problem here, Logan, is that this isn't the same. I wasn't allowed to go camping because I messed up. You not being allowed to get a puppy has nothing to do with you messing up."

"Whoa. What? Puppy? No, I didn't say anything about—"

"You don't need to. It's the only thing you and your sister really want that we aren't giving you. Therefore, it's the only reason you'd suddenly decide you needed to show more responsibility. In this case, though, lack of responsibility has nothing to do with why we're saying no. I'm sure if you get a puppy, you'll look after it. Even Kate will. She may have laughed when her mom asked her to help Jeremy with dinner, but you know what? She went in and helped him. Irresponsibility with her is all about image."

Logan would have smiled at that, but his heart was pounding too hard, seeing his puppy plan dissolve.

"It's not about responsibility, Logan. It's about timing."

"I know." His voice was so soft even he barely heard it, because he did know that, and yet he'd told himself otherwise. Responsibility was something he could fix. Timing was not.

Dad sighed and lowered himself onto a crate opposite Logan. "Sometimes, when your mom says we'll talk about something later, what she really means . . ."

"Is that she doesn't want to talk about it, and she's hoping we'll forget."

"But that's not what she means this time. It isn't *no*. It's *not now*."

Logan nodded.

"What if we laid out a timetable?" Dad said. "Figured out when we might be able to make this happen?"

That was exactly what Logan had been hoping for. *Before* the puppy.

"Maybe the end of the school year," Dad said. "We'd need to discuss it with your mom, but she was already talking about that. Spring's a good time for puppies. She says we can put in our name with a breeder and then pick out the puppy as soon as it's born." Dad smiled. "Apparently, she's done her research."

Logan forced a return smile.

"And that's not what you wanted," Dad said slowly.

"It's just . . ." Logan squirmed.

"Did you see puppies for sale? Is that where this is coming from?"

No, Logan wanted to say. *I already have one. It's out back, and if you come and see it, you'll know it's perfect for Kate, and it would be the best Christmas present, and it would make her so happy, and I really want to give it to her.*

That's why he couldn't say it. Because there was no way his parents would want to say no once they saw the puppy, and then he'd feel as if he'd forced their hand.

Instead, he nodded and said, "I saw a sign. For puppies."

Silence. It was so long he thought Dad wasn't going to answer. Then he said, "I wish I could say yes, Logan."

And that hurt, really hurt, because he didn't want to make Dad feel bad. His parents did have lots going on, and Logan saying, "But I want a puppy!" was selfish and spoiled. He wanted to be mature and understanding and acknowledge that, compared with most kids, he *was* pampered and spoiled. A kid couldn't ask for a better life. Or better parents. He always wanted to remember that, especially when things didn't go his way.

"Dad!" Kate shouted from the bottom of the ladder. "Logan!"

"We'll be down in a few—" Dad started to call back, but Logan rose and yelled, "Coming!" Then he said to his dad, as maturely and sincerely as he could, "I understand," picked up a box, and headed down.

After everyone went to bed, Logan snuck out with leftover roast beef and a hoodie from Kate's hamper. He'd give the puppy her sweater to sleep on, along with the one of his own he'd left earlier. That would get the dog accustomed to both their scents. Not that the puppy would be staying, but just . . . Well, he wasn't sure why. He told himself he was taking Kate's hoodie so, if she did see the puppy, it wouldn't be afraid of her.

He also brought a backpack with a separate set of clothing, which he'd change into and store near the fort.

He tried not to feel guilty about sneaking out. He still did. That was his wolf brain. It wasn't just breaking the rules that made him feel sick. He'd made a mistake. A big one. He should have taken the puppy to the house right away. Told his parents what happened and let them deal with it.

He'd gone behind their backs, hiding it in the fort, and now he was digging himself deeper into a hole. There was no way he could go through with his plan now. He shouldn't even try. Which was a good and mature realization. Except . . . well, that still left the puppy.

As soon as he drew near the fort, the puppy started whimpering. He trudged those final steps, because he didn't want to see it. He wanted to shove the meat through a hole in the wooden walls and run back to the house. That wasn't fair, though. This wasn't the puppy's fault any more than it was his parents'. He'd started it; he had to follow through.

He opened the door and the puppy launched itself at him. He fell back on the snow as it jumped on his lap and wriggled, whimpering and whining in excitement. It licked away the tears on his cheeks, because, yes, there were tears, as much as he'd tried to hold them back. After a moment, when he didn't respond, the puppy's wiggling and whimpering became more frantic, a little panicked.

He wiped away the tears, gave it a fierce hug, and took out the meat. The puppy licked a piece, gulped it, and started to choke, which meant a major freak-out, until he managed to pull the strip out of its throat. That's when the tears threatened again, when he looked at the puppy on his lap, coughing and shaking its head, and all he could think was, *I can't do anything right.*

"Feeling sorry for myself isn't going to help, is it?" he said, his voice echoing in the night.

The puppy whined and licked his face, its whole body shaking with fresh excitement.

"You're not old enough for meat. I should have thought of that."

The puppy kept dancing in place, tiny claws scrabbling against him, just happy to hear his voice, to have his attention.

"We don't have any baby bottles. I don't know what else to use."

How did wolves feed their young once they were ready to start meat? Regurgitation. He made a face. "I can't do *that*. But I guess . . ."

He took a piece of meat from the bag, chewed it, and spit it into his hand. The puppy gobbled it up almost before it hit his palm.

"Well, that works," he said. "Still gross."

He repeated the process, and the puppy ate all the meat in the bag, slowing only as it neared the end.

"Tomorrow I'll grind it up in the house," he said. "I'll research it and . . ."

And how long was he going to keep the puppy in the fort?

"It's just until I have a plan. I'll—I'll figure out what to do. How to get you a real home and . . ."

His voice broke and the tears prickled again, but he blinked them back and cleared his throat.

"You don't need that. You need exercise." He put the puppy down, got to his feet, and started to run, the puppy tumbling along at his heels.

After breakfast, Kate practiced her music. Normally, he'd have stretched out on the floor nearby and read or studied. But while that was perfectly fine for piano and guitar—and even, if he wasn't studying too hard, for drums—Kate had recently decided she needed to add a wind instrument to her repertoire, and of course she hadn't chosen the flute.

Maybe it would be better once she had more practice at the trumpet, but at this point, well, no one expected him to hang around. The trumpet noise also meant he could slip into the kitchen and prepare the meat without anyone knowing. Then he zipped out the back door with a quick, "Going for a walk!" to Mom, who hesitated, as if thinking she'd like to escape with him, but he was gone before she could.

He fed the puppy until its tiny belly bulged, and then they played until the puppy collapsed. He wouldn't be able to return until dinnertime. It was his day for Christmas shopping. Jeremy was taking him later this morning. Mom might pretend she was perfectly fine with crowded malls, but she didn't volunteer to go twice in as many days.

While they shopped, Logan tried not to fret about the puppy problem. Of course, he did. At lunch, Jeremy said, "You're quiet today."

Logan found a smile. "I'm always quiet. You're just used to having Kate around, too."

"True, but there's the kind of quiet that says you just don't have anything to say and the kind that says you have too much to say and don't know how to start." Jeremy cut into his steak. "Your dad used to have that same look, when there was something he needed to say."

"Like: 'I didn't do it'?"

Jeremy returned Logan's smile. "Actually, no. At your age, your dad never had any problem telling me when he'd done something wrong. It weighed too heavily on him. He'd blurt it out like a confession." Another bite of his steak. "You have *that* look, too, though."

Jeremy kept his gaze on his food, but Logan still felt it and tried not to squirm.

Jeremy continued. "Whatever you've done, I suspect you feel worse about it than you need to. There's something you'd like to talk about, but you want to work it out for yourself." He lifted his gaze. "Am I close?"

Dead-on, as usual. Logan could feel the words churning inside him, desperate to escape. *I rescued a puppy, and I wanted to give it to Kate, but I know I can't, and now I have this puppy in the fort, and I should have said something, and the longer I wait . . .*

"Logan?"

He should speak up. Jeremy was the person Mom went to for advice—the person everyone went to for advice. He would keep Logan's secret and help him solve this.

Except Jeremy was right. Logan wanted to figure it out for himself.

"I understand you don't like to ask for help," Jeremy said, as if reading his mind. "*That* you get from your mom. It's not that she doesn't value anyone else's opinion. Or that she thinks she can do everything herself. It's that she *wants* to be able to do it herself. She expects more of herself. Asking for help is weakness." He looked at Logan. "Does that sound familiar?"

Logan said nothing.

Jeremy took another bite of his lunch before saying, "Your mom has learned to ask for help, but it's still difficult. Do you know what she often does instead? She tells me or your dad her ideas and then waits to see what we say. That way, she's not really asking, but we'll still offer advice."

Jeremy waited again, and Logan knew he was hinting for Logan to do the same. Which would be great . . . if he had ideas to share. Instead, he just sat there, fingering his sandwich. Then he said, "Can you tell me a story about my dad?"

Jeremy's lips quirked. "One that illustrates the principles I'm trying to communicate? Or one to distract me from pestering you?"

"I just . . . I need to think some more. A story would help."

"Distract *you*, then. All right. Let's see if I can find one you haven't heard . . ."

When they got home, Kate zoomed into the hall and launched herself at him. Not unlike the puppy, he reflected. Just with less slobber.

"What'd you get me?" she said as she bounced.

"Was I supposed to get you something?" he teased.

"Um, yeah. Only the best Christmas present ever."

He faltered at that.

I did. I tried.

"Oh, I'm kidding. Geez, Lo, you take everything so seriously. Of course, may I point out that your amazing sister *did* get you the best gift *evah*."

"Ignore her," Mom said, walking into the front hall. "We went to town to grab a few groceries, and she talked us into another hot chocolate. Then we made the mistake of letting her run in to buy it herself. She got an extra-large. She's been bouncing off the walls ever since. Too much sugar."

"Sugar doesn't trigger hyperactivity, Mom," Logan said.

"Smarty-pants. Caffeine, then."

"There isn't enough caffeine in hot chocolate—"

"Yes, yes. I'm wrong. Very, very wrong. You do know we're supposed to get a few more years of you thinking your parents know everything, right?"

He smiled. "I never thought that. Sorry."

She smacked his shoulder and waved him into the study. "Your dad needs to talk to you about something. Jer, can I speak to you? And no, you aren't going to just stay quiet and hope to escape Kate's bouncing. If it doesn't work for Logan, it won't work for you. Kate? Go . . . run around the house ten times or something." She steered Logan toward the study and motioned for Jeremy to follow her.

"What's up?" Logan said as he walked into the study. He said it as casually as he could, considering his palms were sweating so hard he had to shove his hands in his pockets.

He's found the puppy. He went for a walk and found it, and now I'm in trouble. He doesn't want to bother Mom about it, not when tomorrow's Christmas Eve.

Christmas was important to Mom. Logan and Kate had always known that. Dad went out of his way to make it perfect, and he was a little more inclined to discipline them himself at this time of year, to keep everything running smoothly. Logan and Kate never asked why it was important. It just was, which meant they had a magical Christmas themselves every year, because that's what Mom wanted for them.

Dad was busy cleaning out the fireplace—his head stuck in it— and he didn't seem to hear Logan's question. Logan had to smile at that and said, "You, uh, don't need to do that this year, Dad. We know. Remember?"

"What?" Dad backed up. "Oh. Right." He rubbed his chin, leaving a smudge of soot, and he looked . . . disappointed. As if he'd forgotten this year would be different, part of the magic left behind in the world of childhood that the twins were quickly leaving.

"You probably should, though," Logan said. "Kate may have been the one to insist on an honest answer, but . . . " He lowered his voice. "I think she still believes."

Dad smiled at him and shook his head. He'd know Logan was humoring him, but he'd do it anyway. It was tradition, and they still believed in that.

As Dad backed out, Logan said, "Should I, uh, shut the door?"

"What?" Dad's face screwed up. "No, no. You aren't in trouble, Logan. I just need to talk to you about something. Before we went to town, your mom, Kate, and I took a walk out back, and we smelled something."

Logan clenched his fists, breath jammed in his throat. *I'm sorry.* That's what he'd lead with. *I'm so, so sorry.*

"A mutt," Dad said.

"What?"

"Yeah, I know. There hasn't been a mutt near Stonehaven in years."

"R-right. They know better." At first, when Dad said "mutt," all Logan could think of was the puppy. It *was* a mutt: a crossbreed. But that was also their word for non-Pack werewolves, and it showed how distracted Logan was that it had taken him a moment to remember that.

"I'm ninety-nine percent sure we're wrong," Dad said. "It was just a whiff, and it passed so fast that all I can say for sure is that we smelled canine and human, and hell, it might have just been some guy walking a dog along the road."

Or a puppy, covered in human scent.

"Your mom is sure it's nothing, but"—Dad shrugged—"I'm not taking any chances. We don't need to go for a run until the Pack Meet, so there's no reason to head out back. We'll be on alert, but Jeremy's still leaving later, and no one's changing any plans. The only thing is that I need to ask you and Kate to stay out of the woods."

Logan went still.

Dad peered at him. "Is that a problem? I know your mom said you've been restless. We can go for a drive later, the two of us. Walk someplace else."

"No, I'm fine."

More peering. Then Dad nodded, not seeming entirely convinced, but only saying, "If you change your mind, day or night, and you need to go out, you just tell me, okay?"

"Sure, Dad."

"Now, if you're still feeling like being extra responsible, you can help me with this fireplace."

The puppy needed to eat. It needed food and fresh water, and Logan couldn't let it go without either until morning. He had to tell his parents.

He should have talked to Jeremy. Stupid, stupid, stupid. Logan might come by his independent streak honestly, but that was no excuse. Now Jeremy had left, and he'd told Logan to call if he wanted to talk, but then Logan hadn't been able to work up the nerve to do it.

His parents kept going in and out, scouting the perimeter, and Logan couldn't stop thinking about the puppy getting lonely and scared. Would it start howling? Would his parents find it?

After dinner, it was time to bake gingerbread cookies, one of their favorite Christmas traditions. Logan couldn't ruin that by bringing up the puppy.

He had to slip out again after dark. There was no mutt. There hadn't been one on the property in years—it certainly wouldn't happen now. Mom and Dad had smelled the puppy, that's all. Logan was safe. He just couldn't get caught, because that would be a serious infraction, worse than anything he'd ever done. Worse than anything Kate had ever done. For this, he'd be punished—not as a boy disobeying his parents, but as a Pack wolf disobeying the Alpha.

He couldn't get caught. It was that simple.

Logan watched the clock tick toward midnight. He had his own bedroom now. He and Kate had shared up until two years ago, when Mom declared they were too old. He stayed in the room that used to be Malcolm's. Kate moved to Mom's old room, from before she and Dad got together. Or before they got together for good.

Logan was a little confused on the exact timeline. His parents had been together and then broken up, but because Mom was Pack, she'd stayed at Stonehaven some of the time, and . . . It was confusing. All he knew for sure was that Mom had kept her old bedroom, though she hadn't used it for years.

Deciding to move Kate in there had been something of a family joke. The room was super girly. Mom said that when she joined the Pack as its only female werewolf, that was the kind of room Jeremy figured she needed. Kate was about as girly as Mom was—which was to say, not at all—and now Kate had the room, and, like Mom, she couldn't complain too much for fear of hurting Jeremy's feelings. Logan figured by now Jeremy knew that it wasn't really their style, but it was like he was in on the joke, and everyone played along. Still, Kate was slowly but surely redecorating, piece by piece, poster by poster.

Logan's room was at the back, across the hall from Jeremy's. Kate's was on the other side of Jeremy's, across from Mom and Dad's.

This meant that, if Logan snuck out, he'd have to pass *everyone* on his way to the stairs. This was a problem. His parents slept soundly, but Kate was overly attuned to his sleeping patterns. He'd need to jump out the window instead.

Being a werewolf meant window-jumping wasn't nearly as dangerous as it might be. Or it wasn't these days, that is. The first time they'd tried it, they'd been three. Logan twisted his ankle, and Kate sprained her wrist, and Mom totally freaked out. They hadn't hopped out any windows for years after that. But now, at their age, it was as simple—and safe—as jumping out a main-floor one.

Logan opened his window, took out the screen, and set it inside. Then he poked his head through to check below. He spotted a figure in the yard and jerked back fast. When he peered out, he saw . . .

Kate.

His sister was making her way across the backyard.

What the hell? He almost said that. Almost shouted it out the window. He started to jump out after her. Then he realized he was wearing his jacket and boots, which would take some explaining. He stashed them under his bed, pulled on a hoodie and slippers, and jumped out the window.

He hit the ground and tore off after Kate. The fresh-falling snow was too powdery to squeak under his slippers, and she had her hoodie pulled tight, so she didn't hear a thing until she was flat on her face in the snow. She twisted, fists clenching. Then she stopped.

"Logan?"

"What the hell are you doing?" he snarled, and she didn't tell him to watch his language. She heard that tone and her gaze dropped, and she pushed up from the snow carefully, her posture submissive, which meant she knew what she'd done was wrong, because there was no submissive or dominant wolf in their relationship. They were twins. Equals in everything.

Normally, he'd have let it go at that. The wolf in him said that if she submitted—acknowledging her error—he should take the high road. She might deserve a cuff on the ears and another snarl, but that was it. Tonight, though, with everything going on, he didn't feel like dropping it quite so fast.

"No, really," he said. "What the hell were you doing, Kate?"

"I . . . I was restless?" Her voice rose in a question, as if looking for the answer that might appease him.

"So, you took off in the night *again*? After what happened this summer?"

"I—"

"No, this is worse than last summer, because this time you were expressly told not to come out here at *any* time. To sneak off in the night—"

"I'm sorry." She stepped toward him, her gaze down. "You're totally right."

He eased back then, grumbling, his temper fading.

She looked up at him. "Are you okay, Lo?"

"No, I'm not. My sister tried to sneak into the forest when there's a mutt—"

"There isn't a—" She swallowed the rest and dropped her gaze again. "Whether there is or isn't, the point is that I disobeyed a direct order."

"From your *Alpha*."

She shifted. They both understood the difference, even if Mom might not. If she told them to brush after meals, that was their mom. If she told them to stay away from a potential mutt, that was their Alpha.

"Are you okay, Lo?" Kate asked again. Then she shook her head. "No, stupid question. I know something's bugging you. It's what happened at school, isn't it?"

It took him a moment to realize what she meant. More than a minute, because he'd honestly forgotten about it. His sister had problems at school with the other girls. Kate was smart and talented and—according to the other boys—pretty. But she hung around with Logan and a few of the other kids who didn't quite fit in, and that drove the popular girls nuts, like she was thumbing her nose at them. They could be mean. The last day of school before the holidays, one of them had tripped Kate, and his sister had hauled off, whacked her, and sent her flying. The girl had been too scared to tattle, but Logan had had a talk with Kate after that.

"I know I need to rise above it," she said. "Ignore them. Never hit them, because I can really hurt them. And because Mom will get a call, and she doesn't need that."

"Right."

"It won't happen again. But you're still mad, aren't you? I disappointed you."

"What? No." He gave her a rare hug. "I actually forgot all about it, Kate. If I'm a little off, it's just that: I feel a little off. Like you did this summer. I'm running behind. Boys *do* mature slower than girls."

She laughed at that and hugged him back. "I don't think anyone would accuse you of maturing slowly. All right, then, as long as you aren't mad at me."

"About the school thing? No. About sneaking out tonight? Yes."

"I know. It was dumb. I'm a kid. I'm allowed to do dumb things. Isn't that what you said?"

"Yeah, yeah. Just get inside before Mom or Dad catches us, or we'll *both* learn exactly how dumb it was."

An hour after giving his sister proper hell for disobeying an order, Logan was doing exactly the same thing and painfully aware of the hypocrisy. But the puppy had to be fed.

He gave Kate time to fall asleep. Then he put on his coat and boots and climbed out the window. Snow was still falling, already obscuring their tracks from earlier. He had a way to go, and he really wanted to get this done quickly, so he circled out to the road, which was easier walking. Any other time he'd have enjoyed the crisp, clear night with lightly falling snow. The nip of the cold didn't bother him at all, and he walked with his hood down, moving between a fast walk and a jog, depending on the depth of the snow.

He'd hit a good run at a plowed section, and he was ripping along, hearing nothing but the wind whistling past his ears. The snow started driving his way, and he narrowed his eyes against it. The cold wind numbed his ears and nose, and he was truly running "blind," all senses deadened. *Just keep moving.* A little farther, and then he'd veer into the woods and—

There was a figure on the road.

It seemed to appear from nowhere, but the truth was, he just hadn't been watching where he was going. Not watching. Not listening. Not smelling. He'd had his eyes on the road, and then he glanced up and there was a man standing ten feet away.

Logan stopped fast. Then he caught the man's scent. His stomach did a double flip.

No, that wasn't possible. It had been a misunderstanding. His parents had caught a whiff of the puppy and mistaken it for . . .

Logan inhaled deeper and swallowed.

And mistaken it for nothing. There was a mutt, standing on the edge of their property.

A mutt, staring right at him.

Logan knew he should run. That's what they'd been taught. But he couldn't, and it wasn't fear—it was something deep in his gut that saw a rogue werewolf on their territory and refused to flee. He planted his feet, lifted his chin, and squared his shoulders. And he waited.

The mutt took three steps toward him. Slow and careful steps. As the mutt drew near, Logan realized he was young. Maybe twenty. Still, twice Logan's size. Both twins were small for their age, one of the more unfortunate traits they'd inherited from their father, who'd been the smallest in his class until he hit his growth spurt in high school.

The mutt stared at him and then inhaled deeply, his eyes widening.

"You smell like a werewolf," the young man said.

"Uh, yeah . . ."

"No, I mean, you're a kid. You shouldn't already smell like a werewolf."

"I'm special. Now, since you obviously know who I am—"

"You're the boy," the mutt said.

"Pretty sure I don't look like a girl."

"No, *the* boy. *Their* boy."

"Three for three. Not exactly genius, considering where you are. You do know where you are, right? Trespassing? On the Alpha's territory?"

"Your dad, you mean."

Logan rolled his eyes. "There's your first strike. My mother is the Alpha, moron."

The mutt's lips twitched. "Sorry, kid, no one buys that story. The Pack would never make a woman Alpha. It's really your dad—they just don't want to scare people by saying that."

"Fine. You're about to meet both of them. You can pick your challenge. Either way, you'll get your ass kicked. That's why you're here, right? To challenge the Alpha."

"No, I'm not stupid."

"Um, yeah. The fact you're here says you are. Now, should I call them over? Or do you want to rethink this particular course of action?"

The mutt's gaze darted to the forest. "They're out here?"

"You think they'd let their nine-year-old wander around at two in the morning? Now, I'm giving you a chance to leave. It's Christmastime. Don't you have someplace to be?"

"Um . . ."

"Never mind. Just go. Head off that way." He pointed. "Don't step on the property or my parents will track you down and make an example of you. If you leave now, I won't tell them you were here. They thought they smelled a mutt earlier, but they weren't sure. Don't make them sure."

The mutt peered at him. "How old are you again?"

"Nine."

"You don't talk like it."

"I take after my parents—both of them. They can think as well as they can fight. It's a lethal combination, and I wouldn't suggest you stick around long enough to find out for yourself."

"Is it true what they say? About your dad? What he did to the last wolf who trespassed here?"

"Whatever they say, it's true. Now just—"

"Do you know what they say? What he did? You must not. Otherwise, you wouldn't be nearly so proud of him. He's a psycho. You know that, right?"

"He is whatever he needs to be to keep us safe. Now get—"

"No, really. He's crazy. You obviously don't know what he did. Him and his buddy, Nick, they found two wolves here, come to issue a challenge. Your daddy was younger than me, and he took those wolves—"

A crash sounded in the undergrowth, and a figure barreled out so fast both Logan and the mutt fell back. Before the mutt could recover, Dad had him by the shirtfront. He threw him onto the road and planted a foot on his stomach.

"Logan?" he said. "Get back to the house."

"I—"

Dad's look stopped the words in his throat. It was the look mutts must get when they crossed him. A look his son never expected to see, and Logan took a slow step back.

"To. The. House." Dad caught Logan's gaze. "Now."

Logan tried. He really tried. This was an order from his father and the beta, but it wasn't the same as an order from the Alpha, and all Logan could think was that there might be other mutts, and he really should stay by his father. Watch out for him.

"Logan . . ."

The mutt slammed his fist into the back of Dad's knee, and it caught his father off guard. Dad's leg buckled. Logan shot forward, ready to throw himself at the mutt if his dad went down. He didn't. He just stumbled, and swung around and grabbed for the mutt, but Logan was already diving at him, and when Dad swung around, his fist caught Logan in the shoulder and sent him crashing into the snowbank.

That distracted Dad for real, and he twisted toward Logan as the mutt leapt up. Logan opened his mouth to shout a warning, but Dad backhanded the mutt down again, and Logan scrambled up as fast as he could, saying, "I'm okay. I'm okay," even as pain stabbed through his shoulder. Dad spun back on the mutt, who was staying on the ground now, his hands raised.

"I'm sorry," the mutt said. "I'm really, really sorry."

"Not yet you aren't," Dad said, taking a step toward him, his fists clenched.

The mutt stayed down. Stayed submissive. His gaze was fixed on Dad's chest, not rising even to his face.

"It was stupid, really stupid," the kid said. "They dared me— my cousins—and I don't have a rep, because I lost my first two challenges, and I thought this would help. All I had to do was get a photo of the house to prove I was here. I wasn't even going to go on the property. Well, not far, because you can't see the house from the road. I tried. But I was going to walk as far on this road as I could, and only go—"

"How old are you?"

"N-nineteen."

"Fuck. Name?"

"Davis. I mean, Cain. Davis Cain."

"Of course. A Cain. Do you guys share a single brain among you?" Dad lifted his hands. "Don't even answer that. Did you set foot on the property?"

"N-no. No, sir, I mean."

Dad winced a little at that, as if the "sir" took it too far, was too submissive, didn't portend well for the kid's future as a werewolf.

"I'm going to check that," Dad said. "In the meantime, you will get into your car, wherever it is, and you will start heading home. You will not stop, even to take a piss, until you are past the state border."

"Yes, sir."

"And you will tell your cousins that you got as far as Bear Valley and turned around, because you realized just how stupid an idea this was, that you weren't just risking your own life but, because you're a kid, I'd hold your family responsible for not teaching you better."

"R-right."

"You decided to go home and start training instead of taking on challenges already. Train until you're ready to beat someone. And maybe, if you can manage it, hit the books and get a little smarter, too, because that will help you fight. And help you not make fucking stupid choices."

"Yes, sir."

"Now, start heading to your car. I'm going to retrace your steps, and if I find you even set foot on our property, I'm coming after you."

"I-I didn't. Honest."

"Good, then you won't be in a rush to get to your car. Walk."

The kid did, heading in the direction he'd come from, which meant Dad followed at a short distance, checking his trail. Dad got about twenty feet before he turned and saw Logan still standing there. He barely had time to open his mouth before Logan broke into a run to catch up, his teeth gritted as the fast movement jostled his shoulder.

They kept going until the mutt turned down another road, and they saw his car. Dad walked a little farther, still sniffing. Once he was satisfied the kid had walked straight down the road—no side trips into their forest—he stopped and watched as the car's tail-lights disappeared from sight.

Then, still silent, Dad walked over and motioned for Logan to take off his jacket. He prodded Logan's shoulder as Logan squeezed his eyes shut, trying not to cry out.

"Can you lift your arm?" he asked.

Logan did.

Dad stepped back. "Do you know how lucky you are that I didn't dislocate it? Or break it?"

"It would have served me right if you did."

Dad gave a disgusted grunt. "Sure, that's what counts: that you deserved it. It wouldn't have bothered me at all. Break my son's shoulder. No big deal."

Logan dropped his gaze. "You're right. I'm sorry. I shouldn't have gotten in the way."

"That was just the last in a very long string of mistakes you made tonight."

Logan could hear the anger in his father's voice. Icy anger, pushed down deep, turning his voice bitter cold. Logan wished he would yell—lose his temper and snarl and shout. He did with others. Even with Mom. Especially with Mom, though they tried to hide it from the kids. But that was just anger. Two volatile tempers clashing, until one of them would stalk off into the woods and the other would follow, and when they came back, everything would be fine.

That's what Logan wanted right now. For his dad to shout and snarl and get it out of his system. To be furious with Logan for doing something stupid, because it had scared him. That's not what he saw, though. This was worse. It was disappointment.

"I'm sorry," he said, trying not to cry. "I'm really sorry, and I know everything I did tonight was stupid and—"

"We told you not to come into the woods. We told you why."

"I-I thought . . . I didn't think it was true. About the mutt."

Dad pulled back, his blue eyes icing over even more. "You thought we *lied* to you?"

"N-no, I thought there was another explanation. I was absolutely sure there wasn't a mutt out here."

"You are nine, Logan. I don't care how smart you are—you are not in a position to make that determination. If *I'm* not sure whether there's a mutt, and your *mother* isn't sure, then *you* aren't, either."

"I know. I'm—"

"Furthermore, I don't care what you thought. It was an order. You do not disobey an order."

"I know, and I'm sorry."

"No, Logan, I mean you *don't*. Not that you shouldn't. You *don't*. You never do. So if you did tonight, then something is wrong, and you are going to tell me what it is, or we are going to spend a very long and cold night on this road."

Logan swallowed. He closed his eyes, and steeled himself, and said, "I'll show you."

"No, you'll tell me."

"I-I . . ." He lifted his gaze. "Please. I have to show you."

Dad gave a wave, looking tired and frustrated, and let Logan lead the way.

Dad followed behind Logan. Maybe watching for trouble. Maybe just not really in the mood to walk with him. When they were halfway to the fort, Dad's hand fell on his good shoulder.

"It's late," he said. "Just tell me what—"

"I have to show you."

"No, Logan." He stepped in front of him, his face drawn in the moonlight, lines deepening around his mouth. "Tell me, because I need to get inside and talk to your mother."

"It's a puppy," Logan blurted.

Dad went still. "What?"

"A puppy. In the fort."

"You found a puppy in the fort?" Dad said slowly.

"No, in the ditch. There were two. In a bag. I thought they were dead, so I was going to move the bag before Kate found them, and I was carrying it across the road when I realized one puppy was still alive."

"One was . . . ?"

Logan nodded, and the look that passed over his father's face . . . It was many expressions, all flickering fast, shock and surprise and anger and outrage, and then something like sorrow and regret as he said, "You were moving dead puppies for your sister."

"I didn't want her to see that."

Dad's expression said he'd rather Logan hadn't seen that, either, but Logan started walking again, still talking. "At first, when I thought the puppy was hurt, I was going to take it to Jeremy. But then it was fine, and I . . . I put it in the fort."

"The fort?"

"I wanted to give it to Kate for Christmas." Again, he blurted the words before he could stop himself. Then he hurried on. "I mean, that was my first thought. I know I can't now. It's a bad time. But I didn't know what to do with the puppy, and I was trying to figure it out while I was looking after it, which is why I went out tonight. I thought you didn't smell a mutt this afternoon—just the puppy. I was *sure* that's what it was. So I was going to feed it." He took the bag of meat from his inside pocket. "Otherwise, I'd never have gone out."

Dad gave a slow nod. They were within sight of the fort when he finally said, "You wanted to give it to Kate. For Christmas."

"I know I can't, so I'm not asking. That isn't fair."

"Isn't fair?"

"To make you and Mom say no. Especially Mom. She wants a perfect Christmas, and a puppy would be, well, perfect. For Kate. So Mom would either have to say no and feel awful or say yes when she really doesn't want to. *That's* not fair."

Dad's hand fell on his good shoulder again, and before Logan knew it, Dad had pulled him into an embrace. Tight and brief and fierce.

"All right, then," Dad said. "Show me your puppy. Before it breaks down that door."

The puppy was indeed trying to break down the door, throwing itself at it as it yipped and howled. Logan opened it, and the puppy flew out. So did the stink of puppy poop, and Logan's hand flew to his nose. The puppy jumped and leapt against his legs, yelping to be picked up.

"I'll clean that up," he said quickly.

"You look after your puppy," Dad said. "I'll handle the rest. I've changed plenty of diapers."

Dad cleaned out the fort while Logan fed the puppy. He came out again as Logan was trying to get the puppy to eat more.

"Food first, then play," he said to the puppy, dancing around his feet. He looked up at his dad. "It likes to play."

"It?" Dad's brows shot up. "You can't tell if it's male or female?"

"I haven't looked. I don't want . . ." Logan busied himself shoving the meat back into the bag. "It's not important."

Not important if they couldn't keep it.

Dad scooped up the puppy in one hand. He flipped it onto its back. "Female."

Logan nodded. Dad tried to put the puppy down, but it—she—climbed onto him, licking his face.

"Okay, okay," he said, handing her back to Logan. "You haven't named her, I'm guessing."

"I didn't want to form an attachment."

Dad snorted, as if to say it was already too late. "Play with your puppy for a while. Tire her out."

Logan wished he wouldn't say *your* puppy. It meant nothing, but it felt like something. He pushed that aside, and he played with the puppy, and Dad did a little, too, feinting and chasing, the way he used to when Logan and Kate were little, wearing *them* out for *their* nap.

When the puppy collapsed, too exhausted even to move, it was Dad who scooped her up and took her back to her bed. Then, as they headed for the house, he called Mom.

"We have a situation," he said.

A pause, as Logan heard Mom's muffled voice. "Yeah, actually there *was* a mutt, but that's taken care of. The problem is our son."

Logan tensed. He tried to fall back, to not listen, but Dad caught him and kept him there, walking beside him.

"He found a puppy by the road a couple of days ago. Abandoned in a bag." Dad went on and explained as they walked.

Mom met them out back. She said nothing as they approached. She didn't stand with her arms crossed. She didn't look disappointed. Not angry, either. Just thoughtful. She looked maybe a little sad, and when Logan saw that sadness, he faltered and felt like he was going to be sick.

"I'm sor—" he began, but she was already there, in front of him, arms going around him in a hug just as tight as his father's— longer, though. Holding him against her, she bent to whisper, "I'm sorry you had to see that," and he knew she meant the dead puppy, and he nodded, and then she backed up, her hands still on his shoulders.

"Uh . . ." Dad said, and motioned for her to take her hand off his left shoulder. "The mutt. He—"

"I got in the way," Logan said.

Mom winced, but Logan said, "I'm fine. Just going to have a bruise. Lesson learned, right?" He tried for a smile, but she didn't return it.

"We'll discuss that tomorrow," she said. "For now, the puppy. It's late, and we're not going to talk about it tonight. I'm just going to say that you don't need to handle things alone, Logan. No one expects you to. No one but you."

She looked down at his expression and sighed. "But that's what counts, isn't it? What you expect from yourself." Another hug, lighter and quicker. "We'll work on that. Go on inside. Your dad and I need to talk."

Logan was almost asleep when his door creaked open. Footsteps crossed the room and even before he caught the scent, those footsteps said it was Dad. He kept his eyes shut until he felt him standing there, beside his bed, looking down at him. Not checking whether he was awake. Just watching him.

When Logan opened his eyes, Dad sat on the edge of the bed. There was a long minute of silence. Then Dad said, "That kid. The mutt. What he said . . . I caught a little of it. I heard you two talking, and I just caught the tail end."

"He was just talking. He didn't threaten me or anything."

"I know. I heard enough to tell . . ." Dad eased back. "I'm not sure if I should say you handled yourself well, because that might encourage you to do it again."

"I got lucky. He was just a kid. A scared kid trying to prove he was brave."

Dad nodded. "But the rest. I caught enough to hear what he said about me."

"I've heard it before. Variations on it."

Dad went still. "What have you heard?"

"That you're crazy. The psycho-werewolf thing. That's how you keep them away. By making them think you're the big bad wolf." A small smile. "Which doesn't mean you *aren't*, just that we don't see it."

Dad shifted on the bed. "He said I'd done something. At Stonehaven. To keep mutts off the property."

"You got there before he told me the details."

Silence. At least two minutes of it. "Do you want to know the details?"

"Not really."

There was a soft exhale of relief. "Okay. Someday, yes, you're going to need to hear them, and I'd rather you did from me, but . . ."

"Whatever you did, it was to keep them away. To keep us safe— Jeremy and then Mom and then us." He lifted his gaze to his father's. "I get that, Dad. You did something—something bad— because it meant you didn't have to keep doing smaller things until they got the message. One big message that lasted a long time. It makes sense."

Dad watched him for a moment, and there was this look in his eyes, like maybe he'd rather Logan didn't understand, like he'd rather his kids lived in a world where that *wouldn't* make sense, because they'd never need to consider it.

Logan sat up and put his arms around his dad's neck and squeezed and said, "Everything's good."

Dad gave him a quick hug back and tucked him in, kissed his forehead like he used to when they were little, and then padded from the room.

There was no resolution to the puppy problem the next day. It was Christmas Eve, and it seemed Mom and Dad didn't want to think about that. Mom said she and Dad would look after the puppy—they needed him and Kate to stay out of the woods, in case the mutt came back.

Logan was fine with that. As much as he told himself she was just postponing disappointing him, he couldn't help but think that, if she really didn't want to disappoint him, she'd get it over with before he got his hopes up. So yes, he did get his hopes up. Way up, if he was being honest.

Then, lying in bed that night, stuffed with hot chocolate and Christmas cookies, he began to feel, well, a little sick, and it wasn't from overeating. He kept thinking about the tree, with Kate's gift under it, and how much he wished he could have given her the puppy, how happy that would have made her. He decided he needed an answer. Just an answer, so he could stop hoping if there wasn't any point in it.

When he snuck downstairs, he heard his parents in the study.

"—don't know how to tell him," Mom was saying, and he stopped short.

"I know."

"I keep going over it and over it," she said.

She's decided against the puppy.

Logan took a deep breath. Maybe it wasn't too late. Maybe he could still talk—

"There isn't a solution," she said.

"I know," Dad replied.

"And you're really not helping."

"I know."

A whack, as if she'd smacked him, and Dad let out a soft laugh, and then there was another sound, another smack—a kiss—and Dad said, "You don't need to figure it out right now, darling."

"I do." A sharp intake of breath. "Distracting me isn't going to help."

"Mmm, yes, I think it will. I'll distract you, and you'll stop fretting, and then we can both come up with a solution later."

"It has to be tonight."

"Which has only begun. Now, come back here and . . ."

A laugh, cut short by a kiss. Logan's shoulders slumped, and he trudged back to bed.

Logan tossed and turned all night. He drifted through nightmares of the puppy in another bag, a new owner tiring of it. Then dreams of him handing the puppy to Kate, which were almost as bad, because he'd wake up and remember that wasn't happening. Couldn't happen.

When he first woke, thinking he heard the puppy, it was obviously more self-torture. He snarled and pulled the covers up over his head. But as soon as he started falling asleep, the puppy returned, howling, the sound muffled, as if she were calling to him from the fort, begging him to come out and play, not to send her away to strangers who might do the same as—

He bolted up with a growl, shaking his head sharply. His room was silent, the puppy only in his head. He looked at the window. It was still dark out.

He reached for the books on his nightstand. There was always a stack. He hunted through the titles for the one least likely to contain canines of any kind. Müller's *A First German Reader*. That would do. He opened the book at random, and his gaze traveled down the page.

Leine: line, rope, or leash.

He slapped the book shut, and he was reaching for another when he heard a yip and the scrabbling of nails. He lifted his head and blinked hard. Then he heard another yip.

No, that wasn't possible.

More blinking. More yipping and scrabbling, like tiny nails against a door. Had the puppy escaped the fort? Maybe Mom had been distracted and didn't quite shut it up right, and the puppy had escaped and followed her trail to the house.

He had to get down there before Kate heard. That would be the worst Christmas morning ever: his sister waking to a puppy she couldn't have.

He raced into the hall, slowing only to tiptoe past Kate's room, and then trying his best not to thump down the stairs. He could clearly hear the puppy now. It seemed to come from the study.

The study?

How did she—?

No time to consider how. She was very clearly in the study.

Logan hurried to the door and pushed it open, and there was the puppy, attacking Jeremy's chair. She'd ripped a hole in it and was tearing out stuffing, the pieces flying everywhere.

"No!" he whispered, and ran into the study. The puppy hurled herself at him, yipping and yelping.

"Shhh!" he said as he scooped her up. "Shhh! Please. We need to get you—"

Footsteps thundered down the stairs. Only one person in the house made that much noise.

"Kate," he whispered. "Oh, no."

He looked both ways, as if he could find someplace to stash the puppy where his sister wouldn't smell it. He went to call a warning, to tell her to keep out, make up some story about wrapping one final present or—

The door flew open. Kate stood there, grinning.

"I see you found your gift," she said. "Or did she find you?"

He froze.

Kate thought their parents had given them the puppy.

This was worse, so much worse.

His mouth opened and closed, and the puppy leapt out of his arms and scrambled over to Kate, who lifted her in a hug, laughing exactly like he'd imagined, her expression even happier than he'd imagined.

"It's not . . ." he began. "She isn't from Mom and Dad."

"Of course not, silly," she said, making a face as the puppy licked her lips. "She's from me. I found her in the fort."

"Wh-what?"

Kate handed him the puppy, who seemed fine with the transfer, wriggling and whining and licking.

"She got inside the fort and couldn't get out, poor thing. Luckily, we'd both left sweaters in there, so that kept her warm, and there was snow to drink. I was out walking with Mom and Dad while you and Jeremy went shopping, and they thought they smelled a mutt, so they were getting me back to the house when we smelled the puppy in the fort. I thought *that's* what the mutt scent had been. I guess not, but, well, that's why I was going into the woods the other night—I thought it was safe, and I had another one of your sweaters, because I wanted to make sure she got your scent most of all." She motioned at the puppy. "Merry Christmas, Lo."

He heard a sharp intake of breath and looked to see their parents in the doorway. Mom was in front, watching him, surprise and dismay on her face.

"Hey, Mom, Dad," Kate said, without glancing their way. "Looks like she escaped from the basement. Logan found his gift early."

"I . . . see . . ." Mom said, that look still on her face, as if frantically trying to figure out what to do, and Logan realized *that's* what she'd been talking about last night. Not how to tell Logan he couldn't keep the puppy—how to tell them they'd gotten each other the same gift. The same puppy.

"Kate," Mom said. "Can I speak to you a moment?"

Kate looked over, and worry crept into her eyes, picking up on Mom's. It was like dousing a fire. She'd been happy giving him this gift. Even happier than he'd imagined she'd be *getting* it. Now they had to tell her it was a mistake—that he'd rescued the puppy for *her*. As her gift.

"It's okay, Mom." Logan looked at Kate. "So, you got me a puppy, huh?"

"*Found* you one. Exactly the kind you wanted, too." Her face lit up again. "When I saw her, I couldn't believe it. It was like . . . well, like it was meant to be."

"She's the kind you wanted, too. Maybe, since you found her . . ."

That light dimmed, just a little, as she nibbled her lip. This was what she wanted: the puppy for him.

"Maybe, since you found her, we could share her," he said. "I think Mom and Dad will agree one puppy in this house is quite enough. One *more* pup, that is."

The light returned as Kate laughed. "Also, giving me half the puppy means giving me half the responsibilities, right?"

"That's what I was thinking."

She laughed again and threw her arms around his neck, and the puppy wriggled between them, and Logan decided that half a puppy was, indeed, the best Christmas gift ever.

BABY BOOM

"See that stroller over there?" I pointed to an elegant one being pushed along the busy Miami street. "It has the best suspension on the market."

"That's important, I take it," Lucas said.

"According to every saleslady we encountered, it is. I am now officially an expert in baby strollers, having spent the entire day being schooled."

"And what was Savannah's role in this outing?"

"Throwing up her hands after the first sales pitch and asking me to handle it. Because 'But, Paige, you're so much better at these things.' Plus, she's got baby brain and can't be expected to make any critical decisions."

"Baby brain? I haven't heard that one."

"Oh, you're going to. For the next five months you're going to, and if she can, she'll stretch the excuse of aftereffects until the poor kid's twenty-one."

Lucas shook his head and opened the restaurant door for me. Yes, Savannah was pregnant. Four months along, which meant she was still fine for joining us on this trip to Miami, especially when Benicio had promised her and Adam a five-thousand-dollar shopping spree as a baby-announcement gift.

"So you had fun?" Lucas asked as the hostess led us to our table.

I rolled my eyes, and his lips curved in a hint of a smile as he said, "The next time, I'll go with you and endure the sales pitches."

"Do that for me and I will thank you in every possible way. Once the baby comes, I'll love it to death. But this part?" I shuddered. "I would rather shop for a new car than a stroller. I swear, they come with fewer options. By lunchtime I'd actually started looking forward to dinner with your dad."

We found Benicio already seated at the back of the restaurant. We were five minutes early—he just always made a point of being there first for Lucas, which was, of course, a point in itself. *You are special, Lucas. You have my undivided attention.* With every year that passed, every step closer Benicio came to retirement, that message grew louder.

You are my heir. You will inherit the Cortez Cabal.

Which was the last thing Lucas ever wanted. Yet if he didn't accept the role, it went to his only remaining brother. Carlos was as inept as he was cruel, and for a corporation employing hundreds of supernaturals, I'm not sure which of those attributes was more dangerous.

Dinner with Benicio was never easy, but at least I could be guaranteed two hours without hearing the word "baby."

Lucas pulled out my chair.

"Carlos's wife is having a baby boy," Benicio said.

I bit back a laugh.

"She had the ultrasound today," Benicio continued. "It's a boy."

"Excellent," Lucas said. "And I believe I know just the person to gift them with the perfect stroller." He opened his menu. "Also, Carlos's wife's name is Annette. You really ought to remember it, Papá."

"I'm not sure Carlos can remember it. I'm still convinced his best man had to prompt him at the wedding vows."

There actually had been an awkward pause at that moment in the service. A few years ago, Carlos had been the very model of a rich playboy—too many women, too much booze, too little responsibility. In the six years since his brothers' deaths, he'd cleaned up his act, preparing to take center stage as heir-elect. Part of that included finding the perfect wife. Model thin and beautiful but lacking self-confidence. Young but not idealistic. Bright but not well educated. Hispanic, from a long and proud lineage going back to Spain. And human. In other words, everything I was not. But I'm okay with that. Benicio remembers *my* name.

"So it's a boy," I said. "But unless Annette is secretly a witch, that was guaranteed."

"There's always the chance of a genetic mishap."

I arched my brows. "Girls are genetic mishaps?"

"For a sorcerer they are, as a son would be for a witch. But she is pregnant with a healthy baby boy, which will help his case as heir. There is only one way you and Lucas can fight that."

Lucas's fingers tightened almost imperceptibly on his menu.

"You need to have a baby," Benicio said.

Silence. One moment of absolute silence. Then the slap of Lucas's menu hitting the table.

I thought Benicio was joking. A poor joke, but a joke nonetheless. Benicio knew we'd decided long ago not to have children. He'd learned to swallow that disapproval or risk torpedoing an already rocky relationship with his youngest son. But when Lucas smacked the menu down, Benicio flinched, and I knew this was no joke.

Lucas pushed his chair back an inch and looked at me. He wanted to go, but he'd never storm out, leaving me to run after him. I rose, and we walked through the restaurant, his hand wrapped tightly around mine.

Outside the front doors, I said, "You knew he was going to suggest that, didn't you? He's brought it up before."

"After he learned Annette was pregnant, he broached the subject with me. I had hoped that the intensity of my response would discourage any future revivals."

"Ah."

"In fact, I made it very clear that resurrecting that topic—"

"Paige? Lucas?" Benicio said behind us, his shoes slapping the sidewalk.

Lucas kept walking, his voice low as he said, "The answer is no, we will not discuss it. As for the question itself, I will not even dignify *that* with an answer. You know it. You have always known it. Not having children is our choice, and it is our right to make that choice. It isn't a medical issue. It isn't something we have tabled for future discussion."

"I'm thirty-four," I said. "Passing the age where it can *be* a future discussion."

"But not past it yet," Benicio said. "Not for a few years. The fact that neither of you has taken steps to permanently prevent the possibility suggests it isn't an absolute decision."

"That would be personal and private medical information," Lucas said, his voice ice-cold. "I suppose I should not be surprised you accessed it, Father. Whether we have made our decision a medically permanent one is absolutely none of your business. What counts is what we are saying. What we have always said. That we choose not to have children."

"Because there's too much else going on in your lives. You don't want to bring a child into that. But no one expects Paige to give up her career for a baby. I can ensure she has the best possible child care."

"Right," I said. "Because our dream is to have a child . . . and then watch her be raised by nannies. The only point to that would be if we were so narcissistic we *had* to reproduce, whatever the cost."

"I'm saying I could help you make this happen at absolutely no inconvenience to either of you."

"Inconven—?"

"With Annette's pregnancy, we're losing the board. They *want* to support Lucas. If you were pregnant, that would decide the matter, and they would recognize the sacrifice you've made."

"Sacri—? Are we still talking about having a child here?"

"I'm wording it poorly. I apologize for offending—"

Lucas cut in. "There is no possibility of phrasing this suggestion in a way that is not unrelentingly offensive. You are asking us to have a *child* to secure the future of a *corporation*. You are asking my wife to lend her *body* to the cause. To bear a child as a political gambit."

"I've upset you—"

"Me? No, Father. My role in this is significant, but it pales in comparison to my *wife's*. To a *child's*. To use them to secure a lineage is beyond appalling."

"Tell that to every monarchy in the world."

"Then perhaps it is indeed a sign of progress that *our* country broke away from that tradition centuries ago. And whatever we might think of that tradition, it is about nationhood. This is about a *company*."

"Which employs—"

"Spare me the statistics, Father. I recite them to myself every time I cannot believe I've taken a role in the Cabal. And now, with this *suggestion*, I suspect I'll spend the rest of the night quoting those statistics to myself and mentally crunching the numbers, deciding yet again if it's worth it."

Lucas took a quick breath and finished with, "Paige and I are going back to our condo. As much as I would love to fly from the city tonight, we have work to do here and our commitment is to that work. But I would strongly suggest that we don't have any more reason to speak this week, or I may rethink that commitment. Good night, Father."

We did not discuss what happened on the drive back to the condo. What would we say? Endless variations on "Can you believe he said that?"

The truth was that I *could* believe it. I was even willing to cut Benicio a little slack in this. Yes, the idea of donating my reproductive system to his business interests was absolutely heinous. But I understood he wasn't thinking of it that way. He believed Lucas and I must secretly want a child. Which is a bit of a head-scratcher, given how his own experience with fatherhood worked out. Three sons born in wedlock, all of whom saw Benicio only as the obstacle between them and unlimited power as CEO of the Cortez Cabal. Then there was Lucas. The so-called bastard son whom Benicio adored. The one who had the most difficult relationship with him. And yet the one who also had the best relationship. Lucas was Cordelia to Benicio's Lear, the youngest child and the only one who truly did love him.

If I had to speculate, I think Benicio saw in us something he never truly had a chance at—the opportunity to bear a child in love and raise it in love. It was also one last chance for him to be a real grandfather, his dead sons having kept their own boys away from him as punishment for not being named heir, with Carlos already threatening to do the same. In Benicio's relationship with Savannah, I see that yearning, and I felt bad that we couldn't fill it for him. But we can't.

It was more than having busy lives. Any child we brought into this world would arrive with a target on her back. Even Savannah, a disavowed child of the Nast Cabal, joked about how often she'd been kidnapped when she was young.

Then there was Savannah herself. She *was* our child in so many ways. As much as we loved her, there'd been a soft sigh of relief when she finally moved out and we had the house to ourselves. When it came to parenting, we'd been there, done that, and it might sound selfish, but I was okay with finally having my husband all to myself.

I understood, then, that Benicio didn't realize he was trying to co-opt my body for his own purposes. To him, this made logical sense, giving us an excuse to satisfy a presumed longing while helping save the company from Carlos and his cohorts. Win-win.

I would tell Lucas that. But not tonight. My husband so rarely lost his temper that I wasn't going to negate his right to be angry over this. Instead, I'd try to take his mind off it, which I did, until both of us fell asleep, too exhausted to fume over Benicio.

"You look like shit this morning," Savannah said when I met her the next morning.

"Thank you. Thank you so much." I collapsed into a coffee shop chair. "And I'd love to say the same back, except it would be a lie. I've always thought that saying about pregnant women glowing was a total lie. Apparently not. Bitch."

Savannah choked on a laugh, but she grinned, too. While she'd been living with us, it'd been hard for me to get past the guardian–ward relationship. We'd always been more like sisters, but it had definitely been an "older sister" vibe. Now we've finally achieved that elusive status of true friendship. The fact that I was okay with calling Savannah a bitch delighted her. Or maybe it was just hearing me say the word.

I caught a whiff of her drink, and my stomach, already unsettled, roiled. "What *is* that?" I said, pointing.

"A decaf cappuccino. Yes, I know it still has some caffeine, but Hope says having one when I need it is fine, and my doctor agrees. Right now, it's the only thing that will get me through another day of shopping."

"The milk's turned. Go ask them for another one."

"Um, it's fine, Paige." She pushed it over. "Smell."

I took a deep whiff and was out of my chair and on the way to the restroom in two seconds flat. Five seconds after barreling through the door, I was bent over a toilet, vomiting up what little I'd managed to eat at breakfast.

"Paige?" Savannah said outside the stall. "Are you throwing up?"

A wave of gagging inelegantly answered for me.

"You weren't feeling well yesterday morning, either," she said. "Are you sick?"

"I wouldn't come near you if I thought I had the flu."

"I know that. But you don't *get* sick. Ever."

"It's food poisoning. Revenge of the cheap sushi from the other night."

Silence answered, and I wondered if the smell of the vomit had her racing out before *she* threw up. But when I exited the stall, heading straight for the sink, she was there, her face drawn with worry.

"Food poisoning doesn't come and go like that," she said. "Believe me, Adam and I have eaten our share of bad-decision street food."

"Well, then, maybe it's sympathetic morning sickness."

"I don't have morning sickness."

"Bitch."

She didn't grin this time. Didn't even smile.

"You really *don't* look good, Paige. I figured it was just a late night with Lucas. Otherwise, I wouldn't have teased you about it. But you look . . ."

"Like shit?"

"Exhausted. That's not normal. You can get two hours' sleep and you're little miss sunshine, raring to go."

I finished rinsing out my mouth. Then I took my toothbrush and toothpaste from my purse. When Savannah didn't rib me for carrying a toothbrush and toothpaste, I knew her concern was serious.

"Maybe I have caught something," I said. "If so, I shouldn't be around you. Let me call Adam. He'll jump at the chance to reschedule his meeting. He might like doing research, but that doesn't mean he likes hanging out with other researchers."

I smiled, expecting her to roll her eyes and make some comment. She only watched me as I brushed my teeth.

"Is there any chance . . .?" She patted her stomach and then pointed at me.

I choked on my mouthful of minty water. "Absolutely not."

"No form of birth control is one hundred percent. You gave me that talk, complete with statistics I can still recite."

"I'm on long-term birth control. As close to foolproof as possible. So no, pregnancy is not the answer."

"Have you had a period since Seattle?"

I capped my toothpaste. "What?"

"You had to do an emergency drugstore run when we were investigating in Seattle. I remember it because I joked about getting nine months of freedom from that particular joy."

"Right, then. It was Seattle, which was last month."

"Six weeks ago."

"Then I'm a couple of weeks overdue. It's happened before. As you love to point out, I have hit middle age."

"You're at least a decade from menopause, Paige."

"I'm not pregnant. It isn't possible."

"Why?"

Because just twelve hours ago Benicio was telling us we need to have a baby. Waking up the very next morning to discover I'm pregnant is too coincidental to even consider.

A woman with two toddlers walked in, the kids shrieking and giggling, the mother looking harried but happy. She admonished them to make sure they wiped up. Then she spotted us and offered a wry smile and an apology as she bustled past.

I've seen other women watch little ones with the hunger of unsatisfied maternal yearning. Even Savannah, who hadn't planned to get pregnant until she was older, had begun watching babies with that look in her eye, until Adam finally asked if there was any particular reason she wanted to wait.

I've also seen women watch little ones and shudder, unable to imagine the horror of that life. I've never felt either emotion. I see little ones and I smile, the same way I would at a puppy. I love puppies. Never had one. Never considered getting one. Just because you think something is wonderful doesn't mean you want it for yourself.

"Paige?"

I took out my cell phone and waved her from the bathroom, saying, "I'm calling Adam to come shop with you. Then I'll go see the doctor and make sure whatever I have isn't contagious."

She plucked the phone from my hand. When I tried to snatch it back, she just held it out of my reach, a strategy she's been able to employ almost from the day I took custody of her.

"Let's pop by a drugstore first," she said.

"I'm not preg—"

"You're going to the doctor while you're here, right?"

"I only go to the Cabal doctor for my annual physical." And apparently, given what Benicio said last night, even that was a mistake.

"I mean that you're going to a doctor and telling her you've been sick for two mornings in a row. You're thirty-four. Happily married. And your period is two weeks late. The first thing she'll do is give you a pregnancy test. So maybe you just might want to get that out of the way, in private, beforehand."

She had a point. I knew I wasn't pregnant. The coincidence alone almost made me suspect this morning's nausea was psychosomatic. But I'd rather walk in with my negative test strip and say, "I threw up this morning and *this* isn't the answer." The pharmacy it was, then.

An hour later, I was standing in our condo bathroom, staring at the double blue line on a white strip.

"Paige?" Savannah rapped at the door.

"Hold on."

"Unless it takes you ten minutes to pee, I've been waiting long enough."

"It didn't work. I have to try again."

She sighed and slumped at the door, like she used to when she was a teen and suspected I'd retreated to the bathroom to avoid a fight I didn't care to continue.

I took out a second box—a different brand—pulled out the kit, and started over.

Another ten minutes later, I was sitting on my bed with Savannah, both of us staring at two strips, bearing identical results.

"I'm calling Lucas," she said.

I reached for her arm. "No, he's in a meeting. This isn't . . ."

I was about to say it wasn't important. But it was, wasn't it? So incredibly important. And yet . . .

If we'd been trying for a baby, like Savannah and Adam, I wouldn't have made that call. I'd have sped to him, and stood outside that meeting door, eagerly waiting. That was how it should be.

I felt the pain of that, the loss of that, the realization this was an experience I'd never know, the joy of running to my husband and throwing my arms around his neck and screaming, "We're having a baby!"

This would be a very different conversation.

"I know it's not urgent," Savannah said. "But you need him. Now. If you can't call, I will."

I kept hold of her arm. "Not yet. I . . . I need to see Dr. Mendez. This must be a mistake."

"Two positive tests plus morning sickness plus a late period. It's not a mistake. I know this isn't the answer you want, Paige, but you're the one who's all about the proof. This is the proof."

I took a deep breath. Then I told her what Benicio said last night. When I finished, she said, "God, he can be such a shit-heel. I'd say I can't believe he'd suggest that, but I can totally believe it.

And then . . ." She trailed off and looked at me. "Wait a second. Right after you refuse, you find out you're pregnant? That's way too coincidental."

"Exactly. If I knew of a spell that caused pregnancy, I'd be thinking he was guilty of more than suggesting it."

"But there's not. There's magic to help get pregnant, like your mother used, but there's nothing . . ."

She trailed off again, gaze going distant as her hand rested on the bump of her stomach. I'd noticed her doing that lately, resting her hand there. I had no doubt Savannah was ready for motherhood. She'd never been the most mature young woman, but she wanted this and would be mature for her baby. Now, seeing her instinctively connecting with her unborn child, I felt a pang of grief for that, too, that I had a child in my womb and didn't feel that way, feared I never could.

I blinked back tears and said, "If that look means you're wondering whether there *is* a spell, there's not. Pregnancy still requires a sperm and an egg."

"Oh, I'm sure there's *plenty* of that going on. Probably even more than when I lived at home, when you guys napped so often I worried you were suffering from chronic fatigue syndrome."

"Yes, but there's no *magic* that can get me pregnant. A seventeenth-century spell can't counteract modern birth control. Which is why I need to see the doctor who prescribed me that birth control."

I'd been at Dr. Mendez's office for hours. It began with a pregnancy test and other samples, all sent to her in-house lab. Supernaturals have enough anomalies in our blood that she needs a dedicated lab, also staffed by supernaturals. Yet even putting aside everything else, processing my test took time. Savannah stayed, no matter how often I insisted she didn't need to.

Finally, Dr. Mendez called me back in for the results.

"I'm sorry, Paige, but yes, you are definitely pregnant."

I managed a wan smile. "Not the usual way you need to give that news, I bet."

She took a seat. "Actually, if patients get their results from me instead of the drugstore, it's usually because they're praying that drugstore test is wrong. It rarely is. In your case, I had to check because of your contraceptive implant. The chance of it failing is so incredibly low, even I thought there must be a mistake."

"So I'm the lucky one-in-ten-thousand chance of failure?"

She shifted in her seat. "Actually, no. You were as likely to get pregnant as any other sexually active, thirty-four-year-old woman."

"What?"

"There's no trace of the birth control in your system."

I shook my head sharply. "That can't be. The implant has been in for five months, and I can't be more than six weeks pregnant. That means it *was* working."

"No, it wasn't. You'd have had residual protection for a while. After that? Well, you *are* thirty-four. Pregnancy isn't going to happen overnight."

"But . . . you're telling me . . . the implant . . ."

"Isn't working. At all. I'm going to remove and analyze it, because I have no idea how this could have happened, and you can certainly sue the manufacturer, but I know that's the least of your concerns right now."

"Have there been other reports of it failing? Is there some way to check now?"

"I did while you were waiting. There's nothing. Somehow, you received a birth control implant that was, for all intents and purposes, nothing more than a placebo."

I texted Lucas as I left the doctor's office. As much as I hated to interfere with his day of meetings, Savannah was right—I needed him. In possibly the only thing that went right that day, he'd not only finished early but was waiting at home.

Savannah dropped me at the condo door. Before I went in, she said, "I won't tell Adam if you'd rather I didn't. Whatever you decide, that's no one else's business."

I nodded.

"And whatever you decide?" She caught my hand as I climbed out. "It's not my business, either, but I'm behind it. I'm behind *you*, Paige. One hundred percent. Always."

I stopped then and leaned across the seat to give her a hug, a tight one, my face pressed against her hair so she wouldn't see my eyes welling up.

I walked into the condo smelling tea. Not just tea, but my favorite blend, one I had to order because I could never quite duplicate it. I was long out of it, too—it'd been on back order for months.

When I walked into the living room, Lucas was there, pouring tea into a china cup. On the end table was a two-tiered tray of English tea pastries and sandwiches. And where we'd once had an ordinary love seat, there now stood one with dual recliners.

When he caught me staring at the love seat, he said, "That *is* the one you wanted, isn't it?"

"It's exactly the one I wanted. The one I've been searching for. But where . . ." My gaze went to the tea. "And also where . . .?"

"Connections," he said. "Quite possibly the only advantage to being a Cortez."

I looked from the love seat to the tea to the pastries, and I managed to say, "Savannah called you."

"Hmm?"

"Savannah called you. To say I wasn't having . . ." I faltered. "Wasn't having a good day."

A wry smile. "She didn't. No one needed to tell me that. After that dinner with my father and a day of shopping, I decided you could use . . ."

He waved at the tableau, and my tears welled again, this time threatening to burst into full waterworks. Lucas hurried over, bumping into the table hard enough to bruise, and saying, "What's wrong?"

"We . . . we need to talk."

"Savannah. Is she all right? The baby . . ."

"The baby's fine. Every—everyone's fine." I stumbled over that last bit, but it was true. There was nothing wrong with me. Just nature, taking its course by leading me *off* course.

I led him to the new love seat. We sat, and I opened my mouth to say *I'm pregnant*, but the words wouldn't come. This wasn't a joyful announcement. Yet neither could I clutch his hand and make a mournful pronouncement.

Instead, I said, "My birth control hasn't been working."

"Your . . .?"

"The implant. It's defective. Has been since Dr. Mendez put it in."

"Someone sabotaged your birth control."

I hadn't said that. Hadn't even suggested that to the doctor. It seemed too outrageous an accusation. But of course it was exactly what I'd been thinking when the doctor told me the news.

"That's one possibility," I said.

"It's almost certainly the *only* one, given the otherwise unbelievable coincidence of timing. My father wasn't asking us to reconsider; he was planting the seed in hopes we'd agree, so that, when it happened, we'd accept it as a happy accident." He shook his head. "After all he's done, how can I still be surprised every time?"

"Because you want better. You know he's capable of better. And you hate being disappointed."

Lucas put his arm around my shoulders and tugged me against him. "I'm only glad you had the forethought to visit Dr. Mendez. I wouldn't have considered checking."

"I . . . I didn't go to her for that. I . . ." Deep breath. "I've been sick the last couple of mornings and my period is late, which I hadn't realized, being so busy. Savannah insisted . . . She insisted I check . . ."

He twisted to look at me. "You're . . .?"

I nodded. Silence fell. One long moment of silence.

No matter how strong our marriage is, there are things I don't know, can't even guess, fear trying to guess. Things like this. We'd agreed to not have children, but I could never really be sure if his conviction exactly matched my own. Was he more open to the possibility, just not *so* open to it that he'd try changing my mind? Or was he even more opposed, and this really would come as the worst possible news?

Silence. Then he said, "How are you doing?" and my eyes really did fill with tears then, as I saw in his face exactly what I felt, that this wasn't secretly joyous news but neither was it a dire pronouncement. When the tears welled, he pulled me against him, and I let them fall before I said, "I think I'm still in shock. I tested twice. Two different kits from two manufacturers. I just couldn't believe . . . still can't believe . . ."

"How do you feel?" he asked as I pulled away.

"Too numb to process anything else."

He shifted to face me. "Whatever you decide, I support it."

I shook my head. "It isn't just about me."

He went quiet for a moment, and then said, "Obviously, it impacts me, but you are the one who would endure a pregnancy and undertake any risks. I don't feel strongly one way or another. I never have. The obvious choice was not to attempt to have children—one *should* care. But if the choice is to continue or end a pregnancy, I will accommodate either way."

"'Accommodate' isn't really the word we're looking for here."

A brief smile. "It isn't, is it? For once I seem unable to find the right one. The most suitably neutral one. It is neutral to me. What you have here"—he pressed his hand to my stomach—"is a collection of cells that could become a child. We know enough about the afterlife to know we are discussing the fate of cells, not a soul. That isn't how it works."

"And you don't lean either way? At all?"

Another moment of quiet. "I don't know. I'd need time to consider more. Even then, it would be only a slight preference and not strong enough to influence your decision, should you already know what you want."

"I don't."

"Then let me suggest that there is no hurry to make that decision. It is a rather large one."

"It is." I looked up at him. "How are you doing?"

"More concerned for you at the moment. As for how this may have come to be, I'm going to postpone thinking about that for a while. This doesn't seem quite the time to lose my temper. It does, however, seem like a fine time for tea. Or a hot bath."

"For two?"

His lips quirked. "The tea?"

"Sure, that, too."

I picked up both cups and headed for the stairs. Lucas brought the pastry tray as he followed.

We had a bath. Not overly hot—I remembered Adam lamenting that they'd bought a backyard hot tub for their new place and now couldn't use it while Savannah was pregnant. Well, *he* could, but he wouldn't, just like he wasn't drinking coffee or alcohol for nine months, and part of that was pure partner support . . . but part was, I knew, self-preservation, because enjoying a nice cold beer in front of Savannah might land him on the couch for the duration of the pregnancy.

So I made the bath lukewarm, and I didn't say why. Nor did I say why I didn't drink the rest of my tea, after remembering it had a caffeine base. I had to proceed as if I was carrying this pregnancy to term, just in case.

We enjoyed the bath. We drank some tea. We ate the biscuits and sandwiches. We made love. Then we sprawled on the bed, naked, and talked. Talked about the presumed sabotage as if it was an investigation for a client. That was how we had to handle it. If someone presented us with this case, how would we proceed?

Discuss the possibilities. Lay them out. Consider each one and how we might prove or disprove it. Come up with a plan of investigation. What evidence did we need to gather? Whom did we need to speak to? Where might we need to go? What might we need to do? Should we bring in Savannah and Adam?

Yes, we discussed that last one. They were investigators at our firm. And they were also that blend of family and friend that makes them closer than either.

We even began a case file. Lucas loves his lists and his files and his notes. I could say that's all him, but before we started the firm, I designed Web sites and software, so I'm nearly as much of a project-management geek. We wrote stuff down. Made those lists. Devised a course of action.

We'd had plans that evening for a late dinner with board members loyal to Benicio. Lucas canceled them quietly, only telling me when it was too late to un-cancel. We both hated those dinners, but we knew how important they were.

I think the fact they *were* important was the worst part. Lucas had spent his life refusing to be his father's heir. Now, he needed not only to accept that mantle but fight for it. That went against everything in his soul . . . everything except the reason he would fight: to provide a decent working environment for supernaturals. He knew a corporation that fully embraced his principles and ethics would see a sharp drop in profits, and the shareholders would overthrow him in a heartbeat. But he did dream of inching toward better, and he'd already fixed some of the Cabal's worst practices, by showing more efficient alternatives.

The problem was that, if Lucas lost the support of the board, the Cabal wouldn't just maintain the status quo. Under Carlos and his supporters, it would begin the downward spiral, where profit ruled and ethics were something you laughed about over your quarterly statements.

We'd already seen that happen with the Nasts. On the death of the CEO, the Cabal split between two successors. One half was run by Sean Nast, the true heir and Savannah's half-brother. Sean was no idealist, but he was a good man, a principled man, and he had implemented improvements. He believed in the greater good. His uncle Josef did not. Like Carlos, Josef Nast believed in profit at any cost. Unlike Carlos, Josef was actually an excellent businessman. The result? Sean was doing fine, but his less committed employees were being lured away as Josef's half flourished. The Cortez board saw that. Which meant we had to reschedule dinner and keep all our other social appointments, however difficult they would be right now.

The next day, Lucas had a breakfast meeting, which was fine, considering I was in no shape to start investigating that early. When Savannah got pregnant, I'd gone into research mode, which meant, ironically, I now knew all the morning sickness treatments she'd never needed. Crackers and chamomile tea still set my stomach lurching, but I managed to do a decent-enough acting job to convince Lucas I was "much better than yesterday," though he still lingered until Savannah showed up.

The moment he was gone, I was in the bathroom, throwing up those crackers and tea. Clearly, more research was needed. Also, more mouthwash.

I'd talked to Savannah last night about telling Adam. She had, and I'd barely finished conversing with the toilet before he was on the phone, wanting to talk. I got as far as "Later, okay?" before I was back in the bathroom.

It was a fun morning. Eventually, though, my stomach calmed down—or emptied—enough for me to get some work done, which helped distract me. Lucas showed up at ten-thirty with ginger tablets and matzo ball soup and everything else he'd apparently found in his own research.

"How long before she began vomiting?" he asked Savannah.

"I think you were still in the driveway."

He turned to me. "I've rescheduled my morning tomorrow. I don't like you going through that alone."

"Um, hello?" Savannah said.

"I appreciate you coming over, Savannah, but bedside manner is not your strong suit."

"It's toilet-side manner that counts here, and mine is just fine." She looked at me. "Would you rather have Lucas standing behind you, freaking out because he can't help? Or have me chilling in the living room while he gets some work done at the office?"

"Option B." I looked at Lucas. "Sorry, but she's right. Work tomorrow morning and then join me once I'm feeling well enough to continue investigating the case of 'who got Paige knocked up.'"

"That's a mystery that doesn't need solving," Savannah said. "With most people, I'd say it's ninety-nine-percent obvious who's the culprit. With you, I'll go all out and say there is absolutely no doubt." She pointed at Lucas. "Him."

"You know what I meant."

"I'm not sure how much of a mystery *that* one is, either. Benicio's fingerprints are all over this. The biggest question will be what we do about it. I know he didn't think through the implications, but causing you to get pregnant against your will?"

"It's unforgivable," Lucas said.

Savannah and I exchanged a look. If it *was* unforgivable, what did that mean for all of us?

"This is why we're investigating," I said. "To definitively answer the question, rather than pointing fingers. I think I'm ready to tackle that soup. Then we'll get to work."

Our first stop was Dr. Mendez. Lucas questioned her. In Miami, it was his name that carried weight, even among supernaturals who avoided contact with the Cabal. Or *especially* among those avoiding contact.

According to Dr. Mendez, my implant was the correct device, but completely empty, without even a trace of chemicals. She had reconfirmed there were no other reports of problems.

Lucas said, "I'm going to need to ask for a full accounting of your supply and storage procedures, as well as access to the facilities and employees who, in turn, have access to these devices."

"If you're planning to sue the manufacturer—"

"I have no interest in suing anyone. If it is indeed a manufacturer defect, they will answer for that. However, I strongly suspect it was not."

"You think someone tampered with the implants?"

"I think someone tampered with Paige's."

She hesitated. "That seems . . ."

"Unlikely? You know who I am. You cannot be unaware of the succession drama. Carlos has married. His wife is pregnant. Paige and I have chosen not to have children. We have been urged—strongly—to reconsider that. Now she is pregnant, the fault lying with a defective device implanted—here in Miami—shortly after my brother announced his wife's pregnancy." He met her gaze. "Please tell me I have no reason to suspect sabotage."

She granted us full access to her facilities and cleared her own schedule to help. That wasn't surprising. The most obvious suspect was Dr. Mendez herself, colluding to switch the proper device for the faulty one.

We spent the next two hours getting to know far more about the clinic's supply chain than we ever wanted to. It was tightly regulated, considering the street value of the drugs. The doctor didn't keep a large supply—she wasn't a pharmacist—but they were still valuable.

That tight regulation meant no one could slip into the supply closet midday and swap out my birth control. Also, I wasn't the only patient receiving that type of implant. It was cutting-edge technology and difficult to obtain—which is why I hadn't used my Portland doctor. After I'd requested it, though, Dr. Mendez had begun using it for two other patients. She'd contacted both yesterday and tested them, and their implants were working fine. That meant *mine* had been switched. Specifically mine.

By four, we had our culprit: the nurse who'd delivered the implant to Dr. Mendez during my appointment.

When we first confronted her, there were about two minutes of denials, which quickly turned to a teary explanation.

"They promised to get my son transferred to a minimum-security prison. He was supposed to be in minimum-security. It's his first offense. But overcrowding and . . ." Her hands fluttered. "He's young. Naive. Small for his age. That prison . . ." She shuddered. "He's not a bad boy, but that prison was going to make him one. And now he's where he should be, and I don't regret what I did to get him there." She looked at me. "When you have your baby, you'll understand."

"No," I said. "I already have a child. I'd jump in front of a speeding bus to protect her, but I'd never push anyone *else* in front of it."

Her lips tightened. "You say you do not want a baby. That makes you the selfish one."

Lucas looked ready to lose his temper again. I gave him a look and instead he asked, "Have you told your contact that Paige is pregnant?"

"No, I only learned it when you came in today."

"Who is your contact?" I asked.

"I was approached by two men from the Cabal. They work for him. Directly for him. He asked them to do this, and he got my boy transferred."

"And *he* is?"

Her look said the answer should be obvious. And it was. I just needed to hear her say it. After a moment, she did.

"Mr. Cortez. Benicio Cortez."

We couldn't go to Benicio and accuse him yet. We needed hard evidence.

The next step was tracking down the two men who'd hired the nurse. She'd provided names and we knew both of them—executives with the kind of vague job titles that tell everyone not to ask what exactly they do. Problem solvers. Fixers. Both of whom reported directly to Benicio.

Lucas knew one of the two fixers—Heath Denby—very well. As kids, neither boy had been particularly enamored of Cabal life, slipping off together when they found themselves at the same function. As for the other man—John Pearce—I was the one who knew him better, having quietly interceded in a family matter that could have cost him his job. So Lucas met up with Savannah to track Denby while Adam and I went after Pearce.

We tracked Pearce to a gym after his shift ended. While Cabal headquarters had state-of-the-art facilities, Pearce was recovering from a back injury and apparently not keen to let his colleagues see that he wasn't in perfect shape yet.

We parked next to his car, where I planned to intercept him post-workout. When a food truck pulled into the lot and set my stomach churning, we put the windows up and turned on the air.

"So, morning sickness . . ." Adam said. "I'm guessing the 'morning' part is false advertising?"

"It's worse in the morning, but it definitely doesn't vanish at the stroke of noon. I'm hoping it's temporary. Well, if . . ."

"If you decide to continue the pregnancy."

When I shrugged, he said, "You don't need to tiptoe around it with me. Are you forgetting who came to Boston when you had a scare in college? There wasn't any question of what you'd have done then, or any question of who'd drive you to the clinic to do it."

"I know. Thank you. I'm just . . . struggling. I'm not in college anymore, so the decision is tougher. I have a great marriage. Lucas would make an amazing father. We have good jobs and enough money to easily support a family. There's no reason *not* to go through with it."

"Except for the fact that maybe you and Lucas don't want to be parents. Which is kinda the most important reason of all."

"I know. But we wouldn't *mind* being parents, so even that makes it hard. On the other hand, saying we wouldn't *mind* having a baby doesn't seem good enough."

"I think if you decide to continue, that's a perfectly fine place to start. But if you decide not to, that's fine, too."

He eased back in his seat, looking out the window. "There's also a third option. Savannah and I . . . Well, we talked, and . . ." He glanced over. "If you wanted to go through with the pregnancy but not keep the baby, we'd take it. Happily. We could do it however you guys wanted—keep it open and be honest from the start, or stay quiet until the kid's older, or . . . whatever."

"That's . . ." My eyes filled again and I brushed my hand over them. "Sorry. Hormones, apparently. Which you know all about."

"Oh, I do, though I sometimes suspect Savannah just likes the excuse."

I managed a laugh. "Possibly. But . . . the offer . . . Thank you. Really. That's . . . big. Huge."

He shrugged. "Hey, one baby, two babies, doesn't make much difference, right?"

"You might want to talk to Elena and Clay about that."

"We'd survive. Anyway, we just wanted to put it out there. As a third option."

I leaned over the seat and hugged him. "Thank you."

We'd been in the parking lot almost three hours. That seemed excessive. Admittedly, my idea of exercise is an hour of Pilates twice a week, so I'm not exactly a gym rat. But even Adam declared this was longer than he and Savannah spent at the gym. We snuck in under cover of blur spells and split up to hunt. By this point, we figured Pearce would have retired to the sauna or the pool. The sauna was in the men's room, so I got the pool.

I was heading toward my goal when I spotted Pearce in the bar. The juice bar, that is. He'd staked out a table in the corner and had his laptop set up to work, though a woman was making that difficult. He was very clearly trying to do work and she kept hitting on him.

I decided to help. I took out my cell phone, set the call to show up as a private number, and dialed Pearce's phone from the number the nurse had been given. It rang. It continued ringing, and Pearce kept typing on his laptop as the woman chattered to him.

The number connected. A man's voice said, "Cortez Corporation. John Pearce speaking . . ." as I watched Pearce, still typing, his phone on the table, untouched.

"The number I used is also the one I have for John." I was on the speakerphone to Lucas as Adam drove us. "Which makes no sense. Sure, whoever was pretending to be him could reroute it, but he'd notice if he wasn't getting any calls. So how . . .? Wait. Wasn't there something about the Cabal phones about six months ago?"

"Yes, a security breach, which resulted in new phone numbers for a few dozen employees, primarily in the security department, which John technically is."

"That means I have his old number. Which is the one someone gave the nurse, pretending to be him. We need to find out who took that number."

From my office, I hacked into the telecommunications system. Easy enough. Something like the reallocation of a phone number isn't considered worthy of the highest security measures. I just needed to be on the Cabal system to hack it, which I did, in about ten minutes.

"Ralph Daly has Pearce's old number," I said to Lucas, who was waiting quietly behind me. "The requisition order tracks back to him. He specifically requested it as an alternative number, which he asked be left off the main directory."

Daly was a VP and a board member. Also, one of Lucas's staunchest supporters.

"Any possibility it may have been requested in his name?" Lucas asked.

"The note says it was directly requested. Of course, it's not inconceivable that—"

A rap sounded at the front door. When I opened the door, Benicio stood there.

"I saw the light on," he said. "I hoped— Oh. Lucas. Hello."

Lucas gave a stiff nod and stayed in his seat.

"May I come in?" Benicio asked.

I motioned him inside. As he closed the door, he said, "I would like to apologize. To both of you, of course, but mostly to Paige. When I made that suggestion the other night, I didn't see the harm in it. Now I do. It was inexcusably offensive. You have made your decision. I respect that, and I apologize for asking you to change it."

"I have heard," Lucas said, "that the board pressured you to put forward the proposal. Strongly pressured you. Particularly some of those who support me."

Benicio made a face. "Whatever pressure I've gotten, the decision to ask was ultimately mine. The mistake was mine."

"Should I speak to anyone from the board myself?" Lucas said. "My sources suggest Ralph Daly has been particularly vocal."

"Ralph wants to see you take my place, and sometimes, in his zealousness to do so, he doesn't consider the ramifications." A wry smile. "Not unlike your father, it seems. I'll have a word with him. You won't hear any more about it. I understand your decision. And of course, if you change your mind, Paige herself is proof that, with a little magical help, there's no reason you couldn't have a child ten years from now—"

"Papá," Lucas said, squeezing the bridge of his nose. "That is not *dropping* the subject."

Benicio sighed. "Another apology, then. Is there any way I can entice you both to join me in a late dinner? If I promise that the subject is truly dropped?"

Lucas glanced at me. I nodded.

"Dinner would be fine, Papá. Thank you."

The next morning, I was parked in our condo bathroom, Adam having carried a comfortable chair in there for me. He'd meant it as a joke. An hour later, I found myself in it, working on my laptop. It was just easier that way.

At ten, Lucas pinged my computer. I opened a video screen as he ushered Ralph Daly into his office.

Lucas greeted Daly, exchanging the prerequisite small talk along with apologies for disturbing his workday and Daly's assurances that it was fine, just fine.

"I have a . . . sensitive matter to discuss," Lucas said, moving to the chair behind his desk. "I have not yet mentioned it to my father, and I would like to ask you to do the same. Before you do, let me assure you it is personal, not business, and therefore I am not placing you in a difficult position."

Daly quickly agreed to silence.

"Paige is pregnant," Lucas said.

Daly lowered himself into the chair, his eyes glowing, the news clearly welcome even as he responded to Lucas with a more cautious, "Is that . . . good news?"

"For me, yes. The only reason I haven't told my father is that I want Paige to pass the initial trimester to ensure all is well."

"But it's *good* news. So congratulations *are* in order."

"Thank you. I will warn, however, that Paige may not be as open to those congratulations. This . . ." He cleared his throat. "This is the sensitive part of the discussion. My wife did not wish to have children. I was not as decided on the matter."

"I see."

"Which is complicated. If a man wants children and his wife does not, there's little he can do if he loves his wife and wants to respect her wishes."

Daly smiled. "It's a happy accident, then."

"It's not actually an accident. Paige's birth control was tampered with at her doctor's office. Naturally, I investigated. That is what I do for a living. I investigate."

Sweat beaded on Daly's wide forehead.

Lucas met Daly's gaze and said, evenly, "I have tracked the sabotage to its source."

Silence.

"And I would like to thank the man responsible."

Daly exhaled.

"I take it I tracked the source successfully?" Lucas said.

Daly managed a wry smile. "You are the investigator, as you said. It seems we underestimated your powers of deduction. But if you aren't angry . . ."

"As I said, I'm grateful. I will remember your intervention when I become heir. Which will be easier now, with Paige pregnant, robbing my brother of his advantage."

"It will indeed," Daly said, relaxing. "I knew this no-baby thing wasn't your choice. Otherwise, I'd never have cooked up the plan."

"I appreciate that. As I appreciate your assistance in this matter."

"Oh, you're going to get lots of assistance once you become CEO, Lucas. Don't you ever worry about that." Daly leaned forward. "You should have come to us with this, and we'd have made this right. We're here for you. I know you're worried about becoming CEO, but once you are, you won't have to do a thing. We know how to run a company."

"And I am learning."

"Sure, sure. Everyone appreciates the effort. It looks good for those in the lower ranks. But no one at the top will actually expect you to lead. You don't need to worry about that. We'll handle it."

"By 'we,' you mean . . ."

Daly rhymed off a list of nearly every board member on Lucas's side. Then he said, "You'll get all the perks of being CEO and none of the responsibilities. Of course, you will need to do a few things, to make it look good. Some of your pet projects—reforms or whatnot—are excellent ideas, and we'll give you everything you need to institute those. Unlimited resources and unwavering support."

"While you and the others handle the business end."

Daly grinned. "It's what *we* do. And when your father finally steps down, we can do it right."

*

"I am as much a straw man as Carlos," Lucas said.

We sat in our condo living room. Lucas sat upright, staring across the room, me twisted sideways, knees pulled up, watching him, my heart breaking.

"I've spent my life fighting my father's plan," he said. "Then I grudgingly inched toward it and then finally threw myself in, because if I was going to do this, I was going to do it right." He looked at me. "They don't want me to do it right. They never did."

I could point out that, below the board level, Lucas had far more support than Carlos—real support from real employees who expected him to be a real leader. But that wouldn't help right now. Instead, I said, "Your *father* expects you to be that leader. This has nothing to do with him."

"Which makes it worse. He's given his life to this company. He made it the most powerful Cabal in the country. How do they repay him? By biding their time, waiting to feast on the spoils."

"Jackals."

"I knew they were businessmen first, but they've always said they support my reforms. They were humoring me. Nothing more. When Hector and William died, they only saw it as their chance to truly run the Cortez Cabal."

"They'll destroy it."

He nodded. "They'll choose meaningless reforms for me to pursue, and in my way, I'll be no different than Carlos. He would use his position and money to pursue his hobbies; I'd use it to pursue mine. It's not even about which of us they'd prefer nominally in charge—each side has its own agenda, and they've each chosen a brother to push forward."

He turned to face me. "I should say it doesn't matter, shouldn't I? If I was as strong as my father wants me to be, I would use them to gain the position and then strip them of their power and pursue my *own* agenda."

"You can't just fire a board of directors."

"My father could find a way to do it. Deceit, trickery, manipulation, blackmail . . ."

"That isn't you."

"It should be, though, shouldn't it? If I was the man he expects me to be?"

"Then you wouldn't be the man I expect you to be. More importantly, you wouldn't be the man *you* expect to be."

He dipped his chin, his gaze dipping with it. "But walking away feels like more than failure. It feels like abandonment. Am I leaving employees to their fate under Carlos?"

"I have another idea."

Lucas took the next day off. No excuses made. He just canceled his meetings. After five years of moving the Cabal up in his priority list—always aware of how it would look to the board if he "shirked" his duties—he no longer had to care. As much as I wished it could have happened in any other way, I saw a weight lifting already. I'd been holding this solution in my back pocket, watching and waiting for the right moment to broach it. Now I realized that "right moment" should have been "as soon as I thought of it."

We drove to Orlando along back roads so Lucas could pull over whenever I needed, while he fretted and fussed and insisted we didn't need to do this today. But we did. This meeting could change our lives. All of our lives.

My stomach was much better by the time we arrived. After a five-hour meeting, we returned to Miami, on the highway now, as I teleconferenced with a caterer and Savannah, who was making sure dinner would be ready when we pulled into the drive. It was . . . and our guest followed less than ten minutes later.

We had dinner with Benicio. Then, over post-dinner coffee, Lucas said, "I am withdrawing as your heir, Papá."

Benicio winced and put down his mug. "If this is about my mistake the other night—"

"It's not. That is, it's not directly connected, and it is not about you at all."

He told Benicio what had happened. Not the entire story. He fudged the pregnancy part, saying instead that, after our dinner that night and our conversation, we decided to check my birth control and discovered the sabotage. From there, he followed the story accurately, ending with his meeting with Daly and offering to show the video of Daly admitting their plans.

"Then they're gone," Benicio said, getting to his feet. "By Friday, every last person on his damned list is out. I know a way."

"I'm sure you do, Papá," Lucas said gently. "But then Carlos has the predominance of support."

"I'll get replacements. Men I know who are loyal."

"You thought Daly was. We both did."

"Then I'll—"

"No, Papá. Even if we win, the moment you step down, the Cortez Cabal would split, just as the Nast one did. I would be left with half a Cabal, and a tenuous hold on even that."

"I'll—"

"No, Papá," Lucas said, firmer now. "I am not asking you to do anything. We both know nothing can be done. You had two viable heirs. They are dead."

"*You* are a viable heir."

"Not to the board. No more than Sean was for the Nasts. To them, we are boys playing at men. We are soft."

"You are *not*—"

"To them, I am. I'm an idealist. A reformer. That makes me soft. Likewise, Sean may be a shrewder businessman, but he's not Kristof. There's none of his father's ruthlessness in him. And a Cabal is not the most progressive of institutions. Sean came out because he wanted to start his leadership in honesty. Instead, it is seen as weakness—not only because he is gay, but *because* he was honest."

"It doesn't matter. Sean has shown he can lead. He might not have won over as many employees as he hoped, but Thomas and Kristof would both be proud."

"Then you agree Sean has been successful and, with the right support and resources, he could have a powerful Cabal."

"Yes, of cour—" Benicio stopped. "Where is this leading, Lucas?"

"I've proposed that Sean and I form a joint Cabal, as co-CEOs. I would propose that you invest in it. You would offer a work-share program to select employees, as a loan of resources, under fair terms. Sean and I would continue to build our Cabal, and when you do retire, your employees who wish to join our Cabal could do so. My goal by that point is to offer a viable alternative."

Lucas lowered his voice. "But yes, Papá, I realize what I am asking—that you surrender the dream of seeing your legacy remain intact. I understand that might not be acceptable. It's not what you wanted. What you dreamed of. I'm sorry for that."

Benicio took a deep breath and said, "I presume you've spoken to Sean, worked out the preliminary details." Before Lucas could answer, Benicio's lips twisted in a wan smile. "No, that's a silly question. You wouldn't come to me if you three hadn't spent the day hammering through it. All right, tell me what you have in mind."

Benicio didn't agree that night. We knew he wouldn't. He needed time to think and consider and accept that his dream wasn't to be, that there was no plausible way of passing on his legacy wholesale to Lucas. The best he could do was, like anyone in power, pass on what he could and see the core of what he'd accomplished continue.

Lucas and I stayed up into the night planning and talking, and there was an excitement in both of us that I hadn't seen in a long time. Finally, as we grew sleepy, curled up on the love seat, I said,

"I told you about Savannah and Adam's offer, but otherwise we haven't had much time to discuss that or anything else about . . ." I laid my hand on my stomach.

Lucas's arm tightened around me. "That takes precedence, Paige. Whenever you want to talk, I'm ready."

"Is now okay?"

He tugged me closer. "Now is perfect."

"Have you had enough time to think about what you'd like us to do?"

"I have."

"And . . .?"

"The fact that you're raising this subject suggests you've done the same, and as I've said, I believe your voice carries more weight. I'd like to hear your thoughts first."

"I'd rather hear *yours* first."

"Because you fear I'll tailor my answer to fit yours?" He took out his pen and notepad. Then, twisting so I couldn't see, he wrote on it.

"There," he said after a minute. "You tell me your thoughts, and then I'll show you mine. First, let me say that I still do not lean heavily in any direction. I have a preference, but if yours is different, I will change mine."

"You mean we'll *discuss* changing it. That's what I want. A discussion. I want to be sure we're agreed, insomuch as we can be."

He kissed my forehead. "I suspect that won't be a problem. It never is. Now . . ."

I took a deep breath. "I'd like to keep the baby. I'm open to giving it to Savannah and Adam if you'd prefer that, but I would like to continue the pregnancy, not because I have any issues with ending it. I just feel that, in this situation, I would regret it. However, if you would rather—"

He pressed his notebook into my hand. On a blank page, he'd written,

1) *continue*
2) *S & A*
3) *end*

"I made a list," he said.

I choked on a laugh even as my eyes filled. "You did."

He wiped away a falling tear. "It's the right list, I believe."

"It is. Sorry." I blinked back tears. "Hormones. I seem to be crying a lot lately."

"And you never need to apologize for it. With or without the excuse." He leaned in and kissed me. "So, it seems we're having a baby?"

I wrapped my arms around his neck. "A baby and a new Cabal. It should be an adventure." I smiled. "I like adventures. Well, I like them so long as they're with you."

"They always will be."

ABOUT THE AUTHOR

Kelley Armstrong is the internationally bestselling author of the thirteen-book Women of the Otherworld series, the Nadia Stafford crime novels and her new series set in the fictional town of Cainsville, Illinois, which so far includes the novels *Omens*, *Visions*, *Deceptions* and *Betrayals*. She is also the author of the hit e-serialised crime novel *City of the Lost*, three bestselling young adult trilogies and the stand-alone YA suspense thriller *The Masked Truth*. Her Otherworld characters have also inspired the hit TV series *Bitten*. She lives in rural Ontario.

Find out more about Kelley Armstrong and other Orbit authors by registering for the free monthly newsletter at www.orbitbooks.net.